THE
RISING
FLOOD

BOOK 3 OF THE MAREK SERIES

ALSO BY JULIET KEMP

THE MAREK SERIES
1: THE DEEP AND SHINING DARK
2: SHADOW AND STORM

☺ ☺

THE DEEP AND SHINING DARK

"A rich and memorable tale of political ambition, family and magic, set in an imagined city that feels as vibrant as the characters inhabiting it." **Aliette de Bodard**
Nebula-award winning author of
The Tea Master and the Detective

"Juliet Kemp's *The Deep And Shining Dark* (Elsewhen) was one of the best debuts of the year, set in a chewy and thought-provoking secondary world that one hopes to see more of." **Graham Sleight**
Locus

"*The Deep and Shining Dark* is a fast, fun romp of a book, diverse, queer, and deeply entertaining. I'm looking forward to Kemp's next work already." **Liz Bourke**
Tor.com

SHADOW AND STORM

"*Shadow and Storm* is an absolute delight to read, the literary equivalent of sinking into the embrace of a dear friend. Warm and cosy but never short on adventure and intrigue, Kemp's second entry into this series won't disappoint. The characters are real, full of depth, and richly drawn, and you'll wish you had even more time with them by book's end. A fantastic read!" **Rivers Solomon**
author of *An Unkindness of Ghosts,*
Lambda, Tiptree and Locus finalist

THE RISING FLOOD

"Fantasy politics with real nuance and believable uncertainty, characters whose richness and depth has developed over three books, and a growing threat that starts pulling together threads across the series make *The Rising Flood* a fantastic read, while Marek is a textured place that is a joy to return to." **Malka Older**
author of the *Centenal Cycle* trilogy
Hugo Award finalist

JULIET KEMP

THE RISING FLOOD

BOOK 3 OF THE MAREK SERIES

Elsewhen Press

For Laura

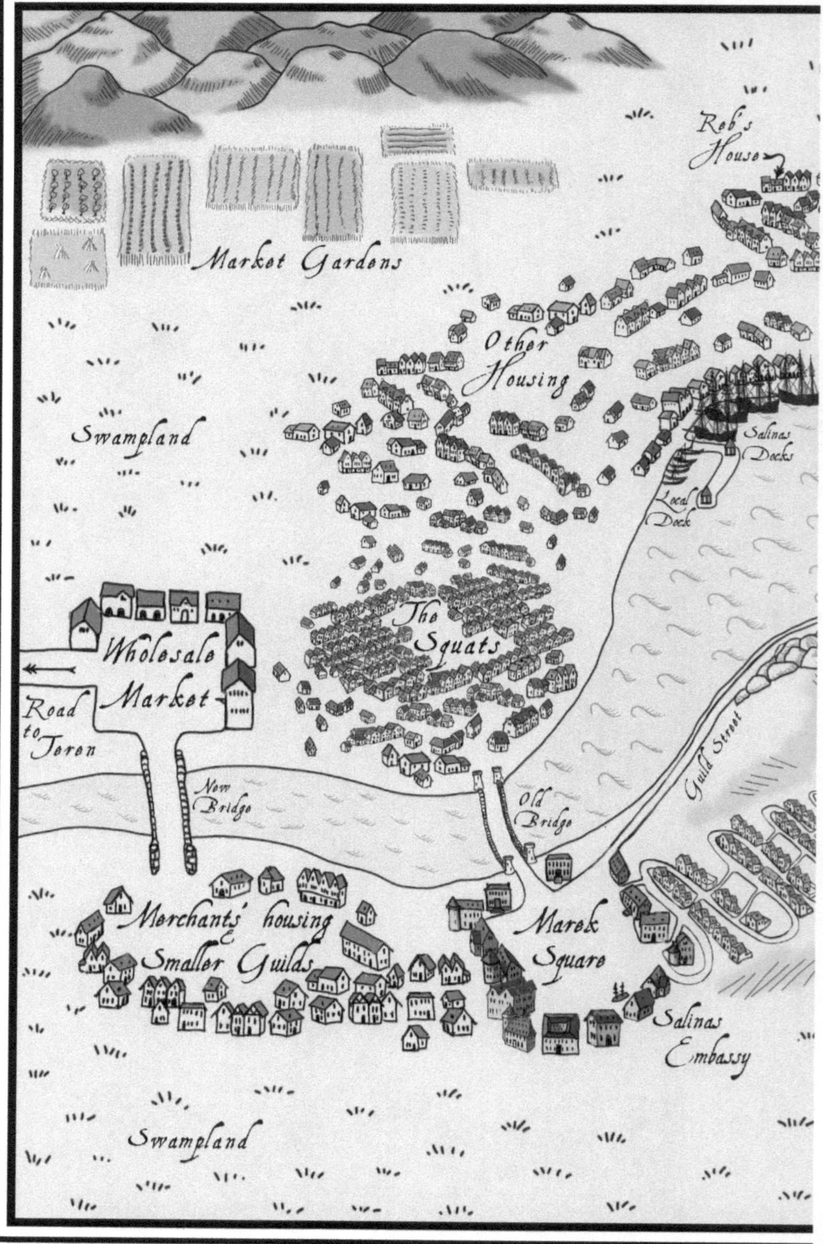

Reb's House
Market Gardens
Other Housing
Swampland
Salinas Docks
Local Dock
The Squats
Wholesale Market
Road to Teren
Guild Street
New Bridge
Old Bridge
Merchants' housing
Smaller Guilds
Marek Square
Salinas Embassy
Swampland

Swamp
Fishers'
Village
Tanneries
Housing
& Shops
Old
Market
Ferry
Oval
Sea
Cliff
Cliff path
Status of
Beckett & Marek
Forum
Leandra
Park
The
Council
Chamber
Shops
Goat
Herders' Village
Marekhill
Marek
© Juliet Kemp and Alison Buck, 2018

ONE

Fireworks were launching from the roofs of the Marek squats as Marcia came over Old Bridge. She barely noticed them; too preoccupied with the confession she was determined to make tonight to her girlfriend Reb. And her concerns about how the sorcerer might take it; especially the part where Marcia had been avoiding this conversation for months.

The bars around Old Market were full with people celebrating the New Year, spilling out into the centre of the market square despite the evening's chill. Marcia skirted the edges of a patch of some unidentifiable but clearly unpleasant liquid, then hastily moved further as a reveller lurched away from her friends to bend over and add to the puddle. Not that the behaviour at the Marekhill party she'd just left had been significantly more restrained.

The noise died away as she left the market and walked up towards Reb's house.

"Happy New Year," Reb said as she welcomed Marcia with a hug and a quick kiss.

"Nice way to start the year," Marcia said, smiling into Reb's brown eyes. "I brought you something from the party." She pulled a small package from her cloak pocket as Reb shut the door behind them. Candles were lit in the small room – Reb, who rarely used magic for mundane purposes, preferred them to witchlights – and an infusion-pot stood on the table. Infusion-sellers weren't out this evening; Reb must have gone to the trouble to brew her own, for once. The small gesture warmed Marcia deeply.

And she was about to break this pleasant moment.

"Oh, lovely," Reb said, unwrapping the parcel to reveal new-year pastries. "Did you just pinch these from the table, then, to bring to your secret lover?"

Marcia laughed. "Yes, absolutely." She mimed furtively sweeping them into her pocket, then sat down in one of the armchairs. "No, I went down to ask the kitchen staff. I used to play at House Pedeli when I was a child; the cook knows me. I don't know what she thought I wanted with them."

"She thought you were off to an assignation," Reb said, sitting in the other chair. "Which, conveniently…"

This was more playful than Reb usually was, and Marcia wanted to bask in it just a little longer before she broke the mood. "So how was your evening?"

"Pleasant. Quiet. Went to Irin's infusion-salon for a couple of hours. Yours?"

"Oh, you know how these things are," Marcia said, then regretted it, because Reb didn't. Sorcerers weren't welcome on Marekhill. "Lots of Heads wandering around looking important, and twenty-somethings overdoing it on pejo and wine."

"You're a twenty-something," Reb pointed out.

"Yes, but I don't take pejo and I don't get that drunk," Marcia said. She didn't like to be out of control. "Not these days, anyway. Daril tracked me down to make snide comments. I'm sure he's planning something. Nisha rescued me, but she does like pejo, so…" She shrugged. "I left as soon as I could."

Reb smiled at her. "And I'm very glad to see you. Was it difficult to get away?"

"Not especially. Midnight's come and gone. Some of the older folk were leaving anyway."

"You're not an older folk. Don't you think – won't someone notice, eventually? If you're leaving things early?"

Marcia shrugged. "I don't think anyone cares all that much."

"Really? Because that's not how it sounds when you start telling me about Marekhill gossip. You lot thrive on it, far as I can tell."

Reb had a point. After all, Marcia's mother Madeleine had realised she was seeing someone, and Nisha kept teasing her. Marcia shifted in her armchair. "Oh, maybe. But even if they were to go beyond speculating about who I'm inappropriately involved with," which neither Nisha nor Madeleine had, "I'm not sure it would matter. Yes, I'd rather not find out. But I've been meeting Cato for years, and everyone knows that, even if no one talks about it. No one cares."

"Cato's your brother," Reb said. "Not your lover."

"Well, like I say, I'm not about to tell the news-sheets about it myself," Marcia said. "But if it happens, eventually – it'll be a five-days-wonder, won't it, and then we won't have to worry so much."

Reb's lips compressed, before she sighed and sat back. "Fine. Your call. Not my reputation at stake."

"Reputation," Marcia scoffed. "You sound like my mother. Honestly, Marekhill needs to stop being quite so much – how it is – about magic anyway."

It wasn't like she was the only one with secrets. The whole of Marekhill revolved around people keeping secrets, or choosing not to. Granted, she'd prefer not to have to hide her relationship with Reb; but it was nice to have something that didn't belong to anyone but the two of them. Something that didn't play into the constant calculations of political clout and reputation management.

"Did you want to sit around and chat for a little longer?" Reb asked. "Because it is quite late, and if we wanted to…" she tipped her head in the direction of the door that led to her bedroom. "Important to start the New Year off right, you know."

"I'd love to," Marcia said, entirely honestly, "but there was something I needed to tell you first." Her stomach dropped, but she couldn't put this off any longer.

Reb's eyebrows went up, and she shifted back in her chair. "Something to tell me. Very well. Have at it, then." Her face had gone still, wary in a way Marcia hated to see.

Marcia swallowed. No point in beating about the matter. She'd been avoiding it for long enough. "My mother wants an heir."

"You are the Heir," Reb said, then visibly caught up with Marcia's meaning. "Oh. Right. Of course. Well, I suppose it can't exactly be a surprise to you." Her voice was calm, but one of her hands was tense on the arm of the chair.

"She says it's up to me how I do it, though she would strongly prefer I find someone I can accept for a child-contract and have a child of my own body."

Reb's face twitched. "And you?"

"I don't know. I – probably would prefer that too. I'm still thinking, but she's pressing me a bit. I mean, I've known it would get more important as time went on. Mother already had Cato and me at my age."

"What a thing to spring on you on New Year's Eve," Reb said. "And yet," her voice slowed, "she's pressing you already?"

Marcia swallowed. "She, uh. She didn't spring it on me today."

"She didn't."

"She made me promise. In the autumn. That I'd deal with it in the next year."

"In the *autumn*. And you only thought to mention it to me…today?" Her calm was visibly cracking.

Marcia couldn't meet Reb's eyes. "I've been meaning to tell you. I have. But – I didn't want to think about it." It sounded so childish, out loud. "But I wanted to tell you now," she hurried on. "To start the New Year off right."

"With telling me you've been hiding something enormous from me for the last three months?"

"With honesty," Marcia protested.

"Yes, well, that works better if you haven't been dishonest before, doesn't it?" Reb scrubbed at her face with her hands. "Look. This is your business, your mother, your House politics nonsense. I don't have a right to have a say in it, I get that."

"You do," Marcia interrupted. "I mean, if we…" She stopped.

"If we what?" Reb asked. "Isn't that part of it? We've

never said what it is we're doing here, have we? Because it's all too bloody complicated. And it's all very well you saying I get a say, but you've made a promise to your mother, haven't you, months ago. You're committed."

"I was always committed," Marcia said. "I've put it off long enough that Mother felt she had to blackmail me into doing it now, but I've always known this was part of the job, however I choose to do it. The House must continue."

"Blackmail?" Reb said, incredulous.

"Bribery, maybe," Marcia said. "In exchange for the House vote with the Guilds business."

"By the angel, your mother's cold," Reb said, reluctantly admiring.

"She has a much better eye on the House's fortunes than I do," Marcia said, grimly aware of just how true that was. "Reb, look, I'm sorry…"

"Fuck that," Reb said, the curse shockingly incongruous from her. "You chose not to tell me this, Marcia, and you can't just say *sorry* to make it all right again. It's been months. You *kept* not telling me."

"It's my decision," Marcia said, bristling. "Like you said."

"Fine. But if you're going to end our relationship, it's hardly kind or reasonable to keep going under false pretences, is it?"

Marcia blinked at her, genuinely taken aback. "End…who said I was going to end our relationship?"

"Oh, be reasonable. We both know this has an end date. How can you possibly be Heir, and have a baby, and keep a secret lover on the side? Especially when I can't even come near Marekhill. We both know…"

Marcia shook her head. "No. I won't accept that." She wouldn't. They *could* make this work, still. She was sure of it.

"Well, it might not be your decision," Reb said. "Right now I'm pissed off enough at how long you've kept this secret, maybe I'm done myself."

The pit of Marcia's stomach lurched. She'd known Reb

wouldn't be pleased, but she hadn't…"Please don't."

Reb looked away. "I don't know. I mean, we've only been involved for half a year. We can't see each other publicly. You're making major life decisions without me, which is perfectly reasonable when we've only been together half a year, but here I am acting like an idiot because I foolishly thought that you'd bring something like this to me. Because I thought we had that sort of relationship." Hurt seeped out at the edges of her voice.

"We do," Marcia said. Pain clutched inside of her chest.

"We obviously don't."

"I didn't know how to say it," Marcia said. "Because I *know* it's going to make everything harder, and I don't want that, and I was hoping something else would come up instead." And that sounded childish too.

"Well, that was bloody stupid." Reb folded her arms, angry lines setting in on her forehead. "Because as you so rightly say, this was inevitable. Which is fine, and maybe we could try, except that if I can't trust you to tell me stuff…"

"Do you tell me everything?"

"I'd tell you if I were planning to get pregnant!"

Marcia flinched. She shifted, to reach a hand towards Reb, but Reb's whole body said she'd be rebuffed. "I'm sorry."

"Don't *say* that. If you were sorry, you wouldn't have done it."

"You're so hard to talk to, though," Marcia said, and cursed herself. She hadn't meant to say that. It was true, sometimes, but…

Reb's mouth twisted. "Stop shifting blame."

"You get all…distant, and I thought…"

Reb was shaking her head. "No. Don't give me that. You lied to me, yes by omission, but that doesn't make it any better. And for *months*. But it just shows up what we both already knew. This can't go anywhere. We were stupid to start it, and we'd be even more stupid to keep it going. I can't do this any more."

She made a visible effort to meet Marcia's gaze. Her eyes had the sheen of tears, which was so unlike Reb that it cut Marcia to the heart. "Reb, please. We can work something out…"

"We can't. I'm done. Please don't make this any harder." Her voice cracked.

"But I love you," Marcia said, and almost bit her tongue. It was true, and she'd wanted to say it, soon, sometime; but not like this.

Reb looked away. "Yes, well. Unfortunately that doesn't fix anything." She looked back, and Marcia saw the depth of hurt in her face before she covered it over. "Will you be safe, getting home this time of night?"

Marcia's heart clenched. She wanted to stay, to make Reb believe that this *could* work, but…

But if Reb was done, she was done. Marcia wasn't going to help anything by hanging around making a fuss like a teenager ditched by her first lover, was she? (Marcia's first lover had been Daril. The comparison wasn't helpful.)

"I'll be fine," she said. She would not cry.

All the way across the room and as she slowly opened the door, she was hoping that Reb would say something, would change her mind, would…

She didn't.

Marcia, against her own will, looked back just before she stepped across the threshold. Reb wasn't looking at her; her head was down, staring at her hands wrapped tight around one another in her lap.

Outside, it had begun to rain gently but steadily; another rocket, white and orange sparks, soared nonetheless over Marcia's head. Marcia shut the door behind her, and walked away.

Tait's room, along the corridor from Cato's in their building in the squats, was significantly tidier than Cato's. Cato maintained that this was because Tait had only been in Marek for two minutes (four months), having arrived with barely more than the clothes on their back, and therefore hadn't had the opportunity to acquire the rich layers of possessions that Cato had over the last decade. Tait maintained that Cato was a slob.

At present, Cato was sprawled across Tait's bed, wrapped in a blanket against the damp grey chill, and eating hazelnuts. He was firing the shells out of the open window with a little flick of magic, and the floor was littered with the misses.

"I am going to make you pick those up, you know," Tait said mildly. They were sitting on the end of the bed, halfway through rebraiding their long dark hair.

"*Make* me?" he challenged.

Tait raised a shoulder, hands still moving. "I'm sure I can find a way."

Cato finished the last couple of nuts, and missed the open window with all the associated shells. For a moment he considered making Tait come good on that threat; but when it came down to it, he didn't *actually* want to upset them. "Pass me a willow twig, will you?"

Tait tied off the end of their plait and passed Cato a twig from one of the jars on the table, all holding bits and pieces useful for basic magic. Nothing as comprehensive as the collection in Cato's room (which he did keep in scrupulous order, because it would be bloody stupid to screw up a spell due to an inability to lay his hand on the correct thing at the correct moment), but Tait was only starting out in Marek magic. Tait watched with interest as Cato braced the twig between his right-hand knuckles, and gestured around the nut-shells on the floor. They scurried together like tiny lodestones, and with a final flick of the twig, Cato levitated the lot out of the window. He snapped the twig with his thumb. Outside, the nut-shells dropped out of sight as the magic disappeared.

"They're aimed at the gutter," he explained.

"Aimed, are they?"

Cato chose to let that slide. "It's neater if you only use the one hand. Bringing the other in shifts the energy, and if that happens before the twig breaks, unexpected things can occur."

Tait pushed themself back along the bed to sit beside Cato, who promptly wriggled round to get his head onto Tait's lap. Tait's leg was surprisingly comfortable, and they found it impossible to keep their fingers still, which meant – ah, there, Tait had already started playing with his hair. Cato fought the urge to purr like a cat.

"Reb doesn't use magic for that sort of thing," Tait said. "You know. Tidying up or whatever. Day-to-day things."

Reb had apprenticed Tait back in the autumn. Cato had assumed Reb would be a terribly organised teacher of magic, and had hoped Tait's lesson reports would help him with his own apprentice Jonas, even if Jonas was quite a different style of sorcerer. Except that…well, Reb was *organised*, that was true, but as time passed, it didn't seem that she was pushing Tait as much as she might. At least, Tait wasn't progressing as fast as Cato had expected. Perhaps he was overestimating Tait's abilities, but he saw them doing magic occasionally, and he knew what they'd done with blood-magic, and…Well. Probably Reb was doing things the best way, wasn't she?

"Yes, well, Reb wouldn't," Cato said. "Very much by-the-book, our Reb. What, does she think it's a perversion of the noble something-or-other of magic? Wasteful?"

"She thinks magic should be saved for when it's truly needed, and that one shouldn't trespass on Beckett's attention more often than that."

Cato pulled a face. "I don't believe Beckett's *attention* is needed for this sort of minor nonsense. I think Beckett can do that without thinking, same as I can, I don't know, scratch my nose without thinking."

Solemnly, Tait reached down and scratched Cato's nose, then smiled when Cato scrunched it up.

"What I think is, the more you practise with small things, the more it's in your fingers and your mind when you need it for bigger things, or when magic really is required," Cato said.

"Also you think it's easier than fetching a broom."

"Do you even own a broom? Do I own a broom?"

"Ser Galten downstairs owns a broom," Tait said. "I borrow it once a week."

"You could probably buy your own damn broom at this point," Cato said, sidetracked. "If you really want one. Fuck, I could buy you a broom, if it would make you happy."

"No thank you. It's a useful opportunity to talk with Ser Galten. You know, she really doesn't think very much of you."

"I know," Cato said smugly. "No one does. That's why no one comes to live up on this floor."

Tait hummed noncommittally. "Well. You get a certain sort of clientele, I suppose, but maybe I'll want a different sort, once I'm done my apprenticeship."

Cato was already clear on the fact that Tait had much more robust morals than him, and was unlikely to take on some of the jobs and clients from which Cato made a chunk of his income. "You might have to move," Cato said, somewhat regretfully. He'd worked quite hard on his reputation, and having to walk past his door might not appeal to the more law-abiding customer.

"Oh, I don't know. I'll manage something." Tait grinned down at him. "You know, having tamed the savage and notorious Cato might do a certain amount for my own reputation."

"*Tamed*, is it?" Cato demanded, sitting up and trying to wrestle Tait down to the bed. "We'll see about *tamed*."

The ensuing tussle was brief, and ended up with Cato pinned down to the bed, wrists held, with Tait sitting firmly across his pelvis. "You were saying?" Tait enquired. Tait was taller than Cato, and stronger than their skinny frame implied.

"I am in your power," Cato said promptly, with a great deal of breathy enthusiasm. "What on earth will you find to do with me?"

Tait bent down and kissed him, then moved to lie down next to him. "Nothing right now. You wore me out already."

Cato sighed dramatically, then turned over to fling an arm over Tait. "Fine, if I'm not getting laid again, tell me about your last couple of lessons. I've got Jonas later. I need ideas."

"Jonas would probably be better off if you did this yourself," Tait said, but it was a form complaint.

"Jonas is fine. Come on."

"Well," Tait said, looking up at the ceiling. "We've been doing scrying this week. Started out with a mirror, because Reb said that's easiest. Moved onto water yesterday, and then right at the end of the lesson she showed me a thing you can do with dust and string and a map."

"Ugh, she would," Cato said. "That's showing-off, that is."

"You mean you can't do it," Tait said, and nipped at his clavicle.

"I'm not great at scrying," Cato admitted. Which was something of a problem, with Jonas and his flickers, since it seemed plausible that there might be a connection there. "I can use a mirror, though. And water, at a push, although ink is more dramatic if you want to give the punter their money's-worth." Perhaps he should try that with Jonas. The lad had been getting steadily more comfortable both with his flickers and with magic; it was probably time to give him a bit of a shove.

"Reb said that about ink, too," Tait said.

"Did she now? Hah. Nice to know the good Reb isn't above a little showmanship."

"She did say it pays to know the person," Tait said. "Some folk are more impressed by water. Simplicity."

Cato nodded. "The more honest they are, the more it pays to keep it straightforward."

"I see why you normally use ink, then."

"I tried quicksilver, once, when I was flush," Cato said. Flush and drunk enough to think that spending most of the rest of his cash on quicksilver was a good idea.

"Really? Did it work?"

"Sort of. I mean, yes, but it was less clear than ink —

something about the curve, I think – and it's so much more hassle. I sold it back on again in the end." For much less than he'd paid for it, which had been annoying, but he'd been fed up of finding tiny pieces in the floorboard cracks. "What's next up in your lesson plans, then?"

"Finding-charms," Tait said. "Fits with scrying, Reb said."

Cato nodded. He'd already done finding-charms with Jonas – who had an affinity for them which might be related to his affinity with Marek's birds – so that was no use. Ah well.

"Oh," he said, remembering. "I had a client by earlier today."

"Mm?"

"Various things they were after. Long and the short of it is, I'll probably be summoning a spirit soon. Want to see?"

Tait shuddered. "Absolutely not. No thank you." Unsurprising with Tait's history, but Cato would have felt bad not offering. "Wait, though. What does Beckett think about that?"

Beckett, as they both had cause to know, did not tolerate other spirits in Marek.

"None of Beckett's business," Cato said succinctly.

Tait rolled over to face him, looking genuinely worried. "Cato. Come on. How can you say that?"

"I'm not, technically, in Marek when I do it."

"Outside the city borders, you mean?"

"No. That wouldn't work, because they need to be able to have an effect in the city. It's a kind of – liminal space. Halfway between here and the spirit plane. Not actually in the city, is the crucial thing."

"That sounds like sophistry to me. Are you sure…?"

Cato ground his teeth, suddenly irritated. "I've done it before. Beckett's never cared." Not that Beckett was, exactly, Beckett, back then. But still.

"Fine, fine. No need to bite my nose off."

Cato wasn't going to apologise. He didn't make a habit of apologising. "Anyway," he said instead. "Thought you might like to learn something."

"No," Tait said firmly. "And…" They hesitated. "And honestly, I wish you wouldn't."

"It's nothing like you did back in Teren," Cato protested. "I *talk* to them. I make deals. With consent."

"Even so." Tait's mouth was set mulishly. "It's not safe. You've got Beckett. Why on earth are you doing this?"

"Because it works better for what I want," Cato said. He sat up, irritated. "And because I learnt it, and if Beckett doesn't mind I don't see why you should."

"Because I don't want you hurt!" Tait said.

"I'm not *going* to be hurt!" Cato folded his arms. "Which of us has been at this for how long?"

"That's not fair. Are you telling me I can't point out when you're doing something dangerous, just because I've got less experience than you?"

"You can point it out. You can't expect me to agree with it, when it's not true." Cato made an irritated noise. "If you cared to *watch* what I did, you'd understand."

"Absolutely not," Tait said again.

They glared at one another, then Tait threw their hands in the air. "Fine. It's your business, not mine. If Beckett doesn't object and you're happy with the risk –"

"There's no risk," Cato muttered.

Tait ignored him. "– then fine. Whatever. Let's drop it."

Cato still wasn't going to apologise, but… "You've a right to your opinion," he said, which was close to an apology, wasn't it? "Agree to disagree, and all that."

Tait shrugged, but they looked less annoyed. Cato leant over to press a kiss to Tait's mouth. "Still feeling worn out?" he asked.

Tait quirked a half-smile. "Oh, I don't know," they said. "Perhaps you can persuade me otherwise."

And, well, that was sort of an apology, too, or at least a way of smoothing things over, wasn't it?

Cato bent to his task.

TWO·

Marcia stared at the note and swore, quietly and furiously. This couldn't wait, and she couldn't keep it from Madeleine. This could seriously affect the House's reputation.

She gathered up the note, her order-book, and her pen-case, and went down to the reception room. Her mother was, at least, not entertaining anyone; she was sitting on the pale-blue upholstered couch by the window, overlooking the cliffside that fell away towards the river, a steaming mug in her hand.

"Ah, Marcia. Good morning." Madeleine smiled at her, evidently in a good mood. Not for much longer she wouldn't be.

"Good morning, Mother. We need to talk. I've just received some bad news about our next shipment to the Crescent."

Madeleine's mouth flattened. "Go on."

"We need to be undisturbed for a while. Shall I...?"

Madeleine rang the bell herself, told the servant who answered that the two of them were not currently at home to visitors, and turned back to Marcia. "Well?"

"The *Heart's Dragon* is due to leave at the end of the week. Our share of the cargo space carries glassware and a selection of knives and silverware to the Crescent. Then she'll take rice, worked cotton, and tiles, whatever our factor has negotiated, over to Exuria. Then back here with raw spices and preserves." For which they had agreements with the Spicers and the Grocerers.

"Yes," Madeleine agreed; it was a standard set of trades. "But...?"

"But I've just heard from the Smiths that very unfortunately they do not have sufficient goods for our order after all." Marcia's jaw clenched so hard her teeth ached. "Not until next month."

"What? But surely we had a contract!"

"That's the thing. We didn't. Not written. I had an agreement with Hagadath, and I thought…"

"You thought that Hagadath's word was good enough," Madeleine finished. "Well. That was careless."

"We've been dealing with the Smiths for years! We were in their order-book!"

"Yes, and even people you've been dealing with for years will, if the price is right, sometimes back out, absent a written contract to hold them to. Although the price must have been very good indeed. Hagadath has always been reliable in the past."

Warden Hagadath liked Madeleine a lot more than they liked Marcia, though. Despite the fact that Marcia, not Madeleine, had helped the Guilds to their extra three seats last year. Hagadath was traditionally minded, getting steadily more so as the Guilds grew in strength, and they disliked Marcia challenging tradition.

"You know better than this, Marcia." Her mother sounded irritated, and Marcia bit her tongue. She did know better than this, but she'd been putting several deals together in a hurry, and they had a long-running connection with the Smiths, and…And she'd thought she could trust Hagadath, especially given that the Smiths were getting a perfectly decent price.

And none of that was any excuse, nor was there any point in saying it to Madeleine, who had no tolerance for attempts to excuse failure.

"Have you any idea what might have happened?" Madeleine asked.

"Not for certain. But I saw Daril talking to the Warden after the last Council meeting, and…I know that the Smiths' current stock was all spoken for."

Madeleine's lips compressed again. "And yet you still had nothing in writing?"

"I didn't think Hagadath would sell us out to Leandra!" But she should have done, because Daril would be delighted to damage Fereno's reputation. They might have worked together briefly when getting the Guild seats, but Daril wanted Leandra to be the one that succeeded off the back of that, not Fereno. *Powermakers* he'd said, when he was agreeing to come in on the arrangement, and *leaders*, but Daril never wanted to share credit. And it wasn't like he didn't have his own parent breathing down his neck, and Gavin Leandra-Head would never hesitate to undercut Daril, whereas Madeleine at least believed in the benefits of a united front. Although Gavin had never fully recovered from his food poisoning in the autumn; Daril was still notionally Heir, not Head, but he was carrying the vote almost all the time now, and Marcia hadn't seen Gavin out in weeks.

"Well," Madeleine said. "It's done. What are our alternatives? Anything from the Vintners?"

"Wine's too bulky, and all their spirits are already spoken for – we've a ship taking some of them week after next, in fact." The Vintners had a set of sweet spirits that were particularly popular in the Crescent. "I thought perhaps the Broderers."

Madeleine tapped her fingers against the arm of the couch, staring past Marcia's shoulder, obviously running it through in her head. "I suppose the space would work, and there's no special packing requirements. Have they anything?" At this time in the season most work would already be spoken for.

"I haven't had the opportunity to ask yet," Marcia said. "I came to speak to you as soon as I received this."

"Don't you have a contact with the Broderers?"

"Aden. Yes." Aden had very recently been taken on as a journeyman, one of the first from the Houses to be accepted to a Guild.

"But Aden may be more inclined to do good to his own House," Madeleine interpreted her doubtful tone correctly.

"And they may not have anything anyway. But I can certainly lean on him to introduce me."

"We can pay for it," Madeleine said, abruptly. She meant: pay above market rate, significantly if they had to.

If they didn't fill their allocated cargo space on the ship, they'd have to pay a fine to the captain, and their reputation would suffer. They'd get a worse deal next time from that ship or any other close to it. It was worth losing on the deal overall to avoid that.

Worth it, but utterly infuriating.

"I'll send a message to the factor in Darem right away," Marcia said. "Warn her that the knives won't be available. Even if I can't yet tell her what will be." At this time of year there were Salinas ships leaving and arriving most days; a messenger could get her note onto the next ship towards Darem, or towards another of the Crescent cities for forwarding by land.

"And then speak to the Broderers," Madeleine said. "When is this ship leaving?"

"Three days," Marcia said. It could be worse, she supposed.

"Do not appear too rushed," Madeleine said. "Whilst this is of course urgent, it won't do our reputation any good to seem as if we are problem-solving in a hurry." Her censure was obvious, and she was right; it was a foolish mistake, a child's error, and Marcia should have known better. "I trust…"

"*Yes*, Mother," Marcia said, her patience finally fraying. "Yes, I understand the mistake I made. Yes, I most certainly do intend to learn from it. Could we possibly leave it at that?" And she needed to find out whether this really was Daril's doing, and if she should be watching her back.

"Certainly," Madeleine said, voice calm, and Marcia wished her mother would *react* properly sometimes. "However. While you're here, I wanted to discuss the matter of a child-contract with you. You did indicate to me yesterday that you were willing to go ahead, and the start of the year is an auspicious time for new beginnings. You can spare a few minutes to discuss the details before you deal with the Broderers; it's early in the day yet."

Marcia absolutely did not want to deal with this right now. But the likelihood of Madeleine letting her get out of here without discussing it was nil.

"I suppose so," she said, ungraciously. "You understand I'm not willing to get married." Reb or not, she wasn't about to lock herself into that.

Her mother's lips compressed, before she made an elegant shrug. "If you prefer not, of course I would be the last one to make you." A tiny pause. "Although, given your recent decisions and the cost to the House…"

"*Mother*."

"Very well. So. Do you wish another parent involved? Or merely a conception-contract."

"I'm not yet certain," Marcia said honestly. "You had only a conception-contract."

"Indeed, and your grandmother before me," Madeleine agreed. "I had siblings living here at the time, though, which eased the burden."

Marcia and Cato, as she remembered it, had been looked after rather more by their nannies than by their uncles and aunts, but it was true enough that House Fereno felt emptier these days. She'd have to engage a child-nurse, wouldn't she, although that was a problem for further down the river.

"Perhaps we should look into extending our hospitality to some of your cousins. It is good, I think, for children to be raised in a busier environment."

"One thing at a time, Mother?" Marcia suggested.

"Yes. The contract. Perhaps then a parenting-contract would be wise."

Suddenly and unexpectedly, Marcia's chest tightened, and for a moment she had the horrible conviction that she was about to cry. She'd always known she'd have to navigate this, eventually, the matter of someone to be Heir after her; and she'd always thought that she would likely choose to birth a baby herself, if she could. She'd thought, over the years, about various possibilities. She'd wondered if she might find someone she wanted to make a marriage-contract with.

And then she'd been with Reb. When Madeleine had pushed her into this, she'd envisaged being with Reb.

She'd assumed she'd make a purely practical arrangement, a conception-contract, because even a parenting-contract would make it hard to keep Reb's existence secret.

Which was – had been – fine, because she had Reb. She'd only have *needed* a practical solution, because she had Reb. Complications and all.

Now she didn't have Reb, and yet she was still facing a wholly practical arrangement. It wasn't even that she wanted a marriage-contract. Of course she'd wondered if it might happen, but…But now that was off the table altogether, because even though she didn't have Reb any more, she couldn't face waiting around to be over her enough to look for an alternative. Couldn't even think of it as likely. It all hurt far too much to think about; she might as well get on with things. Accept the limitations and be done.

But it hurt.

"Marcia?" Madeleine was looking at her closely. Too closely.

"Perhaps it would be best to consider potential candidates first," she temporised. On the one hand, she didn't want to be parenting-contract close to someone just now. On the other hand, having a co-parent would give Madeleine less room to insert herself into Marcia's child-raising.

Best put the matter off. There might not even be a suitable candidate.

"Very well." Madeleine paused. "But first – Marcia, I'm afraid I must ask this. Are you certain that you and your…lover…" she sounded the word with distaste, "will not conceive a child?"

Madeleine was under the – previously correct – impression that Marcia was involved with some unsuitable lover, but didn't know who it was. Or, apparently, anything about them.

"I don't have a lover any more," Marcia said. She looked away, out of the window at the winter-blue sky, the sun shining low off the river.

"Oh." When she looked back, Madeleine, for a wonder, wore a genuinely sympathetic expression. "I am sorry, Marcia." She spoilt it by adding, "Although given how unwilling you have been to talk about them, it is hard not to conclude that it is for the best." She got up and walked to her desk to extract something from one of the many locked compartments, while Marcia considered the merits of matricide. "I took the liberty of making a list."

Of course she had. Somehow, despite all previous experience, Marcia was always surprised when Madeleine blithely assumed the world would reshape itself to her wishes. And here she was, letting it happen again.

That was a foolish way to think. She was Heir-Fereno. She'd always known this would happen. Twenty-seven was already late to be having a child.

"So. Your friend Aden, except that I gather he is now working for a Guild, and thus…"

"Not Aden," Marcia said. She was fond of him, but he would be a terrible parent and even a conception-contract via a doctor would feel peculiar.

"There's a cousin of House Tabriol…a grandson of House Cerit, with very nice manners."

"Have you considered one of the Guildwardens?" Marcia asked, only partly to annoy her.

"*Marcia*. How could that possibly be appropriate?"

"You were talking about building our connections. The Guilds are more important now, remember?"

Madeleine, who had agreed to lend Fereno's vote to that particular change partly in exchange for the discussion they were having now, ignored her. "Our stock with the Guilds is already good. More so after your *decision* in the autumn." Marcia was far from sure she was correct, given the stunt the Smiths had just pulled, but she didn't want to reopen that conversation again either. "Our stock with the Houses, however, has suffered." Madeleine tapped her lips thoughtfully with the paper. "That might be worth a parenting-contract, now I think about it. Since you are unwilling to marry."

"It's not like you or Grandmother married," Marcia said, aware that she sounded like a sulky teenager. Discussions with Madeleine all too often fell back into old patterns, however hard she tried to move on.

How would that work, when she had a newborn? How much was Madeleine likely to take the opportunity to push her back out again under the guise of care? Madeleine had, in Marcia's view, already kept her position for too long, reluctant to hand over the reins and let go of her power even as she grew more hide-bound and started making decisions that looked backwards rather than forwards.

Madeleine, of course, would put the matter rather differently. But surely, soon, she would have to allow Marcia to take the Headship.

It wasn't going to be in the next year, though, was it?

She pushed all those thoughts aside. "Show me the rest of that list."

She knew all the proposed candidates by sight, and some of them from conversation. None of them, now Madeleine had crossed Aden off, were from her particular group of friends.

"Not Kilzan," she said. "That's Nisha's house. No value in strengthening our bonds further there. And he," she tapped the paper on the Kilzan-cousin, "has been gambling rather too deep."

"It's unlikely that it will run in the family."

"No, but I don't want to risk either my child or me being seen as bargaining chips. When I say too deep, I really mean it, Mother. He's going to be in serious trouble in the near future."

"Hmm." Madeleine's eyebrow twitched, putting the information aside for future use.

"I suspect House Athitol will turn us down. You didn't see how Athitol-Head looked at me after the Guild vote."

"She's been perfectly polite to me whenever I've seen her," Madeleine said. "They have long been our allies."

"I wouldn't be averse," Marcia conceded. "It's whether you think she'll take the request well; and if she turns you down, whether she would make that public."

"That would be *very* poor form," Madeleine said.

Marcia shrugged. "Test the waters first, is all I'm suggesting. But you know best, Mother." In this matter, she probably did. Marcia was too close to negotiate this for herself.

Madeleine sat back. "Not Tabriol either. That leaves us with three options. And, of course, we might receive other offers, once it's known that we're in the market. You have no preference, yourself? Nor anyone else in mind?"

"No one else in mind. And no particular preference, not for a conception-contract."

"And if I test the water on a parenting-contract?"

Marcia thought about it. Having scope to manoeuvre would make the discussions easier for her mother. "Only on the clear understanding that I am not committing to anything. But I suppose if there was an offer which was contingent on a parenting-contract, I would be willing to consider it. I don't know any of your list well enough to be certain it would work, but I have no reason to believe otherwise." She stared down at her hands. "I have to say, though, Mother, that my inclination is against. It is a significant tie."

"Yes, indeed," Madeleine said, with exaggerated patience. "Which is why it might be worthwhile. It is a commitment to mutual wellbeing and respect, in a way that a child-contract alone is not. But I would not push you into such an agreement against your preferences."

"Well then," Marcia said. "Let's see what comes of this."

Madeleine stood up from the desk and came over to her daughter. "I am very glad you are doing this, Marcia." She didn't say 'finally'. "It is good for the House, we both know that. But I think it will be a good thing for you, as well."

She laid a kiss on Marcia's forehead. She hadn't done that in years. Marcia, to her own horror, felt tears prickling at her eyes.

"Thank you, Mother," she said, and for once, despite everything, meant it.

Cato frowned down at the sheets of paper he was turning over. Jonas fidgeted on Cato's ratty armchair, feeling uncomfortably exposed. His flickers weren't *him*. But they were and always had been private, his own personal burden, and he couldn't shake the feeling he shouldn't be doing this. Also, Cato was visibly concentrating, and that too was disturbing. Jonas knew now that Cato was perfectly capable of being serious – and indeed *was* more serious, slightly more of the time, than he went to some effort to portray – but it was still unsettling, to see beneath the mask.

Of course, the mask itself was entirely true some of the time; it wouldn't do to forget that.

"Did you see any pattern?" Cato asked, looking up from the last of the sheets. "Also, did you consider making this slightly tidier? I thought you were all in favour of regimented neatness. It's not like I don't *see* you roll your eyes every time you set foot in here."

He tipped his stool onto one leg and swung it around, away from the table, to face Jonas, then kicked away a pile of clothing on the floor and let it clatter down onto all four legs.

"It is tidy," Jonas said, defensively and untruthfully.

"It's a scrawl," Cato said. He grimaced. "Is this giving you…some kind of trouble?" Neither of them were keen for the sorcerer/apprentice relationship to include much in the way of emotional heart-to-heart; but the thing with magic, and also Jonas' flickers, was that you couldn't entirely disentangle them from emotion.

Jonas looked away. Through the window he saw the grey lowering sky that meant that even though Cato had opened the shutters this morning, it didn't make all that much odds.

"It feels dangerous," he admitted, finally.

"Like you're looking directly at it," Cato suggested.

Jonas nodded silently.

"When you've spent a long time not doing that. Right. But is it any worse if you use a proper recording format?"

"More in focus," Jonas mumbled to his hands.

"True," Cato said, after a moment. "May I remind you that that's the *point*. If you have a record of what you've seen, and how long, and when it happened, and so on, then you – we – have a higher chance of working out what's going on and how it relates to your magic."

"I did write down all those things," Jonas said, aggrieved.

"You did," Cato conceded. "It's just hard to compare them, because they're all over the shop. However," he turned back to the sheets, and conjured a witchlight with one hand, as he picked up a metal pen from the desk with the other, "what it does suggest to me is that whilst you do sometimes get flickers spontaneously, you most often get them after you perform magic." He looked over at Jonas.

"Yes," Jonas agreed. "I knew that already."

"Yes, but now you have *data*," Cato said. "The human mind is bad at remembering. You remember what stands out, and forget what doesn't. You remember all the times you did magic and got a flicker, and forget the times that you didn't. Or vice versa. This here," he tapped the pages, "assuming you have been recording *all* of the flickers? Right, good. This, then, shows that you're remembering correctly. The next question, of course, is whether you absolutely always get one after magic, which we don't have on the basis of this, because you've been writing down the flickers and not the magic."

"Nearly always," Jonas said.

"Yes," Cato's voice was impatient. "But you need to write it down. My next question is, whether the sort of magic you're doing is linked to the sort of flicker you have, which is going to take a bit more looking."

Jonas' hands itched to take the papers away from Cato. He didn't *want* it analysed like this, pulled apart and assessed. Except he did, as well; that was why he'd agreed to this in the first place. He wanted to know. He just didn't want to *talk* about it. This was his, not Cato's, or anyone else's. He could handle it himself.

He shifted his weight, and Cato looked at him sharply. "You don't have to do this if you don't want to, you know. And if you do want to, you don't have to tell me about it."

"I thought you said I'd only be able to work out what was going on if I properly kept track," Jonas said, sullenly.

"Yes. I did say that. I even meant it. But you don't, in fact, *have* to work it out. Up to you."

"I thought you said it would be difficult to do magic properly if I didn't know how it interacted with the flickers."

"Yes. That too. Still up to you."

Jonas gritted his teeth. "Then you'd better keep looking."

"Excellent," Cato said cheerfully. "I love a good puzzle. Might take me a little while, though."

Jonas hated this. But he hated not understanding, too. He hated not knowing how his magic worked with his flickers, or if it did. He hated that he'd spent most of his life trying to pretend that the flickers weren't happening. This was the alternative. He might *prefer* it, when it came right down to it, but he didn't have to like it, or the feeling that he needed *help* to sort something out that was *his* alone.

"Right," Cato said. "Well, I'm going to go ahead and take you at your word, and it's up to you to tell me if you change your mind. In the meantime…I had another question."

"What?" Jonas heard the snap in his own voice, but Cato didn't seem to care.

"Can you stop something you've seen?"

"Never tried," Jonas said, which was a lie. But it had been a while.

Cato looked at him narrowly, and Jonas strongly suspected he saw through the lie. Cato could be alarmingly perceptive; which, to be fair, was probably why he hadn't ended up face-down in a gutter at some point in the decade since he'd left Marekhill. That, and a dedication to spreading unpleasant rumours – some of which were even true – about what happened to people who tried to go against sorcerers.

He didn't challenge Jonas, though. He just said, "Well. It might be worth a try. On something tiny, perhaps."

"What do you mean?"

"Right, so, you've talked about seeing something a second or two before it happens. Like, seeing yourself do something just moments before you do it. Double vision, you called it. What happens if you do something else?"

"I've never tried," Jonas said, and this time it was honest. Those tiny double-vision flickers, it had never even occurred to him. By the time he could have done something, it had already happened.

"So, try, next time. Because they're so small, it's a good experiment. Nothing likely to happen if you can't change it. Or if you can."

Predictions. Changing things. "When Tait came. That didn't exactly happen, did it?"

Cato sucked at his teeth. "Well now. You saw doom, you said. Looming over the city. And Tait. Right?"

"More or less," Jonas said.

"Doom did indeed loom. It just didn't land. If you'd seen the city swept away, or Tait being eviscerated, or something, that would be more informative. Because that didn't happen. But the *threat* was real."

"Is it morally right?" Jonas asked, abruptly. "To try to change the future?"

Cato shrugged. "That's at least a step or so down the path. The first question is whether you *can*. The second one – if you care to ask it, which perhaps you don't – is whether you *should*. Or, I suppose, whether you *must*. Now there's a moral question for the philosophers, except that the philosophers can't actually see the future, so sod them. Either way. The first thing is to find out what *is*, isn't it?"

"Fine." Jonas hated the idea, but he did see Cato's point.

"So. You're to try changing the future. I'm to have a better look at all of this. Now then. This is supposed to be a lesson, as well. I know I said I'd talk to you about the spirit-plane and related matters, with an eye to that job I had coming up, but the wretched client has pulled out. *Which* is something of a nuisance but there we go. So. Instead, how about you show me how your spells of protection are coming along?"

Jonas sank, with a sense of relief that would have deeply surprised him five months ago, into the rhythm of magic.

THREE

What Marcia *wanted* was to have a blazing row with Warden Hagadath. Yes, she and Hagadath had had their differences in the past, but House Fereno had always had a good relationship with the Smiths, and to be let down like this was appalling. At the same time, she really should have known better. Which didn't make her any the less furious.

But. She couldn't afford to anger the Smiths. Hagadath was one of – arguably, the leader of – the Guild representatives on the Council. The Smiths were one of the leading Guilds. Word would doubtless get around about what had happened – Daril would make sure of it – and that would do her reputation no favours. It wouldn't entirely look good for the Smiths, either, in that they couldn't expect to do any work on word alone for a while, but having an eye for the main chance was, well. People respected that. It wasn't like the Smiths had broken a written contract.

The point was, losing out was one thing. Looking like a bad loser was very much another. All she could do was to sit tight and smile.

At least she'd managed to lock in a last-minute contract with the Broderers, before the details were public. It had been expensive – the timing had given away that she was up against it, and they'd made the most of that – but the ship wouldn't sail empty.

It did nothing for her sense of grievance to come into the vestibule of the Council Chamber and see Warden Hagadath talking cheerfully – or as cheerfully as they ever managed, which wasn't very – with another of the Wardens and Athitol-Head. Marcia nodded tightly as she passed, and decided she wouldn't stop for conversation with anyone today, even though Piath, Berenez-Heir, gave her a friendly nod. Berenez-Head, next to them, was deep in conversation with the Reader's Clerk.

At least the Council chamber was good and warm, on this damp cold winter day. It was heated by pipes under the floor, and some kind of furnace at the back of the building about which Marcia knew nothing more than that it existed. The ground-floor rooms of House Fereno had a similar system, which Cato had been obsessed with for a while when they were small.

Warm, but dull, today. The first matter concerned the new buildings out on the south-west edge of the city. The builders had come up with a way of creating more land out of swamp, which the Council had authorised the year before. They were reporting back today; it wasn't Marcia's area of expertise, though Piath was asking a series of pointed financial questions which had the builders' representative sweating. It sounded like they'd be able to move people into them soon. She suppressed a yawn. Perhaps, now she came to think about it, it was *too* hot in here. Over the other side of the room, Daril was slouched in the House Leandra seats; no sign of his father.

Once Piath let the builders' representative escape, the only thing remaining on the order paper concerned political printing. Marcia frowned. Did they mean the political gossip and opinion published in the news-sheets? She was aware that some of the older Council members didn't approve of the news-sheets, but there was nothing *wrong* with anything they printed. They weren't always wholly accurate, but it was hardly troublesome. The Reader introduced the matter, and Warden Hagadath stood up. Marcia ground her teeth, and paid attention, if only to listen for things she disagreed with.

Hagadath, it seemed, was concerned not about the news-sheets, but about the moral impact of the pamphlets being produced by unauthorised printers on the other side of the river. How these were to be distinguished from the news-sheets was not entirely clear. Marcia had seen the odd incoherent half-sheet calling for revolution and so on, but it wasn't like anyone could take that sort of thing seriously. And *unauthorised* was a peculiar word to use, wasn't it? Printers didn't need to be authorised. There was no printers' guild, to Marcia's knowledge; though the printers must have some kind of arrangements with one another. Did the printers want a Guild? Was that relevant? She ought to find out, if the matter was spilling out of the Guildhall and into the Council chamber.

"As such," Hagadath said, "we believe that any pamphlets or other printed matter touching on matters of politics should be brought before the Council prior to its distribution."

Marcia was certainly paying attention now. Around the Chamber, she saw others sitting up. A couple of people signalled to the Reader, and Hagadath nodded to indicate that they would allow questions.

"Would that not prove a great burden on the Council?" Jyrithi-Head asked.

"There could perhaps be some kind of delegation of the matter," Hagadath said, "should the Council so decide."

Aha. Was Hagadath angling to control that particular appointment?

"Or, perhaps, a properly constituted Printers' Guild could take on responsibility for this, under Council instruction?" That question – not really a question – was from Warden Ceril. Hagadath was agreeing; so the Printers wanted a Guild, and Hagadath and Ceril were on their side? Marcia glanced around at the other Guildwardens, some of whom looked more dour than others.

She didn't have an opinion on the matter of the printers and their Guild, but overseeing what was printed, that idea bothered her. She replayed in her mind what Hagadath had been saying when she was only partly paying attention. Scurrilous pamphlets, undermining the something-or-other of the city…

"Guildwarden," she said, after the Reader nodded at her. "Is this perhaps not an overreaction? Oftentimes, if one simply ignores these minor irritations, they go away faster than if one takes excessive action." She was quite pleased with her tone.

Hagadath looked annoyed. "House Fereno may not care how much mud is thrown at it," because it's too smeared already, Hagadath's tone suggested, and Marcia's lips tightened, "but the rest of us hold our reputations more closely than that."

"I understand the Warden's position," Daril said from the other side of the room. "It is unreasonable for people to feel that they can print scurrilous criticism of the city's government with no risk. Don't you agree, Guildwarden?"

That really wasn't a question, and the Reader scowled at Daril, but Hagadath agreed enthusiastically and used this as a springboard to move into the next part of their speech – penalties for unauthorised printing.

Marcia listened with mounting concern. Evidently this had gone beyond gossip rags and incoherent calls for revolution. She might not think those were to be taken seriously, but evidently Hagadath did, and had taken her dismissal personally. Which was the last thing she, and House Fereno, needed right now. Madeleine was going to be livid. She'd obviously burnt through any remaining slivers of gratitude over the matter of Council seats; people never did stay grateful for long.

"In any case," Hagadath said, winding up. "At this point I do not suggest any specific order. I merely urge the Council to consider the matter closely, and perhaps to look into these pamphlets themselves. I have a selection at the Guildhall for anyone who cares to investigate them, and to understand more clearly the extent of the problem." That was clearly aimed directly at Marcia. What she *ought* to do was to nod seriously at Hagadath and look concerned, or like she was keen to find out more now this matter had been raised. She ought to extend some kind of olive branch. She couldn't quite bring herself to.

She was concerned, that was true enough. She was

concerned to find out what the hell was going on. She wasn't concerned that the moral underpinnings of the city and its government were tottering due to some badly-typeset rantings and a few crude line drawings.

The Reader called the meeting to a close, and everyone rose to their feet to leave. Daril had gone across to speak to Hagadath, wearing his most charming look, nodding as Hagadath gestured emphatically.

Daril was engaging in a power grab, which wasn't the least bit surprising, and Marcia needed to look to herself to make sure House Fereno didn't lose all their support. Especially once everyone knew that Marcia had let the Smiths renege on an agreement. Of course no one could retaliate against the Smiths, but still; it was going to be months, now, before people stopped trying it on with her. Not all the Wardens had looked like they agreed, which was something to look into; on the other hand, none of them had *said* anything against Hagadath.

"Marcia?" Andreas, Tigero-Head, had come up beside her. He was young, and Marcia didn't know him well; he'd been too young to be part of her social group, and he hadn't been in line for the Headship until it happened. He'd been nervous, at first, but she'd noticed him getting more confident in recent months.

"Andreas. How are you this fine day?"

He nodded. "Well. Well. I wondered though. Have you seen these pamphlets, that Warden Hagadath was speaking of? You seemed not to think very much of them."

"I've seen one or two pamphlets," Marcia said, cautiously. "And posters. Over the other side of the river."

Andreas looked startled. "The other side of the river?" It wasn't a part of the city that most Marekhill folk went to often. "Oh." He sounded enlightened. "Of course, your brother..." He broke off, embarrassed. Madeleine had disowned Cato. It was common knowledge that Marcia was still in touch with him, but no one referred to it, certainly not in the Chamber, due to it also being common knowledge that Cato, besides being a sorcerer, now lived in the squats.

Marcia wasn't about to get offended. She wasn't embarrassed about her brother. Irritated, yes. Embarrassed, no.

"Mm," Marcia agreed, smiling at Andreas to show that she hadn't taken offence. "It is interesting to know about the thinking of *all* the city, you know."

Andreas looked thoughtful. "I suppose you're right. We are sheltered, over here. And it is Marek, the whole of Marek, that we are supposed to be governing."

Marcia did her best not to gape in outright shock. "Yes," she agreed. "Not…the most popular of views, though, in here." She resolutely avoided glancing to see if anyone was listening. They were through the Chamber doors now and into the foyer, and people were collecting their cloaks.

"No, indeed," Andreas said, and turned to favour her with a brilliant smile. "Well. Thank you, Marcia, that has given me some food for thought." He bowed, and left to find his own cloak. Marcia looked after him, unsure what to think. Was nervous Andreas developing not just confidence, but independent thought? He'd voted for the extra Guild seats; maybe he would be a potential ally, after all.

Daril came past her, and smirked. She pretended she hadn't seen him. She had research to do.

If the Guilds were going off out to sea like that, Marcia ought to find out what had worked them up. Which meant going to look for herself. Doubtless people printed all sorts of things; the fact that the Guilds had found some inflammatory nonsense was neither here nor there. What she wanted to know was how much there was, and what else was out there. And she hadn't picked up any of the less reliable news-sheets for a while. If it were up to her, she'd get them delivered along with the Clarion which printed foreign news brought in by the Salinas, and measured assessments of Council matters; but Madeleine absolutely wouldn't hear of getting even the Clarion delivered, never mind the rags. No amount of Marcia protesting that it paid to know what was going on elsewhere in the city had yet convinced her to shift her opinion.

Most of the printers in the city had workshops on what was now known as Printers Street, which ran between the Old Market and the squats. The sort of pamphlet Hagadath had been waving around wouldn't be printed by any of them – not respectable enough – but there were half-a-dozen little stalls in the area that would sell or distribute anything that anyone cared to give them. A fair bit of it was prurient. A certain amount of *that*, Marcia was aware, was produced after hours by the 'respectable' printers and distributed without their mark. Which, come to think of it, might be the case with some of the pamphlets, too.

What was the view of the respectable printers on censorship? Against it on principle? For it, to reduce competition? Or against it because it would limit their under-the-table business dealings?

It was chilly enough that Marcia threw on a thick grey wool cloak and shawl over the down-at-heel tunic and trousers she wore to go exploring on the other side of the river. She wasn't *hiding* as such; it was just – prudent not to wave her position around.

At the corner of Printers Street, a woman with ink-stained fingers and a leather apron stood in her doorway talking to a broad-shouldered person in dirt-smeared trousers. Marcia idled by the tray of books set out under the shop's awning to listen.

"Of course the city won't pay for it, that's the point," the woman was saying. "The printers will. Perhaps. Depending on your quote."

"Couldn't do it 'til the mud's gone. Paving slabs'll sink."

"Isn't the whole point of this to protect against the

mud?" the printer demanded.

"Yes, once they're laid. But we've to get them down first, good and secure, and that needs a dry footing." The builder made a teeth-sucking noise. "O'course, we could do it with plenty of sand, I suppose, but that'll cost."

"If you could give me both estimates, and an idea of when you'd expect to start if you wait 'til the mud's gone, that would be ideal," the printer said briskly. "I'll speak to the others."

Most of the streets on the Marekhill side of the river were paved. Most of the streets on the other side were not. The squats were, Old Market itself, and the docks; though the Council had been haggling over mending streets in the squats for years now. Printers Street was at best tramped mud, and in this weather the mud was more squishy than tramped.

Marcia left the books and wandered on. So, the printers might not have a guild as such, but they were banding together to do things that the city, the Council, wouldn't do for them. She nibbled at the inside of her lip. Had the printers asked the Council about paving? She didn't remember that coming past. If they'd asked and been turned down, that was one thing, but if they hadn't even bothered to ask…was the Council's reputation over here that bad?

Of course, almost all of the Guilds and their members were over the other side too, in the streets that sprawled out at the bottom of Marekhill and out into the new buildings. That was…an interesting thought. If the printers were a Guild, would they have paved streets already?

Most of the printshops along here looked prosperous. Marcia had books from several of them. They all sent catalogues to the Houses, and there was a single bookshop on Marekhill, towards the bottom of the hill, that sold on books and pamphlets. But here, they sold directly to anyone willing to browse, and what they had out was what was popular with those who visited. Very few nicely-bound books; mostly pamphlets, serial romances, folded penny news-sheets. Inside, the shops were primarily taken up with noisy presses, the walls hung with examples of what they could print up.

Clearly they were, as a group, doing well enough to pay for paving. Of course, it would be a sight easier to get their hand-cart-loads of books out and their paper and ink in with paving, especially this time of year.

There was nothing displayed outside this shop for the Guilds or the Council to worry about. She moved along the street to one of the stalls that sold anything and everything.

Aha. Block letters denouncing TYRANNY FROM THE HILL. Next to it was a lurid red-printed pamphlet whose contents were, Marcia concluded from a single glance, titillation masked as shock and concern; another, in dense black, warned of the risks of demons from Teren, and promised 'secret reports from the heart of Ameten!'. Marcia hesitated, then picked it up.

It read like inflammatory nonsense, but the thing was, Marcia had reason to be concerned right now about the Teren Academy and demons. And she'd had real trouble getting any reliable information downriver. Inflammatory nonsense or not, this might be worth a read.

She paid for the revolutionary pamphlet, the Teren demon one, and a handful of news-sheets of more and less sober disposition, turned around to leave the stall, and banged straight into the person behind her.

"Oh, I'm sorry," she said, at the same time as he said, "Oh dear, I do apologise."

She peered up at him – dark hair under a cap pulled well down, a slightly too well-cut tunic over grey trousers now spattered with mud…"Andreas? What on earth are you doing here?"

"Marcia? I mean, Fereno – "

"Marcia is fine," she cut him off swiftly. "What are you – look. Let's not discuss that right here, blocking this poor man's stall. Would you care for an infusion?"

He looked around. "Is there anywhere around here?"

"It's not the wilds of the swamps, Andreas. Don't be

ridiculous." She turned and marched off; when she glanced over her shoulder, he was following.

Irin's infusion-salon was only a couple of streets away. The bell jangled as Marcia pushed the door open; she wiped the mud off her feet, as best she could, on the mat. The place was busy today, but there was a free table on one side wall, and she led Andreas over to it and sat down, unwinding her shawl and taking off her cloak. It was the wrong time of year for flowers, but there were fresh feathery green ferns in the vase on the bright blue wooden table.

Andreas was looking around him curiously.

"Stop looking like you're at an animal-show," Marcia said, sharply. "Have you never been this side of the river before?"

Andreas looked abashed. "I like the mural," he offered. "With the coral."

"Irin's daughter painted it last year," Marcia said. "I like it too. But I like Irin's infusions even better." She raised her voice as Irin came towards them, smiling.

"Very pleased to hear it, Ser Marcia. Ser Reb not with you today?"

Shit. She hadn't thought of that. Hopefully Andreas wouldn't pick up on it and Irin wouldn't enquire further about why she hadn't seen the two of them together for a while, either, because she sure as the river didn't want that conversation now. Or at all. "Not today, no. Could I have some of your rose and chamomile?"

"Certainly. And for you, Ser?"

"Ah, rose and chamomile will do for me as well," Andreas said. "Thank you."

"So," Marcia said. "What are you doing over here?"

"Same as you, I imagine," Andreas said, setting his shoulders and seeming to remember that he was the Head of one of the Thirteen Houses, and not someone to be pushed around, even by the Heir of another House. "Looking at these pamphlets that the Guilds were complaining about."

Marcia's eyebrows went up. "I'm delighted that you

thought to do it."

"And surprised?"

"A little," she admitted. "But I don't know. Perhaps that street is thick with investigative Heads and Heirs and we just neither of us noticed them."

"Can't imagine Athitol-Head managing to go anywhere inconspicuously," Andreas said dryly, and Marcia suppressed a splutter of laughter as Irin set a large pot and two pretty blue cups in front of them.

"Should we be discussing this here?" Andreas asked.

"Not too loudly," Marcia said. "But there's enough background noise to cover us, and it's not as if we've anything to be ashamed of. We're trying to get solid information rather than relying on Hagadath's fear-and-horror routine."

"I'd still rather not be, you know." Andreas waved a hand.

"I don't want to be Fereno here, either," Marcia admitted. "One gets a different view of the world. Which is useful, I think, if we're supposed to be responsible for Marek as a whole, not just our part of it. Cato has been at pains to make that point to me, over the years." She waited to see if he'd react to her mention of her brother; he rose slightly in her estimation when he didn't.

Andreas looked down, fiddling with his cup. "My father always said that when the Houses do well, the city benefits. But what you said, when we voted on the Guild seats, about the need to directly include the Guilds. To work together with our fellow Marekers. That made a lot of sense."

"I'm glad you thought so, given that you voted for it."

He glanced up and smiled at her. He had nice eyes. "I assure you, I don't just toe the line of my allies, whatever might be said of me."

Marcia resisted a surge of guilt; she'd been scathing about Andreas and his backbone, or lack of it, in the past. He'd been very young to become Head, when his father died. Of course he'd taken time to find his feet.

"You were convincing," he said. "And I've thought

more on that since. My father wouldn't have approved. But."

"My mother doesn't," Marcia said. "We have – discussions. From time to time."

"I suppose I am Head," Andreas said. "When it comes to it, no one can gainsay me."

His expression betrayed some ambivalence about that. Well, being catapulted into the Headship at twenty-one on your father's death might well leave you ambivalent.

"So," Marcia said, "you're here to follow up the truth of the Guildwarden's claim."

"I am sure the Warden is telling the truth," Andreas said, sounding shocked. "Those pamphlets were real enough. But I wondered whether they were a reflection of a significant trend, or merely produced by one or two malcontents."

"The Guilds think we should be dealing harshly with them in either case."

"I do not hold with the use of a sledgehammer to crack a nut," Andreas said firmly. "If this is a handful with no following, they're best ignored."

"And if it is more than that? Will censoring their printing be sufficient? Or would it just enrage opinion further?" Marcia asked.

Andreas sipped his infusion. "I thought it best to start with more information before drawing conclusions. There's pamphlets of that sort on all the stalls. Not at the printshops."

"Of course not. They don't want to be associated with it. Doesn't mean they don't print it."

"Some of them, perhaps," Andreas said. "Some were very poor quality, nothing that the big printshops would let go out from their presses, even without their mark on. Unless, I suppose, apprentices after hours…but no, even then, I would think not. Very poor kerning."

"Kerning?"

"The spacing between the letters," Andreas answered absently. He was frowning at his cup again.

"You have an interest in printing?"

"As an adolescent I did," Andreas said. "You may or may not recall, I was not expecting to be Heir until shortly before my father's death."

His elder sister had died that summer too, Marcia remembered, drowned on a pleasure-boat trip. She'd been the Heir; Andreas had expected to do something else with his life. Printing, apparently.

"Although Father was not happy about the idea that I might apprentice," he added. "Especially as it's not even a formal apprenticeship, in the absence of a formal Guild." He gave her a half-smile. "It no longer matters."

Far too many of the younger House members didn't bother to interest themselves in anything meaningful. She was liking Andreas more and more.

"So you think these are produced privately?"

"At least some of them. The thing is, there are a fair few. From more than one press, to my eye. Which either means that they're selling well, or that there's money behind them. You don't run a press, even a private one, for free. Paper, ink, setup…"

"You'd have to find the money up front for that even if people did buy your pamphlets. Of course, that's what the banks are for, but I can't see a bank loaning money for revolutionary printing."

"One doesn't have to be wholly honest to get a loan," Andreas said. "But I agree. There must be some money behind this, even if people are paying their pennies for the things."

"Are they?"

"I saw some of them bought," Andreas said, then grinned at her. "Not only by you."

"I'm more interested," Marcia said, pulling an abandoned news-sheet off the table next to them and smoothing it out on the table between them, "on what the middle-ranking news-sheets are printing, than in a bunch of gutter radicals, even if they have obtained money from somewhere. But look at this."

They both stared at the headline.

IS THE COUNCIL FAILING THE CITY?

"Blunt," Andreas said.

"That's what worries me," Marcia said, finishing her infusion. "If it's the moderates, as well as the radicals — that's when we need to worry."

Leaving the salon, they walked down to the riverside and along the promenade that ran to the north of it, from the docks to Old Bridge. The docks were noisily busy loading and unloading, with Salinas sailors and Mareker porters heaving boxes and crates around. Andreas paused for a while to lean on the rail of the promenade and watch, and Marcia paused with him.

"I wonder sometimes," he said, "about going on a voyage."

Marcia's eyebrows went up. "A voyage?"

"The Salinas islands," Andreas said. "Though that is absurd, I grant you. But the Crescent Cities, now…" He sighed. "But one can't, as Head. Weren't you suggesting it for some House members, though?"

Marcia nodded. "We use factors, over in the Crescent. And in Exuria, come to that. It struck me that sending some of our own over there, to better learn the customs and the opportunities, might not be a bad idea."

"Give them something to do," Andreas agreed. She couldn't quite read his tone.

"Well, yes. I accept that there are some wastrels among the Houses who would rather not, but there are plenty who would like something useful to do."

"Aden," Andreas suggested.

"Well, not any more. He's a journeyman with the Broderers now." Aden was a member of Andreas' house as well as a friend of Marcia. He'd been refused more than once by the Broderers before the deal Marcia had brokered in exchange for getting more Guild seats on the Council. "My cousin Sophia. And I can think of half-a-dozen others."

"Wastrels, or after a useful job…Which category does Daril Leandra fall into, then?"

Marcia looked at him sharply. "Neither, any more. He's Heir now."

"And when he was talking to everyone about this same matter, last summer?"

Marcia shrugged. "Leandra's not my business. Everyone knows that."

"Voted with you, on the Guilds."

"So did you."

"I did," Andreas agreed. "I did indeed." He pushed off the railing and started walking again. "If I can't send myself to the Crescent, perhaps I should look for another family member who'd represent us well." He grinned over at her. "And try not to resent them too much. I do wonder what the factors will think, though."

"I didn't envisage them replacing the factors," Marcia said. "Can't waste local knowledge. More, supporting them. But if you're saying you should send people with some diplomacy, you're not wrong."

"And to Teren?"

Marcia glanced sideways at him.

"The Teren ambassador seemed keen to have the Houses return to Ameten."

"Prancing around in the Teren court isn't exactly useful," Marcia said, more sharply than she intended.

"Oh, I don't know," Andreas said. "Trade isn't only conducted with other traders, is it? That's hardly how the Houses got where we are today."

"Trade and politics are always intermingled," Marcia said, cautiously. It was a truism; it didn't reveal anything.

They were at the end of the promenade now, where it turned into Old Bridge. The river was running high under the bridge, a combination of tide and the recent rains, and the bridge was full of porters with hand-carts and people hurrying to or from jobs and marketing.

"I find myself wondering," Andreas said, "what Teren would think of those pamphlets."

"Is it any of Teren's business?" Marcia countered. She thought of the pamphlet in her bag, railing against Teren demons.

"The Lieutenant suggested they were seeing something similar. Perhaps we should ask them how they've approached it."

Marcia had a lot of things that she wanted to say about that, but absolutely none of them that were admissible out loud, here and now, to the Head of a House who was not a firm ally. "Mmm," she said. "Perhaps."

"Well," Andreas said, as they came into Marek Square. "It's been an interesting conversation. I'd be interested in continuing it another time, if you are? Perhaps we can come to some conclusions together."

"Certainly," Marcia said, taking his offered hand and bowing slightly over it. "I'd be delighted. Do send a message."

"I will. For now, I am away to the carriage-stands." He gestured over to where the public carriage-bearers were awaiting fares, on a corner by one of the Guildhouses. "I look forward to another time." He bowed, and walked away.

Marcia chewed on the inside of her lip, watching him go. Well. That had been…interesting. She wasn't sure where it might go, but it was definitely interesting.

FOUR

Reb stared at the book in her hand and didn't read a word of it. She hadn't read a word of it since she sat down.

It was ridiculous to feel this bad. To *still* feel this bad, four whole weeks, nearly a month, later. It wasn't like she hadn't always known things with Marcia had to be temporary.

"It was always going to end," she said aloud. It didn't help.

But how Reb felt didn't change the truth. They didn't make sense together, and they never had. And maybe, if Marcia had come and said that, or if she'd been honest from the start about the deal she'd made with her mother, *maybe* Reb could have taken that on the chin, could have smiled and shrugged and tried to stay friends. It was that Marcia had *lied* to her, lied for months when Reb thought they were coming to trust one another more. That betrayal was what truly hurt, made her stomach cramp and her throat close.

She should have known. You couldn't rely on people. They always let you down, or went away, in the end. It didn't matter if they didn't *want* to, didn't mean to; it happened anyway, one way or another.

Tait had been due the day before for a lesson; she'd cancelled it, because Tait made her think of Cato which made her think of Marcia, which made her want to punch a wall, which didn't seem like a useful frame of mind in which to approach her apprentice. And besides, she just…didn't want to. She had a stack of requests for charms due, and she didn't want to make those, either. They weren't late, not quite, but they would be soon, yet she still couldn't make herself move. Could barely even bring herself to care.

And she wasn't even reading the wretched book she'd

sat down with as an alternative.

The clock in the market struck the hour, and she counted automatically. Marcia had given her a clock, as a birthday gift, last year. She'd woken up and seen it the morning of New Year, and wanted, with a violence that took her by surprise, to throw it against the wall. She didn't want to be wasteful, or disrespectful of the clockmaker's work, she told herself, repeatedly, until she believed it enough to let herself get up and wrap the clock up and find a messenger (in short supply, the morning of New Year, and twice the usual rate) to take it back to House Fereno.

She'd managed long enough without a clock. The one in the market did the job just fine. And what its chimes told her right now was that Alyssa would be here at the half-hour. Leaving Reb just enough time to send a messenger and cancel. She threw the book onto the other armchair – she'd nearly got rid of that too, but she had apprentices now, she needed it – and went to lean out of the window, looking for a red armband. Instead, she saw Alyssa turn the corner at the end of the street.

Well, shit.

"You're early," she said, ungraciously, opening the door.

"Hello to you too," Alyssa said, leaning on her stick in the doorway. Alyssa was wholly unlike quiet, self-effacing Tait. Alyssa had no deference whatsoever. In theory, Reb was happy with that. Today, it set her teeth on edge.

"I was going to cancel," she said, then cursed herself. Cancelling this late was – well, it would have been bad enough to send the message. It was too late now.

"I can go," Alyssa said, with a careless lift of a shoulder. "Plenty to do today."

"No," Reb said. "You're here now." She heard the flatness of her own voice. "Come in."

Alyssa eyed her curiously; Reb controlled her flinch and turned quickly away to her workroom. Even though Alyssa was doing only tiny magics, it was still sensible to do them inside the windowless workroom with the door barred – and she might as well get on with things, now Alyssa was here, however little the idea appealed.

She shut the workroom door behind the two of them, and turned back to find Alyssa still giving her that assessing look as she sat down on the second workstool Reb had acquired now she had apprentices.

"Are you all right?" Alyssa demanded.

"Fine," Reb said, too quickly.

For a horrible moment she wondered if perhaps, just perhaps, it would be good to have someone, another sorcerer, to talk to. Someone who wasn't a lover or just a casual acquaintance...

But Alyssa was her apprentice. It wouldn't be right. And she didn't want to do that anyway. She didn't need to *talk* to anyone. She was fine. This had always been going to happen. The end of the relationship, and the betrayal. Her *feelings* about it were neither here nor there.

"Show me a witchlight," she said, and folded her arms.

Alyssa rolled her eyes, held her hand out, and conjured a yellow-green witchlight. She obviously didn't have to think about it, though the light was fuzzy at the edges, and less bright than Reb's. It would improve with further practice, and with more use of magic overall, as Alyssa's understanding deepened; Reb really ought to move her on.

The next obvious thing to do was mending-magic – it was easy to practise on your own, because there were always things that needed fixing, and there wasn't much that could go wrong. Unlike heating-magic, more closely related to witchlights but riskier. The trouble was, manipulating matter that way was hard to get a handle on, to start with; and the easiest way to teach it would be to use her own power to guide Alyssa's.

She remembered Zareth doing that with her, when she was an apprentice. She remembered all the times she and he had worked together, as part of the Group. She remembered being out in the barge-yard, Cato's power merging with hers and Jonas' and Tait's, and Marcia behind her, hand on her shoulder, grounding all of them. She remembered teaching her last apprentice, Val, and how Val had looked as they grasped the way they needed to use their magic to hold something together. She remembered Val's corpse-pyre, and felt muscles tighten like steel bands across her chest.

"I thought, today, perhaps a finding-charm," she said.

"Oh come *on*," Alyssa said, sending the witchlight up to bob on the ceiling. "What is this penny-ante shit? I thought magic was powerful. All this stuff coming through Beckett, you said. And now it's just little lights and how to find lost hairgrips."

"You need to learn control…" Reb tried.

"Crap. My control's fine." She snapped her fingers, and her witchlight came slowly back down to her hand. She closed her hand over it, putting it out, then conjured it again and sent it bobbing back upwards. "You know it is. Let's move on. Let's do something useful. Otherwise why am I wasting my time? Half my roof came down today. Can magic fix that?"

Mending-magic, though bigger than apprentices usually started off with. But not impossible. Reb could probably have done it by herself, although if the roof was as bad as Alyssa was suggesting, it would wear her out for a couple of days. It was certainly beyond Alyssa herself right now, but if the two of them worked together, linked so that Alyssa could tell what Reb was doing…

"Magic could, in theory. You can't. Better off paying a roofer." Alyssa wasn't ready. It was only good sense to take things slowly.

"Pay?" Alyssa said incredulously. "With what? You realise that I'm taking time out of my work – my paid work – for this shit? All this slowly-softly-you're-not-ready-yet crap?"

"It takes *time*," Reb insisted. It did. Just because Zareth had pushed her fast, had supported her every step of the way, had helped her do something when she wanted to try it but wasn't quite ready; just because Zareth had done things that way, it didn't mean that was the only way, or the best. She wasn't Zareth. (She missed Zareth; she shut that thought down straight away.) She didn't want to be Zareth to Alyssa's Reb. They weren't those people.

"Fine, whatever. Finding-charm, you said, yeah? But I've not got long. Roofer's coming, and my neighbour that's watching Jina, she's got work later." Alyssa sounded fed up, and Reb felt a distant pang of echoing distress.

She cast around for a better solution. "How about instead of that, you help me with the charms I've got waiting?" she offered. "They're a bit further on than what you're doing, and you can have half the payment for them."

It was more difficult magic for Alyssa, but it wouldn't need Reb to link. That was a good compromise, wasn't it?

"Still penny-ante," Alyssa muttered, but she nodded, a short sharp jerk of her head.

Next time, Reb promised herself. Before next time; or soon, anyway; she'd work out how to help Alyssa move faster.

⊙ ⊙

Madeleine had moved more swiftly than Marcia had expected with finding a child-contract. Not yet a month, and apparently she already had some reasonable offers. Madeleine had offered to make the decision herself, but Marcia drew the line at that. It might not be appropriate to invite contract-offers for oneself, but she wanted *some* say in the conclusion.

When she entered the reception room, Madeleine was sitting on one of the pale blue couches at the end of the room, with papers laid out on the low table in front of her. She looked up and smiled.

"Marcia, dear. Come, sit by me."

That was unusually affectionate, but Marcia could hardly turn it down. Cautiously, she sat down on the other end of the couch from her mother. "Good afternoon, Mother. I hope you have had a productive morning."

"Oh, indeed yes. A banker from the Crescent visiting. Some interesting ideas, which we should discuss later. I've been wondering whether we could use someone out there, in fact..."

"We've got the factor. Oril."

"Yes, and she is excellent, but I wonder whether one of your cousins might be interested in travelling there to get a more accurate picture of the possibilities. The young man I was speaking to today would be very happy to introduce us round."

"Better hope he's not trying to cut Oril out," Marcia said. "Or that he wouldn't be stepping on any existing arrangements."

"Do give me *some* credit, Marcia." But her mother's expression was still fond. "I have been doing this for some decades now."

She'd also nearly got them into serious trouble twice in the last year or so; but perhaps best not to mention that just now. "Sophia," Marcia said, instead. "She might be interested." Sophia was a branch or two of the family removed from Marcia herself, the child of her mother's cousin. Marcia knew her a little – Sophia ran in different social circles – but she also knew that Sophia was involved in running several infusion-salons. Providing funding and trading support to the proprietors, but it was work, and suggested she had some sense.

"Sophia," her mother said, tapping a finger above her lip. "Yes, indeed. I will speak to her father. However." She gestured to the papers spread on the table. "Let us not get sidetracked."

"Child-contracts." Marcia tried to sound enthusiastic. She'd agreed to do this. There was no point in dragging her heels. Even if the idea still made her heart hurt.

"Well," Madeleine said. "As I expected, once I made one or two discreet approaches, word got around and we had a number of further offers. Some for form's sake, which I discarded. One from Leandra, even, of all absurdities. Not that Gavin didn't know I'd discard it. A very junior branch. Almost impolite." She frowned slightly. "But his House is thin, at present. I will assume no ill will was meant."

Marcia wasn't as sure – relationships between Leandra and Fereno were at best complicated, at worst actively hostile – but she knew what Madeleine meant: once it had become known that House Fereno was seeking a child-contract, it would have been impolite not to offer at all, but an offer that was slightly too junior, made in certain terms, was known to be formal rather than sincere.

"Pirran sent an offer, of course – their second son, in fact, which was generous – but really I feel that our links with House Pedeli are already sufficiently close." Marcia wasn't sure they were as robust as Madeleine thought; Madeleine and Pirran, Pedeli-Head, were excellent friends, but Pirran and Marcia had clashed. Not a topic she wanted to pursue. "I would suggest that you consider this from House Jyrithi, and this one from Cerit, which as you may recall was on our original list." She indicated the two sets of papers furthest to her left. "I also," she pursed her lips, tapping the next set of papers in the row, "would not *personally* suggest that you consider this one, but since you made yourself clear during our original discussions – a high-ranking member of the Vintners' Guild has made an offer. In my day…well, never mind. I suppose the world changes. But the offer I find most interesting is this one." She tapped the right-hand papers.

"Which is?"

"House Tigero. Do you know Andreas? Personally, I mean? I was not aware that he was one of your set."

"He wasn't," Marcia said, frowning at the paperwork under her mother's hand. "Isn't. But I have spoken to him recently, a couple of times. He's – interesting. I was wondering whether he might be a future ally, in fact, even though Tigero haven't been historically."

"Well," Madeleine said. "He is offering *personally*."

Marcia's eyes widened. "Really? But he can't, can he?"

"It's not done often," Madeleine said. "It would be

quite out of the question were you seeking a personal contract. But as it is – he proposes a two-child contract, one child for Fereno and one for Tigero. Potentially. Both to be parented between the Houses. He lays out a proposed arrangement, even. It is unusual, but it is a serious offer. And," she coughed lightly, "well-funded."

As well it might be, for a two-child offer which would produce two prospective Heirs. Of course, neither child might, in the end, become Heir; it wasn't guaranteed. You had to earn your place. Andreas would, in all likelihood, make a contract with someone else at some point as well. But it was – interesting.

Marcia picked up the papers from Jyrithi, riffled through them, and made a face. "I know him. I'd really rather not."

"You needn't *do* anything with him," Madeleine said. "We could go through a doctor, and the offer doesn't include parental responsibilities."

"As well it might not. He's a careless fool," Marcia said. "He hides it under nice manners, but he runs through his allowance every month, and borrows. He only gets away with it because, to be fair, he repays his debts scrupulously. But it's sheer wastefulness to be in that position at all. No."

"Very well," Madeleine said. She took the papers out of Marcia's hand, and stacked them on the edge of the table. "This vintner then, Cerit, or Tigero."

Marcia was quite tempted by the vintner. It would significantly strengthen Fereno's links with the Guilds; and though like everyone else Fereno traded the Vintners' products from time to time, they had no significant associations with the Guild. (Leandra did. It would annoy Daril, although that was a bad reason to sign a child-contract. There were easier ways to annoy Daril.)

It would also greatly unsettle the other Houses. Occasionally junior House members contracted with Guild members, but a Head or an Heir? She couldn't think of an example, at least not an open one; some child-contracts were closed, which always gave rise to rumours (including the possibility that the contract occurred, as it were, after a precipitating event). Would reinforcing the link with the Guilds, given their current tension with the Smiths, be worth putting their House relationships under pressure? Especially given that as Madeleine stepped back (when Madeleine finally *did* step back), some of their existing alliances might go with her.

Madeleine didn't want the Guild contract, which also made it more appealing; but she had left it on the table. And Marcia really shouldn't be approaching this in terms of *irritating Madeleine*. She wasn't a sulky child any more. She picked up the papers for closer inspection, and discovered another issue. "Mother. This is a marriage-contract."

"Yes," Madeleine agreed.

"You want me to *marry* a Guild-member?"

"I don't want anything of the sort," Madeleine said. "You were the one who insisted the Guilds should be in consideration."

"I don't want a marriage-contract." It wasn't just about Reb and her own sore heart. She didn't want to be tied to someone she wasn't already attached to. She pushed down a surge of grief.

"Well then," Madeleine said. "I suppose that is an easy decision." There was the tiniest hint of a self-satisfied smirk.

"Mother. Was this the only offer from the Guilds?" She should have known Madeleine wasn't being as accommodating as she appeared to be.

Madeleine hesitated for a moment.

"*Mother.*"

"No. But truly, none are remotely appropriate. The majority of those at the higher ranks of the Guilds are already married, do not wish any kind of contract, or are not suitable for our purposes." By which she meant, wouldn't be able to contribute to a pregnancy.

"Show me," Marcia demanded. Madeleine turned to a much larger pile of papers by her side, and after some rustling through them, produced a smaller stack. Two proposals only, and, fine, Madeleine was right, both would raise eyebrows about whether House Fereno was down on its luck.

"Very well," she said, and set them aside. "I don't want a marriage-contract, so that's that. Cerit or Tigero, then?"

"We needn't stop here," Madeleine said. "A second round is acceptable."

Marcia ignored her, skimming through the papers from Cerit – standard child-contract, with a child of the current Heir. They were perfectly nice as far as she knew. She'd seen them around at social events and didn't know anything to their detriment. They weren't in line to be Heir – a niece was being prepared for that. Fereno were on good terms with Cerit already. It would do, but there was nothing particularly useful about it. She put that down and picked up the proposal Andreas had sent. On the one hand, it was unusual, the Head of one House and the Heir of another. On the other hand…well, as proposed, it was a generous contract, in terms of mutual responsibilities and care for the children, as well it should be, given that Marcia was taking the physical risk. Andreas didn't want any personal commitment, other than as was necessary for the shared care of the children, and he didn't formally propose anything other than what was required in the long term for that. There was an addendum though, in what Marcia presumed was Andreas' own writing rather than that of the lawyer:

Marcia – this is not part of the formal offer, as I would not wish to bind you to it. But I would wish us to be friends, in this endeavour. Andreas.

It would make it clear that House Fereno was not, in fact, friendless.

And she really didn't want to go through a second round of this.

"I am inclined to this offer," she said, finally, looking up at Madeleine. "Subject to detailed negotiations, of course." The proposed contract was generous, but left a significant amount still to be tied down. "If you agree?"

"It is unusual," Madeleine said, judiciously. "But…well, there's nothing wrong with being unusual, is there? And one could hardly criticise his standing. If it pleases you, then by all means."

Marcia nodded. "Will you reply? On my behalf?"

"Of course," Madeleine said. "Will you include any personal response?"

Marcia stood and crossed to the table by the window, which held pen and paper.

Andreas – I too would wish to be friends. I look forward to our next meeting. Marcia.

FIVE

"Are you really sure about this?" Jonas hissed at Cato, as the footsteps of his first client came up the stairs.

"Which of us is the apprentice here and which the qualified sorcerer?"

"*Qualified*..." Cato's qualifications, Jonas had become aware, mostly consisted of him having managed, a decade ago, to become a sorcerer all by himself without also simultaneously becoming dead. On the other hand, Reb, whose qualifications were more traditional, had offered to apprentice Jonas and he'd turned her down; this was his own fault.

"Shut up and relax, Jonas. You'll do fine."

Not wanting to annoy his neighbours by practising sorcery semi-professionally in his own room, Jonas had borrowed Cato's for the occasion. Cato had dragged his battered armchair into the darkest corner of the room, from where he would intervene only if absolutely necessary. Jonas, in a chair borrowed from Tait next door, was seated in front of the bed, which was, for the first time Jonas could remember, properly made. A board over Cato's worktable held Jonas' ingredients and a bowl for mixing. Jonas was not permitted to touch the worktable itself.

A tentative knock. Jonas squared his shoulders. "Come in."

Stay seated, Cato had told him. You're in charge here; make them feel they're intruding. Keep them just a little off-balance. You're the one with the power.

The client, a thin, nervous-looking man in his middle-years, came cautiously into the room. Jonas had arranged things thus far via messages; this was the first time he was seeing the client himself.

"H-hello? I'm Argan Etolin. From the Bakers' Guild.

We've, um. You're…"

"Jonas. The sorcerer." He suppressed his automatic flinch. He and Cato had argued over that. Jonas had wanted to say 'apprentice'. Cato argued that an apprentice sorcerer was still a sorcerer – it was right there in the name – and 'apprentice' would just make people uneasy. In Jonas' view, that rather made the point itself, but Cato had insisted.

Argan Etolin nodded, wide-eyed. "Jonas. Good afternoon."

"What seems to be the issue, then?" It was a truth-charm, he knew that from the messages, but it mattered what it was for.

Argan, shifting from foot to foot as he spoke, unwound a long-winded tale of doubt and worry. Eventually he reached the point: he believed his lover might be straying, and wanted the truth-charm to establish whether this was, in fact, the case.

Jonas thought he heard Cato sigh.

But truth-charms were easy enough, and he had everything ready. They weren't often a good idea, but that wasn't his problem, was it? Except…

"A truth-charm," he said. "By all means. Uh, but. You do realise, right, that the other person will know you're using it?"

Argan nodded several times in quick succession. "Yes. Yes. That will be fine."

Cato had warned him, when teaching him truth-charms, that their primary problem was that knowing you might not be trusted made people more likely to be untrustworthy. In business relationships, a certain wariness was reasonable, but in personal situations, truth-charms tended to lead to distress, at best.

But if the client wanted one, despite the risk, then Jonas' responsibility was just to make sure it worked, wasn't it?

"Very well," he said. "Three demmers. Up front, please." Cato charged between one and five demmers for a charm, depending on the difficulty, the ingredients required, and how tuned it was to the person. Truth-charms needed to be specific.

Argan paid without demur, and Jonas turned to the workbench and to his little pots. Dried river-weed, to take the cityangel's promise; willow-leaf; and a fishbone. Then rose (the expensive part), for family or loved ones. He dropped them all into his mixing bowl, and began to grind them together, reaching out as he did so to catch Beckett's attention, twisting it into the truth-charm to unwind when it was used. His wrists prickled with the tension that held everything together, merging it all into one intention. That was the part that meant magic, the sorcerer's ability. Without that, you could grind away all day and achieve nothing. Power coalesced around him, bubbling along his bones and down into the mixing-bowl as the fishbone cracked under the pestle and cracked again. And *there*, the fragment of Beckett's attention, snagged into the river weed. He ground for a couple more seconds, making sure nothing escaped, then set down the bowl and picked up a tiny muslin pouch. He tucked the mixture into it, a finger-pinch at a time, then tied the string at the top tightly, and turned to Argan.

"There you are. To use it, cut the bag or undo the string, and shake it over the hand of the one you are testing, as they speak."

He couldn't imagine that Argan's lover was going to take that well; unless, perhaps, Argan's suspicions were justified, in which case they still wouldn't be thrilled, but at least Argan would be in the right.

Anyway. Three demmers was three demmers.

Argan took the little bag from him, and as his hand touched Jonas' fingers, they tingled. Had some of the mixture escaped the bag? Had Argan inadvertently used the truth-charm on him? Then something tightened in his head, and he recognised the precursor to a flicker.

Argan, with another figure, their back to Jonas. Argan looking agonised, apologetic. Argan being slapped; the other figure – plump, in a red over-robe – storming out of the room. Tears on Argan's cheeks...

It faded. Jonas was on his knees on the floor, and Cato, in front of him, was speaking rapidly to Argan, as he ushered him out of the room.

"Takes him this way, great strain of doing magic, shows how much he's put into that truth charm of yours. Best of luck. Out."

He came back to kneel by Jonas. "Jonas? Are you well?"

"He won't have any joy of it," Jonas said, inanely. The room still shivered in the corners of his eyes.

"Well, of course he won't, the fool. You don't use a truth-charm on your lover unless you want them to be your ex-lover. He'd be much better off either choosing not to see, or ditching them. But we're sorcerers, not relationship counsellors."

"I mean…" Jonas hesitated, automatically unwilling to say more. But Cato's eyes had already widened in interest.

"Ah! Was that a flicker? Did you see what's going to happen?" He put a hand under Jonas' elbow and helped him to his feet. "Sit down."

Jonas sat on Tait's chair. His legs felt weak, like there were sparks running up and down the muscles in his thighs. Cato handed him a mug of – Jonas drank, and coughed – fairly rough red wine.

"That should probably be water, but I don't have any to hand. Now…"

"Don't want to talk about it," Jonas said, mutinously.

Cato's lips compressed. "You never do. Write it down, at least. If you want to work out what's going on here." He sat on the bed and leant back on his hands.

"You write it down," Jonas muttered.

"They're your notes, Jonas. And, indeed, you're the one that has them, not me." Cato's voice held a sliver of annoyance, then he shifted his weight and changed tone. "You know, if you'd told him what you saw, you could have charged him double, easily?"

"And then what?" Jonas demanded. "I'm not even sure I *can* change something, or anyone can, once I've seen it.

So I tell him, and he does it anyway? Then what?"

"Worth finding out if you can, if you ask me. Because, honestly, the business implications…"

"What about the moral ones?" Jonas felt hollow. The wine wasn't helping.

Cato shrugged elegantly. "I take it the lover reacts badly?" Jonas didn't respond. Cato went on, "In which case, couldn't you save both of them a lot of bother by telling him that? Maybe they'd become the love story of the century. Who knows."

"I don't know what I saw," Jonas said. "I never do, not really. I see it. I don't get an explanation. Maybe it was something else I saw. Maybe it was the threat of the truth-charm. Maybe his lover slapped him to hide their own deceit. How should I know?" He'd said more than he meant to.

Cato's eyes were still bright with interest. "Even so…"

"Leave it," Jonas said, more harshly than he'd meant to, and much more harshly than he ever usually spoke to Cato. He flinched, but Cato just shrugged a shoulder.

"Very well. That aside, you did well."

"I felt daft," Jonas said.

"You looked a little awkward. But our baker was more on edge than you were, so he didn't notice. The charm worked, I felt that well enough, and you didn't waste time with the grinding. All excellent. And three demmers!"

Jonas brightened up. That was two good day's wages, carrying messages, and for much less work. He pulled the notes from his pocket.

"*Of* which," Cato said, neatly plucking the three demmer-notes out of his hand, rearranging them, and taking one, "one is mine, as you are still my apprentice."

"Hey! You didn't tell me that!" Jonas protested.

"I don't tell you a lot of things," Cato said. "I'd shut up if I were you, or I'll charge you rent on the room too."

He probably didn't mean it. But. Best be on the safe side. Jonas took the remaining two notes back. He could get a round in tonight and have some left for groceries tomorrow.

"Take the chair back to Tait on your way out," Cato told him. "And I'll see you in two days for our usual lesson. And make sure you write down the flicker. Well done, though. Excellent start."

Jonas ought to feel good about this afternoon's work, especially the three – two – demmers. Instead, he just felt empty. Empty, and unsure.

Walking back through the squats towards the Dog's Tail, to find Asa and Tam, Jonas found himself slowing, doubt chewing his insides. Instead of turning right towards the pub, he carried on down to the river. He leant on the stone balustrade of the promenade and watched the water flow by below. Tide was on the turn, the water swirling sluggishly.

What would happen, if he tried to stop the flicker? It wasn't that he'd never tried. He had, when he was younger, and it had never worked. But maybe he just went about things the wrong way. Maybe now he was an adult, and a sorcerer, people would listen. Argan Etolin had taken him seriously. If Jonas went to him, told him that it was a bad idea...

...told him that he'd seen the future? Argan's own future? No way that could end well. If the man believed him, he'd want more. (Worse, if he believed him but thought this was something sorcerers in general did, both Cato and Reb would be furious.) If he didn't, it wouldn't make any difference to the flicker, because he wouldn't change anything, and Jonas wouldn't have proved anything.

Cato had said, maybe it was worth trying. Jonas picked at the dry skin around his thumbnail. What if he went back, asked Cato how to go about that?

But this was *his*, his flicker. His ability. His to sort out. Not Cato's. If he was going to do it, he could make the damn decision himself.

Still unsure, he wandered over Old Bridge, towards

Marek Square. Jonas hadn't taken the messages to Argan himself (Cato had firmly advised against that), but he remembered the direction on them. The bakery was over the other side of the river from the squats, a few minutes' walk southwest of Marek Square. He glanced over at the Salinas embassy, and took the other side of the square. It would be just his luck to run into Kia, the ambassador, right now, and whenever he saw her it seemed to end up in trouble for him. Not to mention that he still owed her a favour, and if he avoided her for long enough, it would run out.

He skirted a knot of porters gossiping beside a fried-vegetable stall. Could he try offering Argan advice? *As a sorcerer, I felt an ethical duty to warn you...* but then, why hadn't he offered that warning before Argan left with the truth-charm? Or, *the cityangel warned me...* that could work. Anyone who came to a sorcerer must have some belief in the cityangel.

He would look like a mystical idiot, maybe, but it was better than the other. And much better than the idea of stealing the truth-charm back. Or orchestrating some complicated scenario where it couldn't be used...he'd been watching too many plays. Simple was best. The cityangel had told him it was a bad idea.

Now, of course, he had to *find* Argan Etolin. He might not have gone back to the bakery, this late in the afternoon. Bakers, Jonas was vaguely aware, got up early. Still. It was the only direction Jonas had. He'd try.

The bakery was in a district towards the edge of the city where dry land began to give way to swamp, but not quite out in the newest bits where the more enterprising builders were draining or building over the swamp. Little clumps of shops were scattered among the houses. Jonas passed a grocer's, a candlemaker's, and a haberdashery, and then on the next street a bottle-shop, an infusion-salon, and a bakery that wasn't Argan's. Arches to each side of the street gave onto courtyards where children were playing or laundry drying.

Jonas, consulting his mental map, turned left onto a

cross-street, and nearly went straight past Argan Etolin. He wheeled round and began to run after him, then remembered he needed to be more sombre and sorcerer-like. Which would be difficult; Etolin was walking fast. Jonas spotted a sidestreet, called up his mental map again, turned down it, and then ran like a hare, along and left and left again, to come out, not too much out of breath, just in front of Etolin.

He did his best impression of a sombre sorcerer, and Argan pulled up short in startlement.

"Jonas! My goodness. Is there some kind of – a problem, or, did I, um." He patted at his pockets, then looked up, face worried. "Surely the payment…"

"The charm will work," Jonas said, diction self-consciously formal, "and the payment is sound." Argan sagged in relief. "I have another concern, which I felt obliged to bring to you."

"Another – perhaps we should not discuss it in the street?" Argan suggested, which was a fair relief. "My shop is just back there."

They walked back to the shop in silence – Argan casting worried sideways glances at Jonas – and Argan let them in. The shop was closed, the shelves in the serving-area bare and clean, but the room was still warm from the ovens. Argan spread his hands.

"What, uh. What could possibly be so important as to bring you all this way?"

"The cityangel spoke to me," Jonas said. Best just get this over with. He framed a mental apology to Beckett, who had disclaimed all knowledge of Jonas' flickers and had nothing to do with this at all.

"The *cityangel*?" Argan looked bemused but, at least, not disbelieving.

"The truth-charm works, but will bring you only distress," Jonas said. Was he overdoing the serious tone? "The cityangel wished me to warn you."

"Bring me…what do you mean? Is he…?"

Jonas shrugged. "That is all the cityangel said." He suddenly wondered if Argan would want his money back.

"The cityangel. Really. Well. I suppose." Argan looked deeply flustered. "Well now…"

He pulled the truth-charm out of a pocket, and stood, looking at it. "I don't…Well."

The bell over the door jingled, and they both turned to look. The person who had just walked in wore a rich red over-robe and beautiful orange silk trousers underneath. Jonas' stomach plummeted.

"Argan, sweetheart. You were late. I wondered if there was a problem."

"Geraint. How, um. Lovely."

Geraint turned to Jonas. "And you are…?" He flicked a glance back at Argan.

"Jonas. T'Riseri."

"Salinas. How lovely. Welcome to our city. Geraint Bereni."

I've been here a year already, thank you. Probably not worth bothering, was it. And Bereni – some kind of offshoot of House Berenaz, then. Geraint had already swung back to Argan, who, like an idiot, was still holding the truth-charm.

"What have you got there?" Geraint asked.

Like even more of an idiot, Argan answered him. "It's, um. It's a truth-charm."

Geraint's eyebrows went up. "A truth-charm? Have you a business deal coming up? But you've only just bought this place. Surely – "

Argan went red, and stuttered, and Geraint jumped to what was, unfortunately, the correct conclusion. His eyes narrowed, and his brows came down. "It's not for business, is it. You didn't believe me, the other night. You're *testing* me? I told you already. You've nothing to worry about. Of course you haven't." He grabbed the charm from Argan's hand, and the bag split, its dust drifting across both of their hands. "At least, you *had* nothing to worry about." The charm rang, all the little pieces of dust lighting up at once, showing the truth of what Geraint was saying. "Now, you do. Because I have *had enough.*"

He stepped forward, and slapped Argan's face. Jonas winced.

"If you don't believe me, screw you. That's it. I'm out." He turned on his heel, nodded curtly to Jonas – now deeply grateful that he hadn't identified himself as a sorcerer, still less as the sorcerer who had made the wretched charm – and slammed out of the door.

Argan, face in hands, was crying.

"Um," Jonas said. At least the charm had worked, he supposed. It wasn't a particularly cheering thought.

"Couldn't the cityangel have warned you *sooner*?"

"Um," Jonas said again. "I don't really…have control, over the cityangel." He swallowed. "If you go after him, maybe apologise? He might…Apologise a *lot*, I mean."

Argan wiped at his cheeks, then shook his head. "You weren't there for our last argument. He won't."

Jonas winced. "Uh. I'm sorry. I still – once he's calmed down? Maybe? Anyway. I'll. Um. See myself out."

He slid out of the door as fast as he could, leaving Argan, still weeping, in the shop.

Well. So much for stopping the bloody flicker, then. He hadn't seen himself in it, but the angle he'd seen it at, he wouldn't have. And he sure as anchors wasn't telling Cato about it. Any of it.

But all the way back across the river and to his room, no appetite left for a drink at the Dog's Tail, he kept chewing on the question: if he'd acted sooner, if he'd dithered less, would he have succeeded?

SIX

Marcia was used to doing things that would be public knowledge, but it had never before been this personal. Being confirmed as Heir in the Council Chamber had been an event whose formality was dictated by custom and history. Some marriage-contracts were signed with a great deal of pageantry and celebration, too. But this was a child-contract, involving only a collection of people in a lawyer's room halfway down Marekhill; and then, doubtless, a series of reports in various news-sheets tomorrow. Which, however decorous, she could well do without.

The contract was lengthy. The detailed negotiations – between, firstly, Madeleine and Jamara, current Tigero-Heir, and then lawyers for both Houses – had gone smoothly enough, but there was a great deal to agree. Among other things, it covered the expectations around co-parenting and the settling of disputes – and it laid out the responsibilities of both parties in various circumstances, including if no pregnancy resulted, if Marcia's health prevented a second child, and, of course, if Marcia were to die in the process. (And, to be fair, if Andreas died, but his risk wasn't directly linked to the contract.) It wasn't that Marcia hadn't already known the risks of pregnancy and childbirth, but it was different to see it all laid out in stark black and white in front of her, not to mention to see what was considered appropriate compensation in each case.

Maybe she should have gone for adoption after all.

Andreas signed the final sheet underneath Marcia's signature, and looked up to smile at her as he stepped back. It gave her a slightly odd feeling in her stomach. In his formal tunic, he looked taller, and older than she remembered from last year's Council opening. Madeleine came forward to add her signature. Jamara, current Tigero-Heir and a distant cousin of Andreas', was the last to sign. How did she feel, signing the contract that was intended in due course to bump her out of the Heirship? The witnesses were another Tigero cousin, and Marcia's cousin Sophia.

"There you are," the lawyer said, dusting the ink to dry it off. "All done. Congratulations. I hope all goes smoothly." They bowed particularly low to Marcia, the one for whom that wish was most personally relevant.

"A pleasure," Madeleine said, bowing to the various Tigero representatives. "Delighted."

They made their way out of the lawyer's room onto Fourth Street, where a couple of bearers waited with their litters.

"Sophia," Madeleine said, taking Sophia's arm. "Please do come back to the House for tea." And for discussion of the Crescent; she was due to leave next week. "Marcia?"

"I'll walk," Marcia said, hastily. She wasn't keen on litters at the best of times; and she could do with stretching her legs.

"May I walk with you, perhaps?" Andreas offered.

The honest answer was *no*. She didn't particularly want to make polite conversation all the way up the Hill. But she could hardly say that, here and now, could she? "Of course," she said, and summoned a smile.

They had set off together – the long slow way along the streets, rather than cutting through the steep alleyways that ran straight up the Hill connecting each street with the next – before he spoke. "You could have said no, you know. I wouldn't have taken it amiss." He smiled sideways at her. "Still could. I'll go look at foils or something." He nodded at the window of the shop they were passing.

"You fence?" Marcia asked.

"Doesn't everyone? But I enjoy it, if that's what you mean."

Marcia was sure she'd never seen him at the salle; he

must go to another. "Perhaps we should have a match sometime."

"I would love that. But – truly, if you would rather be alone just now?"

She smiled, appreciating his candour. "I'm sorry if I came across as unenthusiastic. Just a little overwhelmed, perhaps. I promise, it's fine." They'd both expressed a desire for friendship; she should follow through.

"Read any good seditious literature lately?" he asked solemnly, and she laughed.

"No. I'm still thinking about what the Guilds are agitating for. I'm not convinced, I admit."

Andreas held his hand out and tipped it from side to side. "I have, as it happens. I've been back to Printers' Street a couple more times. There's certainly plenty that's – well, I wouldn't say *unobjectionable*, but it's nothing too dangerous. But some people. Well."

"Worse than what we saw the other week?"

"Some of it. Yes." He looked unhappy.

"Perhaps you could send me some?"

"Or you would be very welcome to come to Tigero House to see it now, if you're free. Over an infusion, perhaps. My grandmother would be delighted to meet you."

"Certainly," Marcia said. She'd meant to go straight home, but Andreas wanted to be friends, and she should respond to that. "I meant to ask, by the way – how does your Heir feel about all this?" It would have been rude, except that in the circumstances, she was entitled to be concerned about the future of one of her potential children, and how the Heir might treat them.

Of course, if Andreas died and Jamara became Head *before* the children grew up, likely neither would become Tigero-Heir at all.

"Jamara? She knows she is Heir only in the absence of a younger candidate," he said. "Assuming I remain well, she'll be too old to be Heir before I'm done."

"So she's just happy never to be Head?"

"Well, I don't think she minds enough to do anything

about it," Andreas said. "And it's not like being Heir doesn't come with its own rewards."

In Marcia's experience, most of the 'rewards' of being Heir involved a significant amount of work and Madeleine being annoying, and she said as much.

"Ha! I trust I am not too annoying, and Jamara is being compensated for her work. Part of our arrangement – well, I'm afraid I can't go into details, child-contract or no, but suffice it to say that all is well. There's no need to worry about her attitude to our children, if that is your concern."

Marcia drew family trees in her head and concluded that Jamara must have come from a significantly junior branch; and if she was taking over some of the more lucrative aspects of Tigero's trade and gaining a commensurate income…she might indeed be quite happy. She'd keep an eye open for Jamara pursuing a child-contract of her own, but for now, she waved an apologetic hand and said only, "Of course, forgive my intrusion."

"Not at all. I understand your concern." He looked sideways at her. "As of today, we have also agreed that she will not sign a child-contract of her own whilst she remains Heir."

Marcia's eyebrows went up. Well. That was reassuring. And unusual; though perhaps Jamara would be happy enough not to have a child. It was far from a universal desire.

They'd reached the end of Third Street, and were turning up onto Second; Tigero was at this end of Second Street, furthest from the cliff-edge and the view out over the river. Which, of course, was part of why Andreas was keen for this contract with House Fereno; Tigero was a weaker House, made weaker still by its recent experiences and the time its Head had spent growing into himself. Hardly his fault. He seemed to be getting to grips with it now.

The pretty courtyard was crowded with well-tended early spring flowers in pots, and the building, whilst smaller than House Fereno, was well-kept. The smooth clay tiles in the hallway were laid in an interesting geometric pattern which Marcia admired aloud.

A servant came to take her shawl, and Andreas ushered her through not into the formal main parlour, which Marcia caught a glimpse of through an open door, but into a smaller room further towards the back of the house. A window looked out onto gardens with their spring growth starting. One wall had a geometric mural of a similar type to the floor mosaic, and heat radiated from a ceramic stove. A small elderly lady sat in a rose-pink high-backed armchair by the window, knitting in her lap.

"Grandmother," Andreas said, stepping forward to kiss her affectionately on the hand. "This is Marcia, Fereno-Heir. Marcia, this is my grandmother, Leanne.

"It is delightful to meet you." Leanne was sharp-featured, and very sharp-eyed.

"Likewise, Ser Tigero," Marcia replied with a bow.

"By all means, Leanne." She gestured Marcia to sit down on the couch opposite her. "We have never previously been closely allied with House Fereno," she went on. "I am pleased that this will change."

"Indeed," Marcia said. "It is always good to acquire new allies."

Leanne sat back. "Especially when you're running short on them."

Marcia didn't let her own smile slip. "House Fereno has never been *short* on allies, I assure you, but we are of course always grateful to build new bonds."

"That's not what I heard," Leanne said. "The Smiths cancelled a deal with you, is what I heard. In favour of House Leandra. Gavin must be pleased that Daril boy is finally earning his place. Mind you, I never liked Gavin."

"No one likes Gavin," Marcia said, without thinking, then kicked herself, but Leanne cackled a delighted laugh.

"True, true. Didn't you like Daril once, though?"

"A very long time ago," Marcia said. There was no point in denying it; it had been common knowledge at the time, though what drove their breakup was emphatically not. "We are not well-acquainted now." That wasn't quite correct. But they weren't *friends*.

"And yet he backed the Guilds vote."

"Grandmother..." Andreas interjected uncomfortably, but Leanne ignored him.

"As did your grandson," Marcia said.

Leanne ignored her too. "Backed the Guilds vote, and now he's stealing your deals."

"I am sure Daril has his own reasons for anything he does," Marcia said. "Fereno and Leandra have never been *allied*." As everyone knew.

A servant brought in a tray of infusion-pots, and Leanne pursed her lips and let the matter slide. Marcia was far from sure what the woman's aim was; simply to needle her? To discover something specific? She poured infusions for both Andreas and Marcia, from different pots, without stopping to ask what they wanted.

"Good for babies," she declared cheerfully, placing cups in front of each of them.

"I'd be delighted to hear the recipe," Marcia said with automatic politeness, then regretted it.

"A private blend," Leanne said, smug. "But I can allow my infusion-blender to make you up some, if you would like."

"That would be very kind," Marcia said, and took a sip.

It tasted, of course, absolutely appalling. She kept her expression calm and took another sip.

"You have a good family history, with babies," Leanne said. "I remember both your grandmothers. Two large families. Your mother, not so much." She nodded. "Twins, though, there was that. If you have twins, you'll complete the whole contract in one, I suppose."

"I'll be happy with one at a time, thank you," Marcia said, trying to keep the tartness out of her voice. "And fewer children is more customary now, isn't it?" Andreas had only had the one sister. And if Leanne was going to be this way, she was damned if she wasn't going to hit back.

Leanne's eyes narrowed a little, in acknowledgement of the dig. "Indeed, I am old, and old-fashioned. So, how is your twin?"

"No longer Fereno," Marcia said, managing not to roll her eyes. Cato – and the whole Cato *situation* – was not something it was possible to put her off-balance with, not in a Marekhill context.

"Must be hard, then, now you are on your own," Leanne said triumphantly.

"Oh, it means the only person I have to negotiate with is my mother," Marcia said lightly. "So, I suppose it has its advantages and its disadvantages."

Andreas, watching all this with wide eyes, finally waded in, and not before time. "Grandmother, as ever, I appreciate your thoughts, and your tea. I was hoping you would be able to assist me with some advice on the Spring Festival."

Leanne obviously couldn't avoid that particular lure; Andreas got her talking about rituals and floral decoration, and Marcia sat back, pasted on a look of polite interest, and grimly forced herself to drink her terrible baby-related infusion. She managed a few comments on the matter of Spring Festival – thank goodness Cousin Cara managed it for House Fereno, as it was precisely the sort of thing that neither Marcia nor Madeleine cared about in the slightest – before Andreas neatly concluded things and stood up.

"Thank you for your time, Grandmother," he said, with a little bow.

Marcia, rising to her feet with alacrity, bowed also. "It was good to meet you, Ser Leanne. Do send me a message with the direction of your infusion-blender."

Out in the corridor, Andreas let out a long sigh, and wrinkled his nose apologetically. "I'm sorry. I would have warned you, but she *said...*"

Marcia shook her head. "Don't worry. I can handle a grandmother. Even a spiky one. She's only interested in what's best for you and your House." She was, she felt, being very generous; but Andreas looked worried, and it was hardly his fault. This meeting was supposed to be helping to build their friendship, after all; she should be gracious.

"Well. I suppose so." He sounded doubtful.

"She's your grandmother," Marcia said, touching his sleeve. "It's fine." His grandmother, and his only remaining older relative. No wonder she fussed about babies.

"Anyway. You were going to come and look at these pamphlets, before you go?"

In Andreas' office, they both bent over the pamphlets he pulled out.

"They're getting worse, is the trouble."

"Or you're getting better at finding them."

"That is possible," Andreas admitted. "That one," he pointed, "the printer brought out to offer me. Said he'd noticed I was interested in the matter."

Marcia looked it over, and winced. It began by describing the Houses as tyrannical, and got more polemic from there. The writer felt even more strongly about Teren, to judge from a couple of pointed asides on the first page. "It's not...illegal."

"Not quite," Andreas said. "But it will be if the Guilds have their way."

"I don't like this, not at all, but I still don't think banning is the right way forward."

Leafing through the articles, she could understand the feeling behind them, the fire and the fury. But the way it was expressed...the Council, seeing this, would hardly take it as something to listen to and consider, would they?

"You're quiet," Andreas observed, leaning back against the desk.

"Just thinking about how to bring this to the Council."

Andreas' eyebrows rose. "What, as support for the Guild?"

"No! Not at all. The thing is, some of these ideas are good, and valid, and reasonable." She tapped one of the leaflets. "Why shouldn't more people get some say in how the city works? And the Council should know how people feel."

Andreas was frowning. "Should it?"

"How can we work for everyone's benefit, without

knowing how people experience their lives and what they want?"

Andreas shrugged. "Like my father used to say. When the Houses – and the Guilds – prosper, Marek does too. That's always been the way."

"Just because it's always been *the* way doesn't mean it's the *best* way. The Council is out of touch. This is the sort of thing – put differently, I admit – that it needs to hear. To listen to *all* of Marek."

"I think you must be sitting in a different Council to me," Andreas said, dubiously.

"Maybe." She sighed. "Not all of them listen, I know that. But maybe…" She needed to think about who might be open to listening. Have some discussions. If the Guilds were going to make another push, she needed to be ready to push back. "Anyway. I'd best be off."

"Keep me updated on your thoughts. I may not entirely agree with you, but I'm open to being convinced." He smiled, and Marcia smiled back. He really did have a nice smile. And House-formal suited him.

"I'll see how we go," she agreed.

She let him see her out into the courtyard.

"I meant to say," he said, shyly, as they stood at the top of the steps after she'd turned down the offer of a litter. "I am delighted that we have made this contract. I – a child, I mean. Children. I am glad, to be doing this with you."

"And I you," she said, bowing to him, and meant it. She hadn't had a real friendship with someone at her political level before. Nisha might be be Kilzan-Heir now, and they were still close, but she wasn't willing to discuss politics or to risk rocking the boat with Kilzan-Head. Marcia could *talk* to Andreas.

He held out a hand. "Since we are to have a child together?"

She clasped his hand, an intimacy beyond a customary farewell. "Of course."

When she looked back from the gate, he was still on the steps, looking after her.

⊙ ⊙

These evenings, Daril felt, had been a lot more enjoyable when he'd been able to get raging drunk and behave inappropriately. It was the naming-day celebration of Cerit-Heir's latest baby; he leant on the balcony overlooking House Cerit's large reception room and tried not to sigh audibly. Cerit weren't exactly renowned for their entertainment – Cerit-Head, though decent enough, was unimaginative – but of course, one couldn't just skip these things.

Well, he'd wanted to be Heir, and he'd done a lot to make it happen, one way and another. He had to accept the costs. He sipped the white wine he'd been offered on his way up the balcony steps, and made an appreciative face. At least William wasn't stingy with the drinks. He straightened, turned, and saw Hagadath, of the Smiths, and Fredera, of the Scriveners, coming towards him.

Smiths and Scriveners. Interesting.

"Ah, Daril," Hagadath said, expansively. "How are you this fine evening, then?"

"Oh, well enough, well enough," Daril said. "A good drink and good conversation, always a pleasure." Well, they would be, if the latter was available here. Maybe he'd be able to catch up with Andreas later; Andreas was good value. Even if his taste, apparently, was somewhat lacking, given that he'd just signed a child-contract with *Marcia*, of all people. Good politics, though, Daril couldn't fault that.

Hagadath nodded agreeably. "How's your father? I was sorry to hear he's been so unwell."

Daril wasn't sorry himself; it was, after all, his fault in the first place, and it meant he almost always carried the House vote now. It was only Gavin's hideous stubbornness meant he hadn't yet retired, the old bastard.

"He couldn't make it tonight, unfortunately, but he hopes to be better soon."

"A shame he wasn't in the Chamber the other week,

when we were discussing the matter of these pamphlets," Fredera said.

Aha. The printers. Of course. They were canvassing.

"Ah, but Daril here was, and I'm sure we can count on his support," Hagadath said cheerfully. "We've done good business together lately, haven't we?"

Daril smiled urbanely at him. He wasn't bothered one way or the other about the pamphlets. Why were Hagadath and Fredera so concerned? Was it just rank conservatism, or was there something else?

"Oh, I like to think Marek is strong enough to cope with a variety of views," he said, and paid only a tiny bit of attention as Hagadath went through another version of what he'd said in Council. Smiths and Scriveners. What was going on? The pamphlets themselves were surely just people letting off steam. No need for the Houses or the Guilds to lower themselves to pay attention; and in any case, banning them would clearly just drive the sentiments underground, which would be worse.

But. He'd been in a printshop the other week – the factor in Darem, in the Crescent, had sent word back that foreign hearth-tales and wonder-stories had suddenly become terribly popular with well-off gentlemen. The printer had been more than happy to agree to make up some nicely-bound versions of Exurian and Teren stories, to test the market. Halfway through, an apprentice had come in, talking loudly to a friend through the door, and Daril had heard "but we told those Guild arses where to get off". The printer had ticked her off and sent her out for a new ream of paper, but...

Smiths and Scriveners. The older printers were all one or the other, of course, or had been before they quit. And the Guilds...had turned them down, initially, hadn't they, when they petitioned to become a Guild. That was right. He'd forgotten about that; it was a good couple of years ago now. Now they were doing well, the Guilds wanted in on the action, and the printers had turned them down. That would explain why 'seditious pamphlets' were suddenly such a concern to Hagadath. His proposals would be a massive, and expensive, nuisance for anyone who printed small-scale stuff, whether revolutionary or otherwise. Most of the printers did at least a little of that, bread-and-butter work, serial romances and work for clubs and so on, and some of them did most of their business that way.

That didn't feel like everything accounted for, but he could investigate further later. For now – he needed a way out that antagonised neither Smiths nor printers.

"…And I'm sure you share our concerns, of course, for the wellbeing of the city," Hagadath finished off. Fredera nodded enthusiastically next to him.

"Well," Daril said, mind whirring. "Of course we all want what is best for Marek. However, I'm sure you understand that I need to be certain what *is* best for Marek. For all of us. I don't think, myself, that we need to trouble ourselves about the lower city's freedom to express their concerns – might even be informative, eh?" He put a little disdain for *the lower city* into his tone, making it clear that he saw Hagadath and Fredera on his side of that divide, but they didn't look convinced. "Either way, Marek is strong. We have no need to censor our citizens. I wouldn't want to act as Teren have been." He went heavy on the scorn, and both Wardens automatically nodded. Good. Of course, the Guilds didn't much like Teren, which helped. "And of course, one's business interests…" He trailed off delicately. Hagadath made a face, then hurriedly pasted their smile back on. "But of course I understand your position, and I thank you for taking the time to draw these issues so clearly to my attention. I will consult my father."

Hagadath looked pleased at that. Of course they would be. Gavin would happily come down on both lower city and printers like half a House of dressed stone.

Now he came to think of it, it had been an offhand comment, but maybe he could, at that, learn something from all this lower city outpouring of opinion and emotion. There was power where he was standing now; but there was also half a city of people who were no part of that. If he could tap *that*...

A thought for another time.

"Well, I appreciate that, Leandra-Heir," Fredera said, "and I hope you won't hesitate to come to either of us if you have further questions."

She didn't look too happy, and he needed to keep them both sweet. "Speaking of business opportunities," Daril said, "I was speaking to a Salinas captain the other day, and heard word of a new market opening up, out beyond the islands." Both Wardens looked suddenly interested, as well they might. The Salinas hadn't found anywhere new to sell to for a long time. "Obviously we need to know more, but I am looking to put together some samples, and have a provisional cargo booking for the prospective sailing. Might I call on you both this week to discuss the matter?"

"Of course," Hagadath and Fredera agreed, almost together, eyes bright.

"I'd prefer the matter not get around, you understand," Daril said. "Just for those my House works closely with." Trowel it on. It was a bother to waste that on the Scriveners; though the Smiths he'd have given it to anyway. Good smithwork sold well nearly anywhere.

"In any case," he said, draining his glass and concealing his opinion of the stuff. "I must go find myself a refill. Enjoy your evening, yes? And my thanks."

A great deal to think about.

It had been years since Marcia had had the slightest interest in the younger children of the Houses, those too young to be in consideration as Heir or to attend parties for longer than a dutiful ten minutes wearing best tunics and tutor-drilled polite expressions. Now, she couldn't help but think: if all went well in the coming months, Cerit-Heir's latest baby would be one of her child's close peers.

Which was a shame in that she couldn't bear Cerit-Heir, and the child might take after him.

The baby itself had been shown round in an elaborate frock, and had long since gone off with its child-nurse; this was well into the evening part of the celebration. Cerit-Heir's spouse was established on a couch at the far end of the room, with Cerit-Heir himself looking after them.

When Andreas saw her across the room, he excused himself politely from a conversation with Pedeli-Head, and came across to bow and press her hand. Everyone, of course, knew about the child-contract, and for a moment Marcia felt that nearly everyone was watching them. She smiled back at Andreas – *Fereno does have allies, you see?* – and took him over to join a conversation with some of her friends.

Thankfully it was the height of bad manners to enquire about how someone was going to complete a child-contract; which did not prevent Nisha from raising an eyebrow during a moment when Andreas was at the other side of the room and only she, Marcia, and Aden were present, and saying, quietly, "Well, darling, *I* wouldn't kick him out of bed. Should you wish to pursue that as an option. Should your inappropriate liaison permit."

"There's no inappropriate liaison," Marcia said. She'd been saying that for months; Nisha ignored her. It had stung more than she'd expected that since none of her friends knew about Reb, despite all Nisha's arch comments, none of them knew about the breakup either. "Only six months ago you were complaining that he had all the backbone of an eel," she reminded Nisha instead.

"He's grown up a bit," Nisha said, eyeing Andreas thoughtfully. "Good thing too."

"One might say you have as well," Aden said.

"Wash your mouth out!" Nisha said in mock-horror, and then Andreas was on his way back and Marcia hastily moved the conversation on.

Nisha wasn't wrong, though. Andreas wasn't bad-looking at all, now she'd spent a bit more time with him.

Not that she was going to say as much to Nisha, even if they did have a moment of privacy, because Nisha would never, ever, let up about it if she did.

Later, talking to Madeleine and Jyrithi-Head – Marcia was always uncertain about Jyrithi-Head's politics, but their manners were impeccable whoever they were speaking to – Marcia saw, over her mother's shoulder, Daril at the other side of the room. And in conversation with him, smiling cheerfully, was Andreas.

Andreas and Daril were friends? How had she not known that? Daril was the wrong age, and Andreas, surely, had never been one of his hangers-on during his disreputable years, even once he had been old enough.

But Daril had become more personable of late, hadn't he? Had begun rebuilding his alliances – and House Tigero could use allies of their own. The contract with Fereno was one move, but there was no reason Andreas shouldn't also look to Leandra. It would be a strong move, to be on good terms with both.

She really had to stop underestimating Andreas.

"What do you think, Marcia?" Madeleine asked her, and she hurriedly turned her mind back to the matter of Crescent tariffs.

Both she and Andreas were circulating all night, mixing the more pleasurable aspects of socialising with their House requirements. But every so often Marcia would find Andreas at her elbow, flagging down a passing servant and asking if she could use a glass of something; or he would be in a group she was passing, and would smile and invite her to join the conversation; or would extract himself from a different conversation at the same time as her, and offer a wry comment on, for example, the effort required to remain polite when speaking to Athitol-Head. It was – pleasant, to have someone she felt she could rely on. Not that she hadn't had Nisha, and Aden, in the past, but…Well. She liked Andreas. It was good to feel that someone else was on her side.

Later, she encountered him in the foyer.

"Leaving?"

"I think I'm done for the night, yes," she said. "I know it's a little early, but I have a meeting first thing tomorrow with our factor."

Andreas nodded. "I was about to leave, myself. Were you thinking of taking a litter?"

"Madeleine left already. So no, I'll walk."

"May I walk with you?"

"By all means," Marcia said. Although House Tigero was only two houses along the road from here; it would hardly be a long walk.

Marcia turned down the offer of a torch-bearer from the servant on duty in the courtyard. There was starlight, a little moonlight through the clouds, and torches in front of every House. It was a dry night, if a little chilly, and Marcia tucked her shawl securely round her.

"Or an escort, my lady?" the servant asked.

"I'm fine," Marcia assured them.

"I'm escorting you, after all," Andreas said cheerfully.

"It's hardly dangerous," Marcia said. "Which is just as well, as I've five minutes to walk once you turn in."

"Oh," Andreas said. "I was intending to walk all the way back with you."

Marcia felt a little warmth in her stomach. "Were you now? Well, that will be very pleasant."

It was nice to have someone to go out of their way to spend time with you. It was a good feeling.

They walked together along Second Street, past House Tigero and the rest, talking over the evening. They paused at the turn of the road, just before House Fereno's gates, where there was a waist-height wall on which one could lean and look out over the river. To their left, lights burned outside some of the infusion-salons and late-night clubs further down Marekhill; in front of them, the river was barely visible in the dark behind the even darker outline of the rocks that fell away in front of them. A couple of lights could be seen out to sea; fishing-vessels close in, or Salinas ships further out.

Andreas took a deep breath, as if preparing to speak, and Marcia turned to him. She couldn't quite see his expression, here, away from the torches.

"I've been trying to think of a smooth way to say this," he said, his voice self-deprecatory, "but I'm not getting very far, so perhaps better just to be blunt."

Marcia had a suspicion that she knew where this was going. She could still stop it, if she wanted. If she said, let's not, or if she pretended not to have heard and moved away, Andreas would accept that. And yet…And yet, she didn't think she wanted to stop him.

"Yes?" she said, neither encouraging nor discouraging, balancing in the moment.

He shifted sideways, turning more towards her, the moonlight shining off his dark hair. "I'm attracted to you. You've probably noticed. In other circumstances, I'd say, well, we're both free agents, how about we…entertain ourselves, for a while, together. If you wanted to. But as it stands…"

"As it stands," Marcia said, "why don't we entertain ourselves and deal with the child-contract without involving a doctor?"

"Oh dear," Andreas said. "It sounds rather too pragmatic, put that way."

Marcia laughed. She felt, suddenly, like she was in control of this situation. It felt straightforward, and after everything with Reb, that felt good. "Oh, I don't know. There's nothing wrong with a bit of pragmatism."

In the quiet of the night, she heard Andreas' intake of breath. "I, uh. I really don't want to make any assumptions, here…"

"Yes," Marcia said. "Yes, I am attracted to you, too. And a little…entertainment would be enjoyable. And very practical. But."

"But?"

Marcia chose her words carefully. "I am a free agent, in that sense. But." Ugh, she didn't want to say this, but she had to. Leaving things out hadn't got her far last time, had it? And she liked to think that she learnt from her mistakes. "But that's a relatively recent development. I like you, Andreas, as a friend. I find you attractive. But

I'm not up for anything beyond a friendly fuck, to put it bluntly." Even if she had been, he was the Head of one house and she was Heir of another. They could have something long-term, if they wanted, but they both knew it would never be a marriage-contract. "We've just signed a child-contract, and a parenting-contract. We're both of the Thirteen Houses. We're going to be dealing with one another for a long time. I'd rather we never went any further, than that we destroyed our friendship."

"That's fair," Andreas said. "I wouldn't want that, either."

"But with that established," Marcia turned to face him fully. "And if you are happy with those caveats. I would really very much like to, ah. Get to know you a little better. A lot better."

Andreas shifted his weight, moving a little closer to her. His voice was lower, and she could see the edge of his cheekbone, the shape of his nose, the shadow of his eyes, in the moonlight. "That sounds like an excellent idea to me."

He moved slowly, giving her time to change her mind. She didn't; and their lips met. He didn't feel like Reb; she could feel the tiny edge of his stubble. He didn't smell like Reb, but of a light and doubtless very expensive cologne. But his kiss was sweet, and promising, and, as it continued, a little dirty, and she felt something flare to life inside her.

This felt easy, and uncomplicated; it felt like the solution to a problem. It wouldn't last, but that was just fine. For now, this would do very well indeed. She slid a hand round the back of Andreas' neck, and let herself enjoy it.

SEVEN

It was morning outside, but the drape across Cato's window was heavy, and little light filtered through. Tait thought they'd be out by the time Cato woke, but halfway through putting on their boots, Cato rolled over and made a horrible groaning noise. They turned round to see Cato peering at them under his arm.

"You off out? It's *early* yet." His voice was clogged with sleep.

"Not that early," Tait said, doing up their second boot. "You go on back to sleep."

"That would be easier if you weren't clattering around," Cato grumbled. A blatant lie; Tait had been as quiet as they could. "Where're you off to, anyway?"

"The barge-yard."

"What? What on earth for?"

Tait sighed and sat down on the bed. "Ben. Down at the pie-shop."

"Ben's at the barge-yard?"

"Cato. Hush and let me tell you, if you want to know. Ben at the pie-shop said, there's all of a sudden lots of Teren folk coming in down the river. And a few on carts by the road. Enough that there's people down there, now, trying to help them get themselves sorted when they get here. Ben says, a lot of them aren't really sure what they're about."

"Why on earth did they come here, then, if they don't know where they're going?" Cato yawned, wide enough that Tait heard his jaw crack.

"They're refugees, Ben says." Tait looked down at their hands. "Not *going*, so much as *coming from*."

"Running away from, you mean." Cato looked marginally more awake. "You think things have got worse in Teren since you left?"

Tait nodded. Neither of them mentioned the word 'demons'.

"It's not your responsibility, you know. You don't have to go help them just because you started off in Teren too."

"I don't have to," Tait agreed. "I just want to."

"They might not even need help. You might be going all the way over there for nothing." Cato sounded grumpy, but Tait knew better than to take it personally.

"They might not. I want to offer."

"Instead of just staying here and going back to sleep? Ugh. Well, that's your funeral, I suppose." Cato sat up slightly. "Fuck, it's cold. Didn't you think to do a warming charm?"

"Haven't done one yet," Tait said.

Cato looked surprised. "Really? Oh, well, tell Reb you need to cover that sharpish. Or I'll teach you, if you prefer. Anyway. Off you go. Give me a kiss before you cruelly abandon me?"

"Yes, I am very cruel in leaving you to go back to sleep." Tait leant in to give Cato a kiss. He smelt of sleep, and his skin was warm under Tait's hands. It took an act of will to pull themself away; they were apprehensive about what they would find at the barge-yard.

"Have fun," Cato said, burrowing back under the blankets. "Oh, I've got a client later, so don't come barging in." His voice was muffled by the pillow.

"Do I ever come barging in?"

"Sadly no. See you later, beautiful."

The endearment warmed Tait from the inside, all the way out of the door and down into the street. The air was damp and cold even though the sun was well up. It encouraged Tait to hurry, which was perhaps for the best. If they were going, they should get on with it.

Walking into the barge-yard felt peculiar. They hadn't been there since they, with Reb, Cato, and Jonas, had got rid of the demon that had been chasing Tait through Teren, and trying to break into Marek. 'Peculiar'. That was one word for it. For a moment Tait could see that hazy purple figure again, out on the road; they shook their head and it was gone. They were being silly. The demon had gone, and it wasn't surprising that they didn't like being here, but there was no actual reason to be afraid of it. They were here for a reason, and standing around fretting wasn't going to help anyone, was it?

There was a pale canvas tent over in one corner of the yard, furthest from the river, a few tens of yards from the slightly down-at-heel inn that took up another corner. It hadn't been there the last time Tait was here, so it seemed like a sensible place to start. Somewhere on the way across the yard, something indefinable shifted, and Tait realised they'd stepped outside of the area of Beckett's protection. They shivered, hesitated, then made themself keep walking.

One side of the tent had the canvas looped up out of the way. Tait stepped inside, and saw someone behind a plank-and-trestle table, with a map and a stack of paper on it, and a dozen or so folk with bags sitting on hay-sacks in the other part of the tent. Somebody got up from the side of the table nearest to Tait, and the person at the other side looked up.

"I didn't think there was another boat due," she started, frowning at Tait, then waved a hand. "Never mind. Take a seat, and I'll help you when I can."

"I, um," Tait said. "I'm not from Teren. Well, I am, but not today. I came to help. Um. If you need help."

"Oh." She looked them up and down. "Well, if you're willing, that would be lovely. I'm Jeres. What we're doing here is helping people find somewhere to stay. So what you could do, is find out from those folk over there whether they know someone in Marek and need to be put in touch, or whether they have no idea what to do at all. The ones who don't know, I'll deal with. The ones who do, see if you can direct them. Or a friend of mine will be back soon, he's been walking people into town." She rubbed at her forehead.

"I'll sort something out," Tait promised.

"All right, who's next?" Jeres called over to the huddle

of people, and one of them hesitantly went over to her table as Tait went to see how they could help.

Most of the dozen people had no idea where they wanted to go, and Tait asked them to wait for Jeres. One had a cousin who'd come to Marek some years before, who was an embroiderer, but not a Guild one. She had the cousin's address, even, over on the far side of Old Bridge, in the warren of streets that spilled out from Marek Square away from Marekhill. The other had the name of a friend-of-a-friend, but no address, just the knowledge that they were a member of the Vintner's Guild, having grown up on a Teren vineyard. No one wanted to talk about why they'd left Teren, and Tait didn't ask.

When Jeres' friend Kal came back, he offered to take both the embroiderer's cousin and the vintner's acquaintance back into Marek proper, to drop one at the cousin's place and help the other talk to the Vintner's Guild to see if they could find the acquaintance. "If not," Kal said cheerfully, "I'll bring you back here and Jeres will sort you out."

Jeres had sent another couple of folk off out of the tent, and the others were waiting to speak to her; Tait was, at least for now, at a loose end. They shivered, and realised, belatedly, how chilly it was.

"Oh, what a *good* idea," they heard Jeres say with deep thankfulness, and looked up to see a couple of people wrangling a brazier into the tent. One of them had a walking-stick in the hand that wasn't pulling at the brazier.

"Not really for you," they said cheerfully, and Tait realised it was Alyssa.

"Course it isn't," Jeres said, rolling her eyes. "Thankfully, the brazier doesn't know that, and I'll get the heat anyway."

Tait hadn't spent much time with Alyssa, despite the fact that they were both Reb's apprentices; Reb hadn't encouraged them to work together, or invited them to get to know one another apart from a brief cursory introduction. Tait was slightly nervous of Alyssa, who was the sort of person who Tait associated with…doing things, and making decisions, and a host of things that Tait themself shied away from.

By the time they'd decided they ought to offer to help with the brazier, Alyssa and her friend had dumped it in the middle of the tent, slightly closer to the refugees than to Jeres. The friend nodded and ducked back out of the tent; Alyssa looked up and looked startled. "Tait? What're you doing here?"

"Triage," Jeres said succinctly. "And very useful they've been too. Are you going to light that thing, or just admire it?"

"Good to see you too," Alyssa said.

"Is there, uh. Is there anything else I can help with?" Tait asked.

"You can bring in the rope of logs outside." Alyssa said.

By the time they'd fetched the logs, flames were visible in the brazier, and Tait could even feel the heat if they stood very close. Jeres was dealing with the last of the refugees.

"I'll take this lot over to the squats," she said to Alyssa, getting up from behind the table and stretching.

"I can do it?" both Tait and Alyssa offered at the same time, then looked at one another and grinned awkwardly.

"No, thanks, I need to stretch my legs. And check in at the Guildhall."

Alyssa frowned. "I thought you took leave?"

"Yes, well, that was when I thought this was a temporary situation." Jeres sighed. "I need to go back tomorrow, all else being equal, but I've been having words with some people. Might be able to get the Guildhall to send me down here official-like."

"The Guilds doing something useful?" Alyssa said, mock-wide-eyed. "Say it ain't so. Next you'll have them signing the bottom of your Petition, eh?"

"Oh, hush, you."

Alyssa laughed; Tait wasn't quite sure what they were

missing, but evidently Alyssa and Jeres knew each other well. "There's plenty of folk coming in with Guild links, true," she said. "You think you can convince them it's worth their while to get involved?"

"That's the theory. Whole point of the Guilds is to look after people, right? Anyway. Let's not get into that just now. If you could stay here, for a bit? There's another barge in later. Might not have anyone on it, of course, but on current evidence that's a futile hope. Need someone here if they show up early. Don't have to do anything, just tell 'em to wait for me."

"Right you are," Alyssa said, and poked at the brazier.

Tait wasn't sure whether to stay and help with the next barge, assuming it came, or to leave Alyssa here.

"You're from Teren," Alyssa said, abruptly.

"Um. Yes."

"Know anything about demons?"

Surely Reb would have told them if she'd told Alyssa – everything that had happened? Tait met Alyssa's eyes, but it didn't look like she was asking with any kind of…ulterior motive.

"Some," Tait agreed, then, more accurately, "Quite a bit."

"Right. Yeah." She looked down and poked at the brazier again. She looked almost awkward, although that didn't seem very like Alyssa. She always looked like she knew exactly what she was doing and what she wanted to do. "Don't suppose you'd be up for coming for a drink, then, once we're done here?"

Tait wasn't at all sure they were, if, as they thought might be the case, Alyssa wanted to talk about demons. But they couldn't really see their way to saying no, either. "Uh. Of course."

Alyssa flashed them a smile. "Great. Appreciate it."

Someone else came hesitantly into the tent, canvas sack over their shoulder, and Tait put a welcoming smile on and went to ask them questions.

They stopped at a teahouse near the wholesale market, a few minutes' walk from the barge-yard. It wasn't a place Tait knew, but Alyssa greeted the owner familiarly. The walls were painted a plain, serviceable blue, the counter was old and scarred, and the baskets on the counter held savoury pastries and rolled wraps rather than cake, but the shelves behind the counter held the customary wide range of infusion-jars.

"Ginger and hyssop, please, and one of those cheese pastries," Alyssa requested. "I've a bit of a cough coming on," she explained to Tait. "Hoping the hyssop might knock it on the head."

"Greenmint for me, please," Tait said.

"We come here sometimes for a break, if we're not going to the Bucket."

Tait knew where the Bucket was, though they hadn't ever been. It was a pub, but people held meetings there. Political meetings. Not the sort of thing they wanted to get involved with, but it didn't surprise them if Alyssa was. They made a non-committal noise as the two of them made their way over to a battered table in the corner.

"Do you mind if I take the chair with the arms?" Alyssa asked. "Better for my hip."

"Of course," Tait said courteously, and took one of the creaky stools.

Alyssa let out a short sigh with relief as she sat, and rested her stick against her knees. "How come you're out here, then?" she demanded around a mouthful of pastry once the salon owner had brought their infusions and food over.

"A neighbour told me there were lots of folk from Teren coming in. I thought maybe," Tait plaited their fingers together, "maybe they could, someone could, use a bit of help."

"Yeah," Alyssa said. "Like, there's always been a few people come in, every so often, but that's, you know. People who actively want to move here? And the odd one running from personal problems." Like Tait themself.

"But not like this. These people aren't choosing to come downriver. They're having to."

Tait shivered involuntarily and Alyssa eyed him sharply. "So," she said abruptly. "Demons, then. That why you came here?"

Tait hunched their shoulders protectively, opened their mouth to say something, and then couldn't.

"Shit. Sorry." Alyssa pulled an apologetic face. "Jeres always tells me I'm too blunt. Never mind that, none of my business. The thing is, right, the people who are coming downriver, they say, when they're willing to say anything, they're being chased out, right? A lot of them are radicals, and they say there's police on their doorsteps, there's legislation passed to make it more and more dangerous to speak publicly, or to talk about change." She scowled, with an edge of satisfaction. "The high-ups are getting frightened. But the other thing is, the thing that does worry me, they've started talking about demons. On the streets. No one dares meet in public any more, because they got...set upon. But people aren't all that willing to talk about it? They'll talk about repressive laws, and they'll talk about their printing presses being smashed up, and prison sentences, and all that. But they won't...I dunno. I guess I wondered if you knew anything about it. But if..."

"It's true," Tait said. Their insides felt hollow. But they had to tell Alyssa. Didn't they? "At least...when I was there. In Teren. They wanted me to set a demon on people. Just for...they were outside in the square. A demonstration. Some of them were students, I knew some of them. They weren't *doing* anything. They were just – shouting. You know. But the Academy said, it was, I had to."

Alyssa was silent. Looking up, Tait saw her face.

"I didn't!" they burst out. "They...I sent the demon back, and I ran away. That's why I'm here. But," they shrugged unhappily, "I got lucky. I could have. Um. It could have been much worse. I expect..."

"Someone else will have done it," Alyssa finished.

"Yeah. I expect they would."

"If it's you or someone else," Tait said, staring at their mug. They didn't want to drink it, any more, but they made themself take a sip.

"We should be printing *this*," Alyssa said. Her foot was bouncing restlessly. "The laws and the rest as well, but this is worse. Maybe someone'll talk to me about it, once some of 'em have calmed down a bit."

"Demons can't come into Marek," Tait offered. "That might help people. If they know."

"Because of Beckett," Alyssa said, absently. "Huh. Reb mentioned that, now I come to think of it." She turned her attention back to Tait. "While we're on the subject. Reb. Have you noticed her being a bit…odd?"

"Odd how?" Tait asked cautiously.

"I don't know," Alyssa admitted. "Not like I've known her long, is it? But she made a lot of fuss about needing more sorcerers, and working hard, and all that, fair enough. Except, now all she's getting me to do are charms I got the hang of about two weeks in. She talks about control and all that, but she doesn't *say* anything that I'm not doing already. Is that the same with you?"

Tait thought about it. "I suppose so," they said, slowly. "I just – I've been assuming that it's useful, just repeating the same things? I mean, it's a lot *easier* now to raise a witchlight, you know?"

"All right," Alyssa said, "but wouldn't it be useful to do harder stuff, as well? At least a bit?"

"Cato said something about that," Tait remembered. "And Jonas is doing more than I am. I figured, Jonas is just a stronger sorcerer."

"Jonas is a child," Alyssa said tartly. Tait reckoned Alyssa herself was probably in her late thirties.

"Well, yes," not that Tait was all that much older themself, only a few years, but Jonas did often feel very, very young to them, "but that doesn't mean he's not stronger, magically."

"Maybe," Alyssa said. She didn't sound convinced. "You could ask your Cato what he thinks?"

Tait considered that. Cato would tell them the truth; Cato was happy to lie through his teeth to clients, creditors, people he was trying to pick up, and occasionally Reb, but as far as Tait knew, he'd never lied to Tait themself.

"Because it seems to me," Alyssa said, "that she's holding back. Like," she made a frustrated gesture. "Like she's just not *there*, half the time? It's like she almost does something and then backs off. Look, when I was younger, I apprenticed as a weaver, right? I still do a bit of it now, though I'm not in the Guild any more. And the weaver I was apprenticed to, they really cared about what I was doing. They told me when I was doing it right, and when I was doing it wrong. They didn't spare my feelings, not at all, but I always felt, they wanted me to get better? You know? Not every apprenticeship works that way, fine, but it ought to. This doesn't feel like that. Not at all." She paused. "Unless it does, to you, when you're working with Reb. It might just be me. Bad fit. You know."

Tait, slowly, shook their head. It was the first time they'd thought about it like that, but...

"That wasn't how it was at the Academy," they said. "They insisted we get things right, but it wasn't because they cared about us. But...I do know what you mean. And you're right, it's not like that, learning from Reb." They huffed a half-laugh. "It's better than the Academy, mind. But...Maybe she's just not like that?"

"Well, maybe," Alyssa said. "But even so. That's no reason for her not trying to teach us more, right?"

Tait didn't like to think this way; didn't want to be critical of Reb, who they wanted to believe was doing her best. But... "I'll ask Cato what he thinks. If you like?"

"If you wouldn't mind," Alyssa said. "I'd like – a second opinion, I suppose."

Tait sighed and sipped again at their infusion. They didn't want to think badly of Reb. But they did want to learn Marek magic, properly, and if Alyssa was right...It was worth talking to Cato about, that was for sure.

Alyssa shifted, raising a hand to signal over to someone at the door, and Tait looked up to see Jeres.

"Off duty?" Alyssa asked, as Jeres sat down.

"Radec's taken over," Jeres said.

"Uh. Shall I get you something to drink?" Tait offered.

Jeres smiled at them. "That would be wonderful, if you don't mind. Green-leaf, please." She reached into the pocket on her belt, and Tait waved off the offer of money.

When they came back with the green-leaf, and – after mentally checking their finances – a plate of small sweet biscuits, Jeres and Alyssa were both leaning over the table, deep in conversation.

"But can't the Guilds…Oh, Tait, did you get biscuits?"

"Probably biscuits for *Tait*," Jeres said pointedly.

"Oh, share and share alike," Alyssa said with a shrug. Tait couldn't quite work out how to take that.

"Uh. They're for everyone. Actually," they said instead, which was after all the truth.

Alyssa dug into the biscuits. Jeres blew across the surface of the green-leaf, then took a long slow sip with evident enjoyment.

"And as you were in the process of asking, *can't the Guilds*, what? Produce housing out of thin air?"

"You've those great big Guildhalls," Alyssa said. "Put some blankets down on the floor. Better than tents, surely."

"You can't just house people in the Guildhalls," Jeres said, shocked.

"You *can*," Alyssa countered, taking another biscuit. "You *won't*, is the trouble."

"The Guilds are paying for those bags of food we're giving people," Jeres said. "And they're letting me do this instead of my actual job."

"*Letting* you," Alyssa scoffed. "How's it feel not to decide what you do with your own time?"

"Yes, well, that is the nature of a job," Jeres said. "And what do you do when your sorcerer tells you when to come along for lessons? You're not even getting paid for that."

Tait couldn't quite tell how much of this was genuinely barbed and how much was a well-worn conversation between people who'd known each other for a while – which clearly Alyssa and Jeres had. Alyssa was involved in politics, somehow, wasn't she? Was Jeres a radical too? But Jeres was a Guild member, obviously, so…

"Jeres. Here you are." The newcomer was a big man with a dark beard, wearing a heavy canvas apron stained with what looked like black paint. Or – they were near Printers Street, weren't they? Ink. It was probably ink. His fingers were black-splodged, too.

"Simeon," Jeres said. "How can I help you?" She sounded resigned. "Is this about the Teren pamphlet-writer I sent you? She seemed radical enough for even you, and she had a lot of very hair-raising stories, but if you can't work with her, that is definitely not my problem."

Simeon made an impatient gesture. "No, not at all. I've her first coming out tomorrow, excellent writer. No, I'm here because we've just had someone from the Guildhall down making *threats* about how we should sign up with them or risk their wrath, all that. Blah blah trade, blah blah supplies, blah blah they're in the Council."

Jeres rubbed at her forehead. "You do know, right, that I don't actually control the Guilds? Did the rest of them send you to find me?"

Simeon looked, briefly, slightly abashed. "Tey said she'd come talk to you later."

"But you wanted to talk now," Jeres said. "I'd mention that I've just done an eight-hour shift out at the barge-yard, but I don't suppose it would help."

"Tey," Alyssa said, "would just agree with you that it's all a nuisance and wouldn't it be nicer if everyone would just sign up for a nice new Printers' Guild."

"Well, yes, Tey would like to be back in a Guild," Jeres said testily. "She didn't leave the Smiths because she didn't like them." She paused. "Though she might have changed her mind. She left because they didn't think presses were Smith-business. But, like me, she thinks there are advantages to being in a Guild, and she's *allowed* to think that and to put her view."

"And I'm allowed to think the opposite," Simeon said belligerently.

"Is anyone stopping you?" Jeres demanded. "No, they are not. Not sure anyone *could* stop you if they tried."

"The bloke from the Guildhall. I kept asking, what's the point, and he kept avoiding the question. Then he moved on to the 'if you don't' business."

"Right," Jeres said. "But I don't see why you're telling me about it."

"Because the Guilds oughtn't to be threatening us."

"No," Jeres agreed. "Look, you know fine well that I don't defend everything the Guilds are doing."

"But you tolerate it," Alyssa broke in.

"I don't see the point of a Guild," Simeon said again, arms crossed.

"Then vote against it," Jeres said, temper visibly fraying.

"That was fine until they started coming round and issuing bloody threats. I'm telling you, they won no hearts that way."

"And if they'd asked me before they did it, I'd have told them that," Jeres said. She sighed. "Which they might have done, even, if I wasn't down at the barge-yard all the time right now, but there you go."

"So you're just going to sit around and let them threaten other Marekers for not joining their little *club*?" Alyssa demanded.

"Not like they've ever cared about anyone who isn't in it," Simeon said, jaw sticking out.

"I can't fix the Guilds all by myself!"

"Then *leave*," Alyssa said. "Instead of supporting it by your presence."

"I think there's value in some of what they do, and I think you get further kicking from inside than you do kicking from outside."

"Crap," Alyssa said. "You're either standing against it or you're not."

Simeon sucked air through his teeth. "Come on, Alyssa, Jeres is entitled to her views, right?"

"Oh, so you're defending the Guilds now too?" Alyssa demanded.

"*No*. I'm defending her right to make her own decisions, even when they're wrong."

"Oh, I've had enough of this." Jeres drained her cup and put it down on the table with a sharp click. "Alyssa, thank you for your help today. Tait," her tone warmed as she turned to Tait, who had been listening to all of this wide-eyed, "thank you as well, and for the infusion and biscuits, and I'm sorry for you getting dragged into," she gestured at Simeon, a sharp flick of her fingers, "this."

She was on her way out of the salon before Tait could do more than stammer a demurral that it was nothing, really.

But it did give them the opportunity to push their own chair back and get to their feet. "I, uh, should be going as well," they said. "Please do finish the biscuits, Alyssa." They nodded politely at Simeon.

"I'll catch you another time, alright?" Alyssa said. "It was good to get a chance to talk properly."

"Yes," Tait said politely, not sure if they did truly agree. It was a lot easier just to take Reb, and their apprenticeship, on trust. "I'll speak to Cato." They had to now, then; they'd promised.

As Tait left, Simeon was already sitting down opposite Alyssa, gesturing emphatically. Tait did *not* want to get into Alyssa's politics. But Alyssa was Reb's other apprentice, and they supposed that meant something.

EIGHT

Marcia's bleed was two weeks late now, which for her was very late indeed; she was normally calendar-regular. For the last couple of days her breasts had been feeling tender. And today…She stared glumly at the infusion Griya had brought her. Rosehip and liquorice. Her favourite. She'd drunk it every morning for years. And today just the smell made her feel unwell.

She pushed it irritably away; then got up and moved it to the windowsill and opened the window. Surely it didn't usually smell that strong?

She ought to tell Madeleine. And Andreas. Although, of course, plenty of pregnancies didn't last past the first month or two. She hadn't expected it to happen this quickly. They'd begun to try for the child after that conversation on the way back from House Cerit, a month and a half ago. She'd bled, on time, shortly after that, and she'd expected it to take at least another couple of months.

Still. This was what she'd wanted. What she was contracted for. It was only fair to share the information straight away.

Madeleine, she realised, would know already. The servants would know she hadn't had her bleed, because she'd had no rags needing to be washed; and of course someone would have told Madeleine. She scowled at the table. And Madeleine, unusually for her, was patiently waiting for Marcia to come and tell her.

She didn't want to tell Madeleine. She didn't want to see Andreas, either, though they'd had a perfectly enjoyable evening (a very late evening) four days ago, when she'd already begun to wonder but hadn't been certain enough to say.

She sat down abruptly on the edge of her bed. She

really was pregnant, wasn't she? Which was the *point*, she'd planned this, signed up for it – but now it was really happening, the idea was abruptly and utterly terrifying. Did she want this? For certain? It wasn't – quite – too late, not yet. But this was the last moment when it wouldn't be too late. Once she'd told Madeleine, and Andreas, she'd be committed. Right now, she could go to an apothecary, and this would just become a missed bleed, something that never was. She could take steps to prevent another one, and in due course the relevant contract-clause would come into operation, and there would be no child, no child-contract, none of it.

She put her hand on her stomach. It still felt exactly the same as ever.

No.

She was scared, but she wasn't going to stop now. She didn't want to stop, not really.

What she wanted, with a stomach-turning fierceness that surprised her, was to see Reb. She wanted Reb's calm presence, her solid reassurance. But she couldn't have Reb, now or again, and right now that hurt worse than ever before.

She stood up and began to put on the clothes that Griya had laid out for her. She was supposed to be meeting Nisha this morning, at Petrior's, and it wouldn't do to be late just because she was sad and tired and…all the rest of it.

She was late, in the end, but, predictably, not as late as Nisha, who came into the little private room – the blue one, this time – with a flutter of apologies.

"You haven't ordered?" she asked, then looked properly at Marcia and her eyebrows went up. "Are you all right, Marcia?"

She hadn't been intending to tell Nisha. But… "I'm pregnant."

"Goodness, that was quick. Congratulations!" Nisha smiled warmly at her, then frowned. "Assuming you want congratulations. I mean, if you've changed your mind, I know an excellent apothecary…"

"I signed a contract," Marcia pointed out.

"Yes, you'd need a lawyer for that part, but the apothecary would be a more pressing concern."

Marcia shook her head, reassured despite herself by Nisha's immediate support. And, somehow, by the fact that Nisha had anticipated, unknowingly, those few moments of doubt she'd experienced. "It's fine. I don't want out." She didn't, any more. She was even beginning to feel a tiny kernel of excitement. "I'm just…terrified. Nisha, I'm going to have a *baby*."

"Yes," Nisha agreed. "Or at least, that's the hope. You must be very early on?"

"I'm only two weeks late."

"My sister totally panicked when she first knew," Nisha said. "Showed up at the House and spent two hours going on about it to Mother and me. After that she was fine. It's a big thing. No wonder you're a touch wound up. Let's order an infusion. Rosehip?"

"It smells funny," Marcia said, miserably.

"Ugh, how annoying. Are you feeling ill? Ginger, that's the thing." She rang the bell and ordered two pots of ginger tea. "I'll drink it too, no need to have too many smells around. And – have you eaten? Well then. Plain crispbread with salt, please."

"I'm not hungry."

"Well, too bad. It'll be worse if you don't eat. My sister swore by crispbread the first few months." She paused. "And, admittedly, occasionally *at* crispbread. Ooh, do you remember, Natalia had morning sickness for *six months* with her first?"

"Yes," Marcia said, repressively. "I do remember that."

"Oh, fine, I suppose that's not the most helpful comment. I'm sure it won't happen to you."

The ginger tea and crispbread arrived, and after nibbling cautiously at a corner of the bread, Marcia realised that it was, in fact, helping.

"Right," Nisha said, leaning forwards. "Andreas. Have you been approaching this…the *old-fashioned* way?"

"Nisha!"

"Oh, come on, it was obvious he was making eyes at you, and the last few weeks you've been making them back again. In the circumstances…"

Marcia rolled her eyes, and gave in. She wanted to be able to talk about this. It wasn't that she and Andreas had been keeping things *secret* exactly, just not *public*, either. "Yes, fine, we have been having a bit of a fling. Like you say, in the circumstances…"

"And what does your secret lover think of that?" Nisha's smile was arch.

"There is no secret lover," Marcia said between her teeth. "Not any more."

Damn. She hadn't meant to say that.

"Oh." Nisha bit her lip. "Sorry. I didn't…"

"Yes, well, let's not, shall we?"

"Instead," Nisha said cheerfully, accepting the change of subject, "you can tell me about Andreas! Is he any good?"

"None of your business," Marcia said severely, then, unable to resist, "but, yes, no complaints here."

"Good to know," Nisha said, wiggling her eyebrows to make Marcia laugh. "Are you going to keep it up now you're expecting, or was this just a practical thing?"

Marcia wrinkled her nose. "I imagine I'd puke on him right at the moment, truth be told."

"So you'd *like* to."

"Oh, I don't know. It's not going anywhere, obviously, and I told him I didn't want anything but, you know. Friends."

"The friendly fuck," Nisha said, nodding sagely. "Can work very well."

"I don't think it'll last," Marcia said. "I don't want it to, I suppose. We've got the parenting-contract to fulfil. I don't want to risk us falling out. So perhaps now would be a good time to stop it, especially if I'm going to be tired and sick for a while. But…" But it had been fun, the evenings they'd spent together, and Andreas was entertaining company, and she didn't want to give it up, just yet. It was nice, to be touched. To feel wanted.

"The wanting to puke thing will wear off," Nisha said, sagely. "My friend Gira was *gagging* for it through the second part of her pregnancy. I'd keep him on hand if I were you, in case it takes you that way too."

"Nisha!"

Nisha shrugged. "Just being practical." She looked at Marcia over the rim of her cup. "You're all right, though? With how things are?"

Marcia nodded, slowly. "Yes. I'm fine."

"Good."

"It's complicated. I suppose I feel like…you never know what's going to happen, do you? With any of this." She hadn't expected to meet Reb – had perhaps always halfway expected that the two of them would split up, sometime, but not the way it had been. She hadn't expected her child-contract to work out this way, either.

"With anything," Nisha agreed. "Certainly not with a kid in the mix, as far as I can tell. Even more when you do the," she gestured at Marcia's stomach, "part. I'll be adopting, when it comes my turn to resolve the House succession."

Marcia drained her cup. "Well. I should be away. I ought to tell Andreas about this. And Madeleine." She put her hand over Nisha's. "Thank you."

"For what?" Nisha looked honestly surprised.

"For ginger and crispbread and listening to me," Marcia said. "I feel better than I did."

"Eh, you're welcome, darling," Nisha said. "I'll be at the baths with Aden day after tomorrow, by the way, if you want to come by. I know you can't do the spa or the steam room, but the baths part should be fine."

"Sounds lovely," Marcia said, sincerely. "I'll see you then."

She felt much lighter on the way out than she had on the way in. It was fine. She knew what she was doing. It was all going to be fine.

"They keep talking about demons." The woman standing at Reb's door looked tired, and worried. "We thought – a sorcerer, maybe, might understand better."

"Right," Reb said. She took her cloak, and a shawl, from the peg by the door – it was chilly out. "Let's go."

People had always come in from Teren to Marek, once in a while – Reb herself had, years before. People coming for work, or to escape from something at home, or just because they wanted to. This wasn't the usual time of year for it, though, and it was more often young people on their own. Not families. She'd seen more new families the last time she'd been over in the squats visiting a client, but she hadn't thought much of it; nor when she'd heard from Irin at the infusion-salon about the help someone was providing out at the barge-yard.

Someone was, apparently, this woman Jeres. Who was here, now, and worrying about demons.

It was a long walk out to the barge-yard, and Jeres didn't seem inclined to talk. Which suited Reb fine. As they passed the squats, she wondered whether she should stop to find Tait, who had much more recent knowledge of Teren magic, and demons. But it probably made more sense to gather information first.

She'd rather been hoping that Tait's stories of what the Academy was up to had been – exaggerated, or misunderstood, or something. The lead-feeling in her stomach was telling her otherwise.

When they arrived at the landing-square, Reb stopped short. Half of it was filled with tents.

"What's all that?" she demanded.

Jeres looked unhappy. "Well. Some of it is where we're talking to people. But – we're having to house some of them here, too."

"Can't they go to the squats?"

"Full," Jeres said, succinctly. "Those who have money, there's still rooms available out over the river, in the new part." She gestured across the river, towards the houses being built out into the swamp. "And some of them have friends, or relatives, to go to. But the squats are full."

The squats were never full. There was a more-or-less permanent population of mostly younger people who were quite happy with a small room to keep themselves and their few belongings in, and a shifting, temporary population, who would spend a while in the squats until they had enough money together to find housing of their own. But there was always spare room.

"And they're still coming," Jeres said. "We're meeting with representatives from the Council later, to see what else can be done. It's a difficult time of year, but…Well. We've a number of suggestions. The Guilds are involved here – there's a fair few people coming in to find friends with trades, or who have connections from Teren craftguilds – so we're hopeful. We can hardly turn people away, can we now?"

"No," Reb agreed.

"But you're not here to resolve our housing issues," Jeres said, brisker now she was on her own territory. "Over this way, if you please."

She led the way towards one of the tents, standing slightly apart from the others. It was a decent size, made of thick canvas, and once Jeres held the door-flap open for Reb to step inside, she saw a couple of braziers warming the air. Makeshift tables stood at the far end, with people writing at them or holding discussions over them; at this end, a number of people sat waiting on stuffed sacks, piles of belongings around their feet, some with babies strapped to them or young children playing at their feet.

"This is where we interview people on arrival," Jeres said. "Primarily to establish whether they already have somewhere to stay or someone to meet, if they need directing, or if we need to find them a temporary place in the tents. Some of them just want to go straight down to the docks and negotiate passage onwards, to the Crescent or Exuria, and we help with that if we can. But we've started to ask about why they're coming, to see if we can find out what's going on." She grimaced. "Our hope is that there might be some diplomatic solution. These aren't, most of them, people who *want* to come here, is the trouble. They're running away from something, not coming here to seek a new future. That's never good."

"And they're telling you about demons," Reb said. "That's why they're leaving?"

"Some of them," Jeres said. "Not initially. And not everyone, even now. Mostly it was about – oh, fear of what might be about to happen, I suppose. Some of them are, I suppose you might call them, dissidents. Ameten's never been as tolerant of that sort of thing as Marek, but it was always – it's never been like this, before. That's how we found out about it first of all – the first few were political exiles, and they came to the Bucket. People we've been in contact with for a while, you see." Reb noted that *we*; so Jeres and her friends were part of Marek's own radical political community. Not something she herself was involved in, though she knew Alyssa was and had deliberately avoided finding out anything more about it.

"But these most recent arrivals…" Jeres trailed off. "Well. I don't want to prejudice you. But you'll be able to make more sense of it, I hope."

She led Reb over to a curtained-off corner. Inside, three people were sitting on some more stuffed hessian sacks: two women together; a man on the next sack along. They all looked exhausted.

"So!" Jeres said brightly. "This is Reb, the sorcerer I mentioned."

One of the women jumped up and backed away, eyes wide.

"Marek sorcerers don't work with demons," Reb said, getting directly to what she suspected was the point. The woman backed into the corner didn't look convinced.

"Sit down, Hera," the other woman said wearily, patting the sack beside her. "Isn't that the whole reason we came here? If we were wrong, we're screwed anyway, so why waste time panicking?"

Hera, after a moment of hesitation, came slowly back to sit down next to her friend – partner, Reb concluded, as the other woman took Hera's hand. Reb sat down on another sack, facing all three.

"So," she said. "You're Hera. And you?"

"Dellan," Hera's partner said.

"I'm Patrice," the man slumped on the other sack said. His voice was scratchy.

"Right. Good to meet you all. Welcome to Marek."

All three attempted a smile. Jeres was still hovering behind her.

"You're welcome to stay," Reb said, turning to her, "but could you sit down, if you're going to?" She didn't like people hovering around at her back.

"Oh – no, no, I've other things to do. I'll leave you to it." The curtain fell behind her.

"I'm a sorcerer," Reb said again. "A *Marek* sorcerer, right? Jeres there fetched me because you've spoken of demons, and she didn't know what to do about it."

"There's nothing to be *done* about it, now," Dellan said. "They're in Teren. We're not."

"Marek's in Teren," Patrice said.

"But the demons can't come here."

"'S not what the Academy thinks," Patrice said.

Reb's attention sharpened; but she should start at the beginning. "Could you tell me what you told Jeres, about demons."

"They've set them on people," Hera said. Her voice was quavering. "Bad enough when it was sorcerers, just. I mean – they'd chosen it, at least."

"*Chosen*," Patrice said, snorting. "My brother didn't *choose*. They assessed him, and then they took him."

"Your brother's a sorcerer, in Teren?"

Patrice shrugged a shoulder. "He was. Died a month back. Demon got him. They said it was an accident, that he lost control. I don't believe it. He didn't like what they were doing."

"Which is?"

"Setting demons on people," Patrice said. "Like she said. Dissenters." He shuddered. "At least when they were cutting heads off it was just...well, death's death, isn't it? Who knows what happens when a demon gets you."

"They're using demons for executions?" Reb's spine was crawling.

"Not always," Dellan said. "Not all of them. But there's been a few, big, I don't know, *festivities* around it." Her face showed her distaste, and horror. "It's a warning, plain and simple, we all knew that. Well, anyone who doesn't trust the Archion and the Commission knew it."

"So you left?"

Dellan shook her head. "Not immediately. I don't hardly trust the Archion or his soldiers nor yet the Commission, but we...I didn't think we were at risk. Not until – people went to the Commission buildings, to protest about all those books and presses they burnt. They let the demons out."

"By the angel," Reb swore. The porridge she'd had for breakfast rose in her throat.

"Not for long," Patrice said. "I know people who were there. Not long, but long enough. And it's not...it's that they did it at all."

"We were there. It wasn't an execution," Dellan said. "An execution has a trial first."

Hera snorted.

"In theory, anyway," Dellan amended. "There's...process. This was just terrorising people."

"Of course it was," Patrice said. "They don't want criticism. They want obedience."

"Wasn't the first time, either," Hera said.

Patrice shrugged helplessly. "I thought it was rumours, before. It was only a few people, and you know how gossip spreads, people'll say all sorts. But now..."

"So you left," Reb said.

"Executions. Executions by demon. Demons let loose on a peaceful crowd, just because the Commission don't like what they're saying. What happens next?" Dellan said. "We decided, Hera and me, that we didn't want to find out."

"They were looking for me," Patrice said. "My

brother…we had some conversations, before he died. Got word they were looking for me. Decided not to wait for someone to hand me in."

"Conversations about what?" Reb asked. "You said your brother was a sorcerer?"

"The Academy's got plans," Patrice said. "So my brother reckoned. More control over the demons, more control over the people. They were offering…things my brother didn't like. Didn't want to be involved with. In exchange for the demons giving them more too. Them in power in Teren at the moment, they don't like disagreement."

Reb sat back and thought for a moment. "Would you be willing," she asked eventually, "to come along with me and tell me, and a Teren friend of mine, a bit more about what you heard from your brother?"

Patrice shrugged. "Sure, I guess. If you can tell me that Ameten won't find me here, nor yet the demons."

"Demons can't come into Marek," Reb said. It was true, yet as she said it, she felt a tremor of anxiety. Beckett had held firm against one demon, before, and it had cost them dearly. They'd nearly lost, truth be told. If Teren had *more* demons now, and more control over them; if Teren was offering the demons more…

She really needed to talk this over with Tait, first, and then, if she could, with Beckett.

"Ameten can," Hera said. "Even if the demons can't."

"The Teren Ambassador isn't here at the moment," Reb said, remembering all too clearly the last visit. "Marek's not exactly independent, but it's not *not* independent, either. They're not going to…send snatch squads in, or anything. And the Council wouldn't just agree to hand people over. You're safe here." She was sure she was telling the truth, but…Jeres had talked about a meeting with the Council, to make provisions for housing people. That was all well and good, but the Council weren't going to be listening to anything about demons and magic, were they?

Reb knew one member of the Council who understood

magic; who had been there when Teren tried to send a demon into Marek. Who would understand what Reb needed to say, and might know how to translate it into terms that the Council as a whole could engage with.

Shit. She was going to have to talk to Marcia, wasn't she? *Shit*.

"No demons here," Dellan was saying to Hera in a soothing voice. "That's why we came. Remember?"

Hera didn't look entirely convinced. "We could take ship," she muttered.

Dellan patted her hand again. "Let's worry about that once we've caught our breath, eh?"

"Is there anything else you know about all of this?" Reb asked Dellan.

Dellan shook her head. "I saw them set on the crowd. Then we went home and packed up. I'm not staying around to see that happen again. Or worse. People died at their hands. I was *there*." Her voice was vehement. "I was there, and I saw it. I'm not giving you anything second-hand."

"I believe you," Reb said. "But if there's nothing more you can tell me, best you get on with settling in here. I'm sure Jeres is around, if you need more help." She turned to Patrice. "But if you would be willing to come along with me?"

Patrice shrugged, one-shouldered. "Not like I've anything else to do."

Reb got up and peered out of the corner.

"Hey! Jeres!"

Jeres excused herself from her conversation and came over. "All well?"

"These two," Reb gestured at Dellan and Hera, who had come out behind her, "need help with somewhere to stay. This one," she gestured at Patrice, still sitting behind her, arms folded, "is coming with me to talk to a friend of mine. Does he need to do anything before he leaves?"

"Not at all," Jeres said. "He can always come back if he needs more help."

"I've a cousin, works in the market," Patrice said. "If

the lady sorcerer can give me his direction once we're done, he'll help me out."

"Of course," Reb said. "Come on then."

The sooner she got Tait in on this, the happier she'd be. And then…then, she would have to send word to Marcia. This was far more important than her own wounded feelings.

NINE

The clocks on the Guildhalls along the river were all announcing the hour as Marcia stood by the carved stone pillars that supported the rise of the Old Bridge where it met Marek Square, and looked impatiently around for Cato.

It wasn't full dark yet, but the sun was low and red-tinged, shadows looming across the Square. Stallholders were packing up their wares, or hawking the last of them at reduced prices. Folk with baskets moved purposefully between stalls, snapping up bargains; though even at cut-rate, everything here was expensive compared to the wholesale market or even the Old Market. Those who lived south of the Square, though, even if happy to pay a little extra to save themselves the walk, could still appreciate cut-price over-ripe berries for their evening meal.

An infusion-seller with a kettle on their arm called to Marcia, and she shook her head. Cato had it in mind to go somewhere tonight, she assumed, and she didn't want to be carrying a cup. His message had been non-specific; Cato always preferred a mystery even when one wasn't necessary. He'd said just: *Meet me at five by your side of the bridge. I've an interesting evening in mind.*

She scanned the folk coming over the bridge, the ebb and flow of people in both directions dying away at this hour; there, Cato, slouching across the bridge, the last of the sunlight glinting red off his hair.

"Sister mine. How delightful. Am I late?"

"Of course you are. So. An interesting evening?"

"Well, in a moment, we turn round and go back across the bridge," Cato said.

"Was there a reason why you wanted to meet me this side, then?"

"Because first, I want you to buy me a pastry," he said, smiling sweetly at her. "Berry, for preference."

Resignedly, Marcia pulled a couple of coins from her purse and handed them to him. "Fine, I'll pay, but you can go to the stall yourself."

She tucked her purse back beneath her over-tunic as he went across to a nearby pastry stall whose owner was closing up. He wore a satisfied look when he returned.

"Two for the price of one. You want one?" He didn't return her change.

"No, you have both." The bare idea of the pastry made her gorge rise. And…that was the perfect opening, wasn't it? "Thing is…I've gone off pastries. And nearly all other food, come to that. Lately."

"Ah," Cato said in tones of enlightenment. "Tigero's knocked you up, then?"

Marcia fought back embarrassment. It wasn't like the child-contract wasn't public news. "You've been reading the proper papers? I thought you stuck to the gossip rags, when you bothered."

"Oh, it was all over those too," Cato said cheerfully. "Lots of speculation about whether the child-contract is cover for a hidden relationship that cannot become a marriage-contract, sketches of you and Andreas pining after one another, that sort of thing. I believe there's a barely-disguised play in the offing, too, although presumably they'll have to think up an ending to go with it."

"Ugh." Marcia shut her eyes for a moment, then opened them again. "Well, ignoring all that nonsense – yes, I'm pregnant. You're going to be an uncle."

Cato looked taken aback. "There's a thought. Well. Congratulations." His voice was carefully neutral. "I assume?"

Marcia sighed. "Mother blackmailed me into it." She hadn't mentioned that to Cato, before.

"*Blackmailed*?"

"Her price for supporting the extra Guild seats. I'd have had to do it sooner or later."

"No you wouldn't. Plenty of junior-branch cousins kicking around."

"Mother didn't like that idea. And I wanted to do it this way, rather than adopt." A decision she'd doubted a few times whilst vomiting herself inside out, admittedly. She was still happy, overall. She just wished that…some things were different.

"Well, it's your body," Cato said, then hesitated. "Is…uh. I assumed this was why Reb was stomping about like a dragon-bear. Tait mentioned recently they hadn't seen sign of you over there for a while." His tone was unusually delicate.

She'd seen Cato just after she and Reb split up, and hadn't wanted to talk about it. And then she'd not seen him for a while, partly because she couldn't see a way past having this conversation, and she hadn't wanted to. "Yes. We split up."

"Huh. Well, I suppose it was never going to work anyway, was it, in the long term?"

Marcia shrugged. She didn't want to go into what had happened. She didn't want to admit that maybe it was her fault that things weren't different, that maybe if she'd told Reb sooner…

Well. What was, was. She couldn't go back and do it over, could she? She had a good relationship with Andreas, and he was going to be a good parent, she thought; they could be friendly lovers for as long as they both wanted; she didn't *need* a romantic relationship. She didn't need Reb. She'd have more than enough to keep her busy once the baby came. She was perfectly happy with everything, and that was all there was to it.

Cato was eyeing her middle appraisingly. "How far along are you, then? Not long, I'm guessing?"

"Only about three weeks. What do you know about babies, anyway?"

"I'm a sorcerer, remember? Sometimes people want a hand, one way or another. Early on, I point them to an apothecary. Later…well. I can't make changes to physical matter, but I can," he sliced with a hand, "separate. And then," he cheered up again, "there's charms for a safe delivery and all that."

"Do they work?"

"As much as anything else that vague does," Cato said. "It's asking Beckett's protection, really; and Beckett can't always manage it. It's too diffuse. You could get a much more robust charm for something very specific, but there's so many things that can go wrong in a delivery, and even the good midwives don't understand all of it well enough to put it into a charm."

"Thanks. That's reassuring."

"I'd offer to do you one anyway, though it's not my specialty, but…Marekhill." He shrugged, then got a distant look. "Actually, that does make me wonder whether it would be worth talking to a midwife."

"Or talk to Beckett," Marcia suggested.

"*No*, thank you all the same," Cato said firmly. "Who knows what the result of that would be? Does Beckett even understand child-bearing?"

"Well, if they don't, that might explain why the charms don't work." Marcia had meant to be mostly facetious, but the arrested look on Cato's face suggested that she hadn't succeeded.

"Ugh," he said, after a moment. "I will have to ask, now, won't I?"

"Safety charms don't work that reliably either, though," Marcia said. "Or no builder in the city would ever fall off a roof, and no one break an arm."

"Mm." Cato's eyes were narrowed in thought. "Beckett can't prevent accidents, no. But they can prevent infection, if the charm's made at the right moment. Never been my thing, mind. I did know someone who did medical magic, but only when he was asked by a doctor or whoever." He tapped at his wrist with his other hand, the way he always had when he was thinking. "Can't fix a break, can speed the healing a bit, but really it just takes time. Can't cure the pox. Can lower a fever, sometimes…Ugh. I'll have to talk to Tait. They've got a clearer head for this stuff."

"Surely if it was really likely to help someone would have tried it already," Marcia said. "Your medical friend. Or did he?"

"No, not much with babies, as I recall. But that's nonsense, anyway. Plenty of good ideas no one thinks of until someone does," Cato said. "No one thought of the way I deal with spirits until I did. Although I appreciate the attempt to get me out of having to think about something. Anyway. I do have a plan for the evening, as well as enjoying your delightful company, which I have not experienced lately, presumably because you were avoiding talking about either Reb, or the child-contract, or both." He didn't, thankfully, pause long enough for Marcia to comment. "Back over the bridge we go."

Marcia paid close attention to the sunset on the water – the few small boats tacking in the mouth of the river way over to her right, and the barges clustering around the Salinas ships in the docks – in order to avoid looking at or even thinking about Cato eating his pastries. The river might be, conveniently, just there, but she had no particular desire to hawk up her guts in it. From the north bank, they went east, through the cramped streets that lay between the squats and the docks. He refused to say where they were going.

"Jonas is progressing nicely," he told her, "which is handy as I get a share of his payment if he takes a client. Tait – well. I would have expected your ex to be a harder taskmaster than me, but it seems to me like Tait is working hard but not getting far. Ah, here we are."

The pub they'd stopped in front of had painted-over windows and a crude sign identifying it as THE BUCKET. Marcia frowned at Cato.

"Why the windows? Is this safe?"

"Not everyone who comes here wants to be seen," Cato said. "But yes, it's safe."

"Why? Are they criminals?"

"No. Well. Not exactly. No one's going to hurt us." He paused. "But maybe go easy on the Marekhill accent." He looked her up and down. "At least you're dressed inconspicuously."

This wasn't exactly reassuring. But, when it came right down to it, despite quite a lot of things over the years, Marcia did still trust Cato. Mostly.

He was already pushing the door open, nodding to the broad-shouldered person standing by it with their arms folded.

"She's with me," Cato said, and jerked his head, urging Marcia forwards.

Inside it was dim and warm. Candles flickered in holders around the tops of the walls and on the tables. The place was crowded, and there was a great hubbub of conversation. It smelt of bodies and of alcohol, and for a moment Marcia felt her gut churn, before, thankfully, it settled again.

Cato made his way over to an unoccupied table by the wall with two chairs. He sat down and nodded in satisfaction.

"Get us a drink? Ale for me. I wouldn't recommend the sarak in this place but it won't actually send you blind."

"Pregnant, remember?" Marcia reminded him, and he made a sympathetic face.

Marcia found her way to the bar and ordered an ale and a ginger-shandy, as the least objectionable thing she could think of, with the possible advantage that it might keep her insides behaving. Somewhat to her annoyance, she found herself deliberately slurring her speech to sound less Marekhill.

"You come here a lot, then?" she asked Cato, back at the table. The person at the door had clearly recognised him. "What *for*, anyway?"

"Off and on, off and on," Cato said. "I'm intermittently interested in what people are saying here, let's put it that way. But I thought you might be more interested."

"I can't *hear* what people are saying here," Marcia said irritably. "The only person I can hear is you, and if I wanted to listen to you, we could have gone to your room. Which is marginally cleaner than here, even, and that's saying something."

"Patience, patience." Cato sat back and sipped his ale.

Marcia looked around the room, in lieu of anything better to do. A lot of people here looked like they were from the squats; some looked like reasonably reputable tradespeople. No one who wore Guild jewellery, though that didn't mean no Guildspeople for definite, and certainly no one who was obviously Marekhill. A tall woman with short, curly, dark hair was moving around the room, putting flyers on tables.

DEMAND REPRESENTATION, the flyer headline shouted, in blurry black type. The sloppy letterforms suggested the press wasn't owned by anyone in the not-yet-a-Guild of Printers, and the content was at the more radical end of the genre. It criticised Marek's political setup on the grounds that the Houses only represented themselves, and the Guilds only considered their own members. What, it demanded, of the thousands of Marekers who were neither Marekhill nor Guild members? What of the market traders, the small shopkeeper, the barrow-pushers, the piece-work stitcher who wasn't a seamstress or tailor, the messengers and buskers? Who looked out for their interests? None of it was new to her, but it was better-argued than some, despite the poor quality of the type.

"I've read this stuff before," she said, putting the sheet down.

"Really? You're a reader of revolutionary literature these days?"

Marcia scowled at him. "Unlike, apparently, Teren, one is permitted to have a different political view in Marek."

"Tell that to the Guilds," Cato said.

"Yes, well, I have been. And I know enough to know that this is close to one end of the debate, at that."

"Petitioners and Parliamentarians," Cato agreed. "Please-may-I and Lets-Do-It-Ourselves. There's plenty worse than that, though"

Marcia wrinkled her nose. "True. This wants change, but it's not suggesting anyone storms the Chamber. Have you been down Printers Street lately?"

"Don't be ridiculous. When do I go wandering the streets of Marek?"

"When you're escorting Tait around, or so I gather," Marcia said, and relished the betraying pink that rose in Cato's cheeks.

"As it happens," Cato said loftily, "when I escort Tait around, we go on more interesting excursions than to Printers Street." He wrinkled his nose. "Tait does go on their own, though. They like that sort of thing. And they bring me back the gossip rags, if there's anything the Purple Heart hasn't had in. I skim through Tait's stuff, sometimes. Pays to keep tabs on these things. The tenor of the city, and all that."

"Yes, well, I've been down there too. As has Andreas."

"You and Tigero, hmm? Maybe the gossip-rags are onto something. Keep talking, and I'll flog them a report, keep myself in more of this delightful booze, yes?"

Marcia rolled her eyes affectionately. "Just make sure you cut me in, yes?"

"Wouldn't dream of short-changing you," Cato agreed.

"Anyway. My point is. This is all very well, and I don't think the Guilds are right to be trying to ban it, but it's hardly *right*, is it? The Houses look out for everyone's interest. They say, what's good for the Thirteen is good for Marek, right?"

"Oh, come on, Marcia. You don't still believe that, and I know you don't. The Houses aren't looking out for everyone's interest. They're looking out for their own."

"But Marek being successful, and everyone having enough – that *is* good for the Houses, as well."

Cato sucked in air through his teeth. "Nice theory. Not convinced it's working."

"But it *could*."

"You mean, you could…" Cato stopped, as someone sat down at the table next to theirs, and obviously rethought what he was about to say. "You think if someone with the right ideas, someone worthwhile, was representing one of the Houses, they could do the right thing by the rest of Marek too?"

"Yes," Marcia said. "Well. Perhaps, not a single person. But if the Heads, generally, thought more about the city and less about themselves."

"It's a delightful idea," Cato agreed. "Well. I can see why you think it's a delightful idea, anyway. And I suppose – it's less than even the Petitioners want but I suppose a Petition-inclined Head could keep pushing. But what about when the Heads don't think that way? You know, like now. No one other than a Head of a House gets to choose the next one, and even they only get to choose for their house." He eyed her. "What price Athitol-Head?"

Marcia, chewing on her lip, was saved from answering by someone standing on a tiny raised platform at one end of the pub and thumping a walking-stick against the floor until the room was mostly silenced. The woman leant on her walking stick and surveyed the room. She wore a bright red patterned scarf around her dark hair, and her broad shoulders and hips gave her a solid, commanding look.

With a shock, Marcia recognised Alyssa. Reb's apprentice, Alyssa. Did Reb know about this?

Was it still Marcia's business?

Cato had his blandest look on. He knew fine well who Alyssa was, then. And it wasn't her problem, not any more. She folded her arms, and sat back to listen.

"Welcome, brothers, sisters, siblings all," Alyssa said. "Old faces and new. We're here to talk about what we don't have and what we should have, what they have over the other side of that river there and what they don't want to share."

She was an inspiring speaker, and evidently deeply committed to what she was saying. She criticised the Houses for ignoring the rest of Marek; she argued that since the Guilds came to the Council Chamber, they had started to act on narrower interests than previously; she pointed out that the rest of Marek was held to, and affected by, decisions that were made without their input or opinions being sought. Marcia looked down at that leaflet again, and wondered if she was looking at its author.

And Alyssa suggested alternatives. Not one alternative, but many. The Parliament of the Lower City, which Marcia had seen in more than one pamphlet already, was only one of them, at that. People began to call out, criticising ideas or proposing new ones, and Alyssa welcomed the interruptions, engaged with them, encouraged people to expand on their thoughts. She moved seamlessly from speaking into helping others discuss, and as the room broke up into a series of lively conversations, she looked round, nodded with satisfaction, and stepped down from the platform, leaning heavily on her stick. She took a seat by the bar, with obvious relief, and leant over to talk to the barman, who was already sliding her a glass of ale.

"Well then," Cato said.

"Well then," Marcia echoed. She felt as if her opinions had been turned upside down and shaken vigorously.

"You were on about wanting to change things, a while back," Cato said. "I thought perhaps it would be useful to hear someone who *really* wants to change things."

"I wanted – I wanted to think about doing better for the whole of Marek," Marcia said, slowly.

"But you hadn't got as far as actually *involving* the whole of Marek?" Cato asked, dryly. "Asking people what they want? That kind of thing?"

Marcia narrowed her eyes at him.

"I mean, obviously the Houses know best, and therefore they must know best for everyone."

"Yes, I understand. You can stop now."

"Can I?" Cato was suddenly serious. "Are you actually engaging with this, now? Really thinking about it?"

"But – do people down here understand the whole picture?" Marcia asked. "I mean, asking what people want, yes, but – she was talking about expanding the membership of the Council," *again*, angels and demons, like it hadn't been hard enough last time, "or, or..."

"I don't know," Cato said. "But if you think that the

Heads and Heirs, or the Guildwardens, understand the 'whole picture' either, you're deluded. Up on Marekhill, even if you come wandering around and talking to people, you don't know *shit* about what's actually going on." For once, his customary lazy sarcasm was entirely absent. "You can't know by visiting. You have to be here. You have to live here. Alyssa gets that."

"Does Reb know she's doing this?"

"Don't know, don't care, don't think it's Reb's business. She's not using magic, is she? She's just right."

"Maybe you should be doing this, not me," Marcia said, semi-seriously.

"Oh do fuck off. I haven't the slightest interest."

Marcia didn't believe that for a second; but she did believe that Cato would never get involved in politics. Not any more. However good he'd be at it.

"I just want you to – if you're going to change something, don't just fiddle with the edges. The Guilds get more votes in Council, woo-hoo, how dramatic. Fine, it's *better*, but they're all much of a muchness, and you know that as well as I do. If you're going to make out like you want to change things, you need to actually *change* things."

"It's not that easy," Marcia said. "I can't just say, we should do things differently, and have people listen to me. I already burnt most of my capital on the Guilds; and now they're after shutting down people like this entirely. Maybe the best I can do now is to let them keep talking, rather than being able to do anything with their ideas." Might not even be that, if she was unlucky.

But then…there was Andreas, wasn't there. She still had some allies…At the least, perhaps she could keep the printing presses running.

Cato sat back again, shrugged, and took a long draught of his ale. "Well, whatever. If you can't, then don't. I just wanted you to think."

Marcia, thoughtfully, tucked the flyer, and a couple of others that had materialised while Alyssa was speaking, into her pocket. She, too, wanted to think.

☉ ☉

Cato left the Bucket feeling an ill-defined irritation. He'd done what he'd meant to, hadn't he? Got Marcia thinking. And it wasn't like the whole baby thing was *news*. He'd known about the child-contract (even if Marcia hadn't told him herself), and there was no reason for Marcia to hang about with the matter.

Going to be an uncle. Except he wouldn't be around, would he? Was Marcia going to drag the baby out to meet up with its disreputable uncle in infusion-salons and the occasional bar? She was not. She'd be up on Marekhill, and he'd be across the other side of the river, and he'd see her even less than he did now, and the baby not at all. Which was fine, because he didn't *want* to be anywhere near Marekhill, and he didn't care for babies, and he had no idea why he was in such a foul mood.

He knocked on Tait's door when he got in, and heard "Come in".

"Did you know it was me?" Cato grumbled. "Or do you just let anyone in, whatever?"

"No particular reason to think I shouldn't." Tait had recently acquired a second-hand couch, via some arrangement with the Galten woman downstairs, and they were sitting on it with their feet stretched out, under the window, a novel from the penny-library in hand. They put it down and smiled at Cato. "But as a matter of fact, yes, I did know it was you. I've been practising that twist on the wards you showed me."

"Oh. Good," Cato said, briefly diverted. "It's good practice. Helps with attention." He sat down by Tait's feet on the couch, and Tait leant forward to offer a kiss.

"Though I asked Reb about wards," Tait said, sitting back again, "and she said not to worry about that just yet. I thought – maybe I shouldn't mention you showed me already."

Cato wrinkled his nose. "Wards are easy, though. Not to mention useful. I had Jonas doing them a few weeks after he first managed any magic at all."

Tait shrugged. "I suppose Reb goes about things differently." They hesitated, as if about to say something else, then gave their head a tiny shake. "Anyway. What are you grouchy about?" Their toes poked him.

"'M not grouchy," Cato said automatically. "And never mind that now. What *have* you been covering with Reb, then?" What was Tait bothered about?

"Witchlights, obviously," Tait said. "Finding spells."

"In a room or in the city?"

Tait frowned. "In a room. I didn't know you could do it bigger than that."

"It's more complicated," Cato said. But not that much more difficult. "You need a map." He'd bet Reb had one, too, so that wasn't the problem. "What else?"

"I've helped with her charms," Tait said. "And – breaking things, moving small things, just recently."

"And?" Cato prompted.

Tait shrugged. "That's about it."

"It's been months!"

"She says, best to make the foundations secure first."

"Your foundations are perfectly secure," Cato said impatiently. "I've seen you do magic. Not *much* magic, but I assumed you don't like to practise in front of me."

"Well, I don't, entirely," Tait agreed. "I've been wondering, though – because Jonas seems to be doing more than I am, or, I don't know, moving faster, or something. And I know he started earlier, but, didn't he have a client a few weeks back?"

"Reb won't want you having clients that fast," Cato said, "and I do see her point on that, I just disagree with her. But that's a separate issue to what you can actually do."

"Alyssa's worried too," Tait admitted. "She mentioned it to me a couple-few weeks ago, and I've been meaning to ask you about it, but...I suppose I kept hoping things would change on their own." They looked uncomfortable; worrying about telling tales on Reb, maybe? That was like Tait. But if Reb was holding them back...

Cato sat down with his back against the wall. "Jonas

isn't *that* strong, and he's doing plenty. I mean, Beckett really likes him, which helps. I don't know why Reb's not pushing you harder. Foundations, fine, but..." He thought it through. "Smells like crap to me but I can't think why. It's not like she's the insecure sort herself." He chewed on a fingernail. "Has she ever linked up with you to show you something?"

Tait shook their head. "I don't think so."

"You'd know if she had. That's the quickest way to get a really new idea across. I start Jonas off that way sometimes, when I need to. But. I dunno. Maybe she has reasons to do it differently. I mean, I haven't had an apprentice before, and Reb has. Maybe there's something I'm missing. Maybe I should be tackling things differently with Jonas."

"Maybe," Tait said, sounding a bit doubtful. "I'm sure you're being...sensible, though."

"No you're not," Cato said, feeling suddenly more cheerful. "But. I tell you what. I'll ask Reb about it."

Tait's eyes widened. "I'm not sure..."

"I won't say you've been complaining, don't worry. I'll just ask her about – the theory of apprenticeship, kind of thing." He pulled a face. "I'm sure she'll be *delighted* to tell me everything I'm doing wrong. But if she does have reasons for going so slowly, she'll explain them. And if not, we can think about it afterwards. Yeah?"

Tait nodded, looking reassured. "Yes. Thank you."

"No problem," Cato waved a hand. "Happy to sit through a half-hour lecture from the estimable Reb for you, any time."

Tait laughed. "How was Marcia, anyway?"

"Oh." Cato had briefly forgotten. "Pregnant."

"Congratulations!" Tait sounded honestly delighted. "You'll be an uncle." They squinted at Cato. "You don't look thrilled."

"Eh, well. I won't be an uncle, will I? Not exactly. Her up there, me down here...She's not going to want the precious Fereno offspring to be hanging out with sorcerers, is she now?"

"I don't think Marcia's exactly like that, is she?"

"You mean, she still hangs out with me?"

"Well, yes. And – there was the whole thing with Reb, wasn't there?"

"Yes, but people get strange when they have babies," Cato grumbled. "She'll get all – like…" He stopped.

"Like your mother?" Tait asked gently.

Cato stood up and went to the window, putting his back to Tait. Something was prickling at the corners of his eyes. "Suppose," he said eventually, once he could keep his voice even.

"I don't know your mother," Tait said. "I don't really know Marcia, come to that. But – they seem, from everything you've said, like different people. I don't…it doesn't seem likely that Marcia'll cut you out because she has a baby."

"Tigero might want her to."

"Huh. I mean, obviously you know a different Marcia from me," Tait said. "One who is inclined to do what people on Marekhill tell her to. A Marcia who wasn't out facing down demons by the river last year. Who didn't nurse her brother through the sorcerers' plague. Who wasn't screwing…"

"Stop, stop!" Cato said, hamming it up as he jammed his hands over his ears. "We do *not* discuss that." He turned round to see Tait grinning affectionately at him. "Fine, you've made your point. I don't think I'm being *totally* irrational, but I'll allow that perhaps I'm not thinking quite at my clearest."

"Well then," Tait said. "How about we go get dinner and something to eat at the Purple Heart, and then you can blame it all on the effects of a couple of beers?"

"That sounds very sensible," Cato said. He crooked his arm for Tait to take. "Shall we?"

TEN

It had taken Marcia a while to talk Andreas around to her perspective on the matter of pamphlets and censorship. Finally, he'd agreed that yes, he would vote against the restrictions the Guilds wanted; and in addition, had agreed to host a dinner for those she felt she might be able to persuade to her side.

She'd asked Nisha, but Nisha flatly refused to try to push Marcia's radical agenda onto Kilzan-Head. Andreas thought Cerit-Head was inclined against censorship on principle; Piath, Berenaz-Heir, was a thoughtful type who had seemed interested when Marcia had broached the matter the previous week; and Gil, Jyrthi-Head, had expressed concern in Council.

All of those she had expected. The shock came when Daril walked in. Andreas greeted him cheerfully, and she kicked herself for having forgotten that they were friends.

"Marcia," Daril said, coolly, and she nodded.

"Daril!" Andreas came over. "Terrible weather out, isn't it? You wouldn't think it was supposed to be full summer. Let me offer you a drink."

"You didn't mention him," Marcia hissed to Andreas, as soon as she could.

"Who? Daril?" Andreas looked confused. "Well, the last time I was chatting to him, he seemed pretty down on the idea of doing anything to Printers Street, so I thought…Why? Is there a problem?"

There wasn't much she could say, was there? Their former relationship was over a decade ago; without knowing what had happened, it would seem ridiculous still to be nursing that grudge. Come to that, given that Andreas was younger, and hadn't been in line for Heir at the time, he likely didn't even know. She couldn't talk about what Daril had tried to pull off the year before. And holding the matter of the Smiths against him would seem petty.

"I know your Houses don't agree, but I thought..." Andreas' brows were creased.

"No, you're right, it's fine. We need the numbers. I was just...surprised, is all." She doubted she was very convincing, but William Cerit-Head came up to talk to them, and the moment passed.

Daril, from the other side of the room, raised his glass to her. Marcia gritted her teeth. She'd dealt with him before, she could deal with him again.

Dinner began with social chitchat. Marcia was congratulated on her pregnancy; William made the joke about twins and the child-contract that Marcia was by now quite tired of hearing. It would doubtless be worse if anyone (bar Andreas' grandmother) were willing to mention the fact that she too had been a twin.

"Midwife told m'cousin there was only one heartbeat," William said cheerfully, "and then she had triplets. Triplets!" He nodded sagely, then added hastily, "All did very well, in the end, once everyone was over the surprise. They're eight now, fine children."

Marcia was looking forward to getting to meet her baby in due course, even if she was happy to still have some months before this became a reality, but the idea that 'her baby' might become 'three babies' was horrifying.

"I see," Gil said, changing the subject, "that we have more Teren folk coming into the city. I gather we're to talk about it at the next Council meeting."

"I've heard word of demons," Piath's serious face looked worried.

"I saw a news-sheet mentioned that." Andreas agreed. "Demons set on people in the streets."

Marcia remembered what Selene had said, last year, when that demon was trying to get into Marek. She remembered what Tait had said about the Academy. She hadn't seen anything about this herself yet, but...she shifted in her seat. Perhaps she should make sure Reb knew about this?

"Magical nonsense," William scoffed. "Probably just...wild beasts or something. They dragged a dragon-bear down from the mountains, painted it funny colours, and these panicky radicals called it a demon."

"Be fair," Gil said. "You'd run from a dragon-bear too."

"Damn right I would," William agreed, with a roar of laughter. "No shame to 'em there!"

"No one would confuse a demon with a dragon-bear," Daril said, crisply. There was a small pool of silence, and then Andreas said, hurriedly. "Talking of radicals. That brings us to the matter I brought you here to discuss."

"Preventing these people from printing their nonsense." William frowned. "And it is nonsense, no doubt there, and I don't like to doubt the Guildwardens, but I don't much like the idea of *banning* people from speaking, you know?" William said.

"Well, exactly," Marcia said. "After all," she shrugged, "just because the Guilds have an opinion, doesn't mean we are obliged to agree with them, does it?"

"Absolutely not," William agreed heartily.

Half an hour later, Andreas was wondering aloud why the Guilds were bothering about this now.

"Why are they so concerned about a lot of radicals from the squats? I mean, I don't much like these leaflets either, but is it really a *threat*?"

"You're missing the context on their side," Daril said. It was the first he'd said in a while.

"Which is?" Marcia demanded.

Daril shrugged and poured himself another glass of wine. The servants had long been dismissed. "They're unhappy with the printers."

"Why?" Piath frowned at him. "Is this about whether they get a Guild or not?"

"Yes," Daril said, "but not how you'd think. The printers don't *want* a Guild. Well. Some of them might have been willing. The older ones, some of them are former Smiths or Scriveners, who would quite like to be back in a proper Guild. The younger ones don't see the point, in general. Then there's the links between the Petitioners and the Printers."

"Petitioners?" William asked.

Daril waved a hand. "One lot of the lower city radicals. The less demanding ones, just want more say in the Council. Doesn't matter. The point is, it could have gone either way, but the Guilds made their point somewhat too strongly, and the printers declined to have their arms twisted."

"And the Guilds see that as challenging their power," Gil said, with the air of one suddenly enlightened. "Ah. I see."

"If they can limit the printers in other ways," Daril said, "they demonstrate the peril of being on the wrong side of the Guilds. Especially after the arm-twisting. If one makes threats, after all, one must be cautious not to reveal them to be empty."

And, Marcia realised, we – the Houses – don't pay enough attention to the other side of the river. So we're ripe to be pushed in the direction the Guilds want. Especially when we look down on them. It wouldn't help to say that right now; though she thought Gil might have realised it.

The wine went round again, and the conversation returned to whether anything being printed was truly dangerous.

"I mean; these people who feel there should be *no* government..." Piath tapped on one of the pamphlets spread across the table.

"But they're hardly the majority. Most are simply asking for more input into the Council," Marcia argued.

"Council's plenty big enough already," William said, gesturing with a glass.

"Some of them want to *elect* the Guildwardens," Piath said.

"The Guildwardens are elected. Within their Guilds," Marcia pointed out.

Piath scowled at her. "They want 'the people'," she could hear the quotes like tongs, "to elect those from the

Guilds who go to the Council. Some of them, even, wish to elect which *Houses* are represented."

"However," Gil said, their quiet voice pulling the rest to silence, "what they want isn't really the point. I don't have to agree with them to think that we should permit them to say what they like. Teren may feel it can't handle a little gentle criticism. I would like to think that Marek is more robust than that. Our citizens have a right to express their opinions. Why would we suppress that?"

There was a general noise of agreement though Piath was still frowning.

"If anything," Daril put in, "following Teren's line might give the agitators more ammunition. The more you push, the more they have something to push back against. Leave them to it. There's no sign that they're organised enough – that they even *agree* on enough – to do anything about it."

"Leandra makes a good point," Gil agreed.

Piath nodded, finally, then pulled a face. "This is all very well, but is there really any point, if the Guilds are going to win anyway? Thirteen votes." They spread their hands.

"You talk as if the Guilds are a monolith. They're not." Daril's voice was cool. "I predict at least two Guildwarden votes against the proposal."

"Who?" Piath demanded.

Daril shrugged. "You can hardly expect me to share the details of a private discussion. Let's just say, not all of the Guilds were happy with how the printers were handled."

It certainly wouldn't be the Smiths voting against, Marcia would place money on that.

"Is the only purpose of voting to win?" Gil asked. "It might be possible to force a tie; I would hardly say that all our fellow Heads, or as the case may be Heirs, are wholly predictable in their actions. And in either case. I do not believe this proposal is right. I will vote against it even if I stand alone."

Andreas snagged a piece of paper and a pen – one of

the new ones, with an internal ink-well, Marcia noted approvingly – from a side table. "Well then. Marcia, for House Fereno?"

"You'll be carrying your vote, then?" Daril asked.

"That week, yes," Marcia said. She'd been doing that more often, lately; Madeleine even sometimes stayed away from Council altogether now. "But I'll speak to my mother beforehand, in any case."

Andreas was writing. "Myself. Daril, I assume you'll carry your vote, given your father's health. Piath? William?"

"My Head will vote against," Piath said. "I was given the task of deciding our policy on this matter. I don't like any of this," they gestured at the pamphlets, "but I take your points about the wisdom of banning them."

"I'm convinced," William said cheerfully.

"Gil," Andreas said. "And two Guilds. That's eight against, and presumably eleven Guild votes for. What about the remaining Houses?"

"Nisha wouldn't talk to Kilzan," Marcia said. "But I can try her again. Perhaps abstention."

"Athitol and Pedeli will be for," Piath said.

"Haran?" Marcia said.

Gil made a hand-rocking motion. "Probably for, but might abstain. I'll talk to him."

"I can talk to Tabriol," Daril said. "I doubt I'll persuade her to vote against, but I can get her to abstain.

"Priella and Dintra…" Marcia said.

"For, both of them," Gil said. "Priella has been working closely with the Smiths of late."

Andreas counted them up. "Two Guild and six House votes against. Eleven Guild votes for. Four definite House votes for, three possible abstentions. We can't even pull a tie, unless the Guilds are even less monolithic than Daril expects."

"The morals still matter," Gil said quietly.

"I don't like burning Guild goodwill on a futile gesture." Andreas looked down at the paper, tapping the end of the pen on it, his face creased in a frown.

"Do you like doing what the Guilds want just because they say so?" Marcia asked.

He smiled, a bit reluctantly. "There is that, yes. One wouldn't like for them to think they can convince us to vote against our conscience, would they?"

"One would *prefer*," Piath said, sour, "that they couldn't vote down the Houses. With ten Guild seats, it would have been rather closer. A win, even, perhaps."

"Or not," Daril said, "depending on which way the three newest Guildwarden members vote."

Piath scowled but acknowledged the point.

"Well," Marcia said, getting up. "It has been a delightful evening, but I find myself ready to retire."

"You are undertaking a tiring business at the moment," Gil agreed, smiling at her. "I will be on my way as well, I think."

They left the others behind talking over another round of apple brandy.

"Good work," Gil said quietly to her, as they waited for their litters to arrive – Marcia didn't feel up to walking tonight. She was exhausted enough to feel nauseous again, though the cold air was helping. "We may not win, but I'm glad we're putting the other side. Perhaps we will minimise the harm."

"Maybe we'll do a bit better than that," Marcia said, optimistically. She didn't believe they would, when it came down to it; but there would be discussion before the vote. Quite apart from what they were doing beforehand, maybe the Guilds could be argued out of their ideas on the day itself?

"Maybe," Gil agreed, and handed her courteously up into her litter before climbing into their own. The curtains shut, and Marcia sank back onto the comfortable cushions with a sigh of relief. It had been a long evening. And she hadn't punched Daril, so that was a win in itself.

Reb hadn't quite gotten around to telling Marcia what the

folk coming in from Teren had been reporting. She'd taken Patrice to talk to Tait which had confirmed her suspicion that the Academy of the Court had moved further down the road Tait had seen before they ran. Tait, afterwards, had looked pale and shaky, but had valiantly insisted they were fine. Reb, having never said out loud to Tait that she doubted the accuracy of their story, couldn't apologise out loud either; and her attempts to reassure Tait were, she was all too aware, laughably poor. She hadn't known what to do; hadn't been able so much as to reach out and pat their shoulder, the way she remembered Zareth had patted hers when she was homesick. She couldn't think of any way to help.

And then, after that, she hadn't been able to work out how to tell Marcia. Write it all down and send a message? She'd tried that, written the same two sentences half-a-dozen ways, and given up. Arrange to meet somewhere? But where? She could hardly go to Marekhill; would Marcia be willing to come to, say, Irin's salon?

Now, two weeks later, Marcia had sent her own, painfully polite, message. It said that Marcia had information she thought Reb needed, and suggested meeting at an infusion-salon just on the north side of Old Bridge, close to the river. Rather above her touch, as a rule; but it had private rooms, so the two of them wouldn't be seen together.

That shouldn't still make her grind her teeth. It had been a fact all the way through their relationship, that Fereno-Heir couldn't be seen with a sorcerer. It hardly mattered now they were barely even acquaintances. Her jaw ached from the tension as she made her way over the bridge, cloak and shawl wrapped over her against the rain.

Marcia was already there, although Reb was exactly on time herself. She'd heard the Guildhall clock chime the hour as she reached the door. Neither of them spoke until their drinks were brought. Marcia, Reb noticed, was drinking ginger tea. Well. One might assume – but she wasn't going to ask.

"I'm sorry." Marcia was the first to speak.

"You're...sorry?"

Marcia's cheeks were dark, and her shoulders were tense, but she didn't look away. "I'm sorry for what happened. For what I did. I should have told you before. As soon as I made the agreement. It was – well. I'm not surprised you weren't willing to forgive me. I don't blame you. I lied to you, and I'm sorry."

Reb had no idea what to think. "Was that the important...?"

"No!" Marcia cut in hastily. "No. I wouldn't have...wouldn't have put you to the trouble of coming here just for me to say that. But since we are here...I wanted to say it. I'm sorry."

"Right," Reb said, feeling badly wrong-footed. "I. Uh. Thank you." She couldn't let her heart crack. Couldn't let herself feel this. But she had to ask. "I noticed. The tea. Are you..."

"I'm pregnant," Marcia said. "Yes. A few weeks, now." She grimaced. "Feeling sick most days."

"I could do you a charm," Reb offered, without thinking, then cursed herself.

Marcia smiled at her, a startled, genuine smile, and Reb cursed herself again. "That's very kind. But...I can't. I wish I could."

"Marekhill," Reb said. "I know. Shouldn't have offered. I'm sorry."

"Anyway. That's not what I came for either. So. I was speaking to people the other day, and I read one of the pamphlets they're selling in Printers Street, about the folk coming in from Teren..."

"You're reading that rubbish?" Reb said, startled.

"Isn't your apprentice writing some of the political stuff?" Marcia's chin went up.

"I don't ask. Not my business what she gets up to when she's not doing magic." Or rather, Reb didn't want it to have to be her business, so she ignored it. A decision she was perfectly happy with, thank you.

"My point is. They say, in Teren, they're setting

demons on people. I don't...I mean, you're right. I'm not sure how reliable any of this is, and certainly some of the pamphlets are a bit excessive in other ways, but I remember Selene, and what Tait said. I thought you ought to know." Her mouth pulled sideways into a frown. "Or possibly I thought Beckett ought to know."

Marcia could have told her brother, Reb realised. But she'd come here instead. Was that...deliberate? Or just that she didn't trust Cato to take it seriously, despite Tait?

Best not go there.

"Yeah," Reb said. "As it happens, I spoke to some folk the other day. Heard much the same thing. They were in from Ameten."

"Aren't most of them from Ameten?"

"Well, and maybe that's not coincidence. Since that's where this Academy is. And the Commission, that's the other I hear about."

"The administration, more or less," Marcia offered. She was chewing at her lip. "I wish I knew more about Ameten politics. They were saying the same thing, though? The people you spoke to?"

"They said," Reb remembered, "it's one thing just executing people, it's another getting the demons to do it."

"Fuck."

"Quite."

"Ugh. I want to do something, but it's getting the rest of the Council to listen. The Houses won't talk about magic, the Guilds have other priorities, and no one wants to pick a fight with Teren." Marcia's mouth was set grimly. "My worry is that Teren will pick a fight with us."

"I can't see how the Houses can just not *believe* in spirits."

Marcia shook her head. "It's not that they don't believe. You're right, that would be ridiculous. They just – don't engage. At all. No one would say demons don't *exist*, they'll just...ignore it. Say that the claims are propaganda, or people getting overexcited and thinking soldiers are monsters. Something like that."

"But it's true," Reb said.

"I know. I mean, I suspect some pamphleteers are exaggerating, but I don't think they make it up out of whole cloth; and you got the same story directly from witnesses, and it matches what Tait said last year. But I can't exactly cite you or Tait in Council, can I?"

"I don't think the average Mareker wants to listen either," Reb said gloomily. "They think we're safe here. That we can ignore Teren nonsense."

"Which we are? Safe here?"

Reb couldn't tell if Marcia merely sought reassurance, or had genuine doubt. "Probably," she said, brutally honest. "You were there last autumn. You know what it took to get rid of one. How many have Teren got? What happens if they get bored of turning them on political dissenters in Ameten and ship them all down here?"

Marcia looked down, tugging at the edge of her sleeve. "Yes. I keep worrying about that."

"What could the Council do, anyway?" Reb asked. "Now, or if Ameten starts thinking about us?"

Marcia sighed. "That's the trouble, isn't it? Nothing, right now. Even if our relationship with Teren were stronger, we haven't the power to prevent them from doing anything at all, bluntly. We could remonstrate with them, I suppose. But for all the good it'll do…even if some of the Council are willing to consider those reports seriously, no one will want to make waves for something that won't have any effect. Jyrithi-Head, maybe, on principle. Not many of the rest."

"I don't understand what their end goal is," Reb admitted. "In Ameten, I mean."

Marcia shrugged. "Get rid of all the people who annoy them? I know some Marekers who might quite like to do that too."

"And then?"

"Well. Teren wants more control over Marek, Selene made that clear last year."

"Why?" Reb was almost regretting having ignored

politics all these years.

"Money," Marcia said, succinctly. "We're the gateway to trade with the rest of the Oval Sea. We're richer than the rest of Teren. We pay taxes, of course, but…I wouldn't be surprised if the Archion is looking for a way to squeeze more out of us."

"Is there one?"

"Cut out the middle-operator…Maybe." Marcia sighed. "I don't know. I'm not the Archion, am I? I don't think in country-sized terms. A city's more than enough for me. What I want to know is, why demons? Why don't they use angels for their magic?"

This, at least, was Reb's territory. "The distinction's a human one, really, not all that grounded in reality. Their reality, I mean, rather than ours."

"Go on?"

"I'm pretty sure I've explained this before."

"Possibly. Maybe it didn't stick," Marcia admitted. She cast Reb a rueful smile. Reb pushed away the memory of the last time she'd talked to Marcia about this, naked on top of the bedclothes in the height of summer's heat. "Explain it again?"

"Demons, angels, what the Salinas call elementals – they're all spirits. They just show up over here, on our plane, in different guises and with different interests. The elementals are focussed on a particular kind of matter – water-elementals, air-elementals. I don't know why. Maybe it's just fun for them. Maybe they're, I don't know, researchers. Hard to get close enough to find out."

"And angels?"

"Angels are willing to help, voluntarily."

"Like Beckett."

"Sort of. Beckett's tied to the city, but they chose that deal of their own free will. On a smaller scale, you can call an angel and ask them to do something, usually in exchange for something else. But they're benign. An angel wouldn't kill someone for you."

"Beckett wouldn't kill?"

"Not a human," Reb said, with certainty.

"And demons will kill?"

"Demons aren't limited by being benign, let's put it that way. But in theory it's much the same deal as an angel: you make the deal, whatever it is, you both agree, you're both bound. Your brother, though I wish he wouldn't, does that. Really, angel and demon doesn't make much odds. Human morality doesn't apply to them except if they've chosen it. I suppose in that sense, angels are more interested in humanity, and therefore choose to abide by certain human moral standards."

"Huh."

"But either way – that sort of deal, like your brother makes, is time-limited, and consensual. What Tait says they're doing in Ameten…the other way you can deal with a spirit is to bind it. In which case the spirit doesn't get a say."

"How can they justify that?"

"By saying that all spirits are demons," Reb said. "Basically. Instead of finding a spirit who will agree to what they want, they say, they are inhuman, morality doesn't apply to them, and therefore it is acceptable to make them do what a human wants."

"So they could be binding angels? Who've chosen human morals, or would if asked?"

"Maybe," Reb agreed.

"And they're using them – forcing them – to kill."

"Yes." Reb sighed. "There's always been some of that. Outside of Marek, you get blood-magic, or binding, and there's always been some who'll bind without consent. But it seems, with the Academy, it's become bigger."

"Like they're justifying it? Codifying it?" Marcia suggested.

"Exactly. Not just doing it because they want to and accepting, or anyway not caring, that it's wrong. This is – bigger. Worse, I think."

They both stared at the table in silence for a moment.

"Could you bring one of the Teren folk in to the Council?" Reb asked.

Marcia looked thoughtful. "Huh. Maybe. If I can find

someone who isn't a radical type."

"Mm. I think the people who weren't caught up in that sort of politics weren't there to see," Reb said. "They just believed it when they heard it and decided to get out before it got worse."

"If it gets worse, we'll have more of them," Marcia said.

"There's a grim thought."

Marcia took another gulp of her tea, and made a face. "I'll keep thinking about it. The problem is, if I push too hard, I lose more relationships and more influence."

"And if you don't push, maybe Teren shows up on our doorstep with an army of demons."

"But like I said. Is there anything the Council could do to stop that?" Marcia sounded frustrated.

Reb shrugged. "Cut off trade?"

Marcia blinked. "That's…drastic. I'm not sure they'd do that unless and until the demons were already at the gate." She grimaced. "Actually there's Council members who would just turn around and try to make a deal with the demons."

"With the sorcerers who held them," Reb corrected her. "The demons – spirits – aren't the ones in control, remember."

"Mm. We're discussing the refugees next week in Council – making more housing provision, that kind of thing. I might be able to mention demons and executions then." She shuddered. "It's such a horrible thought."

"I'll think about it a bit from my side," Reb offered. "There's nothing we – the Group, I mean, or sorcerers individually – can do about anything in Teren. But if it might be coming to our door."

"I'd like to think I'm wrong," Marcia said. "I'd like to think Selene was just…blowing hot air, you know, last year. But things getting worse in Teren, that suggests that they're getting stronger, your Academy people. Or getting…I don't know. More practice. Less compunction. Both." She scrubbed her hands across her face. "I would love to be wrong. I really would."

"Me too," Reb agreed. "But. Yes. I'll think about it."
Beckett had struggled with a single demon. She kept
remembering that.

"Well," Marcia said.

She stood up, and Reb couldn't help but notice the way
her weight had shifted, very slightly. And the change
around her breasts. She looked away, blushing slightly.

"I, uh," Marcia said. Reb glanced back at her. She was
blushing too. "I should go. Appointments and things.
Thank you for coming. I really appreciate it." Her tone
was formal once more, and Reb took a deep breath, and
made herself match it.

"Thank you for bringing it to me. You're right; it's
something we should both talk about." She made herself
smile. "Not like there can be *formal* interactions between
the Council and the Group, so I suppose it's just as well
there's informal ones."

"Well, quite," Marcia said. Was she, too, thinking
about previous informal interactions?

Best not go there.

"I'll...we can keep in touch?" Marcia asked, and
without even thinking about it, Reb said, "Of course."

As the door closed behind Marcia, Reb looked down to
see her hand shaking. She hastily put down her cup.

Marcia had apologised. She – hadn't expected that. It
didn't make everything suddenly better. And obviously
Marcia didn't want...

She didn't want. Neither of them wanted. To be back
together. Marcia was pregnant, and she'd moved on, and
she'd apologised. Reb breathed in, right down to her
belly. Her breath was shaky, too.

It was good that Marcia had apologised. Reb hadn't
expected it, but it was the right thing to do, and she was
happy. And now, they would stay in touch, as friendly
acquaintances. Which was perfectly reasonable. She
picked up her cup to finish her infusion. Keeping in touch
was reasonable, actively wise, even, in the circumstances,
and she was entirely able to do it, and everything was
perfectly fine.

Even after all this time. Not just a knee-jerk reaction, trying to get herself out of trouble, but something she'd stopped and thought about and still wanted to do; because she meant it, not to get something out of Reb. Marcia had *apologised*.

ELEVEN

Every so often, Jonas went down to the docks for an evening in one of the pubs there that catered for Salinas sailors on shore leave. It felt good to spend time with people from home. Before Asa he'd sometimes found company for the night, too, but now he was just there to chat and hear news of ships and crews he knew. It'd been a while this time. He'd been busy.

The Bowsprit was generally raucous, but tonight it seemed – not exactly *quiet*, but subdued. By the bar he saw Xanthe, who'd sailed on the *Lion* his last year on her, but now was with – he cudgelled his brains, running over the pennants he'd seen at the docks, and came up with the *Heart's Dragon*.

"Hey, Xan," he said, leaning on the bar alongside her. "Fancy a drink?"

"Jonas! Hey. Good to see you." She put her beer down and, unusually, offered him a formal double handshake. "I'm fine, thanks."

"The rest of the crew?"

She shook her head. "Off elsewhere. I came with a friend from the *Remora*, but he's back on watch now."

She seemed unusually quiet, too.

"Should I leave you be?" Maybe she just wanted to have a drink or two alone, and nothing wrong with that.

"Oh! No, not at all. Get yourself something, and come sit down with me, for sure."

He bought himself an ale, and they found a couple of stools against the wall.

"Uh. Is everything all right?" Jonas asked.

"You haven't heard?"

The ale curdled in Jonas' stomach. "Haven't heard what?" Maybe he should speak to Kia more often, even at the risk of her calling in that favour. Or just come here more often. He was out of touch.

She gazed into her mug. "Storm came up off the coast of Exuria. The *Faithful Wind* went down."

"Shit."

"The *Stormeye* – maybe they're right that's a lucky name, after all – were caught up too, lost a mast, but the crew were safe. They came on the *Wind*'s wreckage the next morning, fished a couple of the crew out, but most of 'em..." She shook her head.

"May their last voyage be peaceful," Jonas said, rote, and they both drank. "Shit. Off the *Exurian* coast?"

"Yeah, well, exactly. And out of season, at that." The sea-storms weren't for another few weeks, or the ships would all be back home already. "But you never get that sort of weather there even in season! The *Stormeye* weren't expecting it either, but their weather-eye spotted it coming up on the horizon. Still didn't have time to get everything down in time."

Obviously not, if they'd lost a mast. "The *Faithful Wind* didn't see it?"

Xanthe shook her head. "The crew who were rescued say the weather-eye'd been ill, but of course, this time of year, and where they were, no one was worried. Someone saw it eventually, of course, but they said it moved in demon-fast."

Any fool could see a stormcloud on the horizon, but it was a skill, to see the very first signs of change – the movement of the water, the feel of the air, the haze across the sea.

"Word is, it was a water-elemental's doing," Xanthe added. "Got everyone nervous. Especially with all I've heard from these Teren folks you've got coming in here. Dock's thick with them asking to buy passage, away to the Crescents or Exuria or wherever. One young lad this morning was after signing up as a sailor. Had to let him down gentle-like."

Salinas ships took only Salinas crew, and Salinas children grew up sailing as soon as they could hold a rope.

"Anyway. Lots of people nervous right now.

Elementals and demons and what-all." Xanthe shivered.

Later, on his way back home, Jonas, chewing things over in his head, detoured via Cato's room.

The light was on in Cato's window, and he answered the door with only his customary irritation. "Jonas? What're you after?"

"I had a question. About magic."

"I'd say, at this time of night, but what do I care." Cato eyeballed him. "You normally keep more conventional hours, though. Why are you not in your bed already?"

Jonas shrugged. "I had a question."

"And it couldn't wait? Oh well, never mind. You may as well come in."

Jonas stepped in, to find Tait sitting in the battered armchair by the window. "Oh. Am I interrupting?"

"Yes," Cato said, throwing himself down on the bed.

"No," Tait contradicted him, and raised their hand in greeting. "It's good to see you, Jonas. How are you?"

"Ah, well enough."

"Question," Cato said. "You had a question. Have at it."

"I can leave?" Tait said, shifting their weight.

"No, no need," Jonas said. "I just wondered – weather magic. Does anyone, do you know if you can, do anything with the weather?"

"The *weather*?" Cato sounded baffled.

"Did you have something particular in mind, Jonas?" Tait asked.

Jonas shifted uncomfortably to his other foot. "Ship went down last week. Sudden storm. Their weather-eye didn't see it. I heard it might have been elementals, so I wondered…"

"Water-elementals?" Cato asked. "You know more about them than me. Do they usually pull up storms?"

"Not storms, not usually. Twisters occasionally. Sometimes they look like they're after being friendly, but we don't go near them. You leave some fish for them, sometimes."

"It's not impossible, though," Tait said. "I read about elementals, at the Academy. There's not much known, because they're hard to get close to even on land, and the sorcerer I read couldn't persuade any of the Salinas to take her on board to try for a water-elemental."

"I'd think not," Jonas said, involuntarily.

Tait smiled at him. "She did one incognito trip, and saw a couple from a distance, but they wouldn't go close. But she thinks – well, it doesn't matter. They could perhaps generate a storm."

"But they *don't*," Jonas said. "And it's the wrong time of year, and the wrong place. Which is why I wondered whether…"

"Would you want to start a storm, or stop one?" Cato asked, with sudden perceptiveness.

"I'm just asking, *could* you. With magic. Affect the weather. If the elementals can."

"I never have," Cato said. "And I wouldn't think that you could here, with Beckett's help, because weather," he gestured, "it's bigger than Marek, isn't it? The storms or whatever don't start here, they start somewhere else and get blown here. Beckett's jurisdiction is Marek."

"They *get* here though," Tait said. "Could you," they brought their hands together then puffed them apart, "break up clouds, or something, overhead?"

Cato looked dubious. "I suppose you could *try*. But clouds are…I don't know. It feels dangerous to me. Too big."

"Says you," Jonas said, grumpily.

"Yes, says me, in which case *perhaps* you should listen."

Jonas chewed that over. He hadn't thought of the fact that Beckett was limited to Marek. Because what he'd been wondering was whether a ship might be willing to carry a sorcerer who could go one better than a weather-eye: who could not only *see* a storm coming, but save the ship from it.

"If Beckett couldn't do it, could another spirit?"

Cato looked at him, narrow-eyed. "I'm teaching you Marek magic, apprentice."

"*Could* they, though?" Jonas appealed to Tait, who

looked uncomfortable.

"I never asked a demon to do anything with the weather," they said, after a pause. "I don't know if they could or not. I don't know much about weather at all. But Cato's right, it *feels* like a big thing."

"Angels can't either?"

"Only difference between an angel and a demon is who's doing the naming," Cato said.

"And how you're dealing with them?" Tait asked.

Cato see-sawed his hand from side to side. "Well. Yes, sometimes, but the point is, they're human names, not different beings, fundamentally."

"Could I *ask* a spirit?" Jonas asked.

"You could ask Beckett, but as per previous statement, I don't think Beckett can reach far enough. And Beckett doesn't like other spirits here, *as* we all already know."

But if Jonas was out on a ship, that wouldn't be under Beckett's jurisdiction, would it?

"You deal with other spirits, sometimes," Tait pointed out to Cato.

"In a very limited way. Too limited to go messing around with weather, within *or* without the city boundaries."

"Well, perhaps, but in theory..." Tait looked thoughtful.

"I don't think it's sensible to experiment. Weather's weather. Just let it happen."

"Easy for you to say," Jonas said. "You're not out at sea in a storm."

"And neither are you," Cato said, which was unanswerable. "Now. In the nicest possible way, could you please sod off and leave us alone? And I'll see you tomorrow afternoon, I believe."

Jonas, stomping down the stairs and across a few streets to his own room, didn't want to leave it alone. If Cato wouldn't talk to him – well, he could always try it for himself, couldn't he? Cato was just being faint-hearted about it.

Because this, maybe, eventually, when he was done in

Marek, would be a way back aboard ship. A way to be useful again; to go home, and have magic, both together.

"So is this simply going to continue?" Gavin Leandra-Head demanded. His voice was hoarse, and to Marcia's eyes he didn't look at all well. This was the first time he'd been in Council in weeks. Today they were due to discuss the refugee situation, then the matter of printing. Marcia was wondering whether, with Gavin here, Daril might not carry the Leandra vote after all; but Daril looked unconcerned.

"With respect, we don't know." The woman in the Chamber answering questions, Jeres Arianden, had dark bags under her eyes. She was a vintner who usually worked in the central Guildhall on cross-Guild logistical issues, and had been seconded to take charge of the refugee support situation. She'd borrowed the Reader's Clerk's lectern for her sheaf of papers, and it was clear that she knew exactly what was going on right now – but hardly surprising that she wasn't in a position to predict the future. "Those arriving are here because they fear for their lives. We must assume that if the situation in Ameten continues as it is, more people will fear for their lives, and more will leave to come here."

"Or they are over-reacting," Gavin said. "In which case we need not expect many more of them, once those prone to unrealistic fears have left."

Madeleine, beside Marcia, made an approving noise, and Marcia managed not to roll her eyes. Marcia was carrying the vote today – Madeleine was letting her do that more often, these days – but she'd insisted on coming along anyway.

"It is true, Leandra-Head, that we would not expect the entire population of the city to come down the river," her voice didn't *sound* sarcastic at all; Marcia was impressed, "and as such, eventually the flow must reduce. However, at present, more arrive every day. We do not think in terms of *over-reacting*; they are all genuinely scared."

"There's no sign of things slowing, then?" Andreas asked.

Arianden shook her head. "We expect at least as many again. Possibly more. Unless things change in Ameten."

"What about the rest of Teren?" Marcia asked, thinking of her conversation with Reb.

"Excuse me, Fereno-Heir?" Arianden frowned at her.

"The refugees thus far are primarily from Ameten, you said. What if whatever is happening there spreads to the rest of the country? Would we expect more Teren refugees?"

"Ah, I see." Arianden pursed her lips. "Well, some might go directly into Exuria, which is possible this time of year for a small group on foot if you know what you're doing. But – for most, yes, the only way out is along the river and through Marek, even if they don't stop here. Many of them, as I said, are only here until they can buy passage out."

"In your view," Marcia said, "bearing the practicalities in mind, should we be making representations to Teren?"

There was a small intake of breath from a few people around the room. Marek was not in the habit of *making representations* to Teren. Marek largely preferred to ignore Teren politics altogether, in the hope that Teren politics continued to ignore Marek. Marcia wasn't sure that policy held, any more. Madeleine shifted irritably beside her.

Jeres Arianden spread her hands. "That is a matter for the Council. But, since you asked my opinion – clearly all is not well in Ameten. The reports we are hearing – "

"Demons. Nonsense," Priella-Head grumbled quite audibly from his place.

Arianden flushed, but carried on. "The reports we hear, even discounting parts of them, describe a city with serious rifts. We, in Marek, understand how a city must work, linked together," she linked her hands, "and we are of Teren, yet not Teren. Perhaps we are in a position to help them. If the Council so wishes."

The Reader banged their staff on the floor. "I believe we have covered as much as Ser Arianden can help us with. If there are no more questions, I suggest we dismiss her, with thanks, that we may continue our discussions."

There was a muttering of assent, and the Reader gestured politely to Arianden, who made a neat bow, gathered her papers, and exited. Out into the rain, poor woman; it had been tipping down for days now, and there was no sign of it letting up any time soon.

The discussion began straightforwardly, with the practical matter of longer-term accommodation for the refugees currently stacking up in tents at the barge-yard. Money was voted to construct some temporary dwellings – which could, apparently, be up in a week, even if they might have to be replaced within the year – out where various speculative builders had already been extending Marek into the marshes; and for the longer term, a committee was formed to assess the costs of extending the squats further towards the mountains behind them.

"Pay them to build," Priella-Head suggested. "Works better than letting them scurry round trying to find their own jobs, still less paying to feed them directly." There was general assent.

The matter of whether to intervene with Teren was thornier. The Council in general felt they could hardly intervene in Teren business without reminding the Archion in Ameten that Marek was, notionally, under his control. In theory, Teren had oversight of Marek: Teren law ought to apply here, and Marek paid tax to Ameten annually. In practice, Marek law superseded Teren law, Marek's annual tax burden was relatively small, and the dominance of the Teren Archion was purely theoretical.

Marcia's concern was that given the actions of the Teren Lieutenant, Selene, on her previous visit, Teren already had its eye on Marek, and that putting their heads under the blanket would not do anything to avoid that. But there was a limit to how obvious she could be in mentioning what Selene had been up to. Especially when it was becoming clear that some of the Heads felt that a closer relationship with Teren, far from being an expensive problem to be avoided, would instead be a positive boon. Evidently Selene's quiet conversations during her last visit had paid off.

It didn't help when, a few minutes in, Marcia put her foot squarely in it.

"If we are to make any representations," Piath said, "we should consider the matter of why they're coming here."

"Feel themselves attacked, I suppose," Athitol-Head said, disapproving. "I gather many of them are *political*."

"Well, that, certainly," Marcia said. "But more pertinently, the Archion – or the Commission, at least – is sending demons after them."

"*Marcia*." That was from Madeleine, in a furious whisper; and a disapproving mutter from around the Chamber echoed it.

Marcia set her teeth, determined to persist. The Council couldn't just *ignore* this. And as Heir she had the right to speak, whether or not Madeleine agreed with her. "I know we prefer not to engage with matters of spirits here, but the reports of the refugees are unambiguous."

"Superstitious fools," Pedeli-Head said. "Seeing soldiers and believing them demons."

Marcia tried to pursue the matter, but even Piath and Gil, who'd looked concerned over dinner, weren't willing to support her publicly, or even to discuss the matter. She did notice Daril leaning forward to have a fierce whispered discussion with Gavin, then sitting back with a scowl; well, she'd have been more surprised if Daril *had* been willing to say something, in the teeth of evident opposition. Even if he did have reason to be nervous of the idea of demons.

The matter of why the refugees were coming was dropped; instead Andreas suggested a delegation to Ameten to urge a more gentle handling of whatever disputes were ongoing. The rest of the Council was firmly against the idea. It was none of their business; if they just ignored it, Teren would doubtless sort themselves out, and not then have anything to hold against Marek. Marcia forced a vote, but only she, Andreas, and Gil Jyrithi-Head voted in favour of sending the delegation, though Piath and most of the Guildwardens abstained. It was *infuriating*.

Across the room, Gavin Leandra-Head got up and began, slowly and with visible effort, to leave the Chamber, leaving Daril behind. He would carry the vote for the printing discussion, then; that was a relief.

"Finally," the Reader said, "the matter of printing."

Marcia took a long, slow, breath, and resolved to keep out of it as much as possible. She didn't think they'd win, but at least she could provide the Fereno vote. She realised, with a sudden jolt, that she hadn't discussed this with Madeleine beforehand, as she'd meant to. Something else had come up; she couldn't even remember what, now. Some matter of lading-bills, perhaps. Never mind.

Warden Hagadath rose to put the case for censorship. Censorship and taxes; the taxation part raised an approving mutter. Marcia grimaced; an extra twopence on the sale of any printed matter would be difficult even for the news-sheets, and make anything less popular nearly impossible to print, if your target audience was the other side of the river.

Which, of course, was the idea. But the Council quite liked taxes, especially when they'd just voted to spend a significant amount of money on housing.

Gil Jyrithi-Head stood up to make a quiet, but convincing, speech about the perils of censorship. "Do we truly believe our system so weak that we dare not hear arguments against it? I have more faith in us, and our people, than that." There were some murmurs of agreement, which cheered Marcia up. "I am also concerned about the risk of suppressing other news. We have just spoken of those coming from Teren, and their treatment. Some of these pamphlets you mention have been printing their stories. I would be distressed if we were to prevent these from reaching a wider audience."

"Even when it's superstitious nonsense? Or stories

twisted out of true, to make us all think worse of the Archion?" Pedeli-Head demanded.

"Not sure I could think worse of the Archion," Marcia muttered. Andreas, in front, evidently heard her; his shoulders twitched slightly.

"Even then," Gil said mildly. "The truth will out, but not when it is suppressed. The superstition may hide real struggles."

To Marcia's surprise, Warden Ilana stood up. "I too am concerned by the implications of preventing our citizens from speaking their minds." They sat down again; but Marcia noted Hagadath's glare. Daril was correct, then; the Guilds were not united on this. And what of their feelings about Teren? Selene hadn't endeared herself to them last year. They might not wish to vote for a delegation now, but they might be persuadable.

"How does this compare with Teren's behaviour?" Marcia asked, once she'd caught the Reader's eye and been given the floor. "I am aware that we have decided against making representations to the Archion, but we are all nevertheless concerned about the refugee situation." Well, most of them were, at any rate.

"We are not suggesting that anyone should *leave* Marek as a result of their views," Athitol-Head said. She looked irritated. "Nor are we setting soldiers on them. Warden Hagadath merely suggests limiting how they can spread those views dangerously around our city. We do not allow people to run around with tapers setting fire to one another's door-sills, do we?"

"It's hardly the same thing…"

"It's worse," Hagadath rumbled. "Minds are more flammable than door-sills." Which was arrant nonsense, but it sounded good.

There was a dispute over taxation between Piath and Warden Tialla of the Accountants' Guild; eventually Piath succeeded in wresting agreement from Tialla to reduce the proposed tax to a ha'penny for pamphlets, with an exception for authorised news-sheets, and tuppence for books. Tialla proposed a separate vote on the taxes, which passed easily; Marcia voted against it, but several of those she was hoping would vote against the censorship rules, including Piath, were obviously happy to support a gain to the city's coppers. Well; with the changes Piath had made, at least that wouldn't be as bad as it could have been.

Which they went right back to discussing; a few more Heads and Wardens stood to make their points, more and less repetitiously, before the Reader finally called a vote. Marcia was fairly certain that Warden Hagadath would win; what she didn't expect was that, when the Reader called for those in favour to stand, Madeleine, beside her, would stand up.

"Mother!" she hissed. "You said…"

"I do not permit you to *embarrass* us when you carry our vote."

"House Fereno?" the Reader said.

"For," Madeleine said clearly, and Marcia, catching the gaze of both Andreas, turned round in surprise, and Daril, smirking from across the Chamber, ground her teeth and roundly cursed Madeleine in her mind. How *dare* she override Marcia without warning? But she could hardly have a stand-up row with her mother in the middle of the Council Chamber.

The vote went off almost exactly as she'd expected, with the exception that Haran voted against – afterwards, she saw Haran-Head say something to Gil, Jyrithi-Head, who nodded courteously. Well; Haran and Jyrithi were allies of long standing, and Gil could be very convincing.

Just not, apparently, convincing enough for Madeleine.

"We will not discuss this now," Madeleine said, quietly, in the rustle of departure. "With anyone."

Which was all very well; but it didn't prevent Marcia from reading the opinions of her allies in their expressions. To be overridden like this, *publicly* – and to think Madeleine claimed to be concerned for the House's reputation.

But what could she *do*?

TWELVE

Five days now it had been raining, off and on, and Jonas was fed up. It was *supposed* to be summer. Marek weather was changeable, fine, and it was nearly the end of summer, but still, this was just unpleasant. Grey and dark and miserable.

But he hadn't expected Asa to be as worried as they were.

"Storm's coming in," they said, sitting on their bed, arms wrapped around their knees. "Here this evening, maybe. Tomorrow morning."

Jonas sat down next to them, puzzled. "This isn't storm season."

"No. I mean, we get summer storms, sometimes, but they blow in and out. Not rain for this long, this persistent, and then with a proper storm on top. You can see it coming down from the mountains." Jonas went to look out of Asa's window, which faced out towards the mountains behind Marek, the other way from his. Dark clouds, darker than he'd seen in the last few overcast days, were massing above the peaks.

Was this the same unseasonal weather that had sunk the *Faithful Wind* and lost the *Stormeye* its mast, come inland now?

"The water comes down from up on the slopes, is the trouble. Not straight into the city, but the river gets higher and it backs up," Asa gestured, "west of New Bridge. And out east, the fishing village." Where Asa's family lived.

"But not here? Or Old Market?"

Asa shook their head. "That's all built higher. Storm surges wash over the embankment by Old Bridge, sometimes, but only enough to get people's feet wet."

"Why isn't everything that high, then?"

"Cheap spread," Asa said, then, catching Jonas' look of incomprehension, elaborated. "The village isn't Marek proper, and we can't afford to build high enough out of the swamp." They shrugged, pretending an insouciance they clearly didn't feel. "It's fine. It happens every so often in winter. Not usually this time of year. But we're prepared for it. Boats and all, you know? The bit out west though – well, it got built on the cheap, the last time Marek was expanding, when there hadn't been a flood for a few years. I suppose we'll see if they've learnt their lesson with the new stuff in the south-west, won't we?"

"Do you want to go check on your family?" Jonas asked, hesitant.

Asa shook their head. "No point. I'd just get underfoot. They know what they're doing. Anyway, I might be wrong. I've been in the city for years now, getting soft and losing my weather-edge. It might not be that bad. And the swamps should have space to soak up a fair bit of water, this time of year, even if it has been raining for a while." They rubbed at the side of their face. "I just don't like the look of those clouds."

"How about I go out and get us something to eat," Jonas suggested, "and a jug of beer, and we stay in here nice and cosy, where we won't get rained on?"

"You'll get rained on," Asa pointed out, but their smile was grateful.

"*I*," Jonas said grandly, "have proper storm gear, unlike you landlubbers," and was rewarded by Asa's laugh.

Much later, he woke from an uneasy sleep, unsure what had awoken him. Asa, beside him, was still soundly asleep, and the room was darker than usual. Low clouds, no moon, Jonas supposed. Then, without warning,

...water everywhere, children crying, someone screaming, a building half-drowned and a crash as something toppled, and that was the tip of the Guildhall he could see behind the buildings, it was Marek...

Afterwards he shivered under the blanket, trying to pull himself together. Asa had slept on undisturbed. He could wake them, if he needed, but...

Floods, in Marek. That was obvious enough. He climbed out from under the blanket – ugh, it was cold – and crossed to the window. In the distance, a lightning-flash lit the mountains, and he could swear the clouds were closer and darker than before. Rain hammered against the window, sheeting down the pane.

Marek was going to flood, and there was nothing he could do about it. The pit of his stomach yawned sickly, and he shivered, then scurried back across the room to shelter against Asa's reassuringly bulky warmth.

There must be something. But he could hardly go running out to find – who, even? the Masons' Guild? the Council? the guard? – to urge them to put up flood protections. They'd done it anyway, most like; it just wasn't going to be enough.

Maybe it wasn't even now that he'd seen. Maybe it was more distant. But either way; what could he *do*?

He turned restlessly on his back and stared up at the ceiling. Elementals. They could summon storms, Tait and Cato had reckoned. And if they could summon, surely they could unsummon? Push the storm away. Like when you outsailed a storm, but in reverse: Marek couldn't go anywhere, but the storm could go away from Marek. Why not? And the only real difference between elementals and angels and demons was the way humans chose to see them.

Cato had said, you couldn't do weather magic. That Beckett was here and the weather wasn't. But now the weather *was* here, and if an elemental could work with it, why not Beckett? Maybe no one had *asked* Beckett before, but people thought of new ideas all the time. Cato didn't understand weather. Cato had never even left Marek, still less spent years out on the sea watching the weather come in and out. It was big, he knew that, but it moved, it was in motion, and surely, surely…

Surely it was worth a go. Given the alternative he'd seen.

He couldn't do it here, though, in Asa's room and without any of his workings. He crept out of bed and into his clothes, careful not to wake Asa, and pulled his rain-slick on over everything. His room was only down the street.

He ought to go to Cato's, if he was doing magic; but Cato wouldn't want to see him at this time of night, and it couldn't wait.

And Cato might not let him. *In that case...* a tiny uncertain voice said in the back of his head, and he squashed it. If he'd seen it, surely he ought to try to do *something* about it? Cato thought he should experiment with stopping his flickers. And they were *his* flickers. He'd messed it up with Argan Etolin. This time, he was going to get it right, and then he could tell Cato. Could show him that he was a competent sorcerer who knew what he was about, that he *did* understand his own abilities. It would work, this time.

Back at his room, he puzzled over his small array of ingredients, and eventually chose salt, a copper nail for the lightning, and a pinch of sandy mud he'd collected from the river foreshore. He held it all in his hand and spat into it, for water and to bind himself. This felt like something he should be close to.

Close to. He grimaced. He should be out in it, shouldn't he? Which meant the roof.

One-handed, he climbed out of his window, rain-slick abandoned as too awkward to move in. Maybe rain-wet clothes would improve the working. He scrambled up into a place between two chimney-pots; he'd learnt his lesson about conducting magic somewhere you might fall. The only place to fall here was between the chimneys, into a little nook that was collecting rain. Jonas dipped his finger into it and used it to stir the mixture in his other hand.

His hand tingled as the rainwater merged with the rest, and he felt a building rightness that told him he was making the right connections. His spine shivered, hairs rising on the back of his neck. Yes. This would work.

He felt for the flicker, the outline of it, the sense of something happening that he associated with both flickers and magic; and then sent it outwards, seeking the building tension of a call to Beckett. The clouds roiled above him, dark and bulging; he reached out to them too, and then raised his hands, instinctively, gesturing them away.

The sudden metallic tang in his mouth told him something was happening, that he had Beckett's attention; and then there was a sense of a great rending inside him, and he threw it up and outwards, dragging the clouds apart and away from the city.

The rain stopped.

Jonas blinked upwards, and saw the moon, and stars in a perfectly clear sky; and around them, like the edge of a soup-plate, frantically boiling dark clouds lit and shadowed both by the moonlight. He felt empty, Beckett and the magic both gone, and his hand stung where he'd held the copper nail. He looked down; it was gone, but it had left a raised mark across his hand.

He looked back up at the moon. He'd done it. He'd shifted the storm. It wouldn't flood the new buildings downtown, wouldn't wash people out of their homes. Cato was *wrong*. You could do weather magic. He could, and he *could* stop a flicker. Satisfaction, and a victorious joy, bubbled up through him, expanding his chest, tingling up the back of his neck.

The clouds were still boiling around the edges of the city. It would be better, he supposed, if they were out to sea, although that might be just as bad for another ship like the Faithful Wind. He couldn't do more, even if he wanted, anyway; no magic at all left to him right this moment, and the workings he'd brought up all gone. But the clouds were out raining on the swamps, and on the mountains. There was nothing to harm there.

He bit his lip, a sudden tremor of doubt in his belly. Although. What had Asa had said? Weather coming in over the mountains, washing down...but there was plenty of space between here and there. Swamp-mess to soak up the water. That was fine.

He looked up again. Was that patch of clear sky smaller now? He squinted at the clouds; and they began to move inwards. Slowly; then impossibly fast.

The stars disappeared. The moon disappeared.

The clouds crashed back together above him, the biggest thunderclap he'd ever heard. As his ears rang and he stared upwards in horror, the skies opened and the water began to sheet down in bucketfuls so strong that all he could do was to cling desperately to the chimney and duck his head down, trying to keep a bubble of air under his hood.

Shit. Shit. Shit. He hadn't prevented anything, had he?

He'd brought it about.

It was pouring down; all Marcia could see in the darkness, as she stood at the window, was the rain beating against the glass. No starlight tonight; and she would bet that beyond the rain there would be very few torches showing on the Hill. Too wet for torches; too wet for anyone to go out, unless they absolutely had to.

Or unless they were avoiding their daughter. Madeleine had gone directly to House Pedeli after the vote that afternoon, and hadn't come back since. Even for dinner, at which the company had consisted of Marcia, Cousin Cara, and two friends of Cousin Cara's whose names Marcia had already forgotten. It wasn't exceptionally unusual behaviour – though Madeleine would usually be back for dinner unless she had a prior engagement – except that Marcia was absolutely positive that Madeleine was staying out because she didn't want to talk.

Perhaps she was hoping Marcia's ire would subside if she stayed away long enough. Not likely. If anything she was getting angrier the longer she had to wait. It had been a peculiar kind of torture to have to control her simmering rage over dinner in order to make polite conversation to Cousin Cara's guests. She wasn't sure how well she'd succeeded; Cousin Cara had made several sympathetic and unprompted comments about the emotional challenges of pregnancy, which hadn't improved Marcia's mood any.

There was a commotion in the hallway, and Marcia was out there immediately. Madeleine was there, her maid helping with her layers of wraps. The outside door was just closing on a couple of litter-bearers, and two footmen were standing around looking attentive.

"Mother!" Marcia swooped in. "Such terrible weather. You must come and sit down and have something warming in the small parlour, before you go to bed."

"It is so late, Marcia," Madeleine temporised.

Marcia smiled at her, broad and fake, and saw with satisfaction Madeleine's tiny twitch. "Indeed, which is why you should take your infusion here rather than fall asleep over it in bed, no?"

She could see the moment when Madeleine calculated that she'd rather give in than have a row in the middle of the hallway in front of the servants. "Of course."

"Mulled ginger, please," Marcia told one of the footmen, and stepped forward to offer her arm to her mother, now divested of her outdoor shoes and re-shod in indoor ones. "Come, Mother. Let me find you something to cover your knees, as well."

"I am not *that* old yet," Madeleine said, but she couldn't refuse Marcia's arm, though her hand on it was feather-light.

Marcia enquired politely after Pirran and the afternoon at House Pedeli while the mulled ginger was brought, with some tiny hot pies, a plate apiece, and the footman added a log to the big ceramic stove.

The door shut behind him, and Marcia got straight to the point. "Mother. What were you *doing* this afternoon?"

Madeleine raised a shoulder a fraction. "Voting to keep the city under control."

"You can't possibly be in favour of that law." That was a foolish thing to say. Quite evidently Madeleine was in favour of it. Marcia was all too aware that Madeleine could be in favour of some wholly terrible ideas. But she kept hoping that if she kept on *explaining*, Madeleine would understand.

"Don't be ridiculous, Marcia." Madeleine's voice was impatient. "Of course I am. Your noble arguments about freedom of speech and our robust institutions are all very well, but these people go too far."

"What's your definition of 'too far'?"

Madeleine sipped her milled ginger. "Calling for the overthrow of the government by force?"

"Why shouldn't they say that?"

"You would like to be attacked by a mob?"

"They're not attacking anyone," Marcia said. "They're suggesting the idea. There is a difference."

"They are inciting riots."

"Unsuccessfully." Marcia gestured to the window. "Do you see any riots?" It was too wet for riots, but still. "Over-excited rag-papers have printed these slogans in capital letters, posters have been pasted on walls over the river, for *weeks*. Months, even. Nothing's happening. They're a tiny minority. We don't need to *legislate* against them. We just need to ignore them. They have no power over the rest of Marek."

"How do you know what's pasted on walls over the river?" Madeleine demanded.

Marcia rolled her eyes. "Because I go there."

"Marcia!"

"Come on, Mother. You knew that. It's useful to know what's going on."

"There's a difference between suspicion and you throwing it in my face," Madeleine said irritably.

"Andreas comes along too, sometimes," Marcia offered as a sop to her mother's sense of respectability, then regretted it as Madeleine's eyes brightened.

"Well, it's nice for you to have a *suitable* lover."

She wasn't going to touch that one.

"In any case," Madeleine went on. "That says only that these people are not being listened to *yet*. We cannot assume that they will continue to be ignored, especially if further problems beset us. We are not as invulnerable as you believe, Marcia."

"We aren't, or Marek isn't?"

Madeleine made a dismissive gesture. "It is the same thing."

"If it's the 'incitement to riot' people you're after," Marcia said, changing tack, "why word it so broadly? Those arguing for peaceful change will be outlawed by this as well."

"There's no real difference," Madeleine said. "They're all the same underneath. I wouldn't be surprised to find that they're the same people writing under different names."

"In that case, you should be even less worried about them, because there's fewer of them. Come on, Mother. They're not the same. I've argued for reform of the Council; are you to put me in prison?"

"No, but it might make my life easier," Madeleine said tartly.

"I think this is bad legislation," Marcia said. "And if you insist that it must be passed, I am unwilling to sit idly by. I will seek to change it. It is far too broad. We cannot imprison Marekers simply for speaking their political mind!"

"We can, and evidently we will," Madeleine said. "Because that is what passed today."

"Because you *overrode* my vote."

"It would have passed anyway. Why be on the losing side?"

"Because I promised! Because I talked people into voting that way! Never mind what you think, Mother, you can't just let me carry the vote and then suddenly go against me!" That was the heart of the matter, really, not the details of the argument.

"I cannot let you run this House into the *mud*," Madeleine snapped, face dark with anger. "You are Heir, Marcia. Not yet Head. And if you cannot make *sensible* decisions..."

"What? You'll disown me? Like you did Cato?"

Madeleine took a sharp breath. They never mentioned Cato.

"Or in favour of the baby?" Marcia indicated her

stomach, fury rising. "Because that'll be a good while yet. I *will* be Head, Mother, and you cannot simply keep holding the reins because you don't trust me."

"I can and will," Madeleine said, voice high. "I have not done all I have for this House…" She broke off, her face suddenly a strange colour. She pressed a hand to her chest. "Oh. Oh dear."

"Mother?"

Madeleine sat back heavily on the couch. "Oh dear." Sweat had broken out across her forehead.

Marcia rang the bell, then ran to kneel by her mother. "Mother? Mama? What's wrong?"

"I really don't…my chest." She coughed, a couple of times, then bent over. "Oh. Oh."

The door opened, and Marcia called over her shoulder, "Send for a doctor! Immediately! And bring some water!"

Madeleine was grey around the mouth, and her breath was coming unevenly. Marcia clutched at her hand, no idea what to do. "Mother?" Fear gnawed at her. The baby felt heavy inside her.

A glass of water appeared, and Marcia fed Madeleine small sips. She could swallow them, at least, even if she still couldn't speak, and her arm was shaking. Only one arm. Was that good?

Time was compressing; it couldn't possibly have been that long since she had demanded a doctor, and yet now here was Doctor Pelligra, wearing the dark coat of their profession, neat grey braids caught together down their back, face rain-damp, boots leaving wet prints across the polished floor.

They knelt down on the rug beside Marcia. "Tell me what happened?"

Their calm presence allowed Marcia to move away a little, give the doctor a little space to work, as they pressed Madeleine's wrist, lifted her arm, laid a hand to the pulse in her throat and counted her breaths.

"She just – she dropped," Marcia said. "It was out of nowhere."

"And you've been giving her water?"

The glass was half empty. Marcia hadn't thought she'd been at it that long.

Dr Pelligra was moving now, commanding servants, insisting that Madeleine be carried to bed, asking for more water and a glass as they dug into their black bag and followed Madeleine, carried on a makeshift litter, up the stairs. Marcia trailed behind the procession up to her mother's room, helpless.

Was this her fault? Had the argument brought this on? Would Madeleine...

Rain battered against the windowpanes in the corridor, harder than ever, drowning out thought.

THIRTEEN

At first all Jonas could do was cling there, shuddering in horror, as the rain drenched him. After the initial deluge, it slackened off, but only to the point that he could breathe without inhaling rain.

This was a disaster.

He had to find Cato. Admit what he'd done. Maybe, somehow, he could make things better. This was his responsibility. He'd chosen to do it. He had to get help.

Sick to his stomach with guilt and regret, he scrambled down to his window. His fingers were so cold he could barely feel them, and water was sluicing down the rooftop; he slipped twice on a climb he'd been doing nearly daily without a thought. He dropped back inside his room, into a puddle on the floor from where he'd left the window open, and stood there shivering and dripping.

Clothes. Dry clothes. Wouldn't be able to help anyone if he was too cold. He closed the window, and went to hunt through the press. He felt like he was thinking through tar, struggling through ideas one at a time. Just finding another jumper wouldn't help. Everything he was wearing was drenched through. Why hadn't he worn his slicker? Climbing, that was right. But he didn't need to climb now. He could change into dry things, put the slicker on. That was supposed to keep the sea off in a storm. It would be up to this. Dry trousers, though his legs and feet would be sodden again soon enough, dry shirt, dry jumper. Slicker back on. Out the door.

He ran the few streets to Cato's room, splashing through streams of water running down the street, huddled under his hood. He glanced up and saw a couple of hurrying figures, bundled up in what passed for Marek wet-weather gear, running down towards the river; going to help? Shit, shit, what had he done.

Cato's light was on, the door open, and Cato was arguing with someone.

"No, I don't know…Oh. Jonas. Have you come to help?"

Tait, inside the room, was wearing some kind of brown coverall – oh yes, they were from the mountains, weren't they? You got proper weather in the mountains – and Cato was standing in the middle of a heap of clothing looking irritable.

"You must have *something*," Tait said.

"I don't normally go *out* when it's raining," Cato said. "Why would I? It's unpleasant." He picked up a hooded jacket. "I'll just have to make do with this."

"And this," Tait said firmly, thrusting a jumper – Tait's, from the size of it – at Cato, who took it with a scowl. "At least you can be warm while you're getting drenched. Hello, Jonas."

"What are you doing?"

"Floods coming in," Tait said. "Most likely, anyway. Cato says just west of New Bridge is most at risk."

Cato emerged from the oversized jumper. "And the fishing village, maybe, but I doubt we can get down there."

"Sorcery ought to be good for something, right?" Tait said. "We can't just sit around twiddling our thumbs, anyway."

"Bloody well can," Cato muttered, doing up his jacket. "Fucksake. You had a similar idea, Jonas? Or is there some other disaster, possibly an indoors one, that brings you here?"

Jonas swallowed. "It's my fault."

"What? It's rain, Jonas. Rain happens. Not quite this much, granted, but we get floods every few years."

Jonas shook his head. "I…I tried to make it go away."

"Oh dear," Tait said.

Cato's expression was incredulous. "Wait. We had a conversation about weather magic, didn't we? And I said, it wasn't a good idea. And you just…went ahead and did it anyway?"

"Yes."

"Great. Great. So – shit, we don't have *time* for this. Tell me, quickly, what you did."

"I tried to make it stop," Jonas said. He stared at the floor. He couldn't look at Cato or Tait. "With, um. Salt, and copper, and river-mud, and spit. And a bit of rainwater."

"What the hell was Beckett thinking?" Cato demanded of no one.

"And it worked, for a moment. All the clouds," he gestured, "just went away. And then, um. They came back."

"Right," Cato said. "Well, it was a stupid bloody idea, but I can't fault your instincts in terms of *how* you executed your bloody stupid idea."

"Cato," Tait murmured.

"I know. We don't have time." Water was still falling in torrents against the window. "Well. What you need to do right now, Jonas, is come along with us and help sort out what you fucked up."

They splashed together along the end of the street and down towards the river. By the docks, people were shifting boxes; but the docks were high, and Jonas didn't think the water would overflow them. They came over Old Bridge and turned right along the wide street that ran beside the riverbank towards New Bridge. Here, the street was built up away from the water, on good solid stone; peering over, Jonas could see the river swirling past far higher and faster than normal, but still well below the level of the embankment. As they neared New Bridge, the street sloped downwards; and once they were past the foot of the bridge, the embankment was gone, the houses crowding far closer to the river, and by the bank the unpaved roadway was already partially underwater. It was very dark; the odd torch shone under makeshift protective coverings. Out front of the houses, by the light of torches suspended from the eaves, people were piling sandbags from a cart with a very unhappy-looking mule in its traces. At least you could get a mule-cart in here – this one had probably come over the bridge from the wholesale market – the older streets weren't wide enough.

"We need to find out what's happening," Tait said, heading towards where someone was standing around and shouting at people.

Before they got that far, though, light suddenly bloomed by the cart, and the horse looked even more perturbed.

"Reb," Cato said with certainty, and grabbed Tait's hand to pull them towards the cart.

Witchlight, Jonas realised, not a torch. To his left, a torch sputtered and went out, overwhelmed by the rain, and curses arose from the people working by the river's edge. Another witchlight appeared where the torch had been.

Reb was standing under the first light, wrapped up in a brown overcoat a bit like Tait's. "Good," she said, as she saw them. "Can you do more lights, first?"

"Jonas," Cato said, waving a hand at him.

It was good to have something to do, even just a tiny thing. He was still tired from the magic earlier, but he could manage it.

Tait began to move their hand as well, and Reb stopped them. "Not you, Tait."

Tait frowned at her. "I can do a witchlight."

"Of course, but it's a continual drain, and I don't think you've got the concentration to hold it while you're doing other things."

Cato looked over at Reb, Jonas' witchlight showing his startled expression, then lifted his shoulders in a tiny shrug, and flicked his hand open. Four or five more witchlights lit the area with their weird yellow-green glow over it.

"What else?" Cato asked Reb. "You've been here longer."

"They're trying to sandbag the houses," Reb said, "which I'm not sure we can do much with. There's someone from the Masons co-ordinating it. But they've also got the guards trying to ditch-and-mound just above where the water is."

"Digging out the bank, you mean?" Tait asked.

Reb pointed. "There, just above the water level. It's all earth there, no stone bank. They're digging a trench and using the earth to build a barrier the far side of it."

"Won't last," Cato said. "It's mud. The river'll just flatten it."

"Indeed," Reb said. "But it'll slow it down, and buy the sandbaggers time, and the householders, too. There's a bunch of Guild folks evacuating people at the moment – the person in charge said they're going to put them up in the Guildhall."

"Shit, what about the refugees?" Jonas blurted out, another shock of worry starbursting in his stomach.

"The barge-docks should be fine; it's all built up off the bank. The rehousing area..." Reb grimaced. "It's in the swamps, yes, but the other side from the mountains, and further from the river proper, so the water'll take a while to get down there. And if we're lucky they built it up high enough." She didn't sound convinced. "Let's sort this out first and then see what's happening elsewhere."

"You want us to dig their ditch for them?"

Reb shrugged. "Making a ditch is easy. The mound is harder, but if we can shift the earth, the folks with the spades can pile it up."

"Isn't it a physical change?" Jonas asked, doubtfully.

Reb shook her head. "Nothing changes. Just moves."

Cato scowled, then marched over to the people digging, pushing his soaking wet sleeves up. One of his witchlights bobbed above him.

"Sorcerer," he said loudly. "Out of the way. Let's see if we can get this done for you."

He bent down and picked up some of the mud, rubbing it between fingers and thumb and pulling a face. With his clean hand, he hitched up the oversized sweater and dug about in the bags tied at his waist. "This isn't my sort of *thing*," he muttered to no one in particular.

"I've some mole-fur," Reb offered.

"Right. Yes. Good. And...periwinkle, yes, I've plenty of that. Give me some of your mole-fur? I'd ask where you got it, but maybe not right now."

Reb passed him a pinch of something, and Cato mixed it into the mud in his hand, shut his eyes, and moved his lips. Jonas couldn't hear what he said.

At his feet, the soil erupted sideways, and all four of them jumped backwards. Once there was about six feet of trench, Cato opened his eyes, and the earth settled.

"Right," he said. "You lot, with the spades, turn all of that," he gestured at the untidy piles of earth to each side of the trench, "into a mound. We'll dig you some more ditch." Without bothering to see if they were listening, he turned to Jonas and the other sorcerers. "Right, so, that's bloody tiring. We'll need to take turns."

"Would it be better if the earth all came out this side?" Tait asked.

"Obviously yes, and if you can work out how to do that, feel free."

"Pass me the periwinkle, then," Reb said.

"Good job none of this needs to stay dry," Cato said. "Probably helps, actually, doesn't it." The rain was coming down so steadily that Jonas had almost forgotten about it. "Here. Periwinkle for all. Grab some mud. Some of that mole-fur of Reb's. Let's dig more trenches. Reb, Jonas, Tait, me again. Off we go."

To Reb the night felt eternal. There had never been a time when she wasn't either shifting earth or waiting, mind blank and exhausted, to shift it. She'd never been dry before and never would be again. She didn't have that much mole-fur, and the apprentices needed the focus more than she did, so without comment, she'd taken the tiniest of pinches each time. She thought Cato was doing the same. And each time she pulled power again she felt the exhaustion seeping further into her bones. Everyone looked about the same way. Alyssa had turned up at some point, leaning heavily on her stick and looking like she'd already put in a full day's work, and taken her own turns.

Tait had found her something to sit on before Reb had even asked.

The water rose higher. Reb shifted more earth. The rain kept coming. The sky had begun to lighten, just a little, when there was a scream, and she looked up, blinking, to see someone pointing upriver. For a moment, she couldn't work out what she was seeing, and then Cato swore, and swung a witchlight out over the river, and with a hideous jolt of realisation she saw, outlined by its yellow-green light, the wall of water coming in.

"*Run,*" someone shouted, and they all ran for the higher ground beyond the houses they'd been protecting.

The wave spread almost gracefully straight over the mound they'd just spent so long putting up, and smashed against the fronts of the houses. The spray hit Reb in the face, tasting of river and of the rain that she'd been wiping away for the last however-many hours.

"Shit," Reb said. The exhaustion dragged at her harder with the realisation that, after all that, they hadn't succeeded. "I thought we were going to save them. I really did."

"All the people are out," Cato said, without turning to look at her. He was watching the wave. "Heard the guard captain say. Could be worse." Then, "Oh. Shit."

The wave hadn't stopped at the houses. It had gone on, crashing into the supports of New Bridge where they were dug into the riverbank. The sides of the river were higher from there; the wave wasn't quite big enough to overtop the walls around and after the bridge. But it was higher now, and faster, the water frothing and speeding down towards the sea, and it wasn't *stopping*.

"It's going to take the supports out," Tait said, their voice thin. The dawn light had strengthened just enough to see what was happening without a witchlight.

There were already people down there, frantically piling things around the base of the bridge, where the ground hadn't quite yet been washed away.

"It might not," Cato said, flat and unconvincing. "They might be able to stabilise it."

Tait was already moving, running down towards the riverbank at the base of the bridge. Jonas started after them, and Cato swore viciously and went too.

Reb, unsure what else to do, followed. They all stopped in the shadow of the bridge, on the edge of the crowd of people trying to help.

"Can we do anything?" Jonas' voice was urgent.

"There's no *room*," Tait said, agonised.

"Well. That's the advantage of magic, isn't it?" Cato said. He threw up another witchlight with one hand, brightening the bridge's shadow. It didn't have quite the casual ease that Cato's magic usually did. "No need to be right in there. Same kind of deal as the trenches, right, but in reverse. Try to hold things in instead of pulling them out." He glanced round at Reb, then turned to Jonas, grabbing his shoulder and pulling him round to squint at his face. "Yeah. Thought so. You're too done in to be doing this on your own. Remember how we linked up, the other day, when we were talking about poisons?"

"Poisons?" Reb asked, and Cato grimaced.

"Never mind," he said. "We weren't poisoning anyone, but let's discuss it later, hey?" His attention was back on Jonas. "Remember?"

"Linking," Jonas said. He sounded about as exhausted as Reb felt. "Yes. I remember."

"Right. We can do that but just for power, not for showing you anything. All right?" He turned from Jonas to Tait. The witchlight cast strange shadows over his face. "I've not linked with you before, so now's not the time to try it. How about you sit down for a moment. You look done in."

"I'm fine," Tait said, tightly.

Linking. She ought to offer to link with Tait, as well, except...they'd never done that, because Reb hadn't wanted to. She bit the side of her mouth, hard. It didn't matter. Cato was right; Tait was done in anyway. She'd already sent Alyssa to rest, before the big wave had come in.

"You need a break," she said, firmly. "I insist. You can

stay here if you'd rather. Cato, can you and Jonas manage? I want to find out what's happening in the rest of the city."

"It's a small space," Cato said. "Even not having to get in there physically, I'm not sure another sorcerer would help. Go."

She didn't have to go far before she found the guard captain, rapping out orders, with someone else standing next to them in a dripping cloak, asking questions. They looked round and Reb recognised Jeres, from the barge-yard. Reb had seen her earlier organising evacuation; by now she looked about as tired as Reb felt. A soaking-wet messenger, spattered with mud, stood nearby, shifting anxiously from foot to foot. Reb didn't have to listen for long to find out: problems out at the south-west. Flooding, which was one thing, but the foundations of the new houses seemed to be shifting, which was rather another.

"We'll have to get the Masons over there," Jeres was saying grimly to the guard captain, "although given who did the work in the first place…"

Could magic help? The bare idea of it filled Reb with exhausted horror, but…

She went back to Cato.

"Messenger just came in. There's problems out at the new build housing, out in the south-west. It might be sinking."

"Fuck," Cato puffed. The light had strengthened enough he'd let his witchlight go, and she could see the exhausted shadows around his eyes. "I'm not cut out for this. And the south-west too? I'm not sure we're doing anything here other than delaying things."

The earth was crumbling almost as fast as people could ferry stone and rubble in to fill in its footing. Tait, over to Jonas' right, was slumped against a lump of stone behind them, eyes barely open.

"We can't be everywhere at once," Reb said. But where should they be? Here? In the south-west? If the buildings were sinking anyway, was there anything useful they could do?

Cato dropped his hands and wiped at his face, leaving smears of dirt behind. "Jonas – over there. Fuck, this is at least as hard as doing it by hand."

Reb saw a stone sliding away from someone at the foot of the bridge, and then saw it stop and slide back up again. Jonas took a gasping breath. "At least your footing's a bit better," he panted.

"Right," Cato said. "You take your two, go out there, link up, see if you can – I don't know, whatever seems helpful. Jonas and me handle the bridge. No room for more anyway."

Linking up. Reb's heart sank even further. But she couldn't take Tait and Alyssa out and get them to work alone; she could see neither of them had the reserves for it. Linking might have worked, like it was working, just about with Jonas. But.

"They can't link up," she said, flatly. "Tait and Alyssa."

"They...why the fuck not?" Cato's voice was incredulous, and he stared at Reb. "What've you been doing the last however many months?"

Reb didn't say anything.

"Angels and demons. Fine. You on your own won't help much, and neither of them are up to working alone just now. Better we all stay here. If you help Jonas and me with this, maybe we can get it well enough supported, that we can leave them to it."

"What can I do?" Alyssa asked, from over Reb's shoulder. Reb managed not to jump, but she was sinkingly sure that Alyssa had heard what Cato had said.

She looked round. Alyssa's face was drawn, her shoulders sagged with exhaustion, and she was leaning far more heavily than usual on her stick, favouring one leg.

"Nothing, for now," Cato said firmly. "You've run yourself far enough into the ground already, and we'll need you again once we get over to the south-west. You and Tait are best off resting." He summoned a grin from somewhere, the effort visible. "If there were anyone around with a pastry-cart, I'd say get one of those, but as it is…" He turned to Reb, and held out a hand. "Reb. Link in."

For a moment Reb thought of insisting she'd help alone, but that was stupid. They'd do better together. She took Cato's hand, and felt the wash of his power, the lighter feel of Jonas' flowing with it. "There," Cato said, through his teeth. The three of them pushed at another lump of stone the workers at the foot of the bridge were moving, and it slid in where it ought.

"If we could scrape mud off the bottom," Reb said, as the thought occurred to her, "I don't know, slide it in somewhere, to shore it up…"

"The water'll speed up," Jonas said, through gasps of breath. His shoulders had straightened a little since Reb linked in, but he was nearly as exhausted as Alyssa and Tait. Linked, he was at least safe from wiping himself out altogether. "Like when they dredge a dock."

"Shit." Cato's eyes were wide with worry, and he gestured a witchlight down towards the footing of the bridge. All three of them saw more of the bank crumble away, felt the earth shiver underfoot

"It's going to go," Jonas said, voice rising in panic. "There's no way…" He yanked his hand away from Cato, to cup his hands around his mouth and shout down towards the people at the bridge, "Get out! Get away!"

With a rush, the rest of the bank fell away and the bridge began to crumble downwards. Reb felt Cato yank power through her and almost lost her own footing, but she could feel what he was doing, trying to hold the whole thing up by sorcery alone. And he was doing it, too, the bridge crumbling far more slowly than it should as people scattered away.

"Fuck," Cato said through gritted teeth. "Not going to be…able…for long…"

"A few seconds more," Reb gasped, her chest hollowed-out. "Almost clear."

The last couple of people were scrambling up the bank, scrambling out from under – and one of them lost their footing, and fell into the water.

"Shit! Shit! I can't…"

Cato fell to his knees and the power dropped. Reb dropped it at the same time; no way could she even try to hold that alone. The rest of the bridge fell away; only half of it was left now, sticking out from the far bank, and she wasn't sure how much longer the supports in the middle of the river would hold.

"Can't see them in the water," Cato was muttering.

"They're gone," Reb said. Her heart ached. It would have been far worse if they hadn't been there, she knew that, but to lose even one…

Then someone shrieked behind them, and Reb turned to see a soaking wet person, face down on the floor as if they'd been dropped, rivulets of water spreading all around them, with someone running towards them.

"What the…"

Behind that, where Cato had told Alyssa and Tait to wait, Tait was on their feet. They were even paler than usual, hand clamped over their arm. They folded gracefully forwards, then backwards, and slumped to the ground in slow motion. Cato, lungeing up the incline towards them faster than Reb would have thought possible, caught their head just in time to keep it off the ground.

"They opened a fucking *vein*," Alyssa said. "Just…that person just reappeared, right out of the river."

"Translocation," Cato said. "They've done it before…stupid idiot, they don't have the *resources*."

"Blood magic…" Reb began. Her apprentice…

"Do not even start," Cato hissed at her. "Trust me, you do not want to go there."

Reb swallowed and raised her hands. "Not criticising. Desperate situations and all that." She rubbed a very tired hand across her face. "There's nothing more we can do here. What about the south-west?"

Tait's eyes blinked open. "The…"

"Not you," Cato said with great firmness. Tait let their eyes close again. Cato looked around. "Not any of us, I don't think. That bridge was fucking heavy. I don't think I *can* do anything else right now. Tait's lost blood. We're all done in."

"I've rested," Alyssa said, face set stubbornly. "I can…at least we can go and see what's needed."

"Reb?" Cato looked up at her. "Don't be heroic, if it'll mean you pass out yourself. We might be needed again, later today."

"I can go and look," Reb said. She could still feel the smallest flicker of power inside her. Not enough to do much, but if she'd taught her apprentices better, Tait might not have needed to do that. She had to make up for it somehow, didn't she? "Can't do much," she added, reluctantly. "But…I'll see what we'll be needed for. Come back here, once you've rested."

"I don't think I can," Jonas said, his voice small. He'd sat straight down on the wet ground.

"You rest," Cato said. "You've done a lot." He looked around. "Not that one can rest all that well in the pouring rain."

One of the guards came up to them, exhausted-looking herself and covered in mud. "We've rooms requisitioned in the Lion, up the road. You can rest there. That one saved Bracken. Anything we can do. Anything." She took a closer look. "Bloody hell. Is that Tait?"

"Ye-es." Cato flicked a nervous glance up at Reb.

"They looked after us in the mountains last year. Should have known." She sounded awed. "Saw them do that trick before, with a dragon-bear. Other way around though, if you see what I mean. Away from us, not towards." She shook her head in alarmed admiration. "Anyway. Let's get you sorted. Something to eat."

"We'll report back," Reb said. "Come on, Alyssa."

Jonas helped Cato get Tait to their feet, and Reb watched the three of them stagger after the guard, before she turned towards the road to the new district, Alyssa trudging silent beside her. Reb felt like a wrung-out rag – and guilty. Very, very guilty.

FOURTEEN

The rain was still coming steadily down. As Marcia descended Marekhill towards Marek Square, cutting through alleyways running with water, the grey morning light showed puddles and lakes everywhere. Her good leather boots weren't designed for walking through this sort of thing; water was seeping in around the edges. This early, there was hardly anyone around; who would be out in this if they didn't have to be?

She took a wide step to avoid a puddle, and almost shrieked at the sharp jab of pain in the front of her pelvis. Yet another thing that she'd discovered was *normal* during pregnancy. She put her hand on the still-small hard bump of the baby, and felt too-ready tears climbing the back of her throat, prickling in her nose. The baby that Madeleine had pushed her so hard for, worrying about the future of the House, and would they ever meet their grandmother now? Yesterday, after the debacle in the Council, Marcia might well have said, *and good riddance*; now the feeling in her chest was almost as painful as the grinding of her bones.

She couldn't think about this now. She was out to find Cato. She had to concentrate on that.

The river was running high under Old Bridge, lapping almost at the top of the embankment walls either side of it. She cast an eye westwards and stopped short in horror. New Bridge…wasn't there any more. Or half of it wasn't. The bridge was crumbled halfway along its length, only the northern part still sticking out jagged over the fast-running river.

"Impressive, ain't it?" She startled, and turned towards the voice. A young messenger, red armband as soaking wet as the rest of them, was looking in the same direction, lips pursed assessingly.

"Not sure I would say *impressive*, exactly, but…Was anyone hurt?"

"I dunno for sure, but they say as the sorcerers were there. They say one of 'em pulled someone right out of the river with magic, just like that." The kid sounded impressed, or doubtful, or both at once. "They say things is worse over the south-west, though, and the sorcerers di'n't make it over there." They shrugged, and took off again into the rain.

Marcia hesitated. Sorcerers by the bridge. Would Cato have gone out into the cold and the wet to help? Reb would have, but…Maybe. She remembered Cato needling at her about Marekhill and the rest of the city.

And Tait. She'd only met Tait a couple of times, but Tait would help, she'd place money. And if Tait wanted Cato to come along, Cato might grumble, but he'd do it.

It would be quicker to go look by New Bridge, and then come back to the squats if she had to. She began to slog westward through the puddles.

She only got part of the way along the river embankment; as she got closer to the bridge – to where the bridge had been – the embankment walls were lower, and parts of the street were underwater. Mounds of earth and a few sandbags protected some of the houses, but they were clear of the flooding, protected by the road and a row of trees, all now wet-footed, between them and the river. Marcia dodged sideways, came out on the wide new road that went between New Bridge and the south-west part of the city, and turned down it towards New Bridge.

A bunch of guards were huddled under a portico outside a pub close to the bridge end of the road, eating pastries and drinking out of tin mugs.

"Excuse me," she said. One of them looked up, and she recognised Captain Anna Barcola, who'd worked for her before.

"Ser Fereno! What are you doing here?"

"Looking for sorcerers," Marcia said.

Captain Anna's muddy eyebrows went up – Marcia was Marekhill, and thus presumed to be unenthusiastic about sorcerers – but she nodded, and gestured to the door of the pub. "You mind that sorcerer came with us over the mountains, that time? Tait? I told you about the dragon-bear? Pulled the same trick again, didn't they? Pulled our Bracken right out of the river, when the bridge went. He's in there, with a doctor looking to him. Sorcerer fainted clean away." Her voice was tired and hoarse.

"Are they all right?"

"Eh, they've come round again. Other sorcerer reckons they're just tired out. We've to go down the south-west in a bit, but can't haul people out of houses on an empty stomach, can you? I've sent a messenger after boats to take round."

"If there's anything – if you need money?"

Captain Anna pursed her lips. "Mostly people are just helping. But if I can call on your tab, if needed…?"

"Absolutely," Marcia promised.

Inside the pub she peeked into a door on the left, and saw someone sitting at a table, head pillowed on their arms. They looked up, and she recognised Cato.

"Marcia? What the hell are you doing here?" He looked exhausted, face drawn, clothes steaming gently from the roaring fire just behind him.

She meant to, ought to, ask about Tait, but… "Mother. It's Mother."

His body tensed, shoulders hunching. "What about her?"

"She's alive," she said, realising what he must think. "She's – for now, anyway. I think. Oh, shit, Cato…"

"Marcia? Are *you* all right? Come in, come on." He was on his feet, had come round the table and had his arm round her. She – was she shaking? She didn't know, any more. She wasn't in touch with herself, somehow; everything felt blurry around the edges. Her mama might never see the baby. Marcia might not see her mama again, whatever Doctor Pelligra had said, she might get home and…

"Tait, though, they said…" she gulped air, overcome by things to worry about.

"I'm fine." It was a moment before she saw Tait,

slumped in an armchair by the fireplace. She hadn't noticed.

"You're tired out is what you are," Cato sniped gently over his shoulder as he guided her to the other armchair. "Right. Wait there."

She stared at the floorboards, unable to think, caught by the tiny whorls in the grain, the gaps between the boards, the…A mug was thrust into her hand. It wasn't hot, so it wasn't an infusion.

"Drink that," Cato directed.

She was halfway through a swig before the smell of alcohol hit her. The liquid hit the back of her throat a fraction of a second later and she choked, swallowed, choked again.

"What the *hell*?"

"Shit brandy," Cato said. "This place doesn't have the good stuff."

Forewarned now, she took a second, more measured sip. It was horrible, Cato was right, but the burn in the back of her throat was bringing her back to herself.

"I'm pregnant, remember," she said, handing the mug back to him.

"Couple of sips won't do you any harm." He took a healthy swig himself, and made a face. "Fuck, this really is vile. Certainly hope it doesn't affect the baby's taste in booze. Right. Are you able to tell me what's going on?"

Marcia closed her eyes, then opened them again. "Mother had some kind of – I don't know. A fit, maybe, or a seizure. The doctor said, something in the brain or the heart, but sometimes people recover. They said, used to be you'd let some blood, but this doctor doesn't believe in that, thinks your blood does more good inside you."

"Seems reasonable," Cato remarked. His tone was pointed, although Marcia didn't understand why. Tait made a noise from the other armchair. "Otherwise why have it there in the first place?"

Marcia shrugged. "I'm not a doctor. But there's no point paying them then arguing with them."

She paused, waiting for Cato to say something. He

didn't. "She's, um. She's still conscious, but she hasn't said anything. Yet."

"When did this happen?" Cato's voice was cool, but he'd sat down on the arm of the chair and his arm was around her shoulders.

"This evening. Yesterday evening, I mean." She rubbed a hand over her eyes. "We were arguing."

"There's a surprise."

"We were arguing, and maybe it was my fault." Marcia's voice cracked.

"You've always argued. Was this any different?"

"No," Marcia admitted. "But maybe..."

"And maybe not."

"Oh, shit. I feel sick."

"You – the window. The window!"

Marcia made it to the window and threw it open just in time. Thankfully it opened onto an alleyway, not onto where Captain Anna and her people were sitting.

"Sorry," she said, after she'd sat down again, and Cato had found her some water and a clean rag to wipe her mouth. "It's – the baby, you know."

"They tell me that happens, yes." Cato pulled a face.

"And the shock, too," Tait put in. "Maybe the brandy wasn't such a great idea."

Marcia looked up at Cato. "What am I going to *do*?"

"What do you mean?"

Marcia shrugged helplessly. "She's Head, but she can't speak. I'm not sure if she understands...Do I act without her? Do I just wait? How long do I wait for? I don't know what to *do*."

"Right."

There was a long pause. "Cato?" Marcia said eventually, and hated the tone of her own voice.

"No. Nuh-uh. No way." He pulled away from her and sat with his arms folded. "I'm not House any more, Marcia. You are. You stayed, and you're Heir, and all the rest of it. I'm not getting involved."

"Cato..." His refusal stabbed her under the breastbone.

"I thought you were telling me...I don't know. Just to

tell me, I suppose. Or because you're upset, and you're my sister. Not because you wanted political advice."

"I am upset!"

"I know you are. And of course I'll always offer you comfort. But I was disowned, Marcia. I am not House any more and I will not have an opinion to make life easier for you." His voice was iron-cold.

"But I don't know what to *do*!"

"Yeah, that's rough. I didn't know what to do when I got kicked out, either."

"And I helped you!"

"I'm helping you. Just not with the politics part. I love you, Marcia. You're my sister. You can sit here and cry on my shoulder and all that – just as long as you don't expect the same emotion of me – but you can't expect me to look to the House." His voice hardened. "Especially not when I've just spent the night trying to deal with fucking floods, and I haven't seen hide nor hair of anyone from bloody Marekhill."

"I just offered Captain Anna…"

"Yeah, but you weren't here when we were digging ditches at two in the morning, were you?"

"I was with Mother!"

"Why is she any more important than the people who live down by the river? Too close to the bloody river. Or out in the south-west, no *idea* even what's going on out there…"

"Cato," Tait said; that was all, but Cato stopped.

"I'm sorry. You've got your responsibilities too. I get that. But they're not mine. And she disowned me, remember? She's not my mother any more, and it's sure as hell not my House. Deal with it yourself, Marcia."

A sob clawed its way violently up Marcia's throat, and Cato sighed and put his arm round her. "I'm sorry," she said, struggling to stop the tears. "I shouldn't, I know, but…"

But he was her brother, and they'd grown up together, and…And she hadn't thought; that was the nub of it. And now she felt more alone than ever. If Madeleine…*if*, it would just be her and the baby, wouldn't it? Cousin Cara looked after the house, not the House. Andreas was Tigero, even if he was her co-parent. It would be her, alone, and she couldn't...

But it wasn't Cato's problem.

"If there's anything House money can help with," she said, once the tears were under control again. "With the floods. I've told Captain Anna, and I'll convene the Council, as soon as I can, but in the meantime."

"Thanks," Cato said.

Footsteps in the hallway, and Reb came through the door, looking even worse than Cato.

"Half the south-west corner's under water," she said, then saw Marcia and stopped dead. "What are you doing here?"

"Fereno-Head had some kind of attack," Cato said, very precisely.

"Your mother?" Reb looked between the two of them.

"Her mother," Cato agreed. It bit into Marcia's heart, however much Madeleine had earnt it.

"It's fine," Marcia said. "I...this is more important, obviously."

Reb was frowning at her, familiar expression of concern. Marcia wasn't sure she could bear it. "But you must..."

"It's fine," she said again, and ignored all the ways in which nothing was fine. "I said to Cato. The Council will help, but in the interim, if House money can resolve any problems."

"Thanks," Reb said. She looked awkward, unsure, her eyes flicking between Marcia and Cato. "The south-west, we really do..."

"Need to get over there, right." Cato pushed himself up off the chair. For a moment, looking up at him, Marcia saw unutterable weariness on his face; then he took a deep breath and it was gone. "Let's go."

"I can come," Tait said, starting to get up. Both Reb and Cato turned and snapped "No!" at the same moment.

"You'll stay here," Reb said. "You've nothing more in

you. Don't worry. There'll be more to do later today, not to mention tomorrow. The rain's easing off, but the water's still coming in from upriver."

"I'll, uh," Marcia said. "Leave you to it."

She tried to slip past Reb, but Reb stopped her with a gentle touch to the elbow that felt far stronger than it was. "I'm sorry," she said. It nearly did Marcia in.

"Thank you," she said, and left before the tears came again.

She should never have come here.

Jonas trudged after Reb and Cato across to the swamp extension in the south-west, without letting himself think. Once he got there, he sat down on a low wall above the water level, hunched his shoulders against the now-lighter rain, and waited for someone to tell him what to do.

"Most of this is just shifting stuff," Cato said. "I've not got the power to do that any better now than any of this lot can by hand."

"It's not that," Reb said. "It's finding whether there's still anyone in the buildings." She pointed over where the worst of the flooding was, water lapping right up to the first floor of some places.

"If there was, wouldn't they be hanging out of the windows?" Cato objected.

"They've already rescued those. They're worried about people who aren't well enough to have moved."

"Ugh. Right." Cato scrubbed at his face. "It's a bugger to run, that spell."

"I thought, both of us," Reb said. "And Jonas. I've sent Alyssa home to rest. She was done in."

Cato turned to look at Jonas. "Huh. I should have sent you home with Tait, not dragged you over here."

"I can do something," Jonas said, even though his legs felt like they wouldn't support him any more. "I…"

"No," Cato said.

"You've done enough," Reb said. She looked drained.

"Go on home. Rest."

"But…" Jonas started. "There's things to do."

"We can do them," Cato said. He pulled a face. "Though I think that's probably all I can do. Jonas, can you get yourself home?"

Jonas had no idea. "Yes," he said, hopefully.

Reb scrubbed a hand through her wet hair. She'd given up trying to keep her hood up at some point during the night. "Give me a minute."

She squelched across the sodden mud – Jonas thought there might once have been grass here, but you couldn't tell it now – to the makeshift command station for the volunteers, someone sitting on the back of a cart. The horse was missing. Hopefully it'd been stabled somewhere dry. There was room out this side of Marek for horses and carts and such, not like the older parts. Room to expand. And then to get flooded.

"There's a cart taking people back to Marek Square in a minute," Reb reported. "It can't go further than that, but…"

"I can manage," Jonas said.

"If you're sure," Cato said doubtfully. He turned to Reb. "Look. I'm nearly done in too. After we've done the house check, I need a couple of hours sleep and a very large breakfast before I can do anything else. I'm sure you're willing to drive yourself all the way to your knees, but it's a bloody stupid idea. Let's ask the cart to wait for us, yeah?"

"Yes," Reb said, reluctantly. "You're right. Very well. You go tell them that, and I'll get the finding-spell started."

Jonas didn't pay attention as Cato and Reb did whatever it was that would find people, nor did he have any idea what the outcome was. Eventually, Cato shoved a hand under his elbow, and dragged him off towards a cart, which he sat dully on all the way to Marek Square, where he had to get off and make his feet trudge across Old Bridge. He didn't look over towards New Bridge. Didn't have the energy. Reb and Cato didn't speak, either.

Over the other side of the bridge, Reb nodded and muttered something that sounded like thanks before she turned towards the market.

"We still have to talk," Cato said, when they reached Jonas' street. "But not now. However, to be clear: absolutely no more magic without my supervision until I tell you otherwise. Do you hear?"

Jonas, too cold and tired and dispirited to say anything, just nodded. In his room he managed only to take off his slicker and wet trousers before collapsing onto his bed.

He hadn't been asleep nearly long enough when a knock woke him.

"Jonas?"

Asa. "'S open," he mumbled into the mattress. He could still hear rain outside. Only a gentle patter now, but clearly it was just never going to stop.

"Jonas? Are you all right?"

He tried to turn over, and couldn't. Nothing wanted to move.

"Jonas?"

"Tired," he managed.

"Wait. Everyone was saying, *sorcerers*, but I thought…" Jonas had a fleeting moment of terror that Asa knew already that this was *his fault*, before they carried on, "I thought all the work must be being done by the full sorcerers. The ditch, and the sandbags. And someone said, one of the sorcerers pulled someone right out of the river when the bridge went."

"We couldn't save the bridge," Jonas said into his pillow.

"Was that you?"

"I helped," Jonas said. "Not – the river person. That was Tait." He finally managed to turn over and squint at Asa.

"You need something to eat. I'll be back."

In barely an eye-blink they were back, holding a bowl that smelled absolutely amazing. "Bacon, eggs, bread," they said, handing it to Jonas once he managed to sit up. It was jumbled in the bottom of the bowl, but it didn't matter even slightly. By the time Jonas had got through the food and the attendant infusion, he felt significantly more human.

"You saved those houses along by New Bridge," Asa said. Their eyes shone, and Jonas' stomach lurched. Asa didn't know. He'd have to tell them, and then they'd look different, they'd… "You and the others," Asa carried on, unaware. "Even if you couldn't save the bridge itself – no one was hurt, and they would have been, without you. Everyone's talking about it."

"What about the fishing-village?" Jonas asked. Breakfast had become an uncomfortable lump in his stomach.

Asa sighed. "No word yet. But…they're used to it. We used to evacuate twice a year, even without that sort of flood. I'm sure everyone's fine." They didn't *sound* sure. "They'll send boats down to check, as soon as it's safe."

"It was my fault," Jonas blurted out. He had to own up to it.

"What? No, Jonas, you helped. It's a flood. It happens."

Jonas shook his head, miserable, unable to look Asa in the eye. "No. It was – I made it worse."

"I don't understand."

"I saw – in a flicker. Horrible flooding. People dying. I." He stopped. "I tried to stop it. By magic. It did, for a moment, and then it was worse again. It's my fault."

"But people didn't die," Asa said. "The bridge went, yes, and houses flooded, and plenty of folk wet, poor sods. But Tam says, everyone got out."

"It was still my fault," Jonas said.

"I thought you were trying to stop it?"

"Yes, but…I should have known better. Cato said weather-magic wouldn't work."

Asa sat down on the edge of the bed. "Let me get this straight. You saw a disaster, in one of your flickers. And then you tried something Cato advised against, to try to fix it? And then when you didn't fix it, you went to help?"

"I guess," Jonas said. "I don't know I would've gone to

help, though, if it weren't for Cato. I went to tell him, and he and Tait were going down there."

"So you went with them."

"Yeah." Cato had told him to go, and he'd gone. Would he have thought of it himself?

"And you helped with all the," they gestured, "sorcery stuff?"

Jonas nodded.

"It was stupid, to try something Cato'd warned you about, on your own," Asa agreed. "That was your fault. But...you were trying to prevent something. And you did. No one died, Jonas, and they very well might have."

"Not how I meant, though." And it could have been him had made it as bad as it was.

Asa pursed their lips. "Well maybe that's the thing to remember? You can change things, but it won't work out how you intended?"

Asa meant well. But it wasn't like they understood this. Magic, or flickers. It was his fault, even if Asa was – thankfully, unbelievably – willing to forgive him. Still his fault.

Two hours later, he and Asa stood halfway down the embankment, and watched the river racing past. Upriver, the flood-waters swirled over the lower parts of the embankment, right up to the houses and their protective sandbags. Further down, the remains of New Bridge slumped ever closer to the water; beyond that, Jonas knew, the ditch he and the others had spent so much time and effort over was gone altogether.

And if he turned just slightly to his left, he could see the tip of the Guildhall over in Marek Square. He'd seen that, in his flicker. But it was daytime now. There were no people here. No one caught in the water in the dark, swept out of reach. It was his flicker, but it wasn't.

"Won't be able to get to the village for a while," Asa said, with a sigh, turning to look back towards Old Bridge and out to sea. "I'm sure they'll be fine."

His flicker, but not his flicker. Still his responsibility.

FIFTEEN

For Reb, the following days were a blur of moving people and things and earth and stone around. When she wasn't out in the city shifting things, she was in her workroom making charms. No one, as far as anyone knew, had died. Quite a few people were very uncomfortable, and even more had lost belongings and would have a lot of work to dry their houses out. The swamp extension area was going to be a major problem; no one got swept away there but the water rose straight up through the landfill the builders had used. Reb received a note from Marcia while she and Jonas were helping drain water temporarily out of various areas (incredibly tiring work) which had made her grin viciously. Apparently the Council would be *speaking* to the builders.

They finally heard from the fishing village that day, too, and she saw Jonas' shoulders sag in relief: houses had been lost, but the villagers had taken to their boats, and were accustomed enough to being flooded out that they'd had time to gather up nearly all of their possessions.

But once there was nothing left that couldn't be more readily done by hand than by sorcery, it was time for Reb and Cato to deal with Jonas. They agreed to conduct the meeting in Reb's front room. Not the most formal of settings, but it would suffice.

Cato rarely came to her place. He didn't exactly look *uncomfortable*; Cato put some effort into looking relaxed in all situations. But he was pointier than normal around the edges.

Of course, that could be because he was about to rip Jonas a new arsehole.

Cato sat in her spare armchair, the one she'd got so

Marcia had somewhere to sit, which was something she was not going to think about. Reb herself took the other, older, chair. Jonas stood in front of them, looking like he wished he was anywhere else.

"Weather magic," Reb began. "What *exactly* did you do?"

"I went up to the roof," Jonas said, twisting his fingers together, and Cato groaned.

"Because that's a safe place to try something dangerous?"

Jonas' jaw squared. "I like roofs."

Cato sighed, and waved a hand for him to continue. It might have been an utterly stupid idea, but what Jonas described was a relatively well-conducted piece of magic, given that he was still an apprentice and he was making it up on the spot. Reb couldn't envisage either Tait or Alyssa being able to do that.

Because you're not allowing them enough scope to even begin to think that way.

"Right," she said. "Not sure what Beckett was thinking, but, fine. So. *Why* did you do it?"

"Um." Jonas' eyes were wide, and he looked hopefully over at Cato, who just shrugged. "The storm was coming in," he said. "I thought...I thought maybe I could help."

"On your own? Just like that?" Reb demanded. What had he been *thinking*? "You just...saw the storm coming in, and thought you'd play around? Without even consulting Cato?"

"Cato said weather magic wouldn't work."

"So you...just ignored him?"

"I wanted to be able to save Salinas ships, maybe." Jonas' shoulders were defensively hunched. "I thought...I thought I could try it out. Here."

"That's it? That's your answer?" Her teeth clenched, and she turned to Cato. "I'm sorry. I know you wanted to give him a second chance. But this is too much. We can't have him just doing what he feels like, whenever he wants, without so much as a by-your-leave or a pause to think."

"He helped sort things out. After," Cato said. He flicked a look sideways at Jonas, and Reb narrowed her eyes, suddenly sure she was missing something. What weren't they telling her?

"That's not good enough."

"So what are you going to do?" Jonas demanded. His voice shook, and Reb repressed a surge of sympathy. This was too irresponsible, this casual, thoughtless, recklessness. They couldn't, she couldn't, let him carry on.

"You'll no longer be an apprentice," she said flatly.

"So he won't even *have* someone to come to if he wants to try anything?" Cato's brows were crimped together.

"If he isn't an apprentice, he mustn't use magic here."

"And if he does?"

Reb hesitated, and Cato's mouth compressed.

"I'm not being involved with taking someone's magic against their will." His eyes met hers in challenge. "Didn't you tell Beckett you wouldn't let them do that to me?"

"And if it's worse, next time? If someone dies? Where's your limit? We haven't the power to banish him. What else can we do, if he won't *listen*?"

"Marcia could banish him," Cato said. He sounded uncharacteristically unsure.

She didn't want to involve Marcia. She didn't *want* to prevent Jonas from using magic, either. But what other option was there, if he was just doing whatever he wanted and never mind the consequences? They were responsible for sorcery in Marek, and that included rogue sorcery, and Jonas, as far as Reb could see, was well past that point.

"I was trying to save people!" Jonas burst out.

Reb sighed. "Oh, come on. At least try to be convincing."

"They were going to *die*. I *saw* it." His voice was high, and there was a ring of truth...but he was being ridiculous.

"You *saw* it." Reb rolled her eyes; then heard Cato suck air thoughtfully through his teeth, and stared at him.

"I see the future," Jonas said. His voice was flat.

"You see the *future*?"

Cato sat up slightly and raised a questioning eyebrow in Jonas' direction, then half-shrugged, turning to her. "He sees the future," he confirmed.

"*What.*" Reb looked between them.

"No idea how it works, but I believe him," Cato said. "Little kind of," his hands shaped something small in the air, "mini-visions. Flickers, Jonas calls them."

"You knew about this already." And he'd been keeping it from her. The *shit*.

"Yes. I promised him not to tell." There might, perhaps, have been the barest shadow of an apology in Cato's tone. "You or anyone else. But you specifically."

Reb took a long, slow, breath, pushing down the impulse to shake one or both of them. She needed to get to the bottom of this first; then, afterwards, in private, she could give Cato her unvarnished opinion. "Right. Well. Let's try this again then, shall we. What were you doing, and why? *All* the information, this time."

"I saw it," Jonas said. He still sounded reluctant, like he was pulling the words out by force. "I had a flicker, and I saw it. Water everywhere. Much further than it went, in the end. People – there were dead people. All down by where we were, where we dug that trench." He swallowed. "I had to try to stop it."

"But you didn't think to come and ask Cato?" Reb was impressed with how level she was keeping her voice.

"Cato said weather magic didn't work."

"But you tried anyway."

"They were going to *die*," Jonas said again. "And on the ship, already…there was a ship sank, last month, in unseasonable weather. Most of the crew lost. I had to try."

"The fact that I didn't think it would work didn't mean…never mind." Cato sighed.

"We'll come to that in a moment," Reb said. "So you

had to try. And you went up to the roof?"

"Everything else is just as I told you." He was staring down at the floor. "It was worse, and I caused it."

"But people didn't die," Reb said, with sudden realisation, as she thought it through. "The flood came to pass, but the deaths you saw didn't."

Cato had leant right back in the armchair, and was sucking at his teeth again. "If it hadn't been for that gigantic crash, Reb, do you think you'd have woken up and gone down to the river?"

"Maybe. Maybe not," Reb admitted.

"And he came to me, afterwards," Cato said. "Was there *more* water, in the end, or just differently timed?"

"Most of the flooding was upstream," Reb said.

"Which would suggest that Jonas' crash overhead didn't affect that part," Cato said. "But it did affect whether we got down there, and when, and what we were able to do." He scratched at his chin. "And, of course, now there's been three days of headlines about how tremendously wonderful the sorcerers are as compared to the Council..."

"Cato."

"...Which is a little unfair, if it was only coincidence that we happened to be there, but..."

"*Cato.*"

Cato shrugged. "I'm just pointing it out. We came out on top, in the end. So did the city."

"You changed it," Reb said to Jonas, ignoring Cato. "That's what we're trying to say."

He blinked at her, looking confused, and then his eyes rolled, and he began to sway. Cato stuck out an arm and broke his fall magically – show-off – and between the two of them they got him sitting on the floor with his head between his knees.

"I am very interested," Cato said, throwing himself back into the armchair, "in the limitations of prediction and what can be changed."

"Maybe later, Cato." Reb felt very tired, all over again.

Jonas, finally, looked up again.

"Right. Well." Reb sighed. "I accept that you were trying to do something to prevent something terrible. Which is all well and good, but you still should not have done it on your own, and without supervision."

"You're going to kick me out," Jonas said. His voice was dull.

Cato caught her eye. "I will veto, Reb, if I have to."

Reb rubbed her hand across her eyes, and weighed it all up. "I'm not insisting," she said, eventually. "In the circumstances…Jonas, I can understand why you felt driven to it, and it's possible that despite what went wrong, you saved lives. Maybe. But. If you ever, *ever*, do unsupervised magic on your own again, that is it."

"Unsupervised or unauthorised?" Cato asked.

"What do you mean?"

Cato shrugged. "If I've signed him off on something…are we stopping him from making a witchlight unless I'm there to supervise?"

"I see. Yes. If you've done something with Cato, and he's authorised you to try alone, that's fine. Otherwise. This was your one chance."

There was silence. "Yes?" Jonas said cautiously, then, more certainly, "Yes. I understand."

"Also," Reb said, "Cato undertakes to assist you with anything reasonable you wish to attempt, and to explain properly why something isn't reasonable if it isn't. Which weather magic isn't, for the record."

"I did explain," Cato protested.

"Obviously not well enough."

"It's not Cato's fault," Jonas said to his knees. "It was mine. I just…ignored him."

"How about, don't do that again," Cato said. His tones were as pleasant as ever, but there was steel under them.

Jonas looked up and met Cato's eyes. "I'm sorry. I won't."

"Well then," Cato said. "Is this all resolved, then, Reb, to your satisfaction?"

"Yes," Reb said. "Although I should also like to know more about these *flickers*."

"No," Jonas said, quietly enough to be automatic, then hunched his shoulders. "I mean…"

"It's fine," Reb said, with only a tiny effort. She wanted to *know*, but – it was his privacy, and he wasn't even her apprentice. "I said *I should like*. I didn't say you were obliged. To me or to Cato, just to be clear. But. It sounds like you need to work it out, one way or another."

"And if I ever have cause to haul you in front of us again," Cato said, "we won't *get* that far, because I will have kicked you right out of Marek. Power to do so or not. Understood?" He was smiling. Sort of. There were a lot of teeth.

"Yes," Jonas said, fervently, and pulled himself to his feet.

Reb had expected Cato to go with Jonas, back to the squats, but he just sat and watched Jonas leave.

"Well," Reb said, after the door closed. "Not the most pleasant experience I've ever had."

Cato hooked a leg over the arm of his chair. "I think he paid attention."

"It's not the first time you've had that sort of discussion with him, right?"

"No. Evidently I was insufficiently *robust* in my terminology before. He's not a bad kid, though. And a reasonable sorcerer, too. Just…"

"Stubborn?" Reb offered.

"Well, that's not exactly an uncommon sorcerer trait, is it now?" Cato took his hand away from his face and looked very directly at her. "Which brings me to another matter. What the fuck is going on with Tait and Alyssa."

Reb's stomach sank. "What do you mean?"

"Don't give me that. You know fine well what I mean. You've been holding them back."

"I've been teaching them slowly and patiently. Not just letting them run on ahead trying things past their ability and sense." Even to herself she sounded unconvincing.

"No. No way. You are not going to twist this around. Yes, Jonas screwed up, and yes, I should have done a better job of explaining why I thought it was a stupid idea. But if Tait and Alyssa had been further on – if they'd been able to act like apprentices of over half a year, not rank beginners. If they'd been able to *link* properly. Then we'd have been able to save more of the city. That's all there is to it." He scowled. "And I promised Tait I'd ask you about this three weeks ago, and I didn't get around to it, and now I wish to fuck I had done."

"No one died." Reb regretted that the moment she said it.

Cato looked incredulous "No one *died* because Tait opened a fucking vein to prevent it! And nearly knocked themself flat doing it. If we'd been at anything approximating full strength, we might have been able to save the bridge." He shook his head. "This isn't like you, Reb. Sliding out of things is my job. What's going on?"

Reb's stomach lurched. She looked down at her hands, clenched tightly together. "How can you do it?" she asked abruptly.

"Do what?"

"Everyone died," Reb said. Her insides were hollow. "Everyone died. In the plague. My friends. Zareth – well, that was before. Every sorcerer I've ever trusted, or worked with, has died."

"Thanks."

Reb shook her head. "Come on. We've never liked each other, have we? Fine, we're working together now, but I don't kid myself that you like me now. Beckett pushed you into being part of the Group. And we've worked *together* precisely twice, and only because the alternative was disastrous. Demon or flood. Everyone I ever worked closely with has died. The same must be true for you. How can you move on from that?"

Cato was silent. When Reb looked up, his expression was thoughtful, almost sad.

"I never worked with anyone the way you did with Zareth," he said, eventually. "Remember? I didn't have an apprenticeship. I had to talk the Group into accepting I was a sorcerer all by myself. You were there."

Reb remembered; cocky Cato, barely twenty, performing spell after spell and making it impossible not to acknowledge him, despite the fact that they all knew what he'd been up to in the squats and who he'd been working for, and that none of them trusted him as far as they could throw him. But they couldn't deny he was a sorcerer.

"I worked with a couple of people, off and on, after that, but…let's just say, none of us were exactly *friends*." He screwed up his nose. "We just worked with a similar sort of client, and those were never *friends* either."

"You were doing illegal things."

"Well, I always prefer not to discuss the details," Cato said, with a faint smile.

"So you're saying there's no one you missed, when they died."

"I wouldn't go that far either." He shifted restlessly. "Only the two of us survived. Of course I felt that. And it's not – I liked them fine. Of course I miss people. But," Reb caught his gaze, and couldn't look away, "but I never made myself vulnerable. So the plague never took that from me." There was an ache in his voice; a truth. "You were vulnerable, and it hurt you. And now you don't want to be vulnerable again. You don't want to work properly with Tait, or with Alyssa, because if something happens to them, you don't want to feel it." His eyes narrowed, and Reb still couldn't look away. "And you're not going to like me saying this, but…that's why you and Marcia aren't together any more either, isn't it?"

"Shut up," Reb said, suddenly furious. "You don't know *shit* about that. She lied to me." And then she'd apologised. Months later, yes, granted, but at the time Reb hadn't waited, had she? Hadn't waited around to see if it could be fixed. Because Marcia had betrayed her, and Reb wasn't going to wait for a second time, and she'd been right to do it.

"Eh, well, that happens sometimes, with people," Cato said. "But fine, we'll leave that aside. Not my business. But Tait and Alyssa are." He looked away, finally, releasing her gaze. "I'm right. Aren't I?"

There was a long silence. Outside, Reb could hear footsteps in the street, a child complaining to a parent.

"Yes," she said.

"Zareth had to…allow you in, I suppose, we could say, in order to teach you. You owe them the same. Or you stop pretending." Cato's words were blunt. But he was right. "And I am sure as fuck not going to let you keep screwing Tait over this way."

"Talking of vulnerabilities," Reb said, wanting to put a knife in Cato the way he was putting a knife in her. She wasn't expecting it to work, though; she was startled when he physically flinched.

"Well," he said, voice a hair unsteady. "If you're not letting me go there with my sister and you, how about you stay clear with me and Tait?"

Obviously a keener shot than she'd intended. She opened her hands, a nearly-apologetic gesture. "Very well. So what now?"

Cato raised an eyebrow. "Can you do it? Actually teach them? Properly?"

"Yes." She hated the idea, and it was going to be horrible, but. "Yes."

"Well, that's good, because honestly I don't know what the alternative is." He looked over at her, mouth quirked sideways. "Because there's only you and me left, remember? I can't teach all three of them."

"Yes," Reb said. "I'm…sorry." She had to drag the words out.

Cato shifted uncomfortably. "Yes, well. Are we all done, then? Because I think that's about as much heart-baring as either of us can cope with, don't you?"

Reb nodded fervently. "Would you like…an infusion, or something?"

"I appreciate the thought, but I really think that both of us will be happier if I just leave now. Won't we. And, you know, how about we never speak of any of it ever again?"

The words were light, but when she looked over at him,

she could see the shadow of genuine sympathy in his eyes. "Works for me," she agreed.

"Right, well then. I am going to go and sleep for a long time." He went to the door, then paused. Without turning round, he said, softly, "I'm sorry. For all of them. Truly I am." The door banged behind him.

Reb sat heavily back in the armchair. Yeah. It was time to sort her shit out, wasn't it?

If only because there was no way she wanted to have a conversation like that ever again.

Madeleine looked so small and pale in her huge bed, propped up by stacks of cushions and pillows.

It was a shame she was just as bloody infuriating as ever.

"Oh, don't look so stricken, Marcia," she said, irritably, then coughed. "I'm sure I don't know why my breathing is so bothersome when they tell me it's my heart that was the trouble." Her voice was thin and reedy. "How is the baby?"

"Fine."

The baby probably was; Marcia herself was exhausted, and her nausea was getting worse. She'd mentioned it to Doctor Pelligra, since they were there; they had shrugged and said that many people felt nauseous in the first few months, but as long as Marcia was still eating and drinking she and the baby would both be fine. It wasn't that she didn't believe the doctor; she just could have wished for something more than 'deal with it' as medical advice. "But the baby isn't important right now. We need to talk about you."

Madeleine flicked dismissive fingers. "I'm fine, too."

"Not if you stay here," Marcia said, and folded her arms. "Not according to the doctor."

The problem was two-fold: first, a strong recommendation for a less damp climate during Madeleine's recovery. Second, despite Marcia's best efforts, it was impossible to keep Madeleine out of politics. It had been fine for the first couple of days, when she was mostly asleep. Marcia had issued strict instructions to the servants that all correspondence was to come through her. Madeleine, the moment she was well enough to sit up, had issued counter-orders, using her authority as Fereno-Head. The servants, understandably, had buckled.

"Doctor Pelligra says that you need to *rest*, Mother. You're not resting."

"Here I am, in my bed," Madeleine said, peevishly. "Of course I'm resting."

"You're writing messages, and reading messages, and the factor says you contacted her to make trade arrangements the other day. That's not resting."

"I am Fereno-Head," Madeleine said. "I cannot simply let the House go to rack and ruin simply because my *heart* is troublesome."

Marcia ground her teeth. "You don't have to be."

The words hung in the air. Madeleine looked away. "There is no other Heir. If you take over now, what if things – go badly, in six months time?" Six and a half months, in fact, by Marcia's count, were left of the eight.

"If I don't," Marcia countered, "what if you drop dead of a heart attack between now and then? I'll have to name some interim Heir anyway. One of the cousins. We've *talked* about this."

Madeleine shook her head. "No. I will not retire until after the baby is born. We risk leaving the House without leadership, and then," she made a gesture, "everything is gone."

"Fine," Marcia said tightly. Getting into a proper row about this wouldn't help Madeleine's recovery either. "You won't resign. But you could take some time off."

Madeleine scowled at her. "No."

"Mother. Doctor Pelligra says you're inhibiting your recovery."

"Doctor Pelligra is a quack."

"No, they're not. They're well-respected in their Guild

and they've been looking after us for two years now. You don't think that in the slightest." *Stop being obstreperous,* Marcia managed not to say.

Madeleine folded her arms. "So, what? You will take my pen away? Imprison me in my room? Refuse me company?"

Marcia held tight to the fraying threads of her patience.

"The doctor recommends a trip to a better climate, especially given that the sea-storms will come in before long. Ideally, inland Exuria, where it's drier and warmer. Failing that, Teren is at least warmer." And if not dry like Exuria, not as damp as Marek in the autumn and winter, either, lacking the swamp that surrounded Marek. "You could go for autumn and winter, perhaps."

"On my own? For *months*?"

"Of course not on your own, Mother. I'm sure you could find someone to accompany you. And in the meantime, you remain Head, but I stand for you."

"I want to be here when your baby is born."

"Which as you keep saying, is six months away. In the spring. If you were to stay in Teren until, say, early winter, you'd be back in plenty of time, and Doctor Pelligra thinks that by then you'll be in far better health. *If* you look after yourself properly now." Doctor Pelligra would have preferred Madeleine to stay longer, but given that the baby was due in early Fein, Marcia couldn't see Madeleine staying away past the New Year at the outside. Likely not even that long.

Madeleine's jaw set mutinously; then she began to cough. It was a couple of minutes before she was recovered. Marcia helped her to a sip of water, and settled the shawls more firmly around her mother's shoulders. Madeleine wasn't meeting her eye.

"Mother," she said, more gently. "I would like the baby to know you. Not to hear stories of the grandmother who died through overwork in the months before its birth. If you're concerned about the wellbeing of the House, I need you to be *well* next spring. I need you, the House needs you, to be well and capable when I am recovering after the baby is born."

Madeleine sighed. "Very well. I take your point. I refuse to go to Exuria, though. I will stay in Teren, at the estates. I will take Cousin Cara."

Marcia made a mental note to warn Cousin Cara.

"You must keep me up to date on everything."

"Of course, Mother."

She'd have to, as well; Madeleine would doubtless be getting reports from everyone else she knew in the city. But at least, unable to engage directly, Madeleine would get *some* kind of rest. Marcia hoped.

Of course, official resignation or not, this now meant that she, Marcia, would be dealing with everything on behalf of the House, just when she was exhausted, sick, and finding it impossible to concentrate. What wonderful timing.

"I'll let you know once I've made your travel arrangements," she promised Madeleine, and on an impulse, leant in to kiss her cheek. Madeleine looked startled, but pleased. "Meanwhile – please can you rest, just for a little?"

"Oh, very well," Madeleine said, then hesitated. "You are a good daughter, Marcia, you know that. And a good Heir."

"Thank you, Mother," Marcia said, and let herself out of the room, to rest her head just for a moment against the cool wall.

Two hours later, she was wishing she'd stayed in Madeleine's room. The main thrust of today's Council meeting was the formation of a committee to address the matter of the new builds out in the south-west, now much wetter underfoot than they had been. The Guilds, via the refugee structure, had found temporary housing for those affected, and the Council was united in its intention to force the builders to fix the problems. Piath had been tasked with establishing exactly which corners the builders had cut, why, and how they were to compensate. Piath had the look of someone who was going to greatly enjoy taking the builders, their accounts, and their planning, fully apart. The Guild of Masons, probably to cover up the fact that they hadn't been conducting any oversight on their members, were falling over themselves to assist.

That was all easy enough. However, now the river was dropping, more refugees were coming in again from Teren. Marcia had hoped that someone else would see fit to raise that particular issue with the rest of the Council; but it looked like it was down to her.

"Of course," she said, when it was clear that the meeting was drawing to a close, "we haven't addressed what continues to happen in Teren. In Ameten, in particular. The barges are coming in again, now the floods are subsiding." She looked around the room. Most of the Council looked uncomfortable. "We discussed this before, and concluded that we were unwilling to engage directly with Teren. Should we revisit that decision?"

"Does it matter?" Athitol-Head demanded. "As you say, nothing has changed, and we discussed this before."

"In one sense, nothing has changed, no, but that is in itself part of the problem. It is clear that the flow of people is not stopping. Of course we welcome them, but," she gestured at the clerk recording their deliberations, "it places a burden on us, no?"

"People make Marek strong," Haran-Heir said cheerfully.

"Indeed. But should we not be concerned about *why* so many of them are coming here? What is going wrong in Teren?"

"Are you with the pamphlet-writers, then?" Athitol-Head sounded peevish. "Cease all interactions forthwith, and all that? We *are* Teren, remember."

"Not exactly," Andreas said.

"Well, of course Marek is Marek, but…My point is, what business is it of ours?"

"We're having to look after their citizens," Marcia said.

Haran-Heir shrugged. "We get the best of that. We get the ones who can make shift to move themselves from a situation they don't like, and in a while, they'll be

Marekers too and we thrive on it. It's not our problem if Ameten is losing half their competent people."

"Isn't it everyone's responsibility to look to their fellow human?" Gil Jyrithi-Head asked.

"We've enough on our plate right here," Warden Bradley, of the Broderers, said firmly. "Let's not go borrowing trouble by intervening with Teren business."

"Which is all very well; but what if they mean to intervene with us?" Marcia demanded. "What if, for example, they don't like us taking in their dissenters, and would like us to stop?"

There was an uncomfortable rustle around the room.

"There's no indication of that," Warden Bradley said, but his tone lacked conviction.

"Look at what the Ambassador tried last time she was here," Marcia said. "Speaking at our formal discussions, for the first time in centuries. Telling us what to think. Would you care to be certain that she wouldn't have voted, if it would have swung the decision?"

"Ah, surely not," Haran-Heir disagreed. "I agree, it was unconscionable interference even as it was, but…no, surely not."

"We made our own decision,"Athitol-Head put in. "I see no need to worry."

"But clearly, something is wrong in Ameten," Marcia argued, frustrated. "Listen to the refugees."

"Is this about *magic*?" someone demanded, but for once, the usual rustle of performative dismissal at the word was absent, replaced by a visible discomfort.

"I'm the first to call talk of the cityangel superstitious nonsense," Tabriol-Head said, speaking up for the first time, "but this is different. We know spirits *exist*. It's always been hard to do much with them, is the thing – we've all heard the stories of Teren sorcerers and their bad bargains. But if they're doing things differently…" She shook her head. "I wouldn't say I trust every word said by panicked people fleeing their home, but something is going on there."

"So shouldn't we find out what?" Marcia demanded.

"And then what?" Tabriol-Head spread her hands.

"We could cease dealing with them." It was a long cast, she knew that, and she could hear that she sounded tentative.

Dismissive laughs from around the room.

"And bring down their ire on us? Without us, Teren *has* no trade, or next to none," Warden Ceril of the Vintners pointed out.

"Precisely! So we have a great deal of influence on them, if we choose to use it."

"But our trade, our trades, too rest on their goods." The Vintners' oldest tradition, barley wine, came from Teren barley, though mostly now they dealt in Exurian grape wines and in the more complicated beverages they created themselves.

"That's all very well, but remember, the other year, those Teren crafters tried to bring their goods and have them stamped as Guilded? And the new recipes the Apothecaries had to ban?" That was Warden Zeril, of the Woodworkers, but Warden Amanth of the Haberdashers was nodding along with him as well.

"Earlier, Fereno-Heir, you were worrying about Teren attempting to exert influence on us. I know of no better way to force their hand than to refuse trade." Athitol-Head shook their head, obviously choosing to ignore the Guild points. "Our position must be neutral. That is our strength, and our safety."

Around the room, heads nodded. Andreas and Marcia glanced at each other.

"If we wait too long, we may find that they are no longer prepared to tolerate our neutrality in any case," Andreas said. "The Ambassador last year gave every indication that Teren would prefer Marek to be – more directly under its wing, let's say. If we don't know what is going on there, if they are growing in strength…what is to prevent them from enforcing that? The longer we wait in ignorance, the more dangerous our position, surely?"

A couple of the Guildwardens were looking thoughtful. Selene hadn't made herself – or Teren – friends in the

Guilds, last year.

"If Teren – or anyone else – come here with force, we have no hope of standing against that," Gil said. "Our only hope is to make it not worth anyone's while. We are not vulnerable by sea. The Salinas would not permit a sea-army. And the swamp protects us to north and south. Only Teren have unprotected access, and if they brought a true army, we *could not* stand against them, and it would be foolish to try. If we wish to retain our liberty, we must give them no reason to do so. As such, I would see it as foolishness to stand against them unless we are truly forced to do so."

The rest of the room rumbled again in agreement, although Marcia saw a few mildly discontented faces, especially among the Guilds.

"Well then," Athitol-Head said. "A productive discussion, and I am glad that we are all in agreement." Her tone left no room for anyone to disagree with the conclusion. "I look forward to seeing you all next week." She nodded to the Reader for the formal bang of their staff that concluded the meeting.

Marcia left the room with the sinking feeling that they were all walking with their eyes shut straight into trouble; and there was nothing she could do about it.

Alyssa, sitting on the spare stool, stick propped against her knees, looked doubtfully at the large tub of water in the middle of Reb's small workroom.

"Generally," Reb said, hearing the stiffness in her own voice, "we don't do things together often. Linked, like Cato and Jonas and I did at the floods."

"The bit Tait and I couldn't do," Alyssa said, arms folded.

What Reb wanted was to do the lesson, teach Alyssa how to link, and not talk about any of it. That…wasn't going to work, though, was it.

She sighed, and sat down on her workstool. It creaked

under her, sounding about as old as she felt. "Yes. That's my fault, and I'm sorry."

"Right."

"I..." She couldn't talk about the plague, or Zareth, or any of the others. Not here, and now; not to Alyssa, not yet. "I should have done things differently," she said, instead. "I've been holding both you and Tait back, when I should have been encouraging you to stretch yourselves." She didn't have to give a reason, did she? Maybe another time. She was doing the important bit already. "So. We're going to start doing things a bit differently."

"Right," Alyssa said. Her voice was cautious, but her body had relaxed a little.

"Linking can mean more power, and it can be protective. But its main advantage to an apprentice is to follow what I'm doing, which can help you learn new things faster. We won't do everything that way, mind, but it can be useful."

"And the water?"

"So. You already know you can move something with magic. Small things. And you already know that larger things, it's usually not worth it."

"Easier to do it by hand," Alyssa said.

"Exactly. Takes about the same amount of effort, maybe more, to do it by magic. Not worth it. Save magic for things you can't do another way. But it *is* useful for learning to link. Physically, we could shift this between us, right? But we'd struggle to do it alone, either of us."

Alyssa pushed herself upwards, took a step to the tub, and tugged experimentally at one of the handles. She scowled at it, then propped her stick against the wall – Reb didn't say anything; Alyssa was quite capable of deciding for herself what she'd risk for and with her body – set her feet and shoulders, and pulled at it with more commitment. She shifted one side slightly off the floor. "Right."

Might as well continue the practical demonstration. Reb stood and took one handle. "If you'd care to try now?" Between them, they lifted it up, then put it down again.

"So, it's heavy, but we could, for example, move it out into the main room, if we really needed to."

"Yes," Alyssa agreed, sitting back down.

"Works the same with magic. I'm not going to ask you to try lifting alone. The heaviest thing you've moved so far was an empty tea-cup. Too much of a jump, and you might hurt yourself. Minds are vulnerable just like bodies." More complicated than that, but that would do for now. "But we're going to link, with me in the lead, and lift it together."

She still didn't want to do this, but it was necessary. She couldn't keep failing her apprentices. They both deserved better than that.

"Right," she said, shifting her stool a little closer, braced herself, and held her hand out to Alyssa. Cautiously, Alyssa took it, her hand warm against Reb's.

"Reach out," she said. "Through the hand if you need to. You don't need physical contact but it makes things easier, especially at first."

She reached out herself, and met Alyssa's power coming the other way. Alyssa felt spiky, unlike Cato's cool wary smoothness. Unlike Zareth's rugged warmth, but she wasn't going to think about that.

Spiky, and too thinly-spread. She'd already known that Alyssa wasn't especially strong; though raw power wasn't the only measure of a sorcerer, and different sorcerers had different abilities. But she hadn't realised Alyssa's lack of focus wasn't just lack of practice, but her not grasping what she was supposed to do. That was Reb's fault, too; both not explaining sufficiently clearly, and not noticing the problem.

"You need to…tighten up your thinking," she said, seeking for the right words. "Focus on the goal. Follow my lead."

Alyssa, eyes shut, was frowning. Reb felt her power solidify, pulling together. "Much better," she said. "Now. I'm going to lift. Stay with me. Like holding hands, or holding the tub together. Yes?"

With her free hand, she took a pinch of chilli and crushed rowan bark from the pouch at her waist. "Hot pepper and rowan bark." Her voice sounded odd in her own ears. She scattered it between them and the tub. "Now. Lifting."

It wasn't so much that she put her thoughts under the tub, as that she thought of the tub lifting, and reached for Beckett, senses sharpened by the pepper, pushing with it against the floor…and the tub went up.

It was heavy, even like this.

"You feel?" she said, breathless. "The lift, against the pepper and rowan. Beckett's power coming through. Yes?"

"Yes," Alyssa said. Her voice sounded wondering.

"Putting it down again," Reb said.

The tub thumped down, and she dropped Alyssa's hand. "Did you understand that?"

Alyssa nodded slowly. Her eyes were bright. "Didn't feel like that, before. Doing things myself. It was all less – I felt the power, this time. Coming through you, but it felt different."

"Right then," Reb said, suddenly warm with the glow of teaching, with the look of understanding on Alyssa's face. "Think of it like that, and summon a witchlight."

Alyssa frowned, held out her hand, and did so. The little light was brighter than before, and clearer, its edges sharper. She turned her hand back upside down, and it vanished immediately; turned it palm up, and resummoned it, then flung it up into the air to bob in front of her face.

"Huh. I could feel…a source?"

"Beckett," Reb said. "That's Beckett's power, coming from Marek, and focussed through you."

"It'll be easier next time," Alyssa said, with conviction.

"I'm sorry," Reb said. "I should have tried harder." It was easier to say it, now that she could see the change in Alyssa. Now that she'd *taught* her properly, finally. "I…It's a long time since I've had an apprentice."

Alyssa looked over at her, and for the first time, Reb saw understanding in her eyes.

"That'll do for today, I think," Reb said, past a thickness in her throat.

"Right," Alyssa agreed. She pushed herself up off the stool, started towards the door, leaning a little more heavily than normal on her stick, then turned back. "What I'd really like to be able to do, if it's possible..."

"Yes?" Reb said, encouragingly.

"I want to be able to protect people."

"Safety charms? They're harder than you'd think, but we can look at them..."

Alyssa shook her head. "No. Well, yes, but that wasn't what I was thinking of." She hesitated. "Demon-protection."

Reb frowned at her. "Demons can't come into Marek. We're already protected."

"In Marek. Yes, I know. But people in Ameten – have you *seen* the reports?"

"Yes. Jeres came and asked me. I know."

"I want to protect them. Not the ones here already. The ones who can't leave."

Reb grimaced. "I'm sorry. Marek magic only works within our own borders. That's the limits of Beckett's power. If you want to help the people who are here, we could look into that...though really they need houses and jobs and food, and that's not something magic can help with. But we can look at safety-charms, next time."

Alyssa looked dissatisfied, but nodded. "All right. Better than nothing, I suppose."

It was a shame, Reb supposed, that they couldn't do things outside of Marek; this whole business with demons was worrying. But there it was; the limits were what they were, and at least she and Alyssa were *inside* Teren. Reb had done Teren magic, a long time ago, and had no intention of doing it again.

Marek, and Marek sorcerers, those were her responsibilities. And for the first time in a long time, she felt like she truly was fulfilling them.

SIXTEEN

Madeleine had been writing regularly from Teren, which was reassuring. She'd been at the estate for nearly eight weeks now, and claimed to be recovering well. Marcia was reading her most recent letter in the reception-room, while Andreas politely stood at the window, looking out at the river – largely empty, the Salinas having returned to their islands a month before to wait out the sea-storms – to give her privacy. She'd offered to leave it until his visit was over, but Andreas had insisted she open it immediately.

"Or you'll just be thinking of it while we're talking," he said, which was true enough.

The letter opened with the customary assurances about Madeleine's health (improving) and the state of the estates (which Madeleine maintained had been terrible on her arrival, but Marcia suspected was just an excuse for her to have something to complain about and then harry the estate staff over). There were trade reports halfway through, in their private code, and a few notes of things happening in Teren – weather, mostly, but also some notes about trends in Ameten. How did Madeleine know about that, from her country estate? Marcia read further down.

I have had a visit from Grainne, a dear friend when I visited Ameten in my youth. Not that we have been in touch regularly since; I was surprised that my presence here was known to her, but of course when she wrote to suggest a visit, I said that would be delightful. Which indeed it has been – I assure you that it has been a boon to my health to have some interest in my life.

Marcia rolled her eyes.

Grainne told me a great many interesting things about Ameten trends – see above – and politics. Fascinating to hear of another city, and one so closely allied with our own.

That was a warning to Marcia to pay attention, though she already was.

The Archion's health is widely rumoured to be failing – I trust he recovers soon, as he is not an elderly man. As yet, no successor has been directly named. Grainne tells me there is a great deal of interest in the matter.

The candidates are circling, Marcia translated, and there's extensive intrigue.

The Archion, I am told, talks a great deal of Marek, and is particularly enthusiastic about Marek goods. He regularly expresses the wish that, if he cannot see Marek again himself, due to his responsibilities, Marekers might return to the Court. Grainne assured me I would be very popular were I to come to Ameten. I invited Grainne to visit us in Marek once

I return, but she regretted that her own family responsibilities and duties at court would prevent her.

Grainne, Marcia concluded, did not wish to absent herself from Ameten for long while the Archion lingered on his death-bed – well, it might not be quite that bad yet – without a successor. Grainne was also, very likely, hoping to gain more popularity, with the Archion or simply within the court, for having visited Madeleine while she was close enough for it to be convenient.

I mentioned in passing that we have had a great influx of people from Ameten to Marek lately – though not, of course, those of the court – but we did not discuss that in any depth.

Grainne didn't want to talk about the refugees; perhaps a political sore point. Well, if they all knew about the demons, Marcia could well understand Grainne's unwillingness to consider it too deeply. Even in the privacy of House Fereno's estate. That might also explain her reluctance to visit Marek, to where all the malcontents were fleeing. One would not want to be associated with that.

In any case. Once I am fully recovered – which I am sure will be soon – I may stop at Ameten before I go home.

"*Mother*," Marcia said aloud.

"Hm?" Andreas turned around. "Is everything well?"

"She's threatening to visit Ameten. She assures me," Marcia looked back down at the letter, "she'll be home before the baby."

"Well, there's time yet," Andreas said encouragingly.

"I don't want her going to Ameten! She says the Archion's not well and there's wrangling about the succession..." And there were demons there.

"I can't imagine you've much chance of preventing your mother doing anything," Andreas said with some feeling. "What's that about the Archion, though?"

Marcia summarised the matter for him.

"The Archion wants Marek back," she concluded. "Is my conclusion. Not that that wasn't clear last year."

"We haven't *left*," Andreas protested, then waved an agreeing hand. "But I see your point. And we are richer than Teren. I can see why the Archion might have feelings about that."

"To be fair, they have more natural resources. But no trade, beyond a tiny bit occasionally over the mountains. I mean, that was the whole point of founding Marek. A route to the sea."

"They tax us," Andreas, perching on an arm of the sofa, countered.

"Yes, but only on trade that involves Teren." A large chunk of what went through Marek never touched the rest of Teren at all, and the Houses therefore didn't see the need to involve it in Teren taxation. She shifted her weight to ameliorate a twinge of discomfort in her bump, and thought. "Oh. Do you remember when the old Lieutenant tried to negotiate a new arrangement?"

Andreas shook his head. Thinking about it, he'd still have been a child. She'd only been in her teens.

"I wasn't Heir then," Marcia said, "but I was old enough to be attending events, and I remember overhearing discussions. I asked Mother about it a few years back and she said the Archion had finally realised how much of our trade was untaxed, and wanted a change."

Andreas was looking puzzled. "But that's been the case for decades. Why then? It can't have been *news*, can it?"

"I asked that too, and Mother said, she suspected that the fact that no one visited the court any longer with elaborate gifts, the way they did in her youth, made a difference. Plus, over the last few decades Teren has become more of a centralised country, rather than a loose agglomeration of towns. Gives them more of a sense of power." She pursed her lips. "Gives the *Archion* more of a sense of power."

"Right. Right." Andreas rubbed at his nose. "But the last Lieutenant didn't get anywhere. With the taxes."

"No. He predated your elevation to Head, but I met him several times, and he didn't seem terribly effective, to be honest. Quite a gentle man. Did a lot of nodding and smiling." She paused. "Huh. I wonder how much of that situation influenced the Guilds getting Council seats? They're a significant part of Marek's prosperity, after all." She waved a hand. "Doesn't matter."

Andreas was nodding, as if he'd solved a puzzle. "So that's what Selene was after. Bring Marek closer first, put on the thumbscrews, tax-wise, after. Teren's wellbeing is your wellbeing too, all that. Just as well that didn't go as planned."

Marcia forbore to mention all the aspects of that particular visit to which she had been privy and Andreas hadn't, which also hadn't gone as Selene had planned. She wasn't up for having a discussion about demons with Andreas right now.

"Do you think she'll try again?" he asked.

"If she wants to be Archion, she'll have to, won't she? Mother says the Archion has gone all misty-eyed over Marek. If Selene were to bring Marek back under his wing, that would be a significant boost for her, even without the revenue increase."

"But she failed last time," Andreas said comfortably. "She's got nowhere to stand to try again."

Marcia wasn't so sure. Selene hadn't struck her as the type to accept one knock-back and give up.

"And surely, returning without any success," Andreas continued, "she couldn't have been popular."

Marcia shrugged. "Or she spun it into success, somehow. Building bridges. I don't know. Either way – she might be chastised, or she might be motivated to try harder." She was sure it would be the second. She just wasn't sure what that might look like.

"Eh. What can she do, though, really?" Andreas waved a dismissive hand. "It'll just be a repeat of last time."

Last time had been much closer than Andreas thought. And she had the nasty feeling that they were missing some of Selene's options. It wasn't like everyone in the Council had been convinced to mistrust Teren. There were Houses – Guilds, too? Those who relied on Teren steel and copper? – who would have been quite happy to work with Selene.

"I feel like the refugees make things more complicated, but I'm not sure how. How does Ameten and the Court feel about them fleeing downriver? Mother's friend wasn't willing to talk about it, where it sounds like she was relatively open about the Archion and the succession. That suggests it's a very sore point."

"Can't be that much of a problem or they'd be stopping barges."

"There's the freedoms of the river, though. That would be complicated." She sighed. "Maybe I should bring it up at Council again."

"Good luck," Andreas said. He'd had enough of that particular debate, then; and who could blame him. Maybe she should leave it until Selene came for the reopening of Council, and see how she acted then.

She sat back, and felt a strange fluttering in her insides. She'd felt something like it the day before, and wondered if it was gas. This was definitely not gas.

It was the baby. The baby, moving inside her. She looked down at Madeleine's letter, and the letters blurred as she felt water damp in the corners of her eyes.

"Hello," she said, under her breath, and put a hand on her stomach. Her bump wasn't always obvious from the outside depending on how she dressed, but its smooth hardness felt, to her, very different from any other way her body had ever felt. "Hello, baby. That's your grandmother, writing to me, you know. You'll meet her, eventually. Hello."

"Marcia? Are you all right?"

"I think the baby's moving."

Andreas' eyes widened. "Really? Can I?"

"I can't imagine you'll feel anything yet," she warned him. "It's barely anything even for me." But she let him slide to the floor to kneel in front of her and put a gentle, wondering hand on her stomach.

"No," he said ruefully, after a moment. "But that's wonderful that you can." He smiled at her, glowingly happy, and she felt overwhelmingly fond – and at the same time, achingly desolate.

Andreas was a decent person, a good friend, a good lover. He'd be a good co-parent to this baby. But right now she wanted – unusual though it felt to admit this – her mother to be here. And even more than that, she wanted Reb.

Neither of which were available. So she would smile back at Andreas, and be glad that he was a good friend and a good lover and a good co-parent, and not repine for what she didn't have.

☉ ☉

Daril had briefly considered inviting Andreas over to House Leandra, but his father was still occasionally haunting the reception rooms like some kind of ill-tempered ghost, and Daril couldn't quite get comfortable there, constantly looking over his shoulder. So they were in the comfortable large reception room at House Tigero instead. Burgundy upholstery and newly painted grey walls, and a whole forest of candles in little glass wall-holders. Tigero was going up in the world.

"I'd use the smaller one," Andreas said apologetically, pouring Daril a glass of wine, "but my grandmother's in there with some friend or other. As she always is, it seems."

It was reassuring that other people had their own annoying relatives. "This is perfectly pleasant," Daril said honestly, and sat back in the armchair. He took a good sniff of the wine, then a sip of it, and nodded approvingly. "Very nice. My thanks, and your good health. How are you, then? The whole heir-project coming along well?"

"Marcia seems fine," Andreas said. "Irritable from time to time, but fine."

"Marcia's often irritable," Daril said dryly. Andreas frowned at him, but with good humour. There was no point in pretending the pair of them got on well; Andreas might not remember their personal history (though plenty of Marekhill gossips did), or care much, but their present animosity and their House history was well-known.

"Talking of irritable," Andreas said, "how's your father?"

Daril scowled and took a slug of wine. "Still insisting he can keep the Headship despite being confined to his bed every other day."

Andreas grimaced sympathetically. "Well, I suppose you get to make decisions for the House anyway, if you're carrying the vote?"

"He likes to discuss it afterwards," Daril said, which was a tepid way of describing the raging arguments that Gavin would conduct until he coughed himself into breathlessness and had to retreat. Daril *won* all the time these days, but the whole process was infuriating. The sooner Daril could ignore him altogether the better.

"He must find it hard, being knocked over so thoroughly by whatever it was, when you bounced back," Andreas said, in sympathetic tones. Daril didn't personally think Gavin had earnt much sympathy during his life, but Andreas was fundamentally kind-hearted.

And unsuspicious, given that not once had he so much as raised an eyebrow to indicate that he might wonder how accidental the food poisoning was; and Daril knew that one or two gossips had speculated, though it didn't seem to have spread successfully.

"It was pretty unpleasant for me too," Daril said, which was true; and he'd made sure the whole household knew exactly how unwell he was before he took the antidote, which was probably why the gossip hadn't stuck. "But three decades younger, you know…"

He hadn't, as it happened, intended for Gavin to be hit that badly. Just knocked out for long enough for that particular vote. But given that he *was* now that consistently unwell, it was infuriating that he wouldn't give up and bloody *retire*.

"Anyway," Daril said. "How's your collection of revolutionary literature?"

"Getting more revolutionary by the week," Andreas said, ruefully.

"Oh, well, perhaps they have a point. Not like any of us spend much time over the other side of the city, do we, to know what they're about? Give me a look."

Andreas pulled a handful of badly printed leaflets out of a drawer and handed them over. "Marcia said that, too, you know. About them having a point."

"Yes, well, once in a while I suppose even unreasonable people are correct," Daril muttered, leafing through the pamphlets.

He didn't care that much how reasonable any of it was – well, perhaps a little, theoretically. What he had begun to wonder of late was: might there be something he could get out of this?

"My cousin said you were making similar arguments a couple of years ago," Andreas said. "Spread power and all that."

"Yes, well, that was before Gavin finally agreed to make me Heir," Daril said. "Perfectly happy with centralised power if it's me gets to wield it."

Andreas laughed, an edge of doubt in his tone.

It was mostly true. But Daril had genuinely thought, back then, that it was unfair. He still genuinely thought that in fact, because it was true. He just wasn't willing to rock the boat any more. He was doing just fine, himself, now, and that would suffice.

But. What if the boat was about to be rocked anyway? If there was an increasing amount of this sort of sentiment, increasingly supported…it wasn't that he thought they should get *that* much power. But if the lower city wanted its views heard, might there be something to be gained from being the one they trusted, the one to negotiate on their behalf with the Council? That could have payoffs. There were a lot of them, in the lower city, after all, and Marek ran on them, whatever nonsense the Houses told themselves about who was the powerhouse of Marek. If they got organised, they could genuinely be strong. Right now, reading these publications, it looked to him like they were wasting most of their energy arguing among themselves.

Positioning himself somewhere in there, if he could, would also help him keep a lid on the whole thing. Best not let them get away with too much.

The pamphlet at the bottom of the pile had an advertisement on the second page: a meeting, at a pub called the Bucket, in a couple of days' time. Perhaps that would be worth attending. See who he could talk to. Whatever the pamphlets might say about equality, it was the nature of people to seek out leaders. Their current leaders would be the ones speaking at the meeting; and those were the ones Daril wanted looking to him.

Leandra, the voice of the people…it had a ring to it, didn't it.

"Overexcited scribblers with plenty to say and nothing to do about it, if you ask me," he said, handing the stack back to Andreas. "Now, as I recall, you promised me a game of cards. A demmer a point, perhaps?"

"William might drop by later, as well."

"Even better. He's bloody terrible at cards. I could use a little spending-money."

Andreas laughed, and pulled a pack of cards from a side-table drawer; and Daril settled down for a pleasant evening of wine, gaming, and conversation. Sedition could wait for tomorrow.

SEVENTEEN

The Old Market clock chimed the hour. Reb frowned. Alyssa was a whole hour late, which was unlike her. They wouldn't have time for a lesson; Reb had things to get on with. She should have just carried on working on her charms, but she hadn't wanted to get settled into that and be interrupted.

There was a knock on the door. Finally. Unless Alyssa had a very good excuse, Reb would be sending her straight away again.

Except it wasn't Alyssa. It was a messenger, and one Reb recognised – ah yes, Jonas' friend, Asa, wasn't it? They'd helped during that business with Daril and Urso. Reb hadn't seen them in a while.

"Message for you," Asa said, holding out a roughly folded piece of paper.

Reb unfolded it. The writing had the careful roundness of one who didn't use a pen often.

> Alyssa under arrest. Asked me to send you word.
>
> Thea. (Alyssa's neighbour)

"What on earth..." she said aloud, then looked up. "Who gave you this?"

"She said to tell you, she lives in the same close as your apprentice. Is there a reply?"

She couldn't just *reply*. She needed to find out what had happened. "Can you show me where you were given this?" she asked.

"Course," Asa said. "Same cost as a message, though."

"Right." Grimly, Reb fetched her cloak – it wasn't that cold right now, but who knew how long she'd be out – and found the money. She thought about it for a moment, then stashed some basic sorcery supplies in her belt pouches. Not that sorcery would get Alyssa out of jail. She wasn't sure, in fact, what would get Alyssa out of jail, but maybe she'd be able to think of something.

Maybe Alyssa *ought* to be in jail. She didn't even know what had happened yet.

"Let's go," she said to Asa, locking the door behind her and setting the wards.

Alyssa's place wasn't far from Reb's. Reb had even been there once, when she'd first suggested the apprenticeship to Alyssa, but she couldn't have found it again without Asa's help. It was in a close off a narrow lane between her own house and the squats. Chickens were pecking around in the yard of the close, there were a few boxes of dirt with vegetables growing in them, and someone's laundry was drying on a line strung between balconies.

"Here you are," Asa said, knocking on one of the doors.

A harassed-looking woman opened it, carrying a baby against her shoulder. The noise of two children playing, or possibly fighting, came from inside the house.

"This is the reply to your message," Asa said, nodded to both of them, and left.

"Oh, goodness. You're Alyssa's sorcerer?" the woman said, then, to the fussing baby, "Hush, now."

Reb wouldn't exactly have described herself as *Alyssa's sorcerer*, but she supposed it was close enough. "Yes. I'm Reb."

"Thea." The woman bobbed a nervous and unnecessary bow.

"Could you tell me what happened?" Reb prompted, after a moment, when Thea didn't say anything more.

"Of course. Uh. I suppose..." Reb saw her square her shoulders. "Come in, please. I'm so sorry about the mess, but it took me a while to get Jina settled, and I needed to get the meal on..."

Of course. Alyssa had a child, didn't she? Jina. Reb rubbed at her forehead as she followed Thea inside. This could get far more complicated. But first, she had to find out what had happened.

Thea pointed Reb to one of the wooden chairs in the small kitchen, next to a table with a pile of half-chopped vegetables. "An infusion, maybe…?"

"I'm fine," Reb said, but Thea swung the kettle over the black iron stove anyway.

"What happened?" she asked again.

"I don't entirely know," Thea admitted. She sat down on the other chair, shifting the baby onto her lap. "I was out hanging the washing, and all these guards came into the close, and I didn't know what to do, not at all. But they didn't even look at me, went straight to Alyssa's door, and she came to it, which with all the banging I'm not surprised, and they said they were arresting her. And then before they dragged her off, she was arguing about what to do with Jina, and I said, of course I'll mind her, and she said, send word to Reb, I'm her apprentice, you need to tell her."

"Right," Reb nodded. "But what I'm wondering is, did they say what they were arresting her *for*?"

"Oh! For traitorous writings," Thea said. "Which I'm sure I don't know anything about." She nodded sharply.

Shit. She'd *warned* Alyssa, more than once, about that. Especially since the new laws came in. But Alyssa had ruffled up, every time, and said, she wasn't going to back down from the truth. And Reb had decided it wasn't her business what Alyssa did with the rest of her time.

She hadn't actually thought they'd come round arresting people, or she might have tried harder to make the point.

"Do you know what specifically they had in mind?"

Thea shook her head. "They had a piece of paper they showed her, but I didn't see it. And nor I didn't want to neither. I'll mind Jina, of course, and I'm glad to be able to tell you, but I'm not getting mixed up in this."

"Right." Reb thought for a moment. "I suppose I'll have to get on down to the jail, then, try and find out a bit more. You said you can look after Jina for the moment?"

"Oh, yes, she's no trouble," Thea said, obviously relieved that Reb didn't want anything more from her. "And I'm sure you'll be able to sort things out for Alyssa very soon."

"Absolutely," Reb said, heartily, and with no sincerity at all. But no point in worrying Thea, was there? Especially given that she very clearly didn't want any more questions. "Hopefully we'll have her out of there and no harm done, by the end of the day."

She got up and left the house, and walked back out of the close, ducking under the drying clothes, thinking hard.

She wasn't at all sure she'd be able to sort things out for Alyssa. Didn't even know where to start. But she knew who would be able to. And she couldn't hold back from asking a favour, could she? Not when it wasn't her safety and liberty at stake.

☉ ☉

Reb's note, asking to meet urgently, had left the choice of venue up to Marcia; but it would be most straightforward if she went to Reb's place. However odd that felt. Reb couldn't come up Marekhill; they shouldn't (even now) be seen publicly together; and booking a private room somewhere would take time.

Reb opened the door almost the moment Marcia knocked. "Come in."

Echo of a hundred visits before, and yet this was different. Both of them were stiffer around each other; cautious. Marcia resisted the hurt.

"Sit down," Reb said, gesturing at the chair that she'd acquired when Marcia first starting coming over. Marcia dropped thankfully into it. Her feet hurt, and the small of her back. "Infusion?"

"I'm fine," Marcia demurred. Reb didn't like to make her own infusions, and she didn't want the delay of her going down to find the infusion-seller. And Marcia couldn't make it, could she, the way she would have done before New Year. This wasn't somewhere she could comfortably avail herself of pot and stove, not any more.

That hurt, too.

"Right." Reb sat down heavily opposite her, opened her mouth, and shut it again.

A faint feeling of dread stirred in Marcia's gut. "Is there…a problem?"

Reb grimaced, and looked down at her hands. "My apprentice. Alyssa. She's been arrested."

"Arrested? What on earth for?"

"Writing revolutionary pamphlets." Reb's face twisted. "Under the new laws."

"I didn't vote for them," Marcia said. "I was trying to swing the vote the other way, in fact. My mother…"

Reb shrugged a shoulder. "I didn't know. Either way. I thought it didn't sound – anyway. Doesn't matter. The thing is. I hate asking. But you're the only person I know who can do anything about it."

Marcia tilted her head, surprised. She certainly hadn't expected that. "You want me to get her out of prison?"

"Can you?" Reb looked up with unmistakable hope, then shook her head hastily when she read Marcia's expression. "No, I don't suppose you can. I meant, I have no idea how this sort of thing works. Lawyers and such."

"It's not like I do either," Marcia said. "But – I do have more resources, yes." Though the lawyers she knew specialised in contract disputes, and no one got arrested for those until you were a *long* way down the line.

But. *Could* she get Alyssa out? She, herself? What would happen if she marched down to the jail and demanded that? As Heir-Fereno?

The law was supposed to be for everyone, and to apply to everyone. But… this was an unfair law. Still.

"Did she write them?" Marcia asked, turning ideas over in her head. "The pamphlets?"

"No idea," Reb said. "No idea what they claim she's written, come to that. Just that her neighbour said, that was what the guards said when they came to pick her up. In front of her little girl, no less." She paused, and added, with slight reluctance, "She has written some pamphlets, I know that."

"Yes," Marcia said absently. "Cato and I saw her speak in a pub, once." She'd been pretty fiery then, but…was there anything that would have breached the new laws? Marcia wasn't sure that there had been. She tapped her fingers against her leg, mind racing.

Wait. It wasn't getting her out of being charged that was needed, was it? It was getting her out of jail. Non-violent offenders didn't *have* to stay in prison whilst awaiting trial, she was relatively certain; so why was Alyssa there? The obvious answer was, *to scare agitators*, and she didn't like that at all. And even if they did insist Alyssa had to stay, Marcia could get her a lawyer. "Well. I suppose the first issue is to find out what she is claimed to have written. And then to find her a decent lawyer."

"How do I go about that?"

"You don't. I do." Marcia nodded decisively. "In fact, I'm going to go straight down there and start asking some questions."

"Marcia – " Reb looked awkward. "You don't have to… go to all that trouble. I didn't mean. When I asked you here. All I was hoping for was advice. How to get a lawyer, maybe, or something."

"I know," Marcia agreed. "But I'm happy to do it. Honestly." And only a *small* amount of that was because she wanted to…prove something, maybe, to Reb. She wasn't even sure what she wanted to prove. But her feet twitched with the desire to get out there and do something, however tired she might be in other ways.

Even if it was for Alyssa's benefit. Marcia hadn't thought much of Alyssa when she'd met her before, but Reb cared about her, or at least felt responsible for her. So. Marcia could do something. For Reb.

"I might as well get on with it," she said, getting to her feet.

"Marcia – " Reb stood too, and put a hand out, then looked awkward and dropped it again. "I didn't mean…"

"I'll let you know as soon as I can," Marcia said briskly, and left before she did anything stupid like trying to take Reb's hand. She was helping. Because she wanted to use her influence for others. Because she still wanted to be Reb's friend. That was all.

The jail was on the other side of the river, on the wrong side of Marek Square. Marcia made her way down along the embankment and across Old Bridge, wondering what she was going to say. Upriver, a gang was working on the foundations of the replacement for New Bridge.

The jail was an old, blocky building, slate-grey stone with no windows and a big forbidding iron door with a smaller wooden door beside it that was the one people actually used. The door led into a small office, which held a bored-looking guard sitting behind a solid wooden desk nearly as wide as the room.

Belatedly, she realised that she should have come down looking rather more Heir Fereno. Not quite formal robes, maybe, but semi-formal House tunic; not the nondescript clothes she wore to go over to Reb's. Still. She was here now.

"C'n I help you," the guard said, without looking up from the news-sheet she was reading.

"I am here to enquire about the prisoner Alyssa Etolin," Marcia said, with her most Marekhill diction, envisaging herself in full formal even if she wasn't. The guard looked up sharply. "I am Marcia Fereno-Heir. I wish to see everything you have on her arrest."

The guard blinked in horror, and jumped up. "I'm sorry, Fereno-Heir. I didn't realise."

Which was fair enough, but she was on the back foot now, and Marcia wasn't going to let that advantage go. "Indeed," she said, in freezing tones. "The paperwork for Alyssa Etolin, if you please."

"I'll just..." The guard scrabbled through some papers in a tray under the desk and pulled a horrible face Marcia suspected she didn't know she was pulling. "Excuse me, please, Ser. Uh. Fereno-Heir. Ser."

She went to the door behind her desk, unbolted it, and

held a conversation that Marcia couldn't quite hear with someone in the room behind. She turned back with a rictus grin, glanced down at Marcia's bump, visible over the desk now the guard was standing up (and now Marcia had deliberately let her cloak fall open), and looked even more horrified. "M'colleague will just fetch it, if you please. Uh. Would you."

There was nowhere to sit down, unless the guard lifted her own chair over the desk. Marcia briefly weighed up the benefits of making her do just that, then decided against it. "I am happy to stand," she said, and composed herself into her best waiting-in-official-parades stance. It was a sight harder right now than it usually was, and she couldn't let that show. She hoped the paperwork wouldn't take long.

It didn't; it appeared from through the back door via a hand; the rest of the body didn't follow around the corner. Marcia stepped forward and reached over the desk to snap it out of the surprised guard's hand. She read it through – inflammatory literature, dangerous to the city.

She looked up. "Which literature? Specifically?"

"Uh," the guard said. "Is it not there?" She shifted her weight uncomfortably.

Marcia, frowning deeply, shook her head. "Obviously, you cannot hold Ser Etolin on this basis. It is imperative that she know the full charges against her." Which might well be nonsense – it wasn't like she was a lawyer – but the guard looked cowed, so it would do.

The guard opened the back door again, and conducted another whispered conversation behind it.

"Uh. If you'll just, uh, wait a little longer, Ser. M'colleague will. Um."

"Yes," Marcia said, putting as much freezing disdain as she could into her tone. She hadn't grown up with Madeleine for nothing. The guard wilted further.

It was a few minutes, this time, and Marcia's stomach muscles were aching badly, not to mention the small of her back, before the person behind the door handed forward a ragged-looking pamphlet with large badly-set headlines. Obviously the change of law had had an effect; fewer reputable printers willing to take the work on. Marcia laid the pamphlet out and skimmed through it, letting her brain whir. Was there anything she could do, here and now, other than bring in a lawyer?

It was pretty radical, that was true. Disband the Council, let the city govern itself, that sort of thing. It didn't have the tax stamp on, granted, but that wasn't the responsibility of the writer, but of the printer (whose name wasn't on there), and in any case that wouldn't be a matter for arrest but for invoicing. Otherwise – she wasn't sure whether it was within the law or not. It didn't call for outright rebellion; but it was quite scathing about the Council. There was a small box on the third page pointing out how little the Council had done in the floods, compared with the sorcerers, which made her wonder whether it was Alyssa's writing at all; she didn't seem the self-aggrandising type, though it was good propaganda, Marcia supposed. The rest of it matched Alyssa's views, more or less, from when Marcia had heard her in the Bucket.

She straightened up. "Well," she said dismissively. "I see no *evidence* that she wrote this. There's certainly more than one A Etolin in the city, it's a common enough surname. That's if this," she flicked a finger onto the paper, "is the author's true name at all. Even if she did, this arrant nonsense is hardly likely to destabilise the city, is it? This is certainly not the sort of thing we had in mind when we brought in the new law." Well; Athitol-Head might have done, but she herself hadn't, because she hadn't voted for it. "And I see no risk that Ser Etolin – who has a child, a house, a job here – will depart the city before charges are brought. I must insist that you release her at once."

"That's…above my grade, Ser," the guard said, weakly.

"Very well. Then please bring me someone who is able to speak about this matter." She hadn't *really* expected that to work, but she couldn't just back down.

A look of relief came onto the guard's face, as if she were finally on steadier ground. "Can't do that, Ser. Very sorry. Captain's off duty 'til this evening."

"Very well," Marcia said, then had another, triumphant, thought. "But you *can* release the prisoner on my cognisance, can't you?" She showed the guard her ring. "I will undertake responsibility for her."

The guard wavered visibly.

"I trust," Marcia said, "that you are not suggesting that my word is *insufficient*."

"Um," the guard said. "There is. I mean. There's paperwork."

"I am glad to hear it," Marcia said. "Kindly produce it."

The guard could obviously see the prospect of being let out of this conversation; and that appealed. "I suppose, Fereno-Heir, Ser, if you really. Um. If you're sure?"

Marcia waited, smiling, and the guard gave in. After that things went quite quickly. Marcia signed several bits of paper, the guard looking more relieved with each one – a paperwork trail to present to the absent Captain, Marcia supposed. Some minutes later, Alyssa was being led out of a door at the side of the room. She leant on her stick and blinked in confusion at Marcia.

"Now mind, Ser," the guard said, "she's not been *released*, as such. She needs to return every other day, to report to us, and she'll have to stand trial eventually."

"Oh, I very much doubt that," Marcia said. "I will be speaking with my lawyer. However, she will of course return as required. Come, Alyssa."

She swept out, and swept Alyssa, still looking bemused, with her.

Outside, Alyssa began to pull up, and Marcia turned to scowl at her without stopping. "Let's not argue about this *right* outside the jail, shall we?"

They got into Marek Square before Marcia stopped. They were by the fountain; she sank down onto the edge of it with a sigh of relief, and Alyssa did much the same next to her. "Right. You have questions."

"Yes. What the fuck just happened?"

Marcia shrugged. "Reb told me you'd been arrested. I couldn't get you off altogether – although the lawyer may be able to – but I could get you out. There's no reason to hold you pending charge *or* trial. I encourage you to make your reports, though. And to speak to the lawyer I'm about to engage for you."

Alyssa folded her arms belligerently. "Take advantage of something no one else in my shoes gets?"

"Yes," Marcia said. "Take advantage of it, go back to your daughter, and write some more inflammatory articles later, for all I care."

"Just because you still want into Reb's knickers?"

Marcia's jaw clenched. "It's not about that. And no. Reb was worried about you. I've helped. That's it."

"Plenty folk in that jail need help just as badly."

"What do you want?" Marcia asked in frustration.

"Expensive lawyers for all of them," Alyssa said. "Or not to need expensive lawyers if you're arrested for something you didn't do."

"You're saying the law is corrupt?"

"I'm saying I'd have had to stay there 'til trial if I weren't apprentice to someone who knows someone. Is what I'm saying."

"Fine." Marcia folded her arms. "Go back in there. Won't help anyone, including you, but apparently it'll make you feel better."

Alyssa looked like she'd bit on a lemon. "Fine," she bit out. "Obviously I'm not going back. But I'm not stopping writing, either."

"I don't expect you to," Marcia said. "Although you might want to give some thought to what, in fact, best supports your cause. It probably isn't getting arrested."

"Didn't write that one anyway," Alyssa growled.

"But you wrote others," Marcia guessed. "Don't answer that." She sighed. "Look. I'm going home. I'll send a lawyer's details via Reb. Use them, or defend yourself, as you prefer. Reb wanted you out of there, and I've done that. Up to you how you use it."

She pushed herself up off the fountain edge, turned on her heel and stalked off. She hadn't exactly expected gratitude, but the woman was *infuriating*.

At least Reb would be happy.

EIGHTEEN

Selene, Teren Lieutenant, was low – very low – on Marcia's list of Things She Wanted To Deal With Right Now. And, in fact, she'd rather hoped that Selene would have lost her position once she'd returned to Ameten last year without having achieved any of the things she was here to achieve. None of Madeleine's letters of Ameten gossip – Grainne wasn't the only one to have visited her – had mentioned Selene, and when Selene had been several weeks later, this year, than she had before – admittedly last year she'd arrived early – Marcia had hoped harder.

She'd also hoped that at least *some* of the Council would remember how Selene had behaved last year. But no; here Selene was, in the Guildhall, at the first of the formal meetings for her visit, and here the Council members were, and none of the Houses seemed the least bit concerned. At least the Guild representatives were being freezingly polite, obviously remembering the way she had ignored the Guilds last time.

Marcia conceded that she was probably feeling more irritable about everything because she had heartburn and she needed to pee every thirty minutes.

"Marcia. How good to see you." Selene smirked at her.

"I could say exactly the same," Marcia said. Could, but wouldn't, and she knew Selene would spot the difference.

Selene's smirk didn't shift. "I hope all is well with you and yours, Heir-Fereno." She glanced down at Marcia's now-obvious bump. "And I understand congratulations are in order."

"Why, thank you," Marcia said. "All is well with our House, indeed. My mother is sadly away at the moment. Recuperating from a heart problem. But I gather she is doing very well on our Teren estate." All of which was true.

"Ah yes. I stopped at your good mother's estates on our way downriver."

Marcia adopted an expression of polite interest. The message about that, if Madeleine had sent one, obviously hadn't outpaced Selene.

"We shared a delightful meal," Selene added. "She sends her good wishes. And, indeed, a message." She snapped her fingers, and a flunky appeared behind her and handed Marcia a slightly battered sheet of folded paper.

Marcia nodded and folded it into her sleeve. "My thanks. As you said last year, those links between Marek and Teren remain important." Untrue, but sounded good, and they did *have* a Teren estate. What had Madeleine said to Selene? What had she said to Madeleine?

"Indeed," Selene agreed. There was still something about her expression...but Marcia was probably imagining it.

What she wasn't imagining was the extent to which the assembled Heads and Heirs were choosing to see Selene's presence as a pleasant indication that Teren wasn't as bad as all those refugees were claiming. Which seemed wildly illogical to Marcia. Not that anyone spoke explicitly about the refugees. It was all about how important Teren trade was, and the long relationship between them – that, especially, from the couple of Houses that specialised in trading Teren crops and goods. It was all in the implications, nothing said aloud.

"Well," Andreas said, as they stood in a corner together. "I think the idea is that if Teren were on the brink of civil war, Selene wouldn't be out here conducting all the customary ceremonial nonsense."

"But that's absurd. Why shouldn't she be here even if there are demons out in the streets of Ameten enforcing the law? They still have to trade with us."

"The demons?"

"You know what I mean. They need to keep us sweet." Or take us over, but they'd had that argument before.

"Certainly, but," Andreas shrugged. "She's being more

cautious than last year, I think. It doesn't feel like she's preparing to take over."

Which didn't mean she wasn't, it just meant that she wasn't conveying it to the assembled Council members. Or, apparently, to Andreas.

"I still think it's worth being aware of what she's saying to whom," Marcia said. "Much of what happened last year was after hours, private conversations." Deniable.

Andreas flushed slightly; Selene had nearly talked him round. Marcia hoped he wouldn't be vulnerable a second time.

"We are still part of Teren," he reminded her.

"At arms-length," Marcia said. "And we need to stay that way."

If it came right down to it, though…As Gil had said in Council, how could they stand against Teren? Marek wasn't a well-armed city; it wasn't that kind of place. You couldn't trade with people at the end of a sword. The city wasn't fortified, unless you counted Beckett. And after last year, Marcia wasn't sure just how much Beckett could do. Certainly against the army of Teren demons that the refugees kept talking about. Even if you discounted some of that as the inevitable exaggeration of frightened people – five or ten becoming twenty or even fifty – it didn't sound good.

Over the hubbub of conversation, she heard someone asking Selene about the refugees. Her eyebrows went up. She wouldn't have expected anyone to talk about that here…ah, Haran-Head. That would explain it. In its own way, his utter lack of tact was strategically useful, even if he only got away with it because others *were* tactful. Marcia drifted closer.

"I'm sure you too have your dissidents," Selene said, with a smile.

"Eh, who knows what goes on in the lower city," Haran-Head said with a shrug. "Pamphlets and things, I hear, but they don't *leave*, oh no. All welcome in Marek."

"Well, perhaps our radicals are more dangerous than

yours," Selene said. "One must, after all, protect the law-abiding residents."

Which suggested the dissidents were a threat but not why. No specifics.

"Oh yes, yes, of course," Haran-Head agreed. "Perhaps Marek is just that bit calmer, what?"

"If I were you," Selene said, smoothly, "I would be concerned for the stability of your delightful city culture if you continue to take in those expelled from Ameten. I am delighted to hear that your radicals are not dangerous, but it would be terrible for them to get *ideas*, no?"

"Ah, I'm sure they'll just get used to Marek," Haran-Head said, cheerfully. "Settle in, all that."

"I do hope you're right," Selene said, and turned to someone else.

So she was planting the idea that Marek might not want dangerous Teren refugees; that Ameten was dealing correctly with them, however regrettable the need, to protect the innocent (that was, those who didn't challenge the state). Marcia didn't buy either of those ideas. They were using *demons*. This wasn't just a disagreement about how to govern. This was more than that, and of course people might want to fight back. Or to flee.

What she didn't know was how many of her Council colleagues would understand that, given their lack of any firm grasp of magic. They might – perhaps, just – acknowledge the existence of the demons Teren sorcerers were binding, but they didn't understand what they could do. Marcia herself only had a faint idea. Was there any way to share that knowledge? Any way they'd actually *listen* to? The Guilds were less averse to magic, though she'd heard that Warden Hagadath had been making disapproving noises lately. (Hagadath really was keen to move more towards the Houses.) Perhaps she should talk to some of the others. Ilana was always sensible, and they and Marcia had a long-standing working relationship.

She really had to pee again. The Guildhall had, at least, the latest in indoor facilities; which was to say, there were seats, which were only halfway outdoors, in a courtyard at the back of the Guildhall, and some kind of pit underneath them about which Marcia chose not to think too closely.

She took the opportunity of brief, if somewhat smelly, privacy to look at Madeleine's note. It was sealed inside a rough sheet of paper with a couple of scrawls across it that indicated the journey it had made from the Fereno estate in Teren. It would have many more if it had travelled on the river the regular way, rather than coming with Selene, but evidently at some point it had spent time in the general mailbags. When Marcia broke the seal, the letter inside was on much better quality paper, and closed with Madeleine's distinctive letter-folds and her seal. Someone might be able to open the seal (someone almost certainly had already opened the outer seal, if this had come down with Selene's group), but the letter inside was impossible to open without breaking the paper itself and giving the snoop away.

There was no sign of a previous tear in the folds, as Marcia ran a fingernail through them. Which didn't mean there was no possibility that someone had read the letter already, merely that they'd have had to copy it back out again, imitating Madeleine's handwriting sufficiently well to fool her daughter. Madeleine hadn't bothered to seal her other letters this well; this implied she trusted Selene less than the mail-handlers on the barges.

Fair.

The letter was short, and largely in plaintext – an estate update, a doctor's report. A section in the middle was in their private code, with more trade reports and notes on Teren fashions. Perhaps Grainne had visited again, though Madeleine didn't mention it, and it seemed rather soon after her previous visit. The trade reports, code notwithstanding, looked like trade reports; there was no point in disguising them beyond that. Everyone knew what sort of information the Marek Houses would be concealing from one another. But here, in the middle, without any distinction between that and the trade information on either side, Madeleine had written:

Archion heir priority v soon. S win vital.

Marcia rubbed her tongue against the inside of her teeth. Well. Her previous letters of Ameten gossip hadn't made the urgency so clear.

Selene had to get a win in Marek. Whatever it took, she had to do it, if she wanted to be Archion. It would be a solid achievement, if Selene could pull it off. The Archion was responsible for Teren's interests; and it was clear to anyone that the more independence Marek had, the worse that was for Teren. Someone who could pull Marek into line would make a good Archion, on top of the fact that the current Archion had a flea in his ear about Marek. Marcia didn't know if the Archion's nominating a successor was the only qualification one needed, but it had to help. That must be Selene's goal.

So. Best look out for squalls.

The next day, Marcia paused to catch her breath at the top of the stairs in Selene's guesthouse. Stairs were harder than they used to be, and her stomach muscles ached. Once her breathing had slowed, she pushed Selene's door open without knocking.

"Ah, Marcia!" Selene turned from where she was standing by the window. The light silhouetted her, shadowing her face. "How delightful to see you. Thank you for taking the trouble to come."

The whole thing was a power play, and they both knew it. Last year, when Selene had sent Marcia a note to request a meeting, she had left the location politely up to Marcia. Or she might have waited to be invited for an infusion one afternoon, or alluded to some matter of mutual interest during a chance encounter at an evening engagement. This time, she had bluntly asked – no, told, though the phrasing had been suitably circuitous – Marcia to come to her rooms. Her territory.

And yet, still Marcia's city, with Selene in borrowed rooms. She'd toyed with the idea of refusing the

invitation, and waiting to see how Selene would react –
lose her initial power by allowing Marcia to set the terms
of engagement, or lose the opportunity to propose
whatever deal she was after? But there was no point in
revealing her own counters so early in the game. Not
when she didn't know what Selene intended to use as
threat. (She did have one guess. Both of them had been
there when the demon that was chasing Tait had been
sent packing; Selene likely wouldn't want her role in that
known either, but she wasn't subject to a ban on the use
of magic.)

Marcia wanted to know how Selene was going to play
the round, and what she wanted. So she was here; but
there was a limit to how far she was willing to let Selene
feel that she had the upper hand.

"Delightful to see you too," she replied, closing the
door behind her and walking into the room to take,
unasked, a seat on one of the armchairs set around a small
knee-high table at one side of the room. She chose the
one that would put her back to the window, making her
expression harder to read, and incidentally turning her
back on Selene and forcing her to move. "Thank you for
the invitation."

Selene came to sit across from Marcia. There was a
steaming pot on the table, two thin china mugs – Exurian,
from the pattern – and a plate of the guest-house's
afternoon-cakes. Marcia leant forwards to pour herself a
cup of the infusion, despite the fact that she could smell
that it was Teren lemon-balm, which she didn't like, and
helped herself to one of the cakes, which at least she
knew were good. It was all unconscionably rude,
suggesting Selene was so deficient as a hostess that
Marcia was forced to look after her own needs, and
Marcia was pleased to note the tiny narrowing of
Selene's eyes, before she smiled and poured her own
infusion.

"Indeed, please do make yourself at home," she said.

Marcia sipped at her cup, keeping her expression calm,
and waited for Selene to talk. Selene, just as obviously,

was waiting for her to ask the purpose of the meeting.

Selene cracked first. "You and I spoke, last year, about magic."

"More than once, even," Marcia agreed.

"You explained to me the attitude of Marekhill, and your Houses."

Marcia remembered that conversation, held up on the top of the hill, in the park. Marcia had been trying to help Selene, at the time; she'd seen her as a potential ally.

"Indeed," she said. "I also remember a later conversation, shortly before you left."

Selene had threatened to blackmail her. No surprise that the threat hadn't really gone away.

"Yes," Selene said pensively. "Marekhill does not hold with magic, does it?"

"Not exactly," Marcia said.

"I would imagine," ah, here she went, "that your peers would be unhappy to hear that you are consorting with a sorcerer."

Oh. Reb. But that was old news. Hadn't they been through it already, last year? But then; that threat of exposing the relationship had worked, hadn't it, in part, back then. Marcia had been nervous about it, and Selene had seen that. Was she less nervous about it now? Only because she'd expected Selene might threaten her with the matter of the barge-yard, which Marcia was significantly more nervous about. Perhaps Selene wasn't willing to risk her own part in that becoming public knowledge.

Selene glanced pointedly at Marcia's belly. "Especially House Tigero."

As it happened, there wasn't much that could get Andreas out of the contract without her own House's agreement. But there was a large gulf between the enforceability of a contract and a pleasant co-parenting relationship. And in general, Selene was right. The rest of the Houses would not be pleased to hear that Marcia had been with Reb, even if the relationship was over.

But the barge-yard would have been worse. She lifted a

shoulder in a half-shrug. "I'm sure no one would accuse me of *consorting* with my brother. Occasionally drinking tea with, certainly. It's common knowledge."

'An open secret' would be closer, but it was true that it would be hard to use against her. Not everyone had exactly approved of Madeleine's approach to the Cato situation, and in any case, it was a long time ago.

Selene's smile was river-shark wide. "Oh, not your esteemed brother. Your lover. Reb, I believe her name is." She paused. "Does Tigero-Head know?"

Marcia examined her fingernails. "I'm afraid your information is out of date."

"Dumped you, did she? Well. I'm not sure that will keep you out of trouble."

If it came to it, she could deny it outright. That would be the sensible thing. Her word against Selene's. Selene would risk looking foolish, salacious, even. Or Marcia could say that it was over, and brazen it out. It would be higher-risk; but she *hadn't* done magic, herself, and suggesting that she shouldn't even be around a sorcerer was ridiculous. Just one more instance of the disastrous ways in which the Council separated itself from the rest of Marek. But there was no need, yet, to decide how she would play it if she had to.

She let her eyes flicker as though she were thinking it over. She needed to find out what Selene wanted.

Selene caught the flicker, and a small smile appeared at the corners of her mouth. "Unless..." she purred, and waited.

Marcia gave it the appropriate couple of beats before saying, grudgingly, "Unless what?"

Selene shrugged. "Support the proposals I will be laying before the Council, this week. Easy enough. And you'd be better that way than standing alone against them, in any case."

Marcia was certain that she wouldn't be standing *alone* against whatever Selene had in mind. If Selene were that confident, she wouldn't be pulling this. On the other hand, there were at least a couple of Heads on Teren's side. Even a couple of Guilds, perhaps. Marcia wouldn't have said *enough*, yet, but...maybe she was wrong. If Selene really thought that what she did here could make her Archion, that was a lot of potential power to bargain with. She couldn't say it out loud, in public, but that needn't stop her from dropping hints during private discussions in quiet corners.

"Of course," Selene added. "You might think you can brazen your way through the relationship part. Perhaps you should be more concerned about the part where you pulled your lover's – I'm sorry, ex-lover's – apprentice out of jail? When she'd been arrested for treason?" She shook her head in false concern. "I fear that might go down even less well."

Marcia's stomach lurched; but no. She made herself take a long, calming breath. She hadn't done anything wrong there. She hadn't prevented a trial. She'd just prevented Alyssa from having to sit around in jail waiting for it. As far as she knew, Alyssa still hadn't been charged – might perhaps never be charged? – but *she* hadn't done anything to obtain that outcome. (Literally nothing; Alyssa had turned down the lawyer Marcia had asked to contact her. The lawyer had messaged Marcia to let her know a couple of days previously; with, of course, a bill attached for the time taken.) If that was all Selene had, she could jump.

"I fear your information must be faulty. I'm not particularly concerned about that," she said, with a shrug.

Selene's eyes narrowed, but she didn't say anything else. Which didn't necessarily mean she didn't have anything else, merely nothing that she was willing to bring into the open just now.

When it came down to it, Marcia wasn't sure that Selene would do what she was threatening, even if Marcia did tell her to go jump. Spreading this sort of gossip...it was petty, and it risked highlighting Selene's meddling again, which would be unpopular with at least some of the Council. If she did, Marcia wasn't convinced people would care as much as Selene thought they would.

Marcia considered her options, in case the silence might needle Selene into releasing more information. She wasn't going to do what Selene told her to; that, she was certain of. Even if she was wrong, and Selene did follow through, and people did care after all. Was she willing to make it seem that she was considering it? That would be the sensible option, keeping her views hidden for as long as possible. And yet...

And yet, she couldn't bring herself even to pretend like she might agree. She took a deep breath and stood up.

"No," she said. "No, I won't support you in Council. No, I won't make it seem like I think Teren interference doesn't matter. No, I don't care if you tell everyone I had an affair with a sorcerer. Have at it. I can survive whatever you throw at me. And even if I couldn't, I'd rather stand free and fall, than bow down to your demands."

She turned on her heel and left, with Selene's raised voice following her. "Reconsider that decision, Fereno, or, I promise, you will regret it."

When Jonas did manage to prevent a flicker, he had just enough time to react, and not enough time to think it through. It was instinct, nothing more.

He and Tam were on their way up from the river to the Dog's Tail, eating pastries as they went. Tam was telling Jonas enthusiastically about the current prospects of his favourite ifban player; Jonas still hadn't managed to get into the game, even nearly two years after arriving in Marek, but he was happy to indulge Tam. Tam gestured wildly with his pastry, and just for a moment Jonas felt like his vision was doubled.

...this street, he was sure it was this street, and Tam holding half a pastry, and then Tam on the floor, blood running from his head...

Jonas blinked back into the now, with Tam looking at him in concern.

"You all right there, mate?"

"Yeah, I, uh, dizzy for a moment," Jonas stammered, trying to fit it together – this street, Tam's pastry, surely –

Tam shrugged and kept walking, arm flying out again, and there, that was it, that was what Jonas had seen, and Tam was about to be hit…

He barged sideways into Tam, knocking him out of the way, and then something large and dark fell past his other side, and there was a sudden shocking pain in his right arm.

He was aware of swearing coming from above, someone's voice raised accusingly, then Tam staring wide-eyed at him, both of them flattened against a house wall. "Fuckkkk. I never even saw it. Jonas? You all right?"

There was no blood on Tam's head. He was fine.

Jonas opened his mouth to say he, too, was fine, then moved his arm, and grunted in pain.

"You all right down there? I'm so sorry!" Above them, someone was leaning out of an upper window with an expression of apologetic concern. "We were trying to get it across the room, and my mate dropped it against the window and – well, anyway. I'm so sorry."

Jonas looked at the thing that had hit him – the thing that had been going to hit Tam. A huge wooden beam, lying across the roadway. What on earth had they been doing with it up there?

"Mate, you have *reflexes*," Tam said with admiration. "I didn't even see it! That'd have hit me bang on the head, if you hadn't shoved me." In Tam's position, Jonas felt he might have been a bit more taken aback, but Tam, kind and generous person that he might be, was never prone to thinking all that hard.

"You're hurt!" The person above was still leaning out of the window. "Uh. Can we, can I…take you to a doctor, maybe?"

"Yeah," Tam agreed. "You should get that looked at. Think you took a pretty nasty bash there."

Jonas managed to pull one thought from his spinning head: Cato. He should take the injury to Cato, and he should tell Cato about what happened with the flicker. He'd promised.

"Cato'll look at it," he told Tam.

"Oh, yeah, right," Tam nodded. "Healing magic. My mum used to take me to the sorcerer round the corner when I was little and I got a cold or something." He frowned. "We went to a doctor when my sib broke their arm though. You sure…"

"Yes," Jonas said. He wasn't; but if Cato couldn't fix the problem, he'd say so, and then Jonas could try a doctor. "I'm fine," he called up to the person who'd dropped the beam. "Thank you." *Maybe I've had enough of your help*, he didn't say.

"I'll walk you there," Tam said, then visibly rethought. "I mean. Uh. To the front door, anyway?"

It was easier to let him do it than to argue, though Jonas didn't think he needed nursemaiding. His arm hurt, yes, and he was feeling a little shaky, but he was *fine*.

Tam left him at Cato's front door and hustled away again sharpish, calling "See you at the Tail!" over his shoulder as he left, and tying his armband back on. Cato's area wasn't the best, but messengers were protected, and Tam probably wouldn't get called for a job before he reached the Tail and took the armband off again.

Jonas made his way up the stairs – fine, maybe he was more than a little shaky – and banged on Cato's door.

"Jonas?" The door swung open. Cato, inside, sounded startled. "You're not due a lesson?"

"No," he said. "Got a problem."

Cato was sitting on the stool in front of his worktable, things arranged in front of him. He swung round and looked Jonas over. "Well. You'd best sit down. What happened?"

"It's not…I'd have gone to a doctor," Jonas said, sitting down heavily on the edge of the bed, "but…"

"They really are better for most injuries, you know. But if you want to see how healing magic works…"

"No. I mean, yes," it would be a good opportunity, he supposed, "but mostly, I got a flicker."

"You got a flicker of you damaging yourself?"

Jonas shook his head. "No. Of Tam."

"He's injured?"

"I stopped it," Jonas said impatiently. Wasn't it obvious?

"Right. Let's start that again." Cato brought the stool over to sit in front of Jonas. "Nice and slow. You had a flicker. When?"

Jonas marshalled his thoughts. He shouldn't feel this bad, just from an injury, even if it was, as he feared it might be, broken. He'd broken his arm before, on the ship, and it hadn't left him this groggy. But flickers always did leave him feeling odd. "Tam and me were walking along the street."

"Tam and I," Cato said absently, then caught himself and made a tiny face. "Carry on."

"I saw – something falling. On Tam. He was badly hurt. Saw in a flicker, I mean. And then I realised, it was right then. We were in that street, in that place, he had a pastry in his hand…It all just came together. I barged him right out of the way, into the wall, and the thing – it was a beam, a big beam of wood – it fell next to us. Caught my arm as it fell."

"But Tam was unhurt?" Cato was watching his face intently.

Jonas nodded.

"The flicker didn't happen the way you saw it."

"No."

"Well now. That is interesting, isn't it. Now, let's take a look at this."

Cato prodded at the arm, Jonas hissing in pain, and pulled a face. "I'm inclined to think it's a break, but let's take a better look."

He stood up, and began taking things out of pots on his worktable. "Eyebright for clear vision. Powdered bone for the link to the body."

"Powdered *bone*?"

Cato shrugged. "I don't take it from anyone who isn't done with it."

"*Human* bone?" Jonas choked.

"You can go to a doctor if you prefer. They practise on corpses, though, so it's not like I'm doing anything worse."

"Fine," Jonas said weakly.

"Rowan for the binding. And willowbark, that's good for most medical workings."

He came back with a little bowl, stirring it with a carved spoon.

"Is that bone, too? The spoon?" Jonas asked.

"Goat's horn, actually. Stubborn sods, goats. Good for curing. Now, bear in mind that personally, I can't get much clearer of a view with magic than a good doctor can with experience. I used to know a sorcerer who specialised in body-magic, and they were excellent. Only worked with the difficult cases the doctors referred, or they'd have been overrun. Anyway. It's not my speciality at all, but I know the basics." He sprinkled the powdered mix on Jonas' arm, laid his hand on top of it – it was cooler than Jonas expected – and closed his eyes. There was a faint tingling, and Jonas saw-felt the invisible glow he associated with magic.

Cato opened his eyes again. "Broken, yes. So. Magic can't alter matter permanently. I can do some support work, but I can't fix it. Healing magic – you can do the destructive stuff, cutting or cauterising. And you can help the body along. But most of the healing the body has to do for itself. For this, I can do a bit of encouraging, but it'll need splinting and a sling too, for at least three weeks, maybe four. But that's quicker than the six weeks it'll take on its own, and much less risk of healing crooked. Shall I?"

"Uh. Sure," Jonas said.

Cato talked him through the whole process, though he still couldn't properly tell what Cato was doing. He could sense *something*, though, which Cato seemed to think was the critical part.

"If one of your friends damages themself, bring them to me and I'll help you see it yourself," Cato said, once he was done. "Though I doubt it'll be your speciality either. But at least you've seen it from the inside now. Nearly impossible to do it without that. Right. Splint." He dragged a box out from under the bed, foraged around in it, and came out with a couple of bits of wood and a bandage. "I would recommend going to see a doctor to get it wrapped properly, but this ought to do you in the interim."

The resulting bandage was, to Jonas' eyes, as neat as anything the ship's surgeon on the *Lion d'Riseri* had ever done. He told Cato as much, and Cato flushed a little, looking pleased, then sat on the stool and propped his heel up in front of him, hugging his knee to his chest. "So, now we've dealt with that. You were able to stop the flicker, at a cost. That's...interesting."

"Might just have been coincidence," Jonas said. "I mean, we stopped that – thing, last year, and I didn't have any consequence from that."

"The demon, you mean? The one that was after Tait?" Cato sucked air thoughtfully through his teeth. "We didn't, though, did we?"

Jonas frowned at him. "We definitely did."

"No. Wait." Cato turned to the table and took a blue cloth-bound notebook from a pile. He flipped through the pages. "Here. What you saw then, what you described seeing, anyway, was the *threat* of it. Not it actually rampaging through the streets of Marek, or," his foot flexed, though his tone continued light, "eating Tait, or whatever."

"What's that?" Jonas asked.

"My notes," Cato said. "I know you have your own notes about this, but you're my apprentice, and I've kept notes as well. Different perspective." He held the book out. "You're welcome to look, if you like."

Jonas leant over enough to see a couple of pages of notes, in a surprisingly neat hand, with a paragraph about the demon halfway down. He glanced up at Cato, took the book, and turned to the most recent pages. The flicker he'd seen about Argan Etolin was there, though not that

Jonas had tried to change things, because Jonas had never told Cato that. And the flood. Jonas twitched, jerking his arm painfully, pushed the book back at Cato, and sat back.

"Right," he said, for lack of anything else to say.

Cato eyed him, then closed the book. "So, the demon thing. You saw a threat. We reacted to the threat, and neutralised it. But you didn't stop the actual thing you saw, that time. This time, and with the flood, you changed the future."

"And it cost me something." Jonas considered. "Though the flood only cost me – it was exhausting, but it didn't hurt."

"It had costs, though. Different to what you saw, but costs. So. Is that inevitable? Will you – or someone – always have to pay for it?"

"If I'd moved a bit faster..."

Cato hummed to himself, eyes distant. "Something must happen," he said, eventually, slowly. "If the thing you see doesn't happen, something else must. Yes? There can't be...a gap in the world. The beam fell, and hit the ground, and fell through whatever was between it and the ground – what on earth were they doing throwing beams through windows, anyway? Never mind. In your flicker, Tam was in the way. In reality, you were, but less so. You could have been more so."

"I could have been not at all."

"And maybe then it would have hit harder and smashed a stone, and someone trips on the hole the next evening. Or maybe not. There's consequences, is my point. If that thing doesn't happen, something else must."

"I could have gone up and stopped it falling, if I'd had more time."

"And maybe then it knocks whoever was up there out of the window instead, or...I don't know. Maybe not. Maybe they're more careful now because this happened, and if it didn't happen, they'd be careless on another project, another time, with worse results. Or maybe they'll be less careful because it wasn't that bad, and someone else gets a head cracked next month."

"Consequences," Jonas said, turning the idea over in his head. "But do they have to be bad?"

Cato shrugged. "No idea. I mean, in theory, I don't see why. I don't like the idea that you'll be – punished, for trying. Magic doesn't work that way. It's neutral." He smiled brightly. "Otherwise I would have had a far worse adult life. But…there's a cost in the sense of, you stop one thing but you don't know what happens instead. The future is always a gamble, I suppose. Always unknowable."

"That's what happened with the flood, then. I tried to stop it and made it worse."

Cato sucked at his teeth. "Did you, though? No one died. Could well have done. Your flicker, from what you said, wasn't all that clear. It was *different*, I'll give you that. Different harm, perhaps, whether worse or better." He scratched at the side of his face. "You didn't use magic this time. I wonder if that's relevant. Not enough information yet."

At some point he should tell Cato about Argan Etolin, where he hadn't used magic, and hadn't changed anything. For now, he sat, thinking. Cato, for once, was quiet.

Whatever he did, trying to prevent a flicker, it would change what happened next. That was the point. And he'd never know what the consequences could be. "Should I…not, then?" he asked, eventually, looking over at Cato.

Cato shrugged. "That's not for me to answer, is it? That's for your own moral judgement. Are the things you see always bad?"

Jonas shook his head. "I saw Tait climbing out of a window, once," he said. "Except I didn't know it was Tait at the time."

"Huh," Cato said. "I happen to know that Tait did indeed climb out of a window, shortly after their arrival in Marek, and it was probably for the best that they did so, though as previously discussed, I suppose we can never know. They came here afterwards, though, so I'm happy about it." His grin was genuine. "Let's assume that your flickers are morally neutral, and therefore, what you do about them is down to your own conscience."

"I never tried changing them before I got here," Jonas said. "Not that way, anyway. Most of the time I don't even realise what's going on until it's too late. I warned my mum once about a storm coming up, but it didn't make any difference. I guess maybe that rope was always going to fail, and it didn't *look* rotten."

Cato sucked thoughtfully at his teeth. "I suppose all we can do is continue keeping track. Now," he shifted on the stool, the tone of his voice changing. "If you're up to standing, I suggest you go eat something and rest up for a couple of days. Breaks are nasty."

Jonas took himself off down the stairs and towards the Dog's Tail.

Consequences. Ethics. The future. He could have done without any of it, truth be told, but there you were; his flickers were part of him, weren't they, and that meant dealing with them.

NINETEEN

The Council's formal return to session went exactly as Marcia expected, formal robes, parades, and boredom, until halfway through Selene's speech.

Selene had done the customary bit about the bond between Marek and Teren and all the rest of it, paused, and Marcia assumed she would sit down. Instead she looked deliberately around the Chamber. "I was – as was the Archion – pleased to hear about your cracking down on the *radicals* spreading resentment and rebellion through your streets. We made such laws in Ameten some time ago, and we are pleased that you have followed our lead in sweeping away this dangerous refuse."

There was a rustle around the room. Some of those who had voted for the censorship law frowned. Marcia was surprised that Selene was still on this tack; hadn't she realised, last year, that Marek wasn't keen on the idea of following Teren's lead? On being seen as subservient?

Perhaps that was the point. Perhaps Selene – and Teren – didn't want to accept that. Surely it wasn't politically sensible to be this obvious; and yet, if she saw this as her only route to the Archion's seat, with the Archion on his deathbed…Perhaps Selene didn't have time to be subtle.

"I am perturbed to see that many of those who are no longer permitted to remain in Teren, have come to batten onto the generosity of Marek." Her voice was somewhere between 'stern' and 'concerned'. "I must urge the Council to consider this matter most carefully. You take a great risk by letting these reprobates run riot here."

This time the unrest was more obvious.

"Marek does not turn people away," Kiran-Head said from a few seats away, quite audibly, and a few heads nodded.

On the other hand…Marcia glanced around the room, noting those who looked more willing to consider Selene's perspective. She'd heard some rumbling, of late, after the south-west corner flooding put more pressure on housing; people suggesting that 'Marekers' should be supported first. She'd seen no reaction from other Council members, and the unrest should settle once the builders had sorted out their little problem with the foundations. But if Selene was trying to stir up trouble…

"Finally," Selene said, "I am delighted to be able to tell you that the Archion has taken all Teren merchants under his umbrella of protection."

She smiled out at them, and Marcia stiffened. What did that mean?

"From now," Selene continued, "all Teren merchants will be guaranteed by the Archion and the Commission. The Marek Houses need no longer fear that any Teren merchant will fail to meet their obligations. As such, all Teren merchants should be treated as if they are acting on behalf of the Archion himself."

The Heads and Heirs were exchanging wide-eyed looks. That sounded almost as if…

"Hitherto," Selene went on, "the rate charged to Teren merchants has been to protect the Houses against defaulters. There is no longer any risk of defaulters. All merchants will thus be given the same terms as the Archion."

She was. She was telling them that they had to trade with Teren merchants *for free*. And the worst thing was, there was nothing they could do about it. Marek's founding charter laid out that the Archion, together with the leaders of other Teren cities, had special rights, to trade through Marek without a surcharge being levied; because Marek was founded by the loose conglomeration of cities that Teren then was, and at the time, the trade that came through Marek was largely that of those city leaders. Over time, other merchants had begun to trade here; the Houses had sprung up; the other cities had come under the Archion and lost their own city leaders; and other Teren merchants had not been granted the same deal. For decades now, the Archion's trade had been only a few barges a year. And now, at a stroke, every Teren barge would get to trade through Marek for free?

This was going to blow a hole in every House budget.

It was admirable, in a sense. Obviously, it would play extremely well for Selene back home in Ameten. Not only that, but it was going to make it harder for Marek to take so many Teren refugees. Yes, in the long run, new blood was good for the city, but in the short term, they needed support to settle in. Marcia saw the Council's annual budget in her mind's eye. She wasn't sure how willing the Houses would be to keep paying in at current levels when their own profits were down, whatever lip service everyone paid to 'when the Houses flourish, Marek flourishes; when Marek flourishes, the Houses flourish'.

They couldn't even *discuss* it, here; this was the Opening Ceremony, with no scope for discussion, and in any case, what was there to discuss, in open Council? They couldn't prevent Selene – Teren – from doing this. They could hardly express their displeasure, either, not here and now. Not without very careful thought. No one wanted to be the first to comment.

Proposals, Selene had said. Proposals that she was laying before the Council. This wasn't a proposal; it was a demand. A requirement. Would her next step be to make *proposals* about Marek's approach to the refugees? Or did she have more than that in mind – and how did she propose to gain support for it? Perhaps Marcia wasn't the only one she was putting pressure on, one way or another.

Glancing around the Chamber, Marcia saw Warden Ilana sitting back, arms folded, squinting slightly. What was Ilana's perspective, as one new to the Council? How would it play out for the Guilds? Teren merchants bringing raw materials in more cheaply – that might benefit some Guilds, in particular those that worked with steel and copper. And if Selene was playing to be Archion; what else might she be able to promise or insinuate, about which goods she could popularise in Teren? But Ilana must know that the Houses would react by trying to squeeze profits elsewhere. And Marcia remembered a squabble about Teren guilds trying to bring finished goods into Marek. Would the Archion's patronage affect that? That sort of competition was the last thing the Guilds wanted.

The session finished by rote, with everyone's minds visibly elsewhere. On the way out, they all had to come up with something to say to Selene, standing in the antechamber wearing a sharklike smile. At least everyone there had plenty of experience in saying something when you had nothing to say.

Marcia was halfway through her own polite niceties, mind mostly still running through implications, when Selene leant forwards, in a moment, when no one was close enough to hear.

"I wouldn't worry too much about what I just said. Because you will not bear the vote of your House for much longer. Indeed, I imagine you won't *have* a House for much longer. You can go to the squats with your brother and rot there."

She leant back, smiled, and then switched her attention to the next person arriving before Marcia could speak.

How *dare* she. Marcia was going to spike her wheel, and bring the Council kicking and screaming into the cold hard light of reality, if it was the last thing she did.

And, if she got it wrong, it might indeed be the last thing she did as Heir of House Fereno. No pressure.

Cato hadn't raised a spirit in well over a year, now. Not since the whole Beckett...*thing*. It wasn't something he did all that often; he'd had a booking for it half a year ago, just after New Year, then the client had pulled out. A few weeks previously she'd come back again – Cato didn't bother asking why she'd changed her mind – and this time hadn't thought better of the matter before paying her deposit.

Now that the moment was upon him, Cato was slightly doubting whether it was sensible to have invited Jonas to witness it. But even if it had been a while, he still knew how it worked; and in any case, he couldn't defer the matter any further. He'd delayed after the flooding, needing recuperation (loath though he had been to acknowledge how far he'd driven himself into the ground); and then he'd delayed because his client had sent him a snotty note, and he wanted to be awkward. It wasn't in the slightest because at the second client meeting, just before the flooding, he'd realised that the client was Heir to one of the Houses, and had experienced a sudden and unwelcome moment of moral qualm. Before that he'd assumed she was from a Guild, as she'd been referred by a Guildwarden former client. The Guilds didn't have the Houses' issues with magic, though rumour had it some of the more self-important Guildwardens were starting to copy the Houses in that regard.

It wasn't *his* problem if his client wanted to break the rules. She was paying well, and that was all there was to it. He didn't get involved in his clients' *morals*, and he didn't care what they got up to up on the Hill anyway.

He had to get this done, today, and Jonas was here now, so he could stay.

"Do not step into the circle, under any circumstances," he said to Jonas. "Once the spell starts, it's technically in a different plane of existence. Or half of it is, anyway. I'm not sure what would happen to either of us if you breach the boundary, but I'm not keen to find out."

Jonas nodded solemnly. He was perched on a stool on the far side of the room. His arm was still bound up; it was only a week since he'd broken it.

"Don't say anything, either. I won't hear it properly, and it'll be distracting."

"What if something goes wrong?" Jonas asked.

"Nothing's going to go *wrong*. I've done this often enough. But I suppose if it did, you should go tell Reb."

Not that Reb knew sod all about this sort of magic, but if bits of Cato ended up strewn all over the room, she could probably arrange to have it cleared up. "Right. Let's go."

The outer circle was a standard salt-and-rosemary one, there primarily for Jonas' benefit, and also because Cato liked the extra layer of protection. Plus rituals were good for one's frame of mind.

Inside the salt-and-rosemary was the more important circle, the one which would create a space halfway between this plane and the spirit one. If Cato weren't in Marek, he wouldn't need this; there were more effective ways of summoning spirits, politely or otherwise. But Beckett didn't like (understatement) other spirits in Marek, and Cato didn't want to leave the city, so he'd found an alternative. Technically, whatever spirit he managed to attract and negotiate with would never set foot in Marek at all.

It had taken some effort and experimentation to work out this circle. A couple of pinches of Marek dirt (often useful; Cato had a big jar of it), mixed with dried rose petals, powdered ginger, and wood-ash from twigs burnt in a silver bowl. (He remembered, suddenly, Urso and his excessively complicated chalk patterns. To be fair, they'd worked. Harder to set up, though, and less elegant. All those angles and twiddles.) He scattered it neatly, with no gaps. He opened up the small engraved silver ball he used for this kind of thing, wound a couple of hairs around his finger, and pulled them out with a quick jerk. He hated that bit. He dropped them into the ball, with another tiny pinch of the dirt-and-ginger mixture.

The final part required him to pull power through his connection with Beckett, into the circle, to shift it into the half-space between this plane and the spirit plane. He hadn't done this since Beckett had become Beckett, rather than just 'the cityangel'. Not since Cato had *met* Beckett in person. But that shouldn't matter, right? Everything still worked the same. He hoped.

No time like the present. He threw his mind into the circle, pulled at the thing inside his head that he felt as 'power', and let one flow into the other. He cupped his hands together around the open ball as he did it; not strictly necessary, but helpful.

It worked, exactly as it always had. Which was more of a relief than Cato was entirely willing to admit, especially in front of Jonas. Not that Jonas could see him clearly now; the room was blurry around the edges through the curtain of dimensional slip that arose from the dirt-ginger-rose circle and curved neatly over Cato's head. Cautiously, he tied the power off; the circle held. All good so far.

The air around him felt charged, the hair on his arms standing on end. It wasn't exactly that he could see anything different, but his vision seemed to slide across something he couldn't quite see. He had the feeling that if he turned too fast he'd see something he shouldn't. Or couldn't. Or the back of his own head. The air tasted acridly of sparks, and the smell of ginger was in his nose.

This was the bit he couldn't hurry. This little patch of space was a beacon now, in the other plane, and hopefully, an interested spirit would show up. Even more hopefully, it would be one he'd worked with before.

A fuzzy figure stepped through the wall and into the bubble, and Cato took a slow calming breath. The air tasted suddenly different, and his ears felt like they were about to pop.

"Greetings," he said. "How are you this fine day?"

"Cato. How lovely to see you." Ah, excellent. This one he knew.

"Yorick. A pleasure as always. Any chance you might have some time free to do me a little favour?"

"What is it this time?" Spirits didn't generally have much in the way of affect – and it wasn't like they had faces in the traditional sense that one could read, that was a new thing Beckett had taken on – but Yorick was interested in humans, and Cato interpreted them in this case as 'moderately cheerful'.

"Life-force deal. Not the whole thing. Siphon a bit off, give someone a scare, you know the drill."

"Eh." Yorick didn't sound enthused. Not surprising; Yorick's interest in humans meant they preferred the jobs which involved more in the way of listening or observing. Cato and Yorick had once worked together on an information-gathering job which Yorick had felt almost entirely paid for itself in interest value.

"I know, I know, but still, even you must like a little power here and there?" Human-plane life-force held a lot of value in the spirit plane; that was how blood magic worked. Within Marek, Beckett's tie to the city gave them enough life-force to spread their power around, back to Marek's sorcerers. A tax, of sorts, on everyone in the city, but unnoticeable, and costing them nothing; humans gave off life-force simply existing, and Beckett just collected it.

"I suppose so," Yorick said. "But you could sweeten the deal."

"The theatre," Cato said, with resignation. Yorick had encountered the concept of 'theatre' on a previous job, and been wholly enthralled. Cato wasn't massively keen, himself, but at least Yorick didn't need their own seat paid for. "Fine. I'll take you to a performance. After the job."

"Before the job."

"Oh, come on. I'm on a deadline here."

"I can see the deadline," Yorick said, shimmering hand-like appendage gesturing at the silver ball. "Two days. You can take me right now."

"There's probably something on tonight," Cato conceded. "No guarantee there's seats, though, and I utterly refuse to hang around on my feet in the pit."

"You'll try," Yorick decreed. "And if not, I'll do the job, and you'll extend the deadline and take me to the theatre." They paused. "And I get the life force as well."

"Of course," Cato said. Wasn't like there was anything he could do with it.

"Well then. Deal."

"Deal," Cato agreed, and held out the open silver ball. Yorick swirled downwards into it. Cato knew that Yorick didn't *have* form or weight in the human world, but he still felt that the ball was heavier as he snapped it shut. He closed his eyes, feeling out towards the circle surrounding them to gently close it down, then stepped out of the salt and rosemary circle.

Jonas was still sitting on the stool – good, he'd taken 'don't move' seriously – and his eyes were wide.

"There we are," Cato said. "Done and dusted."

"The *theatre*?" Jonas demanded.

Well, Cato himself wouldn't have thought that was the central import of the interaction, but perhaps it was quite compelling. "Yorick likes the theatre. Hence actually having a name." Jonas looked baffled. "Side character from a play that was popular about five years ago," Cato said. "Yorick made me take them to it twice."

"I don't understand," Jonas said, plaintively.

"Right, so, Yorick is inhabiting this ball," Cato hefted it. "More or less, anyway. They can see and hear a certain distance around it. Which, by the by, makes these little theatre trips expensive, because I have to be close enough to the stage, and I can't be doing with standing." He narrowed his eyes at the silver ball.

"They can hear us? Right now?" Jonas looked worried. "Should you be…discussing this?"

"Yes, and yes. I don't go around keeping things from my collaborators," Cato said grandly, and untruthfully. He absolutely did keep things from his collaborators on occasion, and certainly from his clients, but keeping things from a spirit would be unwise, and undermine the possibility of future deals.

"Can they speak to anyone else?"

"Not without opening the ball, which I generally recommend against doing until the critical moment. And my clients are always shit-scared of the whole business, so they do what they're told."

"Critical moment?"

"In this case, my client wants to – look, it's like getting someone big and tough in to beat up the opposition, except it's a sight scarier when there's no visible impact.

The opposition, whoever they are, just feels their life-force draining away. And Yorick here gets a bit of oomph for themself, which is nice, although apparently in this instance insufficient payment. Hence the theatre deal."

Jonas looked a bit sick. "They're going to take someone's life force?"

"Not all of it," Cato said, with a shrug. It was a long time since it had been all of it, and he'd been more desperate then. It was the client's responsibility, anyway, or maybe at a push the spirit's; not his, anyway, any more than Leonora up on Marekhill was responsible when one of her fancy decorated smallswords spilt someone's blood.

"That's horrible."

"No more nor less horrible than when someone shoves a knife into someone else, or punts them into the river. Which, I assure you, does happen from time to time in this city."

"But why..."

"That is very definitely my client's business and not mine," Cato said. "Discretion and all that. I get paid, Yorick gets paid, my client is satisfied, everyone's happy. Apart from my client's opposition, I suppose, but that's not my problem either."

Jonas didn't look reassured, which wasn't surprising. Jonas, Cato knew, had some kind of ethical system going on. To each their own.

"So you take that thing along with your client?"

"Fuck no. I give it to the client. I point out the client to Yorick, who as you recall can see and hear what's going on around them. The client gets the ball into the presence of whoever they're after – not my problem. They indicate the victim, and open the ball. Yorick does their thing. The client closes the ball again, and returns it to me. I return to that half-way place I constructed just now, and disentangle Yorick and the ball."

"What if they don't return it?"

"There's only enough in the ball – you saw me putting it in? The same mixture I used for the inner circle, plus a couple of strands of hair – to keep a spirit here for a couple of days. If the ball goes missing, the connection expires after that anyway."

"But then, you've made a connection, you've got that ball – doesn't all of that mean that Yorick's in Marek? I thought Beckett didn't like that."

"Ah, that's the clever part." Cato concentrated for a moment, balanced the ball on one hand, and carefully passed his fingers straight through the silver. They tingled. "Ugh, I hate doing that, gives me a headache."

Now Jonas looked *differently* horrified.

"So, it's not actually on this plane, it just kind of…has a shadow here. You can see it. I can see it. Because we're sorcerers, and we can see things on the spirit plane, to some extent. My client won't be able to see it, but they will be able to feel it. It's easier to feel it than it is not to, even though it's only sort-of here." He tossed it in the air and caught it again, to demonstrate. "It means that Beckett isn't bothered, because Yorick isn't, strictly, *here*."

"You worked this out?"

"I did a lot of reading," Cato said. "Most of it was worked out for me, I just had to," he waved his hand dismissively, "pull things together. A bit. Sort of." There had been a lot more to it than that, as it happened, but he wasn't in the mood to go into it. "Anyway. That's the deal. I am supposed to be delivering tonight or tomorrow, so I shall have to get down to the theatre now, I suppose, and see what can be done in the line of seats near the stage."

The ball vibrated gently in his hand.

"Want to come?"

Jonas shook his head, still staring at the ball.

"Out, then," Cato said, shooing Jonas out of the door, and leaving after him. He'd clear up later. Oh well. Hopefully the play would be entertaining.

TWENTY

"Marcia! Fancy seeing you here!"

Marcia looked up from where she was lolling in the baths, head back and eyes closed. Nisha stood a few feet away. She frowned. "But…"

"I know!" Nisha interrupted, louder. "I haven't seen you in so long. May I?"

What was Nisha on about? She was the one who had sent Marcia a message asking to meet here. So she'd dashed down to the baths – which, admittedly, now she was here she was rather enjoying – and now Nisha was playing silly idiots.

Nisha slipped into the water next to Marcia. "Hush, darling," she said, much lower. "One wouldn't like to be *obvious*, would one?"

This all seemed absurdly cloak-and-dagger to Marcia, but there, that was Nisha, wasn't it? And presumably she had something to share.

Nisha gestured for tea to be brought over, and kept up a flood of inconsequential gossip which Marcia barely even parsed, while they were waiting.

"How's the baby? You're really quite bulge-y now, you know."

"I noticed," Marcia said, dryly. "It's much more pleasant in the water. I'm considering becoming a dolphin."

"Fair. How much longer now?"

"Four months. I'm due early Fein."

"That long still? It's a long process, isn't it. Practically a year."

"Eight months," Marcia firmly countered her. Forty weeks was plenty long enough without Nisha claiming it was fifty.

"Thank the angel I have no plans to experience the

whole business myself."

"No Heir for you?"

Nisha shuddered. "I will find a suitable cousin, just as I was – eventually – found, thanks all the same."

It wasn't until the two nearest groups of people to them had dispersed that she moved closer to Marcia, under the cover of pouring her more tea.

"You know my Head doesn't like you?" Marcia nodded, and Nisha went on. "Well. He can't stop me from being friends with you," she paused, "let me rephrase that. He won't choose, at this point, to prevent a casual friendship. But I absolutely shouldn't be passing information."

"What was all that just now?"

"Social gossip with no hard value, as *well* you know. Don't play coy, Marcia."

Marcia's stomach felt odd, and this time it was nothing to do with the baby. "So what information should you not be passing on?" she asked, pretending calm. This couldn't be about trade, or any of the other things that the Houses treated as dramatic secrets. Nisha wouldn't risk her Head's ire to share anything like that with Marcia. Indeed, Nisha would happily screw Marcia over in a matter of trade or even Council politics. She had done, just after she became Heir, with the Guild vote. And while there had been a certain amount of semi-furtive discontented chatter in recent days about Selene's announcements, Nisha wouldn't come to her over that, either. This was something else. Something personal.

"Your sorcerer lover. The secret's out."

Selene had gone through with it, then. Anxiety spiked in her stomach.

"What sorcerer lover?" she said quickly, automatically, before she'd stopped to think about how she wanted to play this. It was true, even, now; not that that would help much if everyone believed that they *had* been together.

Nisha shook her head. "That won't work. Everyone knows you were seeing *someone* inappropriate, for ages, as well. You even admitted it to me, after you split up."

Shit, Marcia had forgotten that. She'd been just pregnant, hadn't she? "Unless you can produce a wholly different inappropriate lover...?"

Marcia, desperately wondering whether she could in fact do that, and how Andreas would react – had he heard yet? – left slightly too long a gap before replying.

Nisha shook her head. "Didn't think so. A sorcerer, Marcia, really, did you have to? Couldn't you just shag some nice strong fisher lad or lass like the rest of us? Scandalous but not *that* sort of scandalous."

"It's not scandalous," Marcia said, pretending an unconcern she didn't feel.

Nisha shifted onto her side in the water. "It really is, Marcia. People are *very* concerned. Whether or not you and I think they should be." She sounded like she was talking to a child. "The *Council Statutes*, remember?"

"I've never breached the Statutes. I've never done magic, or had it done for me. And I'm not seeing a sorcerer any more. I'm seeing Andreas." Which wasn't even relevant, and also, Nisha already knew.

Nisha rolled her eyes. "Yes, I remember. As does everyone else." She gestured at Marcia's belly. "Unless you make a lot of stink about doctor's appointments everyone's going to assume you did things the easy way." She raised an eyebrow. "Just between you and me, did the magic make a difference, with your sorcerer? A little extra thrill?"

"There's no such thing as magic," Marcia said, and hated herself as she said it. Especially when she'd just denied doing any. She was just as incoherent about this as the rest of them, wasn't she?

"Oh, come on." Nisha sounded affectionately impatient. "We all know Marekhill is just...Marekhill about it. The sorcerers exist, Teren's summoning demons, whatever. The point is, consorting with a sorcerer. Likely to be unpopular."

"Who...?" As if she didn't know.

Nisha rolled her eyes. "Who do you think? Who's just back in town and absolutely hates House Fereno?"

"Selene," Marcia said. At least there wasn't someone else who was *also* out for her blood. She hadn't been sure Selene would go through with it, but it made sense; if she could take Marcia out, not only would she have one fewer opponent, she'd have demonstrated her own power.

"If the sorcerer's gone now," Nisha said thoughtfully, "I suppose you could deny it altogether, past present or future. It'd be your word against Selene's, and I'm not sure it'd make it as far as the Council, in that case, with no proof. I mean, no one's going to haul a sorcerer up in front of the Council, are they?"

It was true enough. She could deny it, the way she had since the start. She could just keep right on lying, about Reb and magic and all of it. But.

"No," she said, slowly. "No. I won't. I'll say that it's over, and I'll say I never used magic, because that is the truth. But I won't deny that it happened."

Nisha looked incredulous. "Marcia. What do you mean, *no*? It's not even like you're letting down your current fling. I mean, even if it was, it wouldn't be worth it. But she's your *ex*."

"I'm not lying about my ex-lover just because of some out-of-date Marekhill nonsense," Marcia said. A great calm had descended upon her. "I won't deny her that way. It may not have lasted, but it was meaningful while it happened."

"Marcia. You're being ridiculous. Of course it was *meaningful*, darling, and it won't be any the less meaningful to you or to her if you just look blank and say it never happened, Selene's making stuff up. Come on. You know better than this. This is politics."

"I'm fed up of lying and pretending." She'd had enough. She had finally had enough. She wasn't going to play this particular game any more. "Like you just said. Everyone knows magic exists. We've been talking for months about Teren and demons. There's charms hanging at the back door of every House on the Hill."

"Servant superstition." Nisha shifted uncomfortably in the water.

"The cityangel's in the story of our founders. It's carved onto the back wall of the Chamber, for goodness' sake. The Statutes *say* we can't engage in magic, which wouldn't matter if it didn't exist. Marekhill's attitude to magic – especially at the moment, with what's going on with Teren – is outdated, incoherent nonsense."

"Fine, yes, it is, but right now..."

"If not now, when?"

"Marcia. You're being ridiculous. *You* don't have to fix this, and you certainly don't have to do it this way. If you're that bothered about Teren, aren't you better off inside the Council, pushing from within? You can't do anything once you've been *disinherited*, can you?"

"I won't be disinherited," Marcia said. "Only Mother can do that. I'll be barred from my House, is what I'll be." Which was in practice the same thing, but right now she was sailing on some kind of soaring feeling of not-caring.

And it had nothing at all to do with having seen Reb again the other week.

"The Statutes," she added, "say nothing about partners, or lovers, or friends, even. They say about magic. Which I didn't do."

Nisha closed her eyes, visibly frustrated. "Marcia. Whether or not you actually did magic may not *matter*, if you admit to being *with* the sorcerer. It's a, a *legalistic* distinction, which not everyone will pay any bloody attention to. And you have no capital right now. Andreas, maybe. That's it. The people who were interested in supporting you over censorship got burned when Madeleine screwed you over – yes, I know, her fault not yours, but they blame you, and you know it. You will be destroyed. You've pushed one too many bloody crusades lately. You're all out. Shut up, deny it, sit tight, live to fight another day."

Marcia thought she might be able to pull on slightly more capital than Nisha thought – she could at least *talk* to Gil and Piath, for starters, they were both fair-minded types who would want to think about the facts of the matter, even if they were annoyed over what Madeleine did – but Nisha wasn't entirely wrong.

That didn't change her mind.

She shrugged. "Turns out, I don't care. I'm willing to fight this one. Maybe you're wrong. Maybe I have more capital than you think."

Nisha shook her head. "Come on."

"*You've* come to warn me," Marcia pointed out.

"Because we've been friends a long time. Doesn't mean my Head will vote for you."

"The Council need to face reality," Marcia said. "And they need to do it now, before Teren takes advantage of this peculiar blind spot we have. Marek is divided, we all know that, right? And this is one of the ways it's divided: that the Houses, the Council, don't recognise one of the great strengths of our city. The magic. The cityangel. Marek, city of magic, that's how we're known to everyone except ourselves. It's absurd. It's been absurd for ages."

"*Yes*," Nisha said. "So how about you let it lie?"

"We need to resolve this. Same as we need to resolve the other divisions, but it turns out, this one is about to become relevant. So we'll start here."

"This is possibly the stupidest thing you've done yet, you know that?"

Marcia shrugged. "Well, it's got plenty of competition. But I refuse to allow this hidebound nonsense to make me choose – or not choose – my partner."

"Your ex-partner."

Marcia waved a dismissive hand. "That's not the point. The point is, the Council needs to deal with the idea of magic. I stood aside when Cato was disowned," she shouldn't have said that; she was revealing too much, "and I won't deny Reb the same way."

"Ugh. No wonder this is your newest crusade, if you've been incubating it since then."

"Not exactly. But – yes, in a way. I suppose I have." Not that Cato would thank her in the slightest for that.

"You going to reinstate your brother while you're at it?"

"Fuck, no. He'd have my guts. Anyway. That wasn't the Council. It was Mother." It would have been the Council, eventually, of course, if Madeleine hadn't done it herself. She'd made exactly the opposite decision to the one Marcia was making now. Though, to be fair, Cato had, in fact, been doing magic, where Marcia had not. She felt herself bare her teeth.

"Fine. Well. There's obviously no stopping you." Nisha sighed.

"No. There isn't. Will you help me?"

"No!" Nisha looked over at her, then pulled a face. "No. Yes. Maybe. Not overtly. But if there's anything I can pass onto you, *safely*, then fine, yes, I will."

"Thank you," Marcia said, genuinely. "And thank you for the warning."

"Eh, it would have reached your ears soon enough. Selene isn't being *terribly* subtle."

"Still." Marcia reached for the teapot and topped up both of their cups. "We should stay a little longer, for your cover to work."

"All right. But I'm going to need something a *lot* stronger." Nisha signalled for one of the attendants, and two small glasses of spirits replaced the tea within a few moments.

"One won't hurt you. I insist." She raised her glass. "To your latest bloody stupid idea."

"Thanks," Marcia said, and drank.

☉ ☉

In theory it might be unsurprising that Beckett, cityangel of Marek, would turn up while one was peacefully practising magic with one's apprentice. After all, it was Beckett who mediated the power on which one was calling.

In practice, Cato reflected as he tried to pretend calm, it was inevitably a surprising experience. And not one that ever used to happen. Not for the first time, he cursed Daril and Urso for their stupid bloody idea, the consequences of which had included Beckett's new willingness to spend time on the human plane.

It wasn't *his* fault, even if he had been…tangentially involved. He'd helped in the end, hadn't he?

Beckett was not happy.

"CATO," they roared.

"Hello," Cato said, with the best impression he could manage of a relaxed grin. He refused to let himself flinch. "How can I help? Ah, Jonas, maybe put that pot down, yes? We'll take a break."

He didn't spare a glance to check that Jonas had done what he was told. He didn't dare take his eyes off Beckett.

Incandescent with rage was usually an exaggeration. In Beckett's case, it was rather closer to the truth. Cato couldn't *actually* feel heat coming off them, but there was a faint glow around their tall pale face, and although Beckett struggled with human expressions, Cato was in little doubt about their current emotions.

Beckett was very, very angry.

"You invited a *spirit* into *my city*," Beckett said. "My. City."

Oh shit. Yorick must have done their thing – Cato had handed the ball over the day before, the morning after concluding the 'evening at the theatre' part of the arrangement – and Beckett had noticed.

"No, I did not," Cato contradicted them. He had to lay out his position clearly, and quickly. "Yorick has never, technically, been in Marek."

"Nonsense." Beckett's eyes were difficult to look at.

"They were in a space kind of *between* here and there. That's the whole point of that spell. Which, I might remind you, I have done before, without any complaint from you."

Beckett ignored that. "And then that spirit *stole* my power."

"Not *your power*," Cato argued. "They took one tiny little piece of life-force. The human didn't even die!" At least, that was the plan, so hopefully Yorick had stuck to it. "It can't possibly have affected your power!"

"It's mine," Beckett said, stubborn and furious. "My city, my life-force, my domain, and I will not *tolerate* other spirits."

"They weren't *here*," Cato said again.

It was something of a loophole, he was happy to acknowledge that. But he'd been using the trick for years – he'd been very pleased with himself when he discovered it – and he didn't see why Beckett was going off into the river-depths about it now.

"They were here *enough*," Beckett said. "You go against my wishes. My express wishes." Their voice had deepened, shaking Cato's bones.

"I don't!" Cato said. He tasted sudden fear at the back of his throat. "You've always tolerated this before. I even mentioned it, a few months back."

"And I said I could close that loophole," Beckett said.

Beckett was right. Cato remembered that previous conversation well. But he was *buggered* if he was going to put his hands up to this without a fight. The occasional spirit intervention was the best-paid thing he did, and far and away the easiest.

"But you didn't," he countered. "Why complain now?"

"I did not *feel* it, before," Beckett hissed.

"You weren't paying enough attention," Cato diagnosed. It was the first time he'd done this since Beckett started being Beckett, in the current sense. It made sense, sort of. Beckett was, Cato was fairly sure, paying more direct attention these days. He spread his hands. "Is that my fault?"

"You will cease," Beckett decreed. "Or I will withdraw my cooperation."

Shit. There it was. Cato's stomach swooped sickly. "Reb won't have that. And you're bound by your covenant. Remember?"

And Reb would – he hoped – be raging that Beckett had brought it up again. Fuck, he hoped this wasn't going to happen every time Beckett got pissed off.

Beckett, furious or not, paused briefly at that. "You will

stop," they said again, after a moment of silence. "You will *not* do this again."

Cato bit his lip. "You're being unreasonable." He would *not* let Beckett push him around. "I'm not just going to agree to whatever you demand."

"I am the *cityangel*," Beckett hissed. "This is *my* magic."

On the other side of the room, Jonas cleared his throat.

Which was, Cato had to admit, brave of him. Given the choice, he, personally, would be out of the room already, leaving Beckett to rant until they calmed down. If they calmed down. Jonas, instead, was putting his oar in.

Brave or not, it wouldn't necessarily be *helpful*.

Both Cato and Beckett stared at Jonas now. Jonas, perched on the chair and looking a little pale under the tan that a Marek winter hadn't quite lost him, arm still in its sling across his chest, did his best to smile at both of them. "Honoured Beckett. Cato. It seems you have a disagreement."

"Well, yeah," Cato said. Beckett just hissed.

"Which it seems you may be struggling to resolve," Jonas went on gamely. "On board a ship, or if captains differ, we Salinas have a process for this. Between, you understand, people of similar status."

"I am the *cityangel*," Beckett said again.

"And I'm a sorcerer of Marek," Cato said, "and there is a covenant."

"Which you are breaching," Beckett said.

"I am not."

"My point is," Jonas said, loudly, "honoured ones, that another point of view might help to resolve this matter."

"You're suggesting yourself?" Cato said, letting his doubt show in his voice.

"An apprentice?" Jonas sounded horrified, then controlled his voice. "No, of course not. I thought of Reb."

Ugh. It was a good idea. Cato couldn't deny it. Reb was the only other full sorcerer in Marek; the only other person fully bound by the covenant Beckett had made at the founding of the city. (Arguably, of course, everyone in the city was *bound* by it – Beckett was taxing their life force, after all, albeit only what they used up in the course of living anyway – but it was only sorcerers who knew of it.) And she was the other member of the Group, which oversaw magic in Marek.

On the other hand, she didn't approve of Cato working with spirits.

On the other other hand, he didn't have any better options. At the very least, Reb would – hopefully, surely – stop Beckett from withdrawing their power. As long as she agreed that he wasn't in breach. Which he *wasn't*. His mouth tasted sour.

"Very well," Cato said, before Beckett could speak. At least he could have the upper hand for a brief moment.

"Reb," Beckett said. "Reb will understand."

Cato forced himself to smile. "Well then," he said. "We may as well go now."

"Shouldn't you…send a message, first?" Jonas said, hesitantly. "She might be…busy."

For a second, Beckett looked even blanker than usual. "She is not busy," they said, flatly, and Cato suppressed a shiver. It wasn't that he didn't already *know* that Beckett could tell what was happening in Marek – even if they didn't do it all that often, as far as Cato could tell, presumably because even for a spirit that would be too much information all at once. It was just that he tried not to think of it.

"We can go immediately," Beckett said, with finality, and disappeared.

"*Fuck*," Cato said with feeling.

"Have they just…" Jonas' eyes were wide. "Reb's going to be raging."

"Dunno," Cato said. "They might just be waiting to show up once I'm there. They might be at Reb's already giving her their side." In which case Reb would indeed be somewhat annoyed at the unheralded incursion.

Jonas was shifting from foot to foot. "Would it be useful if I went ahead? In case Beckett's not already there."

"Or isn't being clear. Yes, I suppose so," Cato said. Jonas was a messenger; undoubtedly he could get there faster than Cato. "Off you go. See you there."

Jonas was clattering down the stairs before Cato could blink. Cato drew his drapes against the cold air, double-checked his wards, and set off to Reb's. He slammed the door behind him, hard, and swore loudly all the way down the stairs. Neither of which assuaged his fury and frustration.

☉ ☉

Serendipitously, Cato encountered Tait halfway down the street.

"Cato? What are you doing here?" Tait's transparent delight – balm to Cato's soul, even when he was this irritable – transformed into concern when they got a good look at Cato's face. "What's wrong?"

"Summoned that spirit," Cato said, cutting straight to the point. "Beckett went off out to sea. Jonas suggested we take the argument to Reb."

"Well, given Beckett won't have other spirits in Marek..." Tait said slowly. Cato ground his teeth, resentment surging.

"It wasn't *in* Marek. That's the whole point. And I've done it *before*. Anyway. I can't stand here chatting. Beckett's already at Reb's threatening to cut me off."

"Shall I come with you?"

"What for?"

"Because you're my partner, and I want to support you," Tait said, simply, which left a weird hole-like feeling in Cato's chest.

"Didn't sound all that supportive just now," Cato muttered, but Tait either didn't hear that, or chose to ignore it.

"Also, this is sorcerer business, isn't it? And I'm a Marek sorcerer. Apprentice, anyway." They frowned. "Though I suppose Jonas..."

"Jonas was there when this all kicked off. He went

ahead to tell Reb I'm on my way. Given that Beckett just," Cato snapped his fingers, "*disappeared*."

"You can't really want Beckett wandering the streets with you," Tait said reasonably. True, but Cato wasn't feeling reasonable. "Anyway. If Jonas is there, I can be too."

"Reb might kick both of you out."

"Then I'll say goodbye politely and leave," Tait said. "Don't worry, I've more common sense than to upset Reb."

Cato twitched a smile, somewhat against his will. "If you're sure…"

"Unless you'd rather I didn't."

It took him a moment to admit it out loud, but Cato finally managed to say, "I'd rather you did. If you want."

"Well then," Tait said, and tucked their hand through Cato's arm. "Let's go."

Tait's presence next to Cato was deeply reassuring. By the time the two of them reached Reb's street ten minutes later, Cato felt like he might even be able to cope with this.

That feeling didn't survive seeing Beckett again.

The only potential bright spot was that Reb, standing in the middle of the room, arms folded, did not look impressed. Beckett was a few feet from Reb, leaking magic to the point that it made Cato's brain hurt. Jonas stood against the wall on one side of the room, shifting anxiously from foot to foot.

That discussion he and Reb had, after the floods. Was she going to hold that against him now? He'd been right, though, and Reb knew it. And there'd been a point, there, where it had felt like…they were actually listening to one another. For once.

"Cato," Reb said. "And Tait. What are you doing here?"

"Observing," Tait said. "We are," they gestured around the room, "the sorcerers of Marek, are we not?"

"You two," Reb said, "are still apprentices."

Cato heard Jonas mutter something under his breath

which sounded a lot like 'happy to leave', but Reb, if she heard, ignored him.

"I'm sure neither Jonas nor I have any intention of interfering," Tait said. "But if this is a matter of Marek sorcery, are we not entitled to hear it?"

"Fine," Reb said grudgingly. "But keep out of the way and keep your mouth shut."

For a moment, Cato thought Tait might suggest summoning Alyssa, and he wasn't sure he could cope with waiting in a room with Beckett like this for however long it took to find her. But Tait just gave Cato's hand a squeeze and went to lean against the wall by Jonas. They looked a lot more relaxed than Jonas did, which was nice. Apprenticed to Reb, Cato supposed they must be getting the hang of dealing with her. He hadn't asked yet whether they'd been taught anything more useful since the flood.

"Well then."

Cato pulled his attention back to Reb. She crossed the room, dropped down heavily into her patched armchair, and gestured at the other armchair and a wooden spindle-legged stool close to it.

"Perhaps this would go more smoothly if we sat down in a civilised fashion, rather than standing around glaring at one another."

Cato did his best to smile at her – Reb returned his gaze without shifting her expression – and did as he was told.

"I do not *sit*," Beckett said, without moving. They were still leaking magic.

"As you prefer," Reb said. "But do please come over where it's easier to see you. And, uh," she hesitated. She wasn't looking directly at Beckett either.

"You're leaking magic," Cato said, helpfully.

Beckett glared, but the blaze of power subsided.

"So," Reb said. "Cato. Beckett tells me you brought a spirit into Marek."

"I did no such thing," Cato said. "I created a space between that plane and this, and I engaged with the spirit solely in that space. It has never come anywhere near Marek. I've done this countless times before and it's never been a problem."

"You have a *thing*," Beckett said.

"Yes," Cato agreed. "And that doesn't change matters. The spirit remains outside Marek, on this plane; and Marek doesn't exist, on the other plane, so it can't be there."

"It *acts* in this plane," Beckett said.

"Also no," Cato contradicted them. He was on safer ground now that Beckett was asking about facts, rather than just spitting emotional fury. "When released, it creates a bubble of between-space. That's where the action happens."

"It *stole* life-force."

"Whose life-force?" Reb asked.

"Whoever it was used on," Cato said.

"What?" Reb's eyes narrowed. Cato, trying not to shift in his seat, explained the gist of the job he'd provided the spirit for.

"So," Reb said, "you've brought a spirit to Marek to hurt someone. And previously, on other occasions, to kill."

Cato had hoped she wouldn't register that part. "Not *to* Marek," he corrected, sticking to the facts. "The someone, rather, is brought to the spirit. Leaves Marek."

"And you're fine with that?"

"Do you go and tell the Smiths and Cutlers off for making swords? Nothing you use a sword for other than killing someone, is there? It's not *my* fault."

"It's my life-force," Beckett insisted.

"I don't see you complaining when someone walks out of the city and drops dead in the barge-yard," Cato said. "And, to reiterate, this time it was only a tiny bit anyway. No harm done."

"Another spirit takes *my* life-force," Beckett said again. "I don't like it."

"I accept that you don't like it," Reb said. "But are you claiming that it's a breach of the covenant?"

"The spirit comes into the city," Beckett said, sounding almost sulky.

"You say it doesn't," Reb said to Cato. Her eyes were narrowed.

"Categorically not."

She chewed at her lip. "Can you create this space in-between without actually summoning a spirit?"

"I don't exactly summon them," Cato said. "I just open the space up and wait for one to come visiting."

"But if you closed it quickly, it probably wouldn't attract a spirit immediately?"

"Usually takes a few minutes," Cato agreed.

"Very well," Reb said. "If you step into my workroom, you can see if I have the correct ingredients, and you can create this space of yours. Beckett, do you wish to observe as well? Jonas and Tait, stay here."

Beckett hissed again, but when Reb stood up to open her workroom door, the cityangel came with Reb and Cato.

It was one of the more uncomfortable magical experiences of Cato's life, creating the interstitial space with Reb watching intently and Beckett glowering; especially when it came to drawing down the magic. For a horrifying moment, he thought it wouldn't work, that Beckett was fulfilling their threat of keeping magic from him; then Reb said, very firmly, *"Beckett,"* and the power was suddenly there, a cool flow.

"Hm," Reb said, once it was open. "If you close it down, can you do it again with me inside it?"

"Fine," Cato said, through his teeth. His back was tight and his muscles ached with tension; this was difficult, and he didn't normally do it with a furious cityangel a few feet away. He closed the space down, and shook his fingers out.

"Are you sure?" Reb asked. Her eyes flicked to his fingers, which he was positive were not shaking. "If you're tired…"

"It's fine," he said. "I can do it."

He made himself take long, slow, breaths through the repeat. He'd never done this with another human in the circle; but there was no reason it should be a problem.

The energies felt slightly different, true, the balance was altered, but he could manage them, he could…

Reb, inside the bubble of space, grabbed his shoulder, and he felt the touch of her magic, the way he had outside Marek against that damn Teren idiot, and during the floods. "Close it down," she said quietly, and he made himself pull on her magic.

"Next time I say 'can you?' and you're not sure, how about you say as much," she said, once they were safely back in their own plane, but her voice was level. She sounded, even…not sympathetic, no. But something.

Cato shrugged. "Didn't think you'd have asked if you didn't need it." And he'd thought he could manage. He'd *assumed* he could. The way he had through his entire magical career and he'd always gotten away with it; which, *fine*, might be more about good luck than good judgement.

"Come on," Reb said, and led them back to the main room.

Beckett, behind them, hadn't spoken.

Reb locked the workshop behind her, an automatic practised gesture, and went to the tiny kitchen that stood against the far wall while Cato sank thankfully into the armchair. She came back with a handful of nuts, and tipped them into Cato's lap. He considered refusing, but it would be stupid. She was right; he ought to eat. Cracking the first kernel between his teeth, he felt immediately better. Tait looked worried; Cato did his best to smile reassuringly. He wasn't sure it landed.

"Well then," Reb said. "To recap. Beckett argued that Cato brought a spirit into the city. Cato argued was that the spirit was never in the city. Having seen the bubble in question, my ruling is that Cato is correct."

"You dare…" Beckett said, taking a step forward. They were glowing again. Not the best of news.

"You asked me to rule. That is my ruling." Reb had her arms folded again. Her shoulders were tense, but her face was set calm.

"I need not abide by this."

"True, I suppose. But there is a contract, a covenant. Marek is yours. Other spirits may not come into it, nor take power from its citizens, whilst they are in Marek. I accept that is the deal you made at the founding of the city. But Cato is correct that when those citizens are outside, it doesn't apply. Pulling someone into another dimension is no different, conceptually speaking, from dragging them over the city border. It might or might not be *legal* – none of us are, I assume, interested in that." Her eyes flicked to Cato for a moment, and Cato showed his teeth at her. "But it does not breach the covenant."

"I could choose…"

"*You* could choose to breach it yourself, yes," Reb said. "Are you sure you want to do that? I will remind you that Cato is a sorcerer of Marek in good standing. And this is the second time I've heard you make that threat, and I don't like it."

"You cannot do anything to me," Beckett said.

"No," Reb agreed. "But I would really prefer not to be on poor terms. You're concerned about Marek's magic, and Marek's sorcerers. Damaging the relationship between us doesn't seem like the best way of going about that."

Beckett disappeared.

Reb shut her eyes for a moment, and let out a long breath. "Fuck. I should never have gotten out of bed today."

Reb didn't usually swear. Common sense suggested Cato should keep his mouth shut, but that was hardly likely. "Thank you," he said, and once she'd reopened her eyes, gave her a florid bow.

"Shut up," Reb said. "I didn't do it as a favour to you. I did it because it's correct. And that's a very interesting piece of magic…" Her voice had altered; she shook her head. "That's not the point. The point is, could you maybe *not*?"

"I'm not doing anything wrong!" Cato protested. "I've been doing this for *years* and this is the first time there's been a problem."

"Because Beckett wasn't paying that much attention before, were they? This is the first time you've done it since…"

"It's very effective."

"And yet, perhaps, antagonising the cityangel is not the best way to approach your magic?" Tait suggested from the sidelines.

"It's not a breach of the covenant. No other spirits are in the city," Cato repeated stubbornly.

"The letter of the law isn't the most collaborative approach you could take," Tait said gently.

Cato tried not to feel betrayed. "I'm not the one threatening to withdraw cooperation."

"I looked into it, you know," Reb said abruptly. "After the last time Beckett threatened you. They can't. They're bound to the terms they agreed, when the city was founded, and that would break those terms. I don't know what would happen, to be honest, but it's possible that the link would just…snap. I don't think Beckett wants that any more than the rest of us."

"Fucksake, losing the cityangel *again* would be a bit bloody awkward, yes."

Reb didn't say anything, just raised an eyebrow that reminded both of them – and Jonas – exactly who had, and who had not, been involved in that particular disaster. Cato coughed and hurried on.

"The point is. Tait is correct. Not antagonising the cityangel seems like a wise move. If you insist on providing methods for members of the criminal underworld to execute one another," it was years since the last of those, but Cato wasn't going to go there right now, "can't you find ones that don't involve other spirits?"

"That's not the only thing I do with spirits," Cato protested.

Reb shrugged. "Still."

Beckett reappeared in the centre of the room. Cato almost swallowed his tongue, and took only a small amount of consolation from the fact that the other three all jumped too. Shit. What now?

"I apologise," Beckett said, to Cato's great surprise. "I would not breach my covenant. I accept that Cato did not breach it, either. I do not *like* it. But I would not fail in my duty." Very stiffly and awkwardly, they bowed towards Cato, a slight inflection of the upper body. "I should not have said that I might."

"Uh," Cato said again. "That's...okay?" He *really* didn't want to say the next thing, but he knew what negotiations looked like, and he did, in fact, know how to build good working relationships, and Reb was going to kill him if he didn't take his own step forwards. "I regret having caused you distress. Would you prefer it," the words came out slowly, because he didn't want to say them, "if I did not make such arrangements again?"

"I wonder," Tait put in delicately, "if there is perhaps a compromise?"

Everyone turned to look at them. They flushed.

"Go on," Reb invited.

"There seem to me to be two issues that concern Beckett. The first is the matter of a spirit being in Marek; which Reb confirms is not, in fact, the case, with this particular piece of magic. The second is that of the spirit taking life-force from a Marek citizen. My understanding is that that is not the only sort of, uh, arrangement, that you have made with other spirits?" They turned to Cato.

"Yeah," Cato said. "There's other things they're useful for, that's true."

"So. Perhaps, would a suitable compromise be that Cato will continue to perform this kind of work, but avoid the cases where life-force is taken?"

That would put a serious crimp on some of Cato's more lucrative client-work. On the other hand, it would move him further from some of his more alarming clients, which might not be entirely to the bad; and whilst it was none of his business who wanted to kill or otherwise damage whom, it would be marginally more comfortable if he wasn't helping any of them. However well they paid.

"That'll be bad for business," he said, not wanting to bend too fast; then, as both Tait and Reb glared at him, "but fine, I can accept that. If Beckett is happier that way."

"Yes," Beckett said. "That would satisfy me." Cato wished that Beckett sounded more appreciative of the sacrifice he, Cato, was making, but that was a bit of a lost cause.

"Thank you for the suggestion, Tait," Reb said, her shoulders relaxing in visible relief. "And for your cooperation, Cato and Beckett."

Beckett nodded stiffly, bowed again, this time to no one in particular, and disappeared, leaving an afterimage of magic behind them.

"I'm going. Work," Jonas said to the room at large, and bolted.

"You should go," Reb said. "I have work to do, as well. Tait, you were due a lesson today?"

"Yes," Tait said. "But..." They glanced over at Cato.

"Let's defer it," Reb said. "I have things to do, and I'm bloody knackered. Get out, both of you."

"Lovely talking to you, as ever," Cato said, and left with haste.

Out in the street, Tait took his arm again.

"I should thank you for that idea, I suppose," Cato said, aware that he sounded disgruntled.

"Don't worry," Tait said. "I don't expect you to thank me for stopping you from doing something you get paid for." They smiled slightly sideways at him. "But you can't expect me not to be pleased that you're not involved in money for harm, and people being eaten by spirits."

"Trust me, no one's particularly going to miss any of the folk that had that happen to 'em," Cato said. "And in any case. It hasn't been anything that bad for *years*."

Tait shrugged. "Everyone has people that care about them."

"You are too positive by half," Cato said. "But I take your point." He might even accept – quietly, to himself – that there was some value to it. "I won't thank you, and I won't grumble that you're pleased either, how about that?"

"Sounds reasonable," Tait said. "Meanwhile, I could really, really use some noodles. Lunch?"

"Lunch."

TWENTY-ONE

Marcia had sent Reb a message, asking to come over. Once, of course, she wouldn't have bothered with the message. Things were different, now, but – maybe less unpleasantly so than they had been. Maybe she and Marcia could be friends, although she wasn't sure a sorcerer friend was any more acceptable for Fereno-Heir than a sorcerer lover.

In any case. She'd said of course Marcia could visit. She might still be exhausted from all the business with Beckett and Marcia's wretched brother (not that one could hold Marcia responsible for Cato), but she could hardly have said no given that she undoubtedly owed her for rescuing Alyssa. Even Alyssa, once she'd calmed down, had given Reb grudging thanks, though mostly, Reb suspected, for her daughter's sake.

Not that Marcia had made it feel like *owing*. Marcia hadn't asked anything of her. Or of Alyssa. She'd just – helped.

She didn't know what Marcia could want to discuss this time. Part of her hoped it was just an excuse; that Marcia just wanted to see her. But that was a foolish, dangerous, absurd idea…

…which she forgot all about when her table collapsed under the two mugs of infusion she'd just put on it.

When the knock came on the door, Reb was in the middle of mopping up hot water and swearing: not quite the scene she'd envisaged inviting Marcia into.

"Oh, dear," Marcia said. She came in, moving awkwardly – she was about halfway through her pregnancy now, though if you didn't know her well, her bump wasn't obvious under a loose tunic – and surveyed the damage. "What happened?"

"Apparently two mugs were too much for it," Reb said,

gesturing at the remains of the table.

"Well," Marcia said, judiciously, "it's been about to breathe its last for a good while now. Uh. Can I help?"

Reb shook her head. "I'm just about cleared up here. I'm not sure the table can be fixed, but either way it can wait." She squatted back down to mop up the last of the puddle. "You should sit down," she added.

"Thank you," Marcia said fervently, and sank into the blue armchair. "Cato uses magic for this sort of thing. The clearing up, and the mending, both."

"That's because Cato's lazy," Reb said, then sat back on her heels and reconsidered. "No, that's not fair. Doing it by magic uses energy too, just a different sort."

"Cato, like me, probably doesn't know how to do it by hand," Marcia said.

"Nonsense," Reb said. "Anyone can operate a floor-cloth. If you weren't quite so pregnant, I'd insist you give yourself the lie."

Marcia had leant over, and was squinting at the table. "Actually, this can be repaired, I think. There's only one joint that really looks smashed."

"You're a carpenter now, are you?" Reb teased, going to dump the cloth into the bucket by the kitchen-stand; then wondered if she'd gone too far.

But Marcia didn't seem to have taken offence. "I was sweet on the carpenter's apprentice, when I was about thirteen," she confessed, looking a bit pink. "The carpenter brought us new dining-furniture, and spent a week or so out back in the yard repairing all the old kitchen furniture. I hung around a bit. I saw her – the apprentice, Tara, her name was – replacing that sort of joint several times."

"Oh, well, I'll take it up the road, then," Reb said. "For a moment there I thought you might say you could do it yourself."

"Goodness, no. I've no useful skills at all."

"I don't know," Reb said mildly. "You do a lot of things that are useful. Practical skills, those maybe you lack." She sat down and decided reluctantly that she should probably move Marcia onto the main subject of the conversation, whatever that was going to turn out to be. "You said you had something you wanted to talk about?"

Marcia sighed, her shoulders slumping. "Yes."

"Nothing with the baby…?"

"Baby's fine. As far as I know. So am I, physically."

"I'm hearing a 'but' in that sentence," Reb said.

"Selene told everyone I'm involved with a sorcerer," Marcia said.

Reb blinked at her. "Right. But. You're, uh. Not."

"No. Sadly, I don't think the timing will be that important a detail, to the Council."

Reb looked down at her hands, unsure how to feel. "Well," she said. "Can't you just – deny it all? Say you'd never dream of such a thing – or if Selene insists she has evidence, blame me?"

Marcia looked irritable. "Of course I'm not going to blame you," she said. "I'm hardly going to just…throw you off Old Bridge like that. *Nor* am I going to deny you."

Reb lifted a shoulder. "If it gets you out of trouble. It's the obvious solution, isn't it?"

"Have you been talking to Nisha?"

"Who's Nisha?"

"The friend who warned me Selene is spreading this."

"No, I haven't been talking to random Marekhill folk," Reb said. "It's just the obvious solution. As demonstrated by the fact that both your Nisha and I thought of it."

"I don't care," Marcia folded her arms. "I am not denying everything we ever shared just because the Council are a bunch of hidebound idiots who are scared to admit that they believe in magic and just as scared *of* magic. I will *not*. I am not ashamed of our relationship."

Which was news to Reb, given how much time they'd spent keeping it out of sight. Perhaps that was unfair. Marcia hadn't *hidden*, had she? She'd just kept it private. Perhaps that was different.

"And then the Council will cause a great deal of trouble for you," she said patiently. "Which you could avoid."

"By lying. Which," Marcia paused, obviously

rethinking what she was about to say. "Which, fine, I might be willing to do in some circumstances. But not in this one. I have not broken the Statutes. I haven't done magic, and I haven't had magic done for me." She swallowed. "I lied to you. Which I still deeply regret. I won't lie *about* you."

Hearing that gave Reb a shock under her ribs. That Marcia was choosing honesty about her, about what they'd shared. It was – a feeling she really couldn't handle right now. She took a breath, getting herself under control, and looked dubiously at Marcia. "And what is Selene going to say about that? She was at the barge-yard."

Marcia raised an eyebrow. "Which she can't admit without also having to admit what she was doing. Of course, the same goes for me in the other direction.

"Anyway. She can't talk publicly about her presence there, and the only other eye-witness on her side was that sorcerer, who can't be here, because of the demon."

Reb shook her head. "Not true. I mean, most likely he isn't here. But that demon went back, if you recall. And if he hasn't another bound, he could cross into the city without any problem at all."

"Huh. Well. Not much I can do if he crops up other than to deny any involvement. I wasn't part of it. Not really."

"No-o. It's a narrow division though. I'm guessing none of the sorcerers could be called on your side?"

Marcia pursed her lips. "Well, if they call him, I don't see that I couldn't call you, or Cato, or Jonas."

"I'm your lover. Cato's your brother. Jonas is Salinas. A decent lawyer would rip all of us apart."

Marcia screwed up her nose, then made a flicking gesture with her fingers. "Anyway. This isn't actually your problem. I just – thought I ought to tell you. Before," she paused, looking apologetic, "uh, it hits the news-sheets. Which I suspect it will, even if the Council dismiss it out of hand."

"Might they do that?"

Marcia shook her head. "No chance. I've too many enemies, just now."

"Look," Reb said. "Are you absolutely sure that you shouldn't just…deny everything? Pretend it never happened?"

"Yes, I am sure." Marcia's voice was absolute; Reb still wasn't going to engage with her feelings about that. "I won't deny you. But it's not just about that. I won't do what Selene wants."

"Which is?"

"To support her. In exchange for keeping this out of Council. She wants to bring Marek back under Teren control. I won't do it."

"Fine," Reb said, "but you can let her bring it to Council and then just *say you didn't do it*."

"Well, that is what I'll say about the magic. Just not about our relationship. I'm not going to lie."

Reb felt that shock under her ribs again at *our relationship*. Which was over. The fact that Marcia wasn't going to lie about its previous existence shouldn't matter to her one way or the other.

"And the other thing," Marcia went on, "besides the fact that Selene can go fuck herself, is that the Council needs to engage with magic. They have to. They can't just keep pretending none of it's real. So. This is the opportunity to make them engage."

"Alternatively," Reb pointed out, "they'll kick you out."

"For engaging in magic, which they don't believe in," Marcia said. "Yes. That might happen. I don't think it will, but…The thing is, even if they do that. Either way. They have to think about it. They can't just pretend none of it's happening. We can't keep ignoring this. Teren is moving already. It's politics, now, but the demons will follow behind, judging by what's already happening in Ameten."

"And what can we do if that happens? Fight?" Reb knew her horror was showing on her face.

"That's the point, isn't it?" Marcia looked tired. "I don't want that. I can't see how it would work. But Beckett…"

"Can't stand up to a whole horde of demons, can they," Reb said bluntly. "One was bad enough."

Marcia shrugged helplessly. "But without Beckett it's even worse. I've said before that the Council needs to stop ignoring half the city. That includes the sorcerers."

"I'm still not getting involved in politics," Reb said. "Not in the sense of having anything to do with the Council, anyway."

"Define 'anything to do with'. I'm not going to ask you again to take a seat, don't worry. Even if that ship would sail, which it won't. But…why shouldn't the Council be willing to engage with your Group?"

"Other than, because they don't believe in magic?"

Marcia made an impatient movement. "They do believe in it, they just can't admit it. But yes, other than that, because if they take this accusation against me seriously, they have to admit that it matters, and therefore that sorcery is real. Or I *can't* have done anything."

Reb sucked air thoughtfully through her teeth. "That is a good point."

"Everyone's talking about Teren demons now, too. So – why shouldn't the Council liaise with you?"

"Sounds to me like you're getting beyond the initial problem, which would be the bit where you're about to be brought in front of the Council to be kicked out of it."

"I need to deal with all of it at once, that's the trouble," Marcia said. She rubbed at her eyes. "I can't…it feels like *string*, I need to pull it together properly. But I think it matters. And it feels like an opportunity."

"Well, I'm glad to be an opportunity," Reb said, very dry, but she felt a corner of her mouth tick up.

Marcia smiled at her, her expression wry. "I'm sorry. To bring you into it."

Reb shrugged. "Not like I didn't know you were a House-Heir when we first…well. Can't really complain if it comes back to bite me, can I?"

"I don't know," Marcia said. "I complain all the time, and I was born to it." She sighed, and heaved herself up out of her seat. "Anyway. I should leave you to it. Taken up enough of your time already."

"At least tell me you'll take a litter up the cliff," Reb said, somewhat against her better judgement.

"Don't worry," Marcia said ruefully. "I got one down, too. My pelvis feels like someone's shoving knives through it every time I take a step. I'll make it down to the ferry but that's my limit."

Reb stood in the door to watch her go, and had no idea what to think.

It was obvious at the next event Marcia went to, at House Tabriol, that rumours were spreading. People turned to look at her; cast their eyes sideways; muttered comments in corners. No one was quite willing to cut her, if she went up to them; no one was willing to begin a conversation either. Marcia chose to find it interesting, the way people were behaving, rather than to sit down in the middle of House Tabriol's reception-room and scream.

She had an utterly bland conversation with Selene, who wore an infuriating smirk throughout. But Marcia hadn't spent this long in politics without learning how to keep her feelings under wraps, whatever Madeleine might occasionally claim to the contrary.

Madeleine. Should she send word to Madeleine? If she didn't, someone else would. She couldn't work out which would be worse.

Halfway through the evening, Andreas came up to her. He too was wearing a polite society smile, and to anyone watching, would have seemed wholly delighted to see her, but close up, she could see the tightness around his eyes, covered by his face-paint.

"I'm hearing some concerning things," he said, halfway through the conversation, without changing his tone or his casual, laughing demeanour. "Let's not discuss it now, but may I come to visit you tomorrow?"

It didn't have the ring of a request. Which, in the

circumstances, was fair enough. What did the child-contract say about Marcia breaking the law?

"Of course," she said, smiling back at him, aware of the tension in her own back and neck. "Tomorrow mid-morning, perhaps?"

She stuck it out another hour before she left, hand on her bump, saying something in passing to Isobel, Tabriol-Heir about the tiring nature of pregnancy. Isobel, either one of the few people who hadn't yet heard the gossip, or a better actor than most, solicitously escorted her out and waited with her until the servants had brought up a litter. In the general case, Marcia preferred to walk, but she was tired, and her bump hurt.

"There are some nasty rumours spreading about you," Isobel said, just as she handed Marcia into the litter. "I am sure…well. I would look to your reputation, if I were you." She looked genuinely worried. Marcia felt a little guilty; Isobel obviously thought it was all lies.

"Thank you for the warning," she said, sincerely. "I'll look to it tomorrow. I do appreciate you letting me know."

"Well, I thought it would all just die down, but…Anyway. You look after yourself, my dear."

Marcia didn't sleep well. This was going to become a Council matter very soon, and she almost wished it would get on and happen. The wait was worse than the thing itself. Maybe.

It was just as well that Cousin Cara kept her busy between breakfast and Andreas' arrival. Cara, to Marcia's deep surprise, had declined the opportunity to go to Teren with Madeleine, refusing to abandon the household to anyone else, "especially with dear Marcia in her condition". Madeleine had taken another distant cousin instead. This morning, Cara first had assorted matters of household management to discuss – which Cara could happily deal with herself, but felt the need to confirm with Marcia – and then of baby clothes, and the blanket she was knitting. Marcia had the sudden jolting realisation, looking at the neat shelf in the press, that these were *clothes*, real clothes, for someone who was currently in her belly but was all too soon going to be a real person, out in the world. She knew all that, obviously, and yet, holding a tiny linen smock in her hand, it felt real in a way it hadn't quite before.

Andreas was, as ever, exactly on time. They went through the ritual of greetings, of Andreas' enquiries after her health and the baby's wellbeing, of infusions and cakes being brought, before the servants bowed themselves out again and Andreas and Marcia settled on the couches. Andreas took the other couch, rather than sitting on the same one as Marcia, for her to lean against him.

"So," Marcia said. No point in waiting. "Rumours, you said."

Andreas looked extremely awkward. "I don't…Of course, it's not that I *believe* it. But it's said that you have a, a sorcerer lover. That you've been seen together. That you've," he winced, "taken part in her magic. As I say. I'm sure it's vile calumny, but I felt you should know."

"It's not," Marcia said, bluntly. "Vile calumny, I mean. Apart from the bit about taking part in magic. I haven't done that. I'm not a sorcerer."

That was…mostly true. She had been *adjacent* to magic, more than once, but only ever as a resource – grounding Reb, or acting as a link back to the city – rather than technically, herself, performing magic. She was aware that the distinction was paper-thin, but it *was* a distinction.

Selene, who was the source of all of this, had seen her, the second time. On the other hand, at the time Selene had been attacking Marek with a demon, so.

Andreas' eyes widened. "What."

Marcia sighed. "Reb and I were together for getting on for a year. Reb is a sorcerer. One of only two left. The other, as I'm sure you're aware, being my brother. Well, and there's some apprentices now, but…Anyway. That's not important." She paused. "The relationship was over before we became involved, if you were wondering about that."

"I am sure you would have told me if you were in a relationship already," Andreas said, which was at least the correct thing to say, even if she wasn't wholly sure he believed it. "But…Marcia. Sorcery. It's against the Statutes."

Marcia sat up as straight as she could, given her aching hips, and shook her head firmly. "Nothing I have done is against the Statutes. I am forbidden to engage in magic – which I have not done – or to engage someone to perform magic for me – which I have not done. It says nothing about social relations with a sorcerer, whether, ah, physical or otherwise."

"No one is going to believe you," Andreas said, bluntly, sitting back. "I'm not sure I do."

"That I haven't engaged in magic myself, you mean?" She sighed. "How to prove a negative?"

"If you haven't done anything untoward, why did you hide the relationship?"

"Why do you think? For exactly this reason. Because I knew it would create drama and difficulty if anyone found out. Because it would damage my relationships within the Council, given the way the Council feels about magic. And, bluntly, because it wasn't anyone else's business."

"It is now," Andreas said. "There's word of bringing you up before the Council. Athitol-Head is…quite enthusiastic." He grimaced, then added, "Small Council, you understand."

In which case, she wouldn't have support from the Guilds; though in any case she might not get that, given that she wasn't in particularly good odour with many of them at the moment. And then, they might not be quite as wilfully ignorant about it as the Houses, and some Guild-folk would use sorcery, but they could hardly wish to condone an Heir breaking the law. Not that she had. And there could be no evidence, no solid evidence, that she had; that was her best hope.

"There's a surprise," Marcia said. She felt bone-deep exhausted. "I imagine they're already sending mail to

Madeleine about it. Suggesting she treat me as she did Cato."

"Will she?"

"No," Marcia said, with certainty. "Not unless I was in fact a sorcerer myself. Which – to repeat – I am not." She paused. "Also, Mother has been quite annoyed, lately, with Athitol-Head, the business with the pamphlets notwithstanding."

Andreas sat back and rubbed his hands over his eyes. "How do you see this playing out?"

"Why are you asking?" Marcia countered. Tension thrummed through her. "I need – Andreas, I'm sorry, but I have to know where you stand on this."

"Whether I am for you or against you?"

Marcia shrugged assent. She hadn't the patience to skirt politely around the question. They were child-contracted, as well as friends, and still occasional lovers. Or maybe they were neither of those last two any more, now, but she had to know.

"Shit, Marcia, I don't know. We're friends, of course. We share political goals. And I don't – I wouldn't break our friendship, simply over your former relationship. We are child-contracted. But," he exhaled heavily. "If you're found to have breached the Statutes..."

"I haven't breached the Statutes."

"Fine, I believe you. But that isn't the same as saying you won't be found guilty of it." That was all too true. "I must consider the wellbeing of my own House."

"Of course you must," Marcia said. "But there's something bigger at stake here than either of our Houses." Andreas eyed her doubtfully. "Look. We're both worried about what's happening in Teren, right?"

"Demons." He obviously didn't like to say the word. "Yes."

"We can't keep ignoring magic. The Council, the Houses. We need to engage with the fact that magic is part of what makes this city *different*, because we need to know what we're avoiding. What we're trying to protect ourselves from, in Teren. You know why I'm not doing what Nisha told me to, denying everything, smoothing it all over?"

"I assumed because you care about your…former lover. And that you're unwilling to lie."

"Well, yes. That too. But also because this has gone on long enough. It was true when Cato was kicked out and it's true now. The Council needs to engage with the idea that magic is real – which they know, really – and that we have something particular in Marek." She grimaced. "I'm saying 'the Council' but arguably I mean 'the Houses'. The Guilds aren't quite so hung up on this."

"I don't think I've ever spoken to the Guilds about magic," Andreas said.

"Well, no," Marcia said patiently, "because you are of a House, so it wouldn't come up. But Guild people use sorcerers, sometimes, though not for their work. My point is – we need to support our sorcerers, not ignore them. We need to bring them in, the same way we need to bring in the half of the city that the Council largely ignores. We've talked about this before, Andreas; about the way the city is fragmented, and our need to do better. This is part of that. And now – I'm not saying I would have chosen to be in this position, exactly, but I *am*. Which means I have the opportunity to do something about this. To make it so that the Council can't keep ignoring the sorcerers. And I can do it before whatever is happening in Teren truly descends on our heads. Which it will."

"Teren can't risk damaging us," Andreas said, but he sounded uncertain. "Trade…"

"They can take us over," Marcia said. "Selene's clearly trying to. She wants to be Archion, and dragging Marek back towards Teren – not to mention the business with the Archion's barges – will strengthen her hand. But it isn't only that. They're using demons against their own citizens in Ameten. Why wouldn't they use them against Marekers?"

"Because they don't need to?"

"That's the Council's argument for turning a blind eye to what's happening in Ameten," Marcia agreed. "Except the last time I checked, people who want power don't stop wanting it just because they theoretically have something else they want. Just because we continue to trade with Teren doesn't mean that they don't want more direct control. As Selene demonstrated last year."

"And failed. Nothing's come of it."

"*Yet*. Nothing's come of it *yet*. Except for her unilateral announcement that all Teren barges are free now."

"That's not actually a change in the agreement," Andreas said, weakly, but it was clear from his face that he wasn't wholly convincing himself.

"Things are changing in Ameten. Once they start changing in the rest of Teren too, once the refugees start coming in from the smaller towns; that's when we need to start worrying."

"Except there's nothing we can do about it, is there?"

Marcia shrugged. "We can avoid it in the first place, that would be best. We can try to resist it, given that they have to arrive from a single place – by road or river – but only if we're prepared. Or we can engage on a different plane altogether. We have a spirit too."

"The cityangel." Andreas sounded dubious.

"Yes. Who I've met."

"*What?*"

Marcia shrugged. "It's a long story. They're called Beckett, these days."

Andreas' face was a picture. She felt she should be relishing this moment more; but mostly she just felt tired.

"Um. If you're – I mean, I'm sure you're. Telling the truth. But How would that even work? Standing against Teren demons. Demons *plural*. One spirit?"

"No idea," Marcia said. "Because – as I said before – I'm not a sorcerer. Which is why we need to stop ignoring the people who *are*, and who might have better ideas."

"Which is why you're sitting around waiting to be called in front of the Council for screwing a sorcerer," Andreas said.

"It's not exactly how I'd have chosen to do it, but here we are." She leant forwards. "Andreas. You don't have to be involved with this. I'm sure there's a clause in the contract somewhere that releases you." She grimaced. "I would prefer that you wait to exercise it until after the hearing, whenever that will be, but it's up to you."

Andreas hesitated, then shook his head. "No. No. I'm not backing out now."

Marcia heard what he wasn't saying. "But you might later."

"I have to protect my House. But – I think you're right, at least in part. And you tell me you have not, in fact, broken the Statutes."

"I'm not a sorcerer. I can't do magic. Reb has never performed magic on my behalf."

"Have you been there when she did magic?"

"Yes." She wasn't going to lie, to Andreas or anyone else. "That's not against the Statutes."

"You've seen it, but it wasn't done for you."

"Well, except in the sense that it was done for Marek as a whole. It's a long story. But I don't think that can count, or every blessing-charm would break the Statutes for everyone in the Council."

Andreas grimaced, but nodded. "I will stand by you, and I will do my best to help you construct your argument. I still hope this whole business in Teren will blow over, and I still think there is no reason for them to act against Marek, but I do agree with you about the matter of governing the city as a whole. I'm uncomfortable with that including sorcerers, I admit, but...that's inconsistent, I suppose. So. I'll help."

"Thank you," Marcia said. She shut her eyes for a moment as a wave of relief washed through her. She hadn't expected it to matter so much, that Andreas was still on her side.

"So," Andreas said, half-smiling at her, though his eyes looked tired. "How about we get some more of those cakes in – or perhaps something a little more substantial – and start on your battle plan. Because I doubt you have much time in hand."

TWENTY-TWO ☉

"Hang on. Is that my sister's name?"

Tait glanced over from the news-sheet they were skimming. Cato, lying next to them under their blankets, had been staring at the ceiling and humming intermittently. Tait had gone out in search of breakfast and brought a news-sheet back too.

"Oh. Yes. Hadn't you seen this?"

"I don't read news-sheets," Cato said, loftily and inaccurately.

Tai grinned down at him. "Don't you keep saying how important it is to be in touch with the mood of the city?"

Cato waved a hand. "You don't get that from reading the news-sheets. You get that from listening to what people have taken away from the news-sheets. 'Have you heard' and all that. Half of what's in there no one cares about. And of the other half, what matters is what people *think* they know, not what they actually know."

"What about what's actually happened?"

"Well, yes, that too, but that's different again and a sight harder to come by. Anyway. Give me that. I want to know what they're saying about Marcia." He read the snippet, muttering under his breath, then threw the sheet down. "Well. She must have known this whole thing with Reb would bite her in the arse sooner or later. It's not as if they're still together, though. Why not just deny it?"

"That wouldn't be very like Marcia," Tait said, doubtfully. "I mean, I say that. You know her better than I do." But she hadn't ever come across to Tait like that.

Cato hummed again, long and thoughtful. "No, you're right. Denial would be my approach. It's amazing how often you can get away with an outright lie, given sufficient conviction. Marcia's more the head down, charge straight through type, always has been."

"So've you," Tait said, retrieving the news-sheet.

"What? Nonsense. Rubbish. Deny everything and dare 'em to pin it on you."

"It's the same thing, really," Tait said. "Brazen it out, one way or another. You're both just as stubborn as each other."

Cato made an irritable noise, rolled over, and bit Tait's thigh, not very hard. "Shut up."

Tait poked him in the forehead, and he rolled back again. "Ugh. Poor Marcia, though, if it's all landed in her lap. Not that she has a lap just now." He sighed. "Breaking the Council Statutes? How does she intend to defend herself?"

"Maybe she thinks she hasn't broken it. It's about magic, isn't it? Marcia hasn't performed magic."

Cato gave him an incredulous look. "Last autumn?"

Tait shook his head. "She didn't do anything. She was a – conduit, I suppose, back to Marek, or from it, or something. But she didn't actually *do* it." They didn't like thinking back to then, not at all. They repressed a shiver.

"It's a pretty narrow sliver of a distinction."

"Anyway, who was there to say anything about it?"

"The Teren Lieutenant," Cato said, immediately. "*Who* is in town at the moment, because there was all that kerfuffle in the square the other week." He drummed his fingers against the sheets. "I didn't like her."

"She can't say anything about it, though," Tait said. They hadn't liked the Teren Lieutenant either. "Because she'd have to admit to being there, wouldn't she? And then, to what she was doing there."

"She's not in the Houses," Cato said. "But...yes, true, wouldn't do Teren's reputation any good. There's that other sorcerer, though. Dunno what happened to him. If she brought him back...He could say whatever he liked to the Council, keep Selene out of it and claim he was acting alone. Marcia could claim Selene was there, but it'd be one word against another. Mind you. The Council doesn't much like sorcerers. Not sure what they'd do if it was her word against his."

"Couldn't we defend her? We were there too."

"I am not going anywhere near the Council," Cato said. His tone was absolutely implacable. "I don't care what Marcia's got herself into."

"I could." They shrivelled a bit inside, just thinking about it. But they could. If they had to.

Cato's head jerked up, and he looked at Tait, startled. "Why would you?"

"Because it's not fair?" Tait said. Cato really could be incredibly self-focused, at times. "She wasn't involved. It's not fair if someone lies and says she was."

"Doubt it'd help anyway," Cato said. "They don't like us, up there. And it's not about that, not really. Or at least, there's more to it than that."

"Politics?" Tait still didn't understand Marek politics, and wasn't sure they wanted to.

"Yeah." Cato looked glum, and his feet were twitching restlessly under the blanket.

"What's up?"

"What?"

Tait shrugged. "There's obviously something on your mind."

"Huh, and there was me thinking I was all unreadable and enigmatic and so forth."

"You keep thinking that," Tait said kindly, and Cato swatted at them.

"I had a client," he said abruptly, then stopped.

"Mmm?" Tait prompted. Cato wasn't good at talking about certain things. Marekhill was one of them.

"Marekhill client." He sounded reluctant.

"As in, Marekhill in general, or as in, someone from a House." Tait began to have a feeling about where this might be going.

"Someone from a House. You remember all the stuff about spirits, last week?"

Tait suppressed a shiver, remembering Beckett's anger. "That client was from a House? But the Houses aren't allowed to do magic." That was, after all, why Cato was here, now, although he never talked about that and Tait wasn't about to bring it up.

"No performing magic, no having magic performed for you," Cato agreed. "Which, yes, must be the loophole Marcia's trying to squeak through. She hasn't performed magic, she hasn't asked for any to be done, she just spent a few months screwing someone who happens to do magic."

"But your client…"

"Is, was, absolutely breaching the Statutes, yes."

"And they're getting away with it when Marcia isn't? That hardly seems fair."

"Mm."

"Especially given what they were using magic to do."

"That bit I don't care about," Cato said. "But I bet the hypocrite will vote against Marcia." Not just from a House, but a Head or Heir, then.

"Can you report them?" Tait struggled to get to grips with the issue.

"At the cost of my professional reputation," Cato said, gloomily. "And, you know, in the general case, I don't actually care. I worked for Daril Leandra-Heir a while back, you know, though he was b'Leandra at the time. And anyway that…fell through. Still kept the first half of the pay, mind." He stopped, and chewed at his fingernail, making a horrible face.

"So," Tait prompted. "You worked for Daril Leandra-Heir, who absolutely shouldn't be having magic done for him. And now someone else? Or Daril again?"

"Someone else." Cato glanced up at Tait. "You're not passing this onto Reb, mind. Or anyone else."

"Course not. Not my business."

"Didn't think you would," Cato said, sounding almost, and unusually, apologetic. "Just…"

Tait wriggled down the bed and put an arm round Cato, who stiffened, then rolled over into Tait's embrace. "Don't worry. I'm your partner, right? I'm not going to go blabbing your stuff all over the place." Whatever Tait thought Cato ought to be doing, it wasn't their job to make decisions for him.

"It's not that I thought you would…"

"I get it. It's fine."

Cato rested his head on Tait's shoulder. "The thing is. Generally, I don't care in the slightest what that lot get up to. Breaking the rules, not breaking the rules, why should I care." His voice was brittle at the edges. "They pay well, so."

"And you don't talk about clients."

"Exactly. Reputation and all that. I won't *get* jobs if people think I open my mouth. And there's a lot of jobs that I get that Reb wouldn't because everyone knows I don't care what they're getting up to." Cato twisted to look up at Tait. "And, while we're at it, I know you don't approve."

"That's…an overstatement," Tait said, carefully. "Just because I wouldn't do things the way you do doesn't mean I'm looking down on you for them."

"But you'd rather I didn't."

Tait shrugged. "Sure. But it's your decision, not mine." They smiled, trying to convey their affection. "I'm more concerned about your wellbeing than your morals, you know."

Cato smiled back in return, his face lightening. "Well. I suppose I can accept that. Fear not, though, I'm always very careful with my own wellbeing."

"So. You don't care what clients are up to."

"Exactly. Including this client."

There was a long pause.

"But?" Tait prompted, aware that Cato, quite obviously, did care.

"But it *is* unfair, isn't it? Marcia, trying to do something useful with her job, even if she doesn't quite get it, is hauled up for something she didn't do. This waste of space definitely did do it and just gets away with it."

"I thought you didn't care about fair."

"Ugh." Cato groaned and sat up a bit, disentangling himself from Tait's arm. "I don't. But she's my sister."

"What are your options?" Tait asked, pragmatically. No

point in getting too caught up in theory. "Sit tight and say nothing, obviously."

"Tell the Council, or someone associated with it. But – I'm a sorcerer. And I'm…well. Everyone up there knows who I *was*. Might not listen. Almost certainly not."

"Could you tell Marcia? Directly?"

"Blackmail information. Yes."

Tait blinked. "I…hadn't thought of it that way."

Cato shrugged. "Politics. It's not about what she's done – or not entirely, anyway. If she *had* done it and there was cast-iron proof, that would be different. But it's not like that. So it's about who'll vote for her and against her, and that…she might be able to swing."

Tait *really* didn't get politics. Never mind. "But?"

"But it'll cost my reputation."

Tait sat back. "Will it?" They had difficulty accepting that *mattered*, given what Marcia was up against; but it wasn't their reputation at stake, so maybe they just didn't understand.

"Can't see how not. Ugh, this is as bad as Jonas and his wretched flickers. Changing things and not knowing what'll come of it."

"Wait." Tait had the germ of an idea. "You've done the work already, right?"

Cato nodded.

"Can't I report it? Overheard you, saw them sneaking out, something like that? Upright sorcerer disapproving of this breach of the rules, sort of thing."

Cato sucked at his teeth. "It certainly muddies the waters. Why would you tell Marcia and not the Council, though?"

"Um. I hadn't thought of that."

"I suppose, if it's blackmail, that doesn't matter, but it needs some kind of plausible cover story. Aha. You're Reb's apprentice. That's it. You told Reb, Reb told Marcia – we won't actually bother doing it that way, I'll tell Marcia directly – and Marcia puts the thumbscrews on my client."

"And Daril Leandra-Heir?" Tait asked. "From what

you said before?"

Cato's eyes widened. "Shit, I never even thought of that. Of course. And if Marcia were thrown out, she'd have nothing to lose by kicking up the most enormous stink about that. He wouldn't like that at all. If Marcia can't use this, she's not the politician I thought she was. If you don't *mind* being used as cover…?"

"No," Tait said, with truth. "I like Marcia, and I like Reb, and I don't like what's being done to them. I'm happy to help." Even if they thought none of this ought to be necessary.

"Still not going to do *wonders* for my rep, but it's not like I get all that many Marekhill clients anyway. And…ugh, yes, *fine*, it's worth it." Cato sighed deeply. "You're terrible for my worse impulses, you know that?"

"Not gonna apologise," Tait said, and kissed Cato's shoulder.

"Wouldn't expect you to. Right. I'm going to write to Marcia. You're going to apologise to me for coercing me into sticking up for my sister by finding a messenger. And then you're going to come back up here and we are going to forget about the whole sorry business for a while." Cato leant in and kissed Tait, slow and sweet, belying his irritable words.

"Sounds good to me," Tait said into his mouth.

"Pedeli? That… *toerag*."

Cato hadn't seen Marcia this furious since they were fourteen and he'd got drunk, thrown up on her new slippers, and got both of them confined to the House for two weeks.

"Heir," he clarified for the second time. "Not Head."

"Even so! That sanctimonious *arse*. You should have heard what she was saying the other night, the importance of maintaining…oh, never mind, it was crap to start with and now it's not just crap, it's hypocritical crap."

"Well." Cato shrugged. "Colour me surprised. What're

you going to do about it?"

Marcia sat back on the pale-green couch, foot tapping, one hand resting on her bump. She was definitely getting *bigger*.

They were in a private room in their customary infusion-salon. This one was decorated all in pale greens. Cato slouched further into his pale-green chair, hooked one leg over the arm-rest, and considered calling for wine. Or brandy. As he recalled, they had quite nice brandy here, and the thing about Dyesha, Pedeli-Heir, was, hypocritical toerag or no, she had paid through the nose, and Cato's metaphorical pockets were jingling pleasantly.

Which reminded him. "I didn't tell you this, mind."

"Hmm?"

"I have a reputation, you know."

"Yes, as a shithead."

"Fuck you. The point is not the sort of shithead who sells out his clients. Or I won't *have* any clients."

"Do you have many Marekhill clients?" Marcia looked up, eyes narrowing.

"Not often, obviously. Hardly ever, in fact. *Most* of you aren't that sort of hypocrite." He pursed his lips. "Or possibly most of you are too scared of the whole thing."

"Daril been back since before?"

"*No*. Leave over. If you want to screw Daril over you'll have to do it with whatever you have already. My point is, I can't have it known that I am passing information."

"They'll guess," Marcia said. "Wherever I say I got it from – where do you want me to have got it from? – it's not like she didn't know who you are, and everyone knows I'm still in touch with you."

"Not the point. I need plausible deniability."

"Such as?"

"Tait."

Marcia looked sceptical. "Did Tait say you could bring them into this?"

"*Yes*. I'm not going to just dump my um…"

"Your friend?" Marcia suggested, grinning sharply.

"Your *very good* friend?"

"Shut the fuck up. My close acquaintance." Tait had said *partner*, the other day. The word had felt warm in Cato's chest.

"Very close."

"Shut. Up. I'm beginning to regret this. I am not going to drop *Tait* into it without their permission. Point is. Tait lives next door to me, Tait is Reb's apprentice, Tait is a loyal and morally upright Marek citizen. And so on."

"If I say it was Tait, Dyesha won't believe it."

"Come *on*, Marcia, you could do this sort of thing in your sleep by the time we were twelve. You don't say it was Tait. You say it was an unknown source and then say it was overheard, or she was seen on the stairs, and then say something about the moral side of Marek magic."

"Meaning that you're the immoral side?"

"If you could see your way clear to muttering darkly about the terrible behaviour of your own brother, that would be delightful, thank you." Cato paused. "Could we stage a row? Maybe I should storm out in a bit, what do you think?" He would enjoy a good dramatic fake row.

Marcia rolled her eyes. "Whatever works for you." She sighed. "Straight-up blackmail, then."

"Will it be enough? Who's voting for you already?" He was going to regret this if Marcia would end up kicked out regardless.

"Good question. Andreas. And we've been working on some of the others. Talking about what the Statutes actually say, that kind of thing. Gil Jyrithi-Head is legalistically-minded, I'll probably get them; Piath maybe, but they're Berenez-Heir, not Head, and I don't know if they'll care enough to speak to their Head. We're hoping to make it a whole-Council vote, that might help. And there's a couple of votes I might swing if I'm really convincing on the bit about needing to engage with magic."

"To...hang on. What?"

"Come on. I've said this before. Marekhill needs to get past its – whatever the opposite of an obsession is – with magic. The city's divided, along lots of axes, but this is one of them. And with whatever's happening in Teren…we can't just keep on pretending it's not there. Pretending like people don't believe in it."

"Change the Statutes? More clients for me?" Cato beamed brightly at her.

"If we change the Statutes, it'd likely be Reb would get more clients," Marcia said, which Cato felt was unreasonably hard-hearted, especially given how he was being positively helpful right now.

"Wouldn't bet on it. Reb's all upright and that. Not well suited for political backstabbery, which is doubtless what you'd see a lot of."

"Anyway. I doubt that will change, in fact, and that's not what I want. I don't think politics would be improved by magical involvement – and isn't Beckett sworn to keep out of it?"

"Another reason why people might need to come to me," Cato observed. Although of course he'd promised, now, to limit that.

"I *really* don't want to know. My point is. It's not about the Houses using magic, or using magic for political purposes. It's about the city coming together. Everyone being represented. Using all the strength that we have available."

"I'm not sitting on the fucking Council," Cato said, flatly. Best head that one off sharpish. At least he and Reb were already in agreement there.

"Reb said that too. Don't worry. Can't see it happening. But if the Council could *talk* to you – fine, not you. Reb. Find out more about what you know and can do. Understand Beckett."

"No one understands Beckett. Up to and including Beckett."

"Understand *more*. I've been thinking…well, never mind. That's for later."

Cato had a twinge of curiosity, then shoved it back into its box. He didn't want to get caught up in Marcia's politicking, now or ever.

"So I can't just twist arms and get them not to vote me out. I need…more. But this will help."

"You might not *just* be able to twist arms, but a bit of judicious arm-twisting will fit in nicely?" Cato guessed.

Marcia smiled, shark-like. "Something like that. Well. Thank you, Cato. I really appreciate you telling me."

"Thank Tait. I'd have kept it quiet."

Marcia just smiled at him fondly. "I'd get up and give you a hug, but I'm quite slow-moving these days. You can come here and give me one."

"*Ugh*," Cato said, with feeling, but he got up, and bent down to hug her, and felt fondness creeping up his insides. Marcia had always been there for him, regardless of what else was happening and how much she disapproved of whatever he was up to.

"So, did you say you wanted to stage a fight?"

Reluctantly, Cato let go of the tempting idea of that brandy. He could come back another time. If he stayed much longer it would play less well. "Let's do it."

He crossed to the door, flung it open, and shrieked "It's none of your business what I do!" at full volume.

"How dare you!" Marcia shouted over the top of him.

"I will not stay here to be *lectured*!" Cato declaimed in his best theatrical tones, and stomped out into the corridor.

"The worst is having to hear this from someone else!" Marcia called after him.

"Fuck you!" He stomped down the corridor, threw open the door to the main salon instead of taking the private corridor, and exited with a dramatic flourish and plenty of people looking.

A fig-leaf of cover, enough to unblushingly deny everything if challenged.

Shame about the brandy, though.

TWENTY-THREE

Daril was easy. They'd come to one agreement already, in order to save the good name of both of their Houses. If Marcia was thrown out, her part in that agreement became somewhat moot. And in truth, whilst Daril would have been happy to vote against her, Marcia got the impression, during their conversation, that he was just as happy not to. He seemed to have his mind on other matters. Trade arrangements, most like. The Heads and Heirs who might like him less for voting in Marcia's favour already disliked him; and House Leandra's stock was high at present. Most importantly, it was far better than what might happen if Marcia dropped Daril thoroughly in the shit. They both knew she could, without needing to allude to it directly while they were talking. The way Urso had been bundled away out of the city after that little *event* told its own story; and Marcia still had the confession she'd made Kia sign. She'd be reluctant to use it, as it happened, even if she were no longer Fereno-Heir. But Daril, in the same circumstances, would happily burn everything down as he left; it was evident that he assumed the same of her.

So that was done. Dyesha would be more difficult. But she couldn't delay; Athitol-Head had indeed brought the matter formally to the Council, and her hearing was in two days' time. Every shift in the numbers mattered, and she had no *time* to think of other ways to approach Dyesha. She'd just have to play her cards as well as she could, and see how they fell.

Seated in the pleasantly light receiving-room of House Pedeli, after laying the whole thing out as succinctly as possible: what 'Tait' had told her, what sort of magic Dyesha had commissioned, she smiled without warmth at Dyesha. "I suppose the question is where that leaves us."

Dyesha sat in silence, eyes narrowed.

Marci sat back and folded her arms, hitching them on top of her stomach.

"You've no proof," Dyesha said, eventually, but her tone lacked conviction.

"I've a sorcerer who will state you were seen coming out of Cato's rooms, and that they overheard part of your conversation. Everyone knows Cato. It's going to be hard to claim you were there for purely innocent reasons."

"And yet *you* are about to *admit*, in the Council Chamber, to a relationship with a sorcerer." Everyone knew, by now, that Marcia wasn't denying the relationship; she was denying that it breached the Statutes.

"Which isn't against the Statutes," Marcia said. "That being rather my point. You, however, were buying magic."

"Maybe I wasn't. Maybe I was there for personal reasons too."

"In which case we're both in the clear," not that Marcia thought anyone would buy that Dyesha was screwing Cato rather than employing him, "and I would expect you to support my argument that I'm not in breach." Marcia bared her teeth at Dyesha. "Otherwise you'll be the next one called down into the circle."

"If you're found guilty you won't be able to call me down." Dyesha sounded sulky.

"That's fine. Andreas will do it for me."

Not that she'd asked him; but the bluff would hold. She hoped.

"You're called to the circle regardless." Dyesha's expression had shifted further into uncertainty. Good. Nearly there…

"Indeed I am," Marcia agreed. "For sorcerous breach of the Statutes, regarding my relationship with the sorcerer Reb, of the Group of Marek. A relationship which I did indeed conduct, for a short while, and which does not breach the Statutes. I am happy to stand in the circle and defend myself. Your situation, on the other hand, is rather more precarious."

"If you're so certain you've done nothing wrong, I don't know what you even want of me," Dyesha said, watching her narrowly.

Marcia spread her hands. "If you're honestly telling me that you expect mere *argument* is necessarily going to sway the Houses…I don't really know what to tell you. What I want is a promise that your House will vote in my favour. Which requires no moral squirming, since I am not, in fact, in breach of the Statutes. In return, I will overlook your own very definite breach of them."

"I don't carry the vote," Dyesha pointed out, which wasn't refusal.

"But you'll be able to convince Pirran, if you try hard," Marcia said. "I feel confident you'll be motivated to try hard."

"If you hadn't spent so much time antagonising people," Dyesha sneered, "you might not need to go around engaging in *blackmail* to win your argument."

"And if you hadn't engaged my brother to perform sorcery for you," Marcia said calmly, "you wouldn't be vulnerable to it."

She watched Dyesha, and waited, as the other woman's eyes flickered, calculating. They both knew that evidencing Dyesha's breach of the Statutes would be difficult; absent Cato's own testimony, which Marcia had been at pains to indicate she did not have. But…

But mud sticks, even if it did all fall apart, and it would damage Dyesha's reputation. The same way Marcia's was already damaged, of course, but it was too late for that. Marcia had made her decisions. Dyesha, if she made the right choice now, could avoid the problem altogether.

Dyesha made a tiny, infuriated grunt, and Marcia had to fight not to smile. She'd won.

"Very well," Dyesha said, through gritted teeth. "I will vote – will convince Pirran to vote – in your favour. But you'll lose anyway, you know. Regardless of the letter of the law, they all hate magic. They'll vote you out of your House simply from disgust."

"Maybe so," Marcia said. It would be close, she knew

that. But...Well. "We'll see tomorrow, I suppose." She stood up. "I am glad we could come to an agreement. I look forward to tomorrow, in the Chamber."

Which was an outright lie, and Dyesha knew it as well as she did; but the more she said it, the more true it might be.

⊙ ⊙

Xera gave a tiny nod when she saw Jonas on the Embassy's doorstep, which in all honesty Jonas found worrying. Xera was never pleased to see him. Not that she seemed *pleased* exactly now, that was an overstatement. Still.

What did Kia want? The note she'd sent had reminded him, and not subtly, that he owed her a favour. Which he did; from when she'd agreed not to tell his mother about his apprenticeship with Cato. She had the right to call it in; that he'd told his mother himself in the end didn't negate the original agreement. And none of that meant that he was *happy* to be following Xera along the corridor to Kia's study. Again.

"Jonas!" Kia got up from the desk and they clasped hands. "Wonderful to see you. Thank you, Xera, that's all." Two glasses and a bottle of berith stood on the desk. Not reassuring. Kia sat down, gestured him to sit opposite her, and poured a heavy-handed glass for each of them. Jonas raised his glass to her and took a tiny sip for propriety; but downing that much berith wasn't going to help him negotiate.

If Kia noticed his caution, she didn't react. She took a decent sip of her own drink, set the heavy glass back down on the desk, leant back, and smiled at him. "So. Jonas, we've known each other a long time, haven't we?"

"...Yes?"

"I won't sail around the island here. I'm going to be up front with you." Another bad sign. People didn't say that sort of thing about something you'd be happy about. "The last time Selene, the Teren Lieutenant was here in

Marek," Kia continued. "I have reason to believe that something magical happened. Something involving Marcia, Fereno-Heir. And possibly Selene herself, not sure about that. Might just have been a Teren sorcerer. Anyway. My point is. You're a sorcerer. What do you know about it?"

Jonas tried not to squirm. Marcia wasn't supposed to do magic. And he didn't want anything to do with Teren. He shrugged. "Nothing. What reason do you have to even be saying such a thing?"

"Never you mind. I have reliable sources, but I'm hardly going to reveal them to you." He hadn't really expected her to; but there were plenty of ways Kia might be getting information, whether by intercepting post or by suborning people, and if she thought her sources were reliable, they probably were.

Kia gave him a sorrowful look. "I had hoped not to have to remind you, but…you owe me one. Remember? I'm afraid I don't believe you weren't involved, or at the least that you didn't hear about it afterwards. Not given how few sorcerers there are in Marek these days. I'm calling the favour in, and this is the first part. Talk."

Jonas folded his arms, quailing at the implications of 'the first part'. "Of course I acknowledge the favour. But that doesn't include screwing someone over."

Kia looked genuinely surprised. "You're worried about screwing over *Selene*?"

"Selene? No, of course not."

For a moment they stared at each other in mutual incomprehension, then Kia's expression cleared. "Ah. You're worried about Marcia. Who didn't ought to be tangled up in magic, and who's already on the hook for it, if the news-sheets are to be believed. Don't worry. I'm on Marcia's side too."

Jonas must have looked disbelieving, because she sighed. "I owe Marcia – quite significantly so, in fact, and I would very much like to have it out of the way – and you owe me. Selene pissed me off the other night, and I never liked her in the first place, so I'm quite happy if I can settle debts all round and thereby put a hole in Selene's sail. I swear by the Lion, Jonas. There's nothing in this to hurt Marcia. Rather the opposite."

If she was swearing by the ship they'd been crewmates in… "Fine," he said, still reluctant, but she'd sworn. "Something happened, yes. Something magical. Selene was there, in person, and a Teren sorcerer, and, uh. Maybe Marcia was too."

"And you?"

Jonas set his teeth. "Yes."

"Well," Kia said. "The thing is, hypothetically, if Marcia had indeed been there, that Teren sorcerer might be able to say that Marcia was using magic, which obviously I'm sure she wasn't even if she was there, due to it being forbidden by the Covenant."

"She wasn't using magic!" Jonas said indignantly. "She was just…representing Marek." He caught up with himself too late; but it wasn't like Kia didn't sound certain already. "They were trying to invade the city! With a demon! Taking down the cityangel!"

Kia shrugged. "Honestly, I don't much care, and I certainly don't care about all the spirit nonsense. I don't like magic."

"You wouldn't like it if Teren took over Marek properly," Jonas said.

Kia scratched the side of her face. "Well. Perhaps so. The main thing is, Selene is trying to screw Marcia over, and like I said, not only do I owe Marcia, I don't like Selene. Don't trust her, or Teren." She screwed up her nose. "Land-bound. They don't know anything, do they? So. We need to take this sorcerer out of the game."

"We?" Jonas asked, resigned.

"Come on, Jonas. A snip of information I already knew wasn't going to balance that favour. Yes. We."

"And what do you mean, take him out of the game?"

"I'd prefer a nice quiet gentle resolution," Kia said, lips pursed judiciously, "but I suppose we'll have to work with what we have. So. You need to find him. And solve the problem."

"Kia! I'm not killing anyone."

"I'm not asking you to. I'm asking you to find what'll get rid of him. Which, once established, I am very happy to help you get." She leant across the desk, eyes narrowed. "You owe me. We shook on it. Are you challenging the size of the favour?"

Jonas scowled. "I am if you want me to kill him. Or to be involved in his death."

Kia shook her head. "No. But you're better equipped to find him than I am, and to shake some information out of him. Are you challenging?"

"No," Jonas said reluctantly. She was right; it was a fair trade. Just. If he'd wanted something more certain, he should have negotiated it at the time; but he'd been desperate, and this was the price of that, paid late. It was what it was.

Kia sat back. "Find him, find out what he'll take to go away, come see me. And quickly; Marcia's due in the Council day after tomorrow and at a guess, that's when Selene wants to spring this." She nodded, sharp and satisfied. "Drink your berith before you go, my lad, no point wasting it."

Jonas sighed, and drank.

It was harder to track down a single recently-arrived Teren than it once would have been, what with all the refugees coming into the city. When he asked around, no one had heard of a Teren sorcerer arriving – and if Tam hadn't heard, then it wasn't current messenger gossip, which meant the sorcerer wasn't bragging about his sorcery, ruling out the easiest way of finding him.

He likely wouldn't stay long; so he wouldn't be in the squats, or in proper housing, he'd be at an inn. Which Marek had plenty of; but many were full just now, what with all the new arrivals. He asked Tam where people were staying at the moment, people that weren't refugees, just visitors, making out it was something he'd offered to do for the folk out at the barge-yard. At the White Horse, the second place on the list, he called in at the kitchen and got lucky.

"Him, well, yes." Kenton pulled a face. Kenton was the Horse's pastry-cook, and Jonas knew him from the Dog's Tail. "Hira, his name is. Polite enough, I suppose, but won't leave his room. Made a fuss about a room with a view over the city, as if *all* our rooms aren't perfectly nice. He's eating well, though. Keeps asking for more pastries up, not that he's sent a tip back down on the tray yet, the skinflint. By all means set her out at the barge-yard onto him. See if she can screw some donations out of him. He must be able to afford it, staying here."

Jonas thanked him, excused himself, and went round the back and up onto the roof. A room with a view of the city...the rooms out front all had very convenient balconies.

He'd assumed that he'd be able to see Hira from a distance, the way he could see Cato or Reb or Tait or Alyssa these days, that invisible glow that marked them as sorcerers. To his surprise, he couldn't; but he recognised the man's face the moment he peered through the window. Hira, lounging in a chair, hadn't seen him; and when Jonas tried the handle of the balcony door, it opened without him needing to jimmy it.

"What the..." Hira stood up, knocking his chair backwards as Jonas stepped over the threshold. He got halfway through making a gesture then stopped with a jerk, as if he'd remembered something.

Like, for example, that he couldn't call on a demon while he was in Marek. Which was useful, because Jonas had had *more* than enough of that the last time he'd seen Hira.

Jonas put out his hands placatingly. "It's fine. I'm just here for a chat." Keeping a cautious eye on Hira – just because he couldn't do magic didn't mean he might not do something more physical – he reached behind him to pull the balcony door shut again.

"People here for a chat don't usually climb through the window," Hira snarled.

"I wanted to be discreet," Jonas explained. "Because you're a sorcerer, which I'm guessing you don't want to get around just now."

Hira's involuntary hunch told him he was right.

"I didn't tell anyone, while I was looking for you," Jonas offered. "Honestly. I'm just here for a chat."

"My arse you are. What do you want?"

Jonas had hoped to lead into this more gently, but if Hira wasn't going to go for that…"I was there, when you attacked Marek last year. I want to know if you're planning to go to the Council to talk about it."

"Oh, shit, that's where I recognise you from, isn't it?" Hira sounded disgusted. "You were the one who was having a fit all over the floor."

This sounded unfair to Jonas, but it was true that he hadn't been at his best at the time. He shrugged. "Something like that."

"You, and two other Mareker sorcerers," Jonas wasn't, technically, Mareker, but he didn't interrupt, "and the Teren. And the posh one. That's where the Council comes in, I gather." He eyed Jonas. "What's it to you?"

There didn't seem much point in dancing around it. "Selene wants you to testify against Marcia – the posh one – in the Council, doesn't she?" Hira didn't say anything; just watched Jonas. "I want you not to. That's all."

"You…want me not to." Hira sounded incredulous. "Well then. I suppose I won't, since you don't *want* me to." His voice had sharpened into sarcasm. "Sod off, sorcerer-boy."

"I didn't mean to ask you to do it for nothing," Jonas said, rolling his eyes. Had this Teren no idea of a negotiation? "We can pay you."

"You can pay me," Hira repeated. "Well, that's nice. Have you any idea what the Academy will do to me, if I go back and Selene tells 'em I bottled it? Tells them I conveniently forgot what happened or…whatever you're suggesting? Show up in the Council and say oops, I don't recognise anyone here? There ain't no money enough to be worth it. They'll rip me apart, and I mean that quite literally." He shook his head. "No way."

"Then don't go back," Jonas said. "Stay in Marek. With the money. You know the Academy can't get you here. They – you – couldn't get Tait."

For a tiny moment, Jonas saw something in Hira's eyes that might have been hope; then he shook his head violently, and it was gone. "Stay in Marek? And do what? I can't do my magic," a flare of resentment, "and even if I wanted to give up magic – which I don't – it's not like I've other skills. You're going to pay me enough to sit around on my arse for the next forty years?"

Jonas was fairly sure that no, Kia's debt to Marcia didn't stretch quite that far.

"So. Sod off. I know what keeps my soup salted and I'll stick with that, thanks all the same."

"You could stay here and do magic," Jonas said.

"No demons in Marek," Hira said, like he was speaking to a particularly stupid child.

"No demons. Only the cityangel." Again, that tiny flare of hope in Hira's eyes. "Tait came here, and started practising Marek magic. Reb. Reb's, like, the strongest sorcerer in Marek," he was never going to tell Cato he'd said that, "and she was Teren once, and she came here. Why can't you do that? You can get sanctuary. Do our magic instead." He paused. "It's cleaner, I think," he added, very quietly.

Hira shifted nervously in his chair. Jonas, knowing when not to push his advantage, shut up.

"Mareker magic," Hira said, eventually. "You're saying, if I stay away from the Council, I c'n stay here, and you'll get me access to Mareker magic. And give me money, to get myself started." It wasn't a no.

"I'm saying, I'm willing to try to negotiate that for you," Jonas said, cautiously.

"Well," Hira said. "Well. You've got until tomorrow, sorcerer-boy. I'm not saying I'll take it. I'm saying I'll maybe consider it, if you can promise me all of that. But then again, maybe I won't." He eyed Jonas. "So go back to whoever sent you, and tell 'em that. Come back with an actual offer, and we'll talk again. Now, piss off out of it and leave me alone."

Hira turned his back on Jonas, which was a bit lowering – obviously he'd pegged Jonas, correctly, as not a threat – but, well. That was a proposal, wasn't it? Time to take it to Kia.

"I'll be back," Jonas promised.

TWENTY-FOUR

Marcia's curiosity made her fingers twitch as she waited in one of the plushly decorated private rooms at Petrior's. She glanced again at the message.

> *I have information you will be grateful to hear, but best not shared in public. Petrior's, three in the afternoon, tomorrow; or propose an alternate time by return. Kia t'Riseri.*

Neither House Fereno nor yet the Embassy would be *public* exactly, which suggested that Kia wanted to avoid observation. As such, Marcia had taken the back route in – Petrior's hosted a variety of meetings, from those that were deliberately public, to those whose subjects of conversation were private but not the meetings themselves, to those that were secret altogether, and as such, it had an equally wide set of access arrangements.

Kia was ushered in. It was raining again; she pulled the hood of her cloak down and grimaced at Marcia. "My apologies. Shedding water everywhere."

"Not at all," Marcia said. "There's a hook on the back of the door."

"My apologies as well," Kia said, hanging the cloak up and turning back to her, "for dragging you down here in your condition. I hope all is going well in that regard?"

"As well as can be expected, or so they tell me," Marcia said. "By which I mean, it is all tremendously uncomfortable and awkward, but I am not yet enthusiastic for it to be over."

Kia laughed. "You'll know you're nearly done when you get to the point where the discomfort outweighs the nerves. I remember it well."

"You have children?"

"Two. Both grown now; older than our mutual friend Jonas by a good ten years or so. Both on good ships, though my son may be staying home to raise children himself in the next year or so. He was through here just before New Year." She meant Salinas New Year, what Marek called Mid-Year. "Was good to see him."

"I have peppermint infusion," Marcia offered, "or you could order something else?"

"Peppermint will do," Kia said, nodding when Marcia offered to pour. "I'd rather...well. Get on with it, I suppose."

"Of course. I was surprised to receive your note."

Kia grimaced. "Because I didn't want...Well. Before I start. You remember, Fereno-Heir, that I owe you a favour?"

Marcia nodded.

"Well. This will pay back, I think. But you must agree to keep my hand in it quiet."

Marcia frowned. "Very well."

"Right. Well. Time to name names." Kia sighed. "I asked you to come here because Selene would know, if we met at your House or at the embassy, and I don't think you want that. I certainly don't. I can't take sides."

Salina, given their central position in trade around the Oval Sea and beyond, maintained neutrality in any disagreements between countries.

"Of course," Marcia said. "Ah – what is it that Selene is up to, then, that she wouldn't want you to tell me?"

"I'm aware that you're already in trouble, about," Kia looked uncomfortable, "uh. Consorting with a sorcerer, I believe, they're saying."

"Trouble's one way of putting it," Marcia said, automatically deflecting. In any case. She'd hopefully solved that now, hadn't she, after her conversation with Dyesha. Not that it wasn't still going to be tight.

"Well. I have...reason to believe, let's say, that Selene has in mind to make those troubles worse. That you've been more directly involved in sorcery in the past."

"I've never performed sorcery," Marcia said immediately, but her mind went to last year, and the demon Selene's sorcerer had tried to unleash upon Marek. Her stomach lurched. Shit. This wasn't about her having an affair any more. This was direct. Against this, none of her politicking, neither the parts where she'd spoken of the letter of the law, nor the parts where she'd applied other sorts of persuasion, would hold.

Why was Selene doing this, now, when she hadn't even threatened it before? It had seemed Selene couldn't risk her own involvement coming to light; but perhaps, if Selene was under more pressure now herself, her willingness to take that risk had changed. Or if she thought the matter of Reb wasn't enough to get rid of Marcia. Or perhaps she'd just wanted to lull Marcia into a false sense of security, before, and bring this out at the last minute.

"I'm not saying you have," Kia said. "I'm saying, Selene thinks she has evidence that you have. I don't know any more about it than that – not what that evidence is, nor how conclusive, nor whether the Council will believe her. But my information suggests she's confident."

"Information?"

Kia looked at her reprovingly. "Come on. You know I won't reveal my sources. But they're reliable."

Marcia realised she was jiggling her leg, and stopped. "Why are you telling me?" she asked bluntly.

"Because you're more useful on the Council than most of 'em," Kia said, equally bluntly. "Because I owe you. Because Selene has pissed me off once too often, and the last thing I want is for her to get more power. And because I've spoken to some of the refugees from Teren, and I am not at all happy with what's going on there. Marek should be separating itself from Teren, not cleaving closer to it, and you're more likely to do that than any of those who'll merrily vote against you in Council. Not that I can say any of this publicly, you understand. Salina remains neutral." She met Marcia's gaze. "I've been listening, the last few days. You'll suffer for this *consorting* business, but it won't be enough. But actually *performing* sorcery…"

"I haven't," Marcia said again.

"Fine, but you know as well as I do that isn't the point. The point is whether someone can claim you have and be believed. And it sounds to me like she's got someone can swear to it."

Marcia bit her lip. Of the people who'd been in the barge-yard that day…Even if Selene was willing to take the risk of Marcia bringing up her own presence, she wouldn't risk it on just her word against Marcia's. Neither Reb nor Cato would betray Marcia, and she might not know Tait well, but given Tait's history with Teren, she couldn't believe they would speak for Selene either. Jonas? Surely not. Certainly not if Kia was coming to speak to her.

Which left that Teren sorcerer. The one holding the demon. Had Selene brought him back to Marek? (Did that explain the timing, that the sorcerer had only just arrived?) Would the Council really trust the word of a Teren sorcerer over one of their own?

They might. If the sorcerer were swearing that she'd been there, and she couldn't counter it, cleanly and without doubt…And if Kia hadn't warned her, if she'd been caught out in Council itself, she'd have floundered. She and Andreas were planning to force the matter to stay in full Council, rather than Little Council, on the grounds that the Guilds were less concerned about magic; but if it were about the barge-yard, that wouldn't help. The Guilds wouldn't stand for a breach of the Statutes. Whether or not they thought it mattered in itself, the point was the betrayal. And she might not have performed magic, that day, but she'd been treading right along the line of it. She'd been in that circle; she'd let Reb ground through her.

Kia was watching her closely. "I gather," she said delicately, "that there's a Teren, name of Hira, staying at the White Horse. Rumour has it he's a sorcerer. Rumour also has it that he'd rather be a Marek sorcerer than a Teren one, especially if he had a little more in his pockets to ease his way, if you understand me. Couldn't say if that has any bearing on this matter, of course." She looked away, draining her cup. "And if you'll excuse me, I would rather not know anything more. But. I've told you."

"Thank you," Marcia said, sincerely. "This does indeed pay back the favour."

"Good. Good. I don't like to be beholden. You'll burn the paper."

"Or send it to you?" Kia meant the confession she'd given to Marcia, after the business with Urso, that she'd let him use the Embassy for his sorcery.

Kia shrugged. "I trust you to burn it." She stood up, and flung her damp cloak back on. "Well. Good luck, Fereno-Heir."

☺ ☺

The timescale was tight. Marcia fretted as she sat on a coil of rope on the ferry across to Reb's place. (Her bump was visible enough now, even under a cloak, to get her offered what passed for a seat on the ferry, so that was something.) She hadn't wanted to waste time sending messages around; and, messenger-privacy or no, she didn't want to commit any of this to paper.

And she was all too aware that she was asking a lot of Reb. She'd sat alone in the salon, after Kia left, staring sightless at the walls, trying to work out what she should do. Money she could manage; but if what the man really wanted was to be a Marek sorcerer, that wasn't hers to arrange. Cato, notionally, could do it; he was in the Group now. But she couldn't see him being willing to get involved. Especially not when he'd already told her about Dyesha.

Which left Reb, or no one at all. And she couldn't just leave this. If this sorcerer showed up tomorrow and told the Council about what had happened in the barge-yard…there was no way she'd survive that.

"Marcia!" Reb looked surprised, but not unpleasantly so, when she answered the door.

"Were you in the middle of something?" Marcia asked. Her stomach was churning.

Reb shook her head. "Nothing important. What's wrong? You look – anxious." Her eyes widened with worry. "Is it the baby?"

Marcia shook her head. "Baby's fine. As far as I know, anyway."

"What's the problem, then? You definitely look like there's a problem."

Marcia helped herself to an armchair, and hesitated, unsure where to start. Reb sat opposite her and waited, patiently, her eyes on Marcia's. Just her presence was calming, even if she wasn't going to agree.

"So you want me to come round with you and offer him to be a Marek sorcerer," Reb concluded, once Marcia had finished reporting what Kia had said, and paused, unsure how to broach the request. Marcia couldn't read her voice.

"That's about the size of it. If you will." Marcia hunched her shoulders. "It's a big favour to ask. I don't – if you don't want to. But…"

Reb shook her head. "It's not that I don't want to help. And I owe you one, anyway."

For Alyssa. But Marcia didn't want Reb to help because she felt beholden. She hadn't meant Reb to feel that way after she helped Alyssa. She wanted Reb to help because she wanted to; because they were friends who helped one another, not because they were counting favours. But she couldn't be picky right now, could she?

"You realise, though," Reb continued, "it's not up to me? It's up to Beckett."

"But Beckett accepted you, right? And Tait? They don't have anything against Teren sorcerers."

Reb was worrying at her thumbnail. "Neither Tait nor I deliberately attacked Marek. Or indeed Beckett themself. I – I don't think it's going to work. Or. I don't want to make the offer without checking, anyway."

Marcia hunched backwards into the armchair. "You mean – right now?" It wasn't like she was scared of Beckett. Not scared, exactly.

"You can wait outside, if you like?" Reb offered.

Marcia made herself sit properly upright, as much as that was possible in Reb's sagging old armchair. "No. No. I'm fine. Go ahead."

Reb stood up, and closed her eyes. There was that faint moment of discomfort, and then Beckett was standing in the room.

"You need me?" they demanded, their expressionless eyes looking between Reb and Marcia.

"There is – one from Teren, who would be a Marek sorcerer," Reb said, hesitantly.

"Your apprentice," Beckett agreed.

"No," Reb said. Marcia could see her bracing herself. "His name is Hira. He…attacked Marek, once."

Beckett's eyes were distant for a moment, and Marcia remembered with a horrified sick discomfort that they had, in some sense, access to everything that happened in Marek. Their attention returned to the room, rage blazing in their eyes, and the air thickened and grew heavy. Marcia couldn't stop herself from shrinking backwards. Beckett hissed. "Him! I see him, now, and you *dare* to ask me…"

"I believe – he wants to do *better*," Reb said, which was a bit of a stretch, given that she hadn't even spoken to Hira. She was doing this for Marcia, wasn't she? Marcia bit, hard, at the inside of her lip. "To be able to work in the Marek way, to work with you, to do things differently…"

"You expect me to forgive the *insult*? You want me to *work with*, to send power to, someone who attacked me? My city? No. I will not."

"People change," Reb said, tension shivering in her voice. "They change. And we learn to work with them. I'm working with Cato."

"No," Beckett said again. "He is not Mareker. He attacked me. I will not. The covenant binds me to Marek sorcerers. He is not a Marek sorcerer. Nor will he be. I will *not*."

They vanished while Reb was still opening her mouth to try again.

"Shit," Reb said, and sat heavily down.

Marcia rubbed her hands over her face. "Well then. That's that. I suppose…I suppose I'll just have to go and see if money and sanctuary alone will buy him off." If not, she had the edges of another idea, one rather more morally grey, but she wasn't going to share that with Reb. "I'm sorry I bothered you."

Reb shook her head. "I'm glad you asked." Marcia couldn't meet her eyes. "And I do understand why. You didn't use magic, back then, but…"

"But it looked a whole lot like it," Marcia said. "I thought I'd managed things well enough, for the Council tomorrow, but that was about," she gestured, feeling awkward, "you and me. If Hira brings evidence about the barge-yard, I've no hope. But they can't bring it in without him, or it'll just be hearsay."

Reb was jiggling her foot, visibly unsettled. "Right. What if I gave evidence, though? The other way. That you weren't involved."

"But you can't say I wasn't there," Marcia said. "Because I was. You can say I didn't do magic, but the Council won't understand the detail. And I don't want you to lie, any more than I would ask Tait or Jonas to," or Cato, who wouldn't care about lying, but wouldn't come to the Hill in the first place, "but in any case, even if said I wasn't there, against Hira saying I was, no one's going to buy that. Not when I've admitted we were in a relationship at the time. They'll assume you're protecting me." She spread her hands. "My only hope is to keep it out altogether. And I wish I didn't have to do that, either. But I *didn't* do anything wrong. I don't want to take the fall for something I didn't do. I just want to stop this from happening."

Reb sighed, and pushed herself to her feet. "Fine. Let's do it."

Marcia blinked up at her, confused. "But you can't. Becket…"

"I can't offer him magic. But I can come with you."

Marcia swallowed, blindsided by how badly she wanted Reb at her back. But… "You don't have to. Truly, you don't. I – I had to ask you, but I'll understand…"

Reb shook her head, and Marcia's heart lifted, just a little. "Don't be daft. Of course I'll come."

The inn Hira was staying in was over the other side of Old Bridge. Marcia's feet ached horribly by the time they got there. She'd refused Reb's suggestion of a litter from the embankment – there weren't any to be had closer – and now she regretted her pride.

The innkeeper showed them up to the sorcerer's room. When he opened the door, Marcia experienced a shock of recognition. She wouldn't have said she'd paid much attention to him back then, but apparently she had, because this was definitely him. He was better-dressed than he had been. Perhaps Selene was worried about the impression he needed to make on the Council.

His eyes went straight over her and landed on Reb.

"Sorcerer," he said, his shoulders up round his ears.

Reb nodded. "May we come in?"

Hira didn't say anything, just silently stood back and gestured them in. Marcia eyed the chair in the corner longingly, but she couldn't intimidate him from there. She made herself stand up as straight as she could.

"We're told," she said crisply, drawing Hira's attention away from Reb, "that you intend to testify against me in Council tomorrow. Testify that I used magic in front of you. I did not use magic, and never have used magic."

Hira scoffed. "I saw you."

"She was a conduit," Reb said. "She's not a sorcerer herself."

"I'm sure your Council are going to think that a very important detail, yes."

"Which is why I am here to make you an offer," Marcia said. "I am given to understand that, in exchange for sanctuary in Marek, and funds to support your first few months, you are willing to disappear and not report to the Council tomorrow."

"Bribing me not to give evidence? Not all that certain of your innocence, then."

"I didn't do it," Marcia said, again, chin up. "But I've no way of proving that. I'd rather not be kicked out of the Houses for something I didn't, in fact, do."

"Fine. Whatever. Not like I actually care." He looked at Reb again, and Marcia took the opportunity to shift her weight surreptitiously. "But that's not what I wanted. Sorcery. If I can be a Marek sorcerer," there was a brief deep hunger in his eyes, before he controlled his expression, "I'll disappear as soon as you like. That's enough to keep me clear of the Academy. You made that plenty clear last year."

"Unfortunately I can't offer you that," Reb cut in, voice cold.

Hira began to scoff, and Reb cut over him. "And that is not my decision. That is the decision of the cityangel, who knows who you are, and where you are, and who is unwilling to work with one who fought them." Her eyebrow lifted. "Not unreasonably."

Hira swallowed, looking sick and scared, and for a fraction of a second, before his face shuttered, unutterably distraught.

"I can request their presence, if you doubt me," Reb added.

Hira shook his head, reflexively fast.

"Well. That's that. No sorcery for me, no Marek for me, no luck for you."

Marcia ruthlessly tamped down her feelings. She had to get out of this.

She hadn't wanted to have to fall back on straight threats; but that was where she was, so.

"In that case," she said, examining her fingernails. "I suppose I'll have to tell Selene what you were willing to agree to, if Beckett hadn't turned you down. I'm sure she'll be *fascinated* to know. The Academy even more so, when I write to them."

Naked horror flashed onto Hira's face, before he smoothed it away and tried to shrug. "Tell her whatever you like. I'll testify against you anyway, and that's what she wanted. She'll be happy enough."

"Oh, I'm sure she'll be happy with the testimony. I'm just not sure that'll buy you out of the fact that you were willing to screw her over at the last minute in exchange for sanctuary here. You *suggested* it, even, as I understand it." That was a guess, from what Kia had said, but Hira's expression suggested it had landed. Marcia shook her head slowly. "She's not the forgiving sort, Selene."

She was gambling. If Selene had any sense, even if she believed Marcia, she'd ignore the whole business, protect Hira from the Academy in exchange for his help here, and gain his everlasting support. What mattered right now was what Hira *thought* Selene would do, and she didn't think Hira trusted Selene in the slightest.

"I'll deny it," Hira said, but she saw him swallow.

She shrugged. "Well, she'll have to decide who to believe. I wonder which of us will be the more convincing? And then, of course, even if Selene believes you, what will the Academy think, once my message reaches them? Will Selene be able to protect you?"

"Selene's going to be Archion," Hira said, but his voice lacked conviction. That was interesting in itself.

Marcia nodded sympathetically. "I'm sure she's told you that. She might even believe it herself. Ameten politics isn't all that predictable, the way I understand it, and I'm not sure I'd trust Selene's assessment of her chances. That's if the next Archion isn't already in place by the time you get back."

Hira's eyes flickered.

"Never mind," she said soothingly. "I'm sure the Academy will be happy to accept your assurances. Despite your failure last year. I'm sure they won't begin to wonder where your true allegiances might lie." She shifted her weight, as if she were preparing to leave, ignoring the flare of pain in her hip.

Hira flinched, just a tiny movement. He wouldn't look at her. She had him. She was sure of it. She let the silence stretch. To her side, Reb was silent, unmoving.

"Alternatively," Marcia said, when Hira's tension had ratcheted up a notch further, "I could give you the money, and you disappear into Marek anyway. Safe from Selene. Safe from the Academy."

He'd twitched again. "No magic," he said, hoarsely, after a moment.

"Will you still get to use magic, either way, once Selene and the Academy are done with you?" Marcia asked, keeping her voice light, uncaring.

Hira slouched aggressively. "Can't hardly make myself a living here, without magic." Marcia hid her delight. That was it. He'd cracked. "Been at the Academy. Got no trade."

"I can give you a letter of introduction at the Guilds," Marcia said. She'd won. She'd got him. This was just negotiation, now, and she was good at that. "A specific one, if you've a preference. If not, they'll help you find something you prefer. A more honourable living, don't you think, than setting demons on your fellow citizens."

Pain flashed across Hira's face. Marcia wished she didn't feel pride in herself for having found all his buttons. He might keep pushing, but the bottom line was, he wanted out. And the reason he was so scared of Selene and the Academy was that he knew they would believe he wanted out, and they'd treat him harshly to discourage the others. Like they'd tried to do to Tait. Hira should never have spoken to – Jonas, was where Marcia guessed Kia had got her info – should certainly never have let her and Reb in. He'd wanted out badly enough to risk it. And now Marcia was using that to screw him over to save herself.

She ought to feel guilty. She did, maybe, a little. On the other hand, he'd attacked Beckett, even if had been under duress. And she didn't have time for guilt. She needed to save herself, and her House.

She didn't dare meet Reb's eye.

Hira, to give him credit, made a hard bargain. Marcia

paid over most of what she had on her, and agreed to have her factor make up the balance, and sort him out with accommodation.

"In writing," Hira said.

"Absolutely not," Marcia said. It was bad enough that the innkeeper knew they were up here speaking to Hira, even if the innkeeper didn't know who he was. "I'll speak to my factor in the next two hours. Go to her after that for the balance."

"What's to stop you just 'forgetting' to do that?" Hira demanded.

"What's to stop you turning up at the Council tomorrow anyway?" Marcia countered. "We're both at risk here. It's not like you can't find me, if I don't follow through. I live in a bloody great House with my name on it. Go to the Council yourself, anyway, if I let you down." He could do that even with the money in his pocket, but if she could once get through tomorrow, it would be a sight harder for anyone to bring the same thing back again.

It was a risk, still. And if he turned up tomorrow at the Council, with not only his original story but the addition that she'd been willing to bribe him to shut up, it was going to backfire on her. It was a risk; just less of a risk than if she hadn't.

"I could bind you both." It was the first thing Reb had said since Beckett disappeared. Her voice was gruff.

"Marekhill," Marcia said. "I haven't broken the Statutes yet. That's the whole point of this."

Reb shrugged. "I could bind him, then. If he agreed."

Marcia, finally, looked over at her. Reb, clearly, didn't entirely approve of what Marcia was doing here. But she was willing to back her up anyway. Marcia had to swallow past the lump in her throat.

Hira eyed both of them. "Double the money," he said, flatly.

"Double the money so you won't screw me over?" Marcia said, incredulous.

Hira shrugged. "Double the money for the guarantee."

"Another fifty," Marcia said, "and that's it."

Hira sucked his teeth. "Fifty, and that one binds me not to speak to the Council, tomorrow only. Otherwise I've no recourse if you don't speak to your factor."

"Done," Marcia said briskly.

The binding was nothing that she could see, but Hira pulled a horrible face as Reb did it. Marcia didn't know how Beckett's power would feel, to one in Hira's situation, even fed through Reb.

Marcia told Hira, again, to see her factor in two hours, and took her leave.

"I know," she said, once they were a little way down the street. "I screwed him over."

Reb shrugged, letting her feet scuff along the ground. "He was going to screw you over."

"Selene was going to screw me over. Hira's just caught in the middle."

"If you're looking for me to say I don't approve – fine, I don't. But I don't approve of what Selene is doing, either, and I don't think your Council is at all reasonable about magic." Reb still wasn't looking at Marcia. "Hira's better off away from the Academy, even if he might not appreciate that."

"He won't have magic."

"That's the bit he won't appreciate. But his magic is taken from spirits without their consent, so I'm not that bothered." Reb stopped, and turned to Marcia, finally meeting her eyes. "I'm not saying you were right. But then, I'm not sure you were wrong, either. So." She spread her hands. "It's done, either way. We'd both best get on." She reached out and gently took Marcia's hand, her palm warm. "Good luck, tomorrow." That was sincere.

She let Marcia's hand drop, turned, and left. Marcia watched her walk away, her own hand still tingling, before she sighed, and took the turning that led towards the warehouse, and her factor's office. It was done, and she'd had her part of the bargain to keep, even if the bargain hadn't been a fair one. They weren't, always, were they?

TWENTY-FIVE

Walking into the Council Chamber took an act of will. However much she might have planned, however much she'd done to make this work out…well. It was a risk.

Athitol-Head brought the initial charges: 'use of magic', and Marcia's stomach flipped – had they decided to try that even without Hira? Or had Hira found a way past the binding? But it rapidly became clear that the charge was based solely on Marcia's relationship with Reb. On the other hand, as far as Marcia could tell, Athitol-Head did sincerely believe everything she was saying. Somehow that felt better than it being wholly opportunistic or political; not that, if Marcia lost, it would matter *why* this had come to Council.

The next hurdle was Athitol-Head's attempt to move matters to the Small Chamber. Andreas objected, on the grounds that this was sufficiently serious to be of relevance to the whole Council. The Reader sided with Andreas; when planning, Marcia and Andreas had thought that was most likely, but it was nevertheless a relief. Marcia wasn't fool enough to think all the Guildwardens would vote on her side, but it definitely gave her more room in the numbers. Without the pressure she'd put on Daril and Dyesha, it would have been a different matter. If Athitol-Head were, after all, somehow still able to produce Hira later, it still might. Marcia had realised, afterwards (too late), the gap in the binding – if Athitol-Head were to say they would have evidence the next day, ask to postpone, the binding would expire. And Athitol-Head could still be waiting to spring that on her.

Selene was here, which…well. Marcia wasn't, in fact, surprised, but it was unusual. There was a seat in the Chamber for the Teren Lieutenant, but last year had been the first in living memory that the Lieutenant had sat in on anything other than the annual return to session. Was Selene planning to speak again? Marcia almost hoped so; she suspected it wouldn't go down well. Selene narrowed her eyes slightly as Athitol-Head came to a conclusion – had she expected the business in the barge-yard to be brought up? Had Athitol-Head avoided admitting the star witness had disappeared? – then sat back and folded her arms. Maybe she was hoping for something dramatic later on. Marcia sincerely hoped the opposite.

Athitol-Head finished with a rhetorical flourish and sat down.

Marcia's turn.

She rose to her feet, and waited for quiet.

"I could have just denied this, from top to bottom," she began. "Denied that I knew a sorcerer at all, said this was a base and scurrilous rumour about my private life. Perhaps then it would not have come to the Council at all. But that would be untrue. I have never done magic, nor had it done for me. I did have a sorcerer lover, for nearly a year. I have not broken the Statutes." She paused there, to make sure that sank in. "I have never broken the Statutes," she said again. Andreas had strongly suggested she steer clear of the 'magic performed on behalf of Marek as a whole' argument unless she was forced to go into it, for fear of muddying the stream. "But I could have denied all of it. Why haven't I? Because the Council needs to reckon with its relationship with magic."

There was a susurration around the room. Marcia glanced around – some disapproving faces, a few thoughtful, the Guilds at the back looking faintly distant, as though they saw this as a House matter, not a Guild one.

She took a deep breath, and rested her hand gently on her bump. It genuinely helped while she was standing up; but it might also sway some of the older Council members to treat her more kindly, and she wanted every edge she could get.

"The city is split into fragments – Houses, Guilds, unguilded folk, Marekhill, lower city, the squats, sorcerers...We can't carry on like this. We need to do better. And engaging with the reality of magic, and the position of our sorcerers in Marek, is part of that. Right now, it's the part that, by standing here, I'm able to talk about."

"Magic," Priella-Head scoffed.

"If you didn't think magic was a real thing," Marcia said, "none of you would mind that I was spending time with a sorcerer. My brother wouldn't have been disowned. The Statutes wouldn't matter, would it, if none of it was real." She'd found that disconnect infuriating when Cato was disowned – before then, of course, she'd never thought about it, the same way the rest of them didn't. She found that even more infuriating now. "And while I'm mentioning my brother, there's not one person in this room hasn't known I've been meeting with him regularly the last ten years and more. Apparently that hasn't mattered. One does rather wonder why 'speaking to a sorcerer' has become a problem *now*."

"*Speaking*, is it?" someone said audibly behind her, but she ignored them. It didn't matter what she'd been getting up to with Reb, and nearly no one in this room was going to get moral about that part of it.

"In truth, you all know that sorcery is real. That's why we're banned from using it. But over the years, centuries, it's become the norm for us to ignore it altogether. We need to engage with that, now, urgently, before what is happening in Teren descends upon our heads."

"Teren demons, nonsense," Athitol-Head said, waving a dismissive hand.

In the back, a couple of the Guildwardens shifted unhappily in their seats.

Selene's face was tight. She looked as if she wanted to say something and was restraining herself.

"They're not nonsense," Piath said quietly, to Marcia's shock. "I wish they were. I have spoken to people. I have been forced to conclude otherwise. Marcia is right. This is happening in Teren, and if we are to talk clearly about it, can we still ignore Marek magic?"

She'd expected – hoped – that Piath would speak to

Berenez-Head about voting in her favour. They had a strong view of what was legally right, and Andreas had promised to have a word on her behalf. But she hadn't expected them to agree with her publicly. It was hugely heartening.

"Teren magic works differently to ours," Marcia said. "That's one of our advantages. We are protected by the cityangel." It felt transgressive even to say that – still, even after meeting Beckett – and so much more so here in the Chamber. Her heart shivered in her chest, beating fast, the top of her chest tight with it.

"Superstition…" Pedeli-Head said.

"I've met the cityangel," Marcia said. A shocked silence fell across the room. She felt almost weightless, floating on the barely-suppressed panic that vibrated through her tense muscles. "Their name is Beckett."

"Are you suggesting, Fereno-Heir, that Teren demons will come here? To Marek?" one of the Guildwardens demanded.

Marcia avoided looking over at Selene. "I sincerely hope not," she said. "But I have no idea about magic, really. Which is why I think the Council needs to engage with those who *do* know about it."

"What, so we can all break the Statutes and cheat in the Chamber?" Dyesha scoffed.

Marcia took a moment to marvel at her utter cheek; but it was a useful line. "Of course not. I am not arguing that House members should be allowed to use sorcery themselves at all, still less as part of our work in the Chamber. The Statutes as they stand I have no objection to." Not entirely true, but a good line. "I am arguing, firstly, that I personally have not breached it," best underline that as often as she could, "and secondly, that we must all re-examine how we think about sorcery and sorcerers. We must acknowledge that Marek is a city of magic, from our founding onwards. I have done nothing wrong. What I *have* done is to listen to a sorcerer." She'd been listening to Cato, too, for over a decade, as it happened. "I've listened, and so should the Council listen. That's all. I have never used magic, and I defy anyone to prove otherwise."

The room was quiet. She looked around, keeping her head up and her gaze open. Selene was looking expectantly down at Athitol-Head. Athitol-Head, on the other hand, was turned away from Selene, to the point that she looked slightly awkward in her seat. Ha. No, Athitol-Head was not going to suddenly produce Hira, or the threat of Hira. The relief was immense.

Marcia let the moment stretch before she spoke again. "No one brings evidence. I have not broken the Statutes." She looked around the Chamber, meeting as many eyes as she could. "This whole situation, this *claim* against me, is symptomatic of a wider problem. We, the Houses, refuse to talk or to think about magic. We treat it as if it doesn't exist – but if we truly believed that, I wouldn't be here today. It wouldn't matter, if I were spending time with charlatans or the deceived. My brother Cato would not have been disowned, but treated with sympathy and concern, as one deluded. Of course we *believe* in magic. We just choose not to speak of it. And we cannot, must not, keep doing that. Marek was founded on the agreement with the cityangel. They are depicted on that stone there, the one on which we renew our oaths. Magic is part of our city; and yet we look past it. Of course we can't allow magic to be used as part of our duties here. But to cut it off altogether is equally foolhardy. Right now, refugees are flooding into Marek because of the misuse of magic in Teren, and we ignore it. Sorcerers saved people when the bridge fell, and we don't speak of it. We cannot keep ignoring a part of our reality. And to punish me while I try to bridge those gaps – I do not believe that you are all that short-sighted."

"Is that why you took a sorcerer out of prison?" Isobel, Tabriol-Heir asked, earning herself a frown from the Reader.

Marcia hadn't expected that, and kicked herself for it. "I helped her because there was no good evidence against her, and no reason to keep her before trial. The fact that she was a sorcerer was immaterial."

"That she was your lover's apprentice?" Isobel pressed.

"We were no longer together by then. The case was brought to my attention and I assisted."

Isobel, for a wonder, shut up.

"I would do the same for anyone else," Marcia added. "If there had been a case to answer she would have been brought to trial." She still wasn't sure if that *definitely* wouldn't happen, but she thought she'd have heard about it if it *had* happened, and it had been a while now. She shrugged, very slightly. "Everyone is equal before the law." She wanted to point out that the pamphlet made some interesting points, never mind who had written it. But that was an argument for another time.

"I urge you," she concluded, "to vote as you believe."

The Reader looked around the room for other comments. Athitol-Head, apparently, felt she had said enough already, and shook her head. She was still facing away from Selene.

The Reader nodded at Warden Bradley, of the Broderers, who stood. "Whilst I appreciate Fereno-Heir's flights of rhetoric, I think we risk drifting away from the central point at hand. Whether or not the Council should be more willing to listen to sorcerers – perhaps something to discuss at another time – I see no evidence that Fereno-Heir has breached the Statutes. She may, perhaps, have made a bad decision in her personal life, but, truly, who among us has not?" He looked around and got the laugh he was expecting. "The Statutes forbid performing magic, or having magic performed for one. Not social engagement with sorcerers, of whatever sort." He twitched an eyebrow and got another laugh. "I may think less of Fereno-Heir's judgement as a result, but I see no reason to remove her from the Council, nor to encourage her Head to take action."

Dintra-Head was recognised and spoke, briefly and gruffly, about the scourge of sorcery, but Marcia got the impression he had suddenly become aware that by talking about sorcery at all he was giving it credence; his speech was halting and unconvincing.

To Marcia's surprise, the Reader nodded to Warden Ilana. "I agree with Warden Bradley that I find no reason to formally censure Fereno-Heir. I also note that, as she correctly said, it is common knowledge that she remained in touch with her brother. I find myself wondering, therefore, without wishing to cast any prejudice upon good Athitol-Head, whose concern I do not doubt, why exactly it is *now* that this matter has been raised." Warden Ilana cast a long, considering glance over at where Selene sat, arms folded and lips pressed tightly together; then spread their hands and sat down again.

Haran-Head stood. "Don't hold with sorcery," he said, scratching at the beard, fashionable in his youth, that he still wore, "but don't hold with gossip and hearsay either. Even if the girl did admit to it. Not the point. Shouldn't have got this far." He sat down again with a sharp nod, and to a murmur of agreement from a couple of the older, more hide-bound Heads. They might disapprove of her relationship with Reb, but an accusation of breaching the Statutes was a serious matter, and to vote against her they would want concrete proof.

The Reader called for the vote. Marcia dug her nails into her palm while she waited; but it went largely as she'd expected it would once the threat of Hira had been removed. Andreas voted in her favour, as did Haran-Head, Berenaz-Head (obviously Piath *had* spoken to him), and William Cerit-Head. Athitol-Head and Dintra-Head voted against her. Daril, to her surprise, voted in her favour; she'd only agreed with him that he'd abstain. Pirran, Pedeli-Head, abstained, looking faintly irritable; Dyesha must have done what was necessary. A couple of the Guildwardens voted against Marcia (Hagadath, unsurprisingly, was one of them); more, including Ilana, in her favour. There were a number of abstentions from both Houses and Guilds, more than Marcia had hoped for; but the balance was enough in her favour that it didn't matter.

Relieved, and suddenly extremely keen to *leave*, her

legs beginning to shake with the aftermath of anxiety, she waited for the thump of the Reader's staff to conclude the session. Instead, there was a murmur, and she looked up to see Daril on his feet.

"I am delighted that Fereno-Heir has been acquitted of these unfair rumours," he began. "And I am pleased to see her attempting to create new bridges within the city," which Marcia didn't believe for a second. Where was he going? "But there is a more urgent issue to address today. When I began to hear these rumours, I found myself wondering where they originated. By Fereno-Heir's own admission, this relationship has been over for some time. Why, then, was it now that the gossip arose? It did not take me long to establish that the source was," he gestured at Selene, "the Teren Lieutenant. Who is here, in our Chamber, once again, as she was last year when she argued against our friends in the Guilds joining us." He nodded courteously to Ilana and the two Wardens next to them.

He was winding up to something, but Marcia couldn't tell what it was. Her anxiety returned, sharper now.

"For decades, now, longer, Teren has let us manage our own city," Daril continued. "Why now is it attempting to shoulder its way into our deliberations?" He paused, looking up at Selene, eyebrows raised.

Selene took the bait. "Marek is part of Teren."

"So you say," Daril said, nodding slowly. "So you say, and you use it as an excuse to *intervene*, when for so long you have correctly left us to ourselves." He didn't mention the business of the tariffs. He didn't have to. "And I say – very well then. Let's change that."

With a surge of satisfaction, Daril heard the intake of breath around the Chamber. He felt the glorious, uplifting thrill of doing something unexpected, of suddenly holding the whole focus of the room. Selene, sitting in front of the arms of Teren painted on the wall, was frozen in shock, which was satisfying all by itself. Marcia, until moments ago the focus of attention, looked almost as surprised. Ha. This was *his* moment, and he was going to make it count. He would be the architect of the new Marek, and then he would make the most of everything that might mean.

But first, he had a Chamber to win over.

"Hasn't Marek been independent in practice for decades? Centuries, even?" He let his voice ring proudly. "Since the Houses were first founded, and the Chamber set up? What is our notional *link* with Teren worth to us, when we do our own trading and set our own laws?" *Worth*, like *value*, was a word that really focused the minds of the Houses and Guilds.

"Apparently, it gets us told we have to sell Teren merchants' goods for free," Kilzan-Head called out, earning himself a repressive look from the Reader and an irritated mutter of agreement from the rest of the Chamber.

"Exactly," Daril agreed. "Exactly. Teren does nothing for us, and yet Teren swaggers in here and tells us how we are to conduct our business. When we are the ones doing all the work. What has Teren, or the Teren Lieutenant – saving your presence – " he turned and offered a shallow bow to Selene, who, he saw with pleasure, looked absolutely furious, "done for us, that we should extend the owners of Teren goods such charity?"

Warden Bradley rose to speak. "I would note," he said, "that this sudden announcement from the Teren Lieutenant has caused the Guilds significant problems, both in terms of our raw materials, and with regard to finished goods that might now be coming in duty-free and, more importantly, unexamined. We are concerned, as ever, about the quality of goods both in Marek, and outside it. Teren must not be allowed to slip us substandard goods." Daril wasn't sure that the risk of Teren-made goods being sold on as Marek-made was a real one, but the Guildwardens all looked genuinely concerned. Also, the Guilds largely hated Selene after she'd ignored them so comprehensively last year; her attempted charm offensive this time had been wholly transparent. Admittedly, Hagadath might have fallen for it.

The Reader nodded to recognise Pedeli-Head. "Our arrangements with Exuria and the Crescent run officially through Teren," she said, standing stiffly upright. "Our people there are looked after by the Teren Embassy, and our contracts operate under the treaties between those countries and Teren, not directly. We would not wish to sacrifice those contracts."

Andreas gestured to interrupt, and Pedeli-Head nodded politely at him.

"In practice, though," Andreas said, leaning on the rail in front of his seat, giving Pedeli-Head the benefit of his best open smile, "our contracts are all negotiated directly via each House with the various operators in those places. Not with their governments." Pedeli-Head frowned, and Andreas hurried on. "I understand your point about the legal underpinnings. But my point is that those direct contracts are favourable to both ourselves and to those operating out of Exuria or the Crescent. Teren is only one of our country-clients, and they do very little of their own business. Our trade volume around the Oval Sea is several times that of the rest of Teren. We," he gestured round the Chamber, "as Houses, have negotiating experience in those places, and as Guilds, have high-quality goods for which there is an eager existent market. Why should we not negotiate official recognition for Marek, independent city, directly with the relevant governments?"

"Will they care to?" Pedeli-Head asked. "And if they care to, will they not seek to gain advantage?"

"Why wouldn't they care to?" Andreas shrugged. "We have closer relationships with them than Teren does, by our nature and location. Both Exuria and the Crescent have ambassadors here as well as Ameten, because in practice Marek acts independently. And, again, our trade volumes are far higher. The legal treaties may be with Teren, but it's Marek's trade that matters. And of course Salina explicitly does not engage with internal disagreements; our Salinas contracts are safe. As for the matter of them seeking advantage – no doubt they will, indeed. It's not like anyone in this room is unfamiliar with the art of negotiating with someone who is seeking to profit from you, is it?" He grinned, and there was an answering rumble of laughter.

Andreas was good at winning people over. Daril could feel the room starting to shift; belief growing that they could do this thing. "What is the value of being in Teren?" he called, rhetorically, and earned his own glower from the Reader.

Tabriol-Head received the nod from the Reader, and rose to her feet. "What is the value of *not* being part of Teren, though?" she asked.

"They won't get in our way," William, Cerit-Head, called out. There was a general laugh.

Tabriol-Head frowned at him. "My point is, there is always a cost to change. Even if this change is beneficial, is it beneficial enough to be worth that cost – negotiating new treaties, potentially damaging our relationship with Teren, plus whatever we don't think of now that will become clear later. Because believe me, there are always things that you haven't thought of. So. What do we gain? If we have been independent in practice for decades, centuries even, as Leandra-Heir says, why rock the boat now?" She nodded and sat down.

Andreas glanced over at Daril, who gave him a tiny nod. Andreas was handling the reluctant-agreement side of things.

"If I may," Andreas said, looking to the Reader for permission. "Until recently, I would have said that we gain nothing. Because the fact that we are notionally part of Teren was only a matter of official status. A small payment annually. The occasional Archion's barge trading for free. Some official events. But now – the Lieutenant comes here to interfere. Last year, it was the composition of the Council. This year, we're expected to allow all Teren merchants to trade for free. We're asked to turn back their refugees, against all our close-held traditions. And yes, right now that is an ask, but sooner or later they will insist. Do we want to wait?"

There was a murmur of agreement, but looking around, Daril still saw some doubtful faces. His toes twitched inside his boots. He *had* to win this, now he'd launched it.

"It seems to me," Warden Ilana said, "that Teren have taken rather too much *direct* interest in our governance lately." Together with her earlier comment during Marcia's trial, the implication was clear. "If I wished to be ruled by Ameten, I would move there. Marek does not need this interference. If independence is what it takes to get rid of it, then," they shrugged, "by all means, let us do that. It is, after all, merely a formalisation of a long-standing practical truth."

Athitol-Head rose to her feet. "We should give the Teren Lieutenant a chance to speak. If we are to seriously engage with this matter." She sounded dismissive, disapproving. Unsurprising; Athitol-Head was conservative in all ways and Daril had no expectation of obtaining her vote.

"By all means, if I may." Selene rose to her feet. She looked like she'd managed to control her emotions during the previous few minutes; which was a shame, from Daril's point of view, but unsurprising. Selene was a politician, and one from Ameten's High Court, which had its own reputation.

"I am saddened to hear that you perceive our recent requests as so burdensome," Selene began. Her tone was gentle, concerned, and Daril ground his teeth. "Of course, Teren has no intention of overruling Marek in any matter. You are free to take refugees as you prefer; we request, only, that you consider the implications of the matter on the rest of the country. Marek of course has its own character, its own Council, and the Archion would never wish to impose anything upon our cousins. We are only sad that the relationship has atrophied in recent decades, and wish to rebuild that closeness."

"So we don't charge you!" someone called out – Daril didn't spot who. The Reader banged their staff, but there was a mutter of agreement in the room. Still, Daril thought; she was taking the right tack. She might yet persuade them. He caught Andreas' eye; he, too, looked worried.

Selene ignored the interruption. "We would be delighted to see our Marek cousins in Ameten, meeting the Archion, spending time in the High Court. Teren is a power in its own right, and Marek is part of that power, and benefits from it – as Pedeli-Head pointed out, through our treaties with your trading partner. Better, surely, to be aligned with Teren's power than arrayed against it."

There was a rustle of discomfort, and Tabriol-Head gestured a request to interrupt. "Is that a threat, Lieutenant?"

"Of course not," Selene replied, looking performatively startled that anyone would read it that way. "Not at all. Merely a natural truth about power and strength. Teren is a large country, with all the resources that implies. What power does Marek hold?"

"We hold the river mouth." Andreas gave the obvious answer. "We control Teren's trade."

Selene's lips compressed. "Indeed. Yet we have demons."

A ripple of unhappiness ran through the room. Daril did his best to hide his glee. *She fucked up.* She'd nearly had it, too. He caught Andreas' eye, and saw relief and satisfaction that mirrored his own. Selene was already attempting to backpedal and return to the matter of Marek's long history as a Teren city; but she'd lost them. He supposed that she might not quite have meant it as the threat they'd all read it as; but what she'd *meant* didn't matter.

Daril caught the Reader's eye, and stood. Time to summarise. "So. The Teren Lieutenant gives us soft words about close relationships, but means that she wants to enforce special rates. Did she ask nicely before she issued the new rules about the Archion's exemption? Of course not. It was imposed. It takes advantage of an existing agreement which was never intended to cover every barge out of Teren. So much for soft words and cousinship. And then she reveals her true hand, by talking of power. Not a threat? Of course it's a threat." He let disgust slip into his voice. "How foolish does she think we are? When she sees her power and her discounts slipping away, the mask slips too. Why should we give in to this?"

"If the power is real," Athitol-Head objected, "then the risk is real."

Daril, about to reply, saw Marcia requesting to speak. She'd been silent so far; what would she say? Well; magic was the issue at hand. Best let Marcia continue to spend her credibility on that, then he could avoid having to do so himself.

"If the power is real," Marcia said, clearly, "then she's talking about demons. If you accept the demons, the spirits, then surely you must accept that our own cityangel protects us from other spirits, and so their demons are not a threat to us. If, on the other hand, you disbelieve the cityangel, then you don't believe the demons either."

Daril was impressed. Marcia was really committing to the magic bit. Good luck to her, especially if it saved him having to take the political risk.

"Never mind this demon nonsense, what about a real actual army?" Athitol-Head demanded.

A reasonable question, in that everyone in the room was fully aware that neither the guard nor the mercenary troop that lived in the barracks would be up to dealing with that.

"They have to come down the river, or down the road," Haran-Head said, standing and shrugging. Daril remembered that he'd done a year in the mercenary troop, before he'd come to the Heirship. "We're surrounded by swamp. Bottleneck. You can't get an army down here that fast, not one big enough to take a city. Plenty of time to keep 'em out."

"A siege?" Pedeli-Head asked doubtfully. She was twisting her fingers together.

"Who's besieged?" Haran scoffed. "We have the Oval Sea. Everything comes through us. Teren would be besieging themselves if they tried to blockade the river and the road. We're the ones with the power here, and they know it."

Yes. Daril could feel the energy shifting. More points were made, some with more vigour than others, but it was no longer Andreas and him alone defending independence. Others were stepping in to speak. The matter had gained its own momentum. He was going to win.

Selene tried to speak again, possibly to soften her perceived threat, but was shouted down. "This is a Marek matter," Haran-Head said loudly. Selene pressed her lips tightly together, expression betraying her worry. And a deeper anxiety; this mattered more to her than just on a political level, Daril suspected. Not that he cared.

There was a proposal to consider the matter longer, but it was shouted down by those arguing that the sooner they acted the better. Daril could almost taste the febrile enthusiasm in the air, the wish for action.

"Let's vote," Daril called, when he judged the moment to be right.

It was almost unanimous. Far better than he'd hoped. Athitol-Head was the only outlier. He jumped to his feet, only barely awaiting the Reader's authorisation.

"May I ask Athitol-Head, given the importance of this vote, to formally confirm that she will abide by the decision of the Council?" he asked loudly.

Athitol-Head looked around the room, and nodded, tightly.

"Athitol-Head agrees," Daril said.

Selene stormed out. *That* was satisfying. Andreas was grinning across the Chamber at him. Half of the Council looked almost as elated as Daril felt; the giddy joy of having got away with something.

He couldn't remember ever feeling this good. This was his idea. He'd proposed it. He'd shepherded it through the discussion. He'd *won*. His fingertips tingled with power. Never mind magic; *this* was the real deal. And this was only the start.

TWENTY-SIX

Reb knew when Marcia was due in front of the Council; and when, the next morning, she still hadn't heard from Marcia, she found herself far too jittery to settle to anything. Could she message Marcia herself? But maybe there was a reason Marcia hadn't been in touch. They weren't together any more. She might not think Reb wanted to know. She might...

She had charms to make, but there was no way she could do reliable magic while she was like this. Perhaps a quiet infusion at Irin's would calm her down.

Irin kept gossip- and news-sheets on the corner of her counter, for her customers. Today, their front pages all had huge block-letter headlines, impossible to miss, all screaming about...Marek independence?

Reb, confused, scanned further down. The text below each headline varied in degrees of breathless excitement, concern (the most staid of the sheets), and cynicism (the one radical sheet that was managing to keep just the correct side of the new laws), but had the same basic content: Marek's Council had declared the city independent of Teren.

Irin glanced at Reb, then away. Her daughter, Celia, was behind the counter, stacking biscuits onto trays and talking excitedly to her mother. "I mean, if the Council has to make changes *anyway*, maybe now really is the time for them to listen to us about the Petition..."

"I'll thank you to keep your politics out of my salon, young lady," Irin said tartly, and Celia subsided, looking grumpy.

Reb paid for her infusion, and took one of the less-excitable sheets to a table to read it properly. If that was what had happened in the Council last night, perhaps Marcia's matter hadn't been dealt with at all? In which

case, what about Hira and the time limit on the binding?
She took a sip of rose infusion and turned the page.

MAGIC SCANDAL ON THE COUNCIL

Ah. It had happened, after all, then. Well, that explained
the look Irin had given her. She skimmed the article –
brief coverage of Marcia's speech, and some political
speculation about votes and the connection between that
and the independence vote.

If it was in this one, it was probably in the others as
well. Did she want to read them, or didn't she? Well, she
didn't *want* to read them in the slightest; but perhaps it
was wise to know what people were saying about you?
After an inner struggle, she went to the counter and took
a selection of sheets. She gave Irin, peeking over at her, a
glare that sent her scurrying away to the other end of the
counter.

THE HEIR AND THE SORCERER

FERENO GETS AWAY WITH IT AGAIN

Ugh. One or two of them even named *her*. She hadn't
expected that. Mind you, there were only two full
sorcerers in Marek, which the Council and Marekhill
might not know but the rest of the city certainly did, and
the other was Marcia's brother. He was in the most
gossipy of the sheets, under a section providing
'background colour'. Cato's banishment had been a
scandal of its own, although that was before the news-
sheets.

The reporting wasn't *wholly* inaccurate. It still made
her squirm. Even if it weren't for all the political
complications, Reb didn't know how to deal with how
public this was. It wasn't like she'd had that many
relationships before, never mind ones spoken of all over
the city. Presumably Marcia was more accustomed to it.
Did one get accustomed to it? Her skin felt itchy.

"Uh…are you all right, Ser Reb?" Irin asked, coming
cautiously up to her table. "Can I get you another

infusion?" Her eyes darted down to the news-sheet and then back to Reb's face.

"I am fine," Reb said, repressively. "And yes, it's true, if you were wondering." Might as well just admit it.

Irin opened her mouth, eyed Reb, closed it again, and nodded.

When she left, the baker on the corner dashed out to offer her yesterday's stale bread-crumbs (useful for certain magics and also for baking), and after exchanging pleasantries, visibly tried trying to find a way to ask without actually having to ask. Reb didn't help.

Marcia still hadn't sent a message by the time Alyssa turned up for her lesson later that morning. Alyssa was a lot less subtle than the baker.

"So, the whole city knows you were screwing the Heir," she said, walking through Reb's front door. She looked appallingly cheerful.

"The bits of the city that bother to read rubbishy news-sheets, yes, I suppose they do," Reb said. If she *had* to talk about it at any point, she'd concluded, it was best just to be straightforward and boring. The more prickly she became the more it would seem like news.

"Not just the rubbishy ones," Alyssa contradicted. She helped herself to one of Reb's armchairs. "The good-quality ones too. Marcia's Heir-Fereno, after all."

"I was aware," Reb said. "And it's not happening any more." Not all of the sheets had made that clear, which made her uncomfortable in a different way.

"The revolutionary ones are interested too. Says something about the Council, doesn't it, that they're turning a blind eye to this? Things are changing, up on the Hill."

"It wasn't a breach of the Statutes," Reb said. "The Statutes say that Council members may not involve themselves in magic at all, for any reason, political or otherwise." She had read them. "And, by the by, Beckett's own covenant from the founding of the city bans them from engaging directly in politics, although that wouldn't say anything about the Houses using magic privately. In any case, the Statutes don't say anything about friendships with sorcerers."

"I thought they just didn't believe in it, up there."

Reb rocked her hand from side to side. "It's more that...they refuse to engage with it. 'The cityangel is a lower-city superstition', 'don't speak about magic', all that sort of thing. If they truly believed it doesn't exist, they wouldn't have to ignore it so hard. And they acknowledge the existence of elementals and sorcery in Teren, if they have to. It's Marek sorcery they're confused about."

"That doesn't make sense," Alyssa said.

Reb rolled her eyes. Not that she wasn't right. "If you go round expecting people to make *sense* all the time, you're going to be sadly disappointed."

Alyssa screwed up her nose. "Anyway. I'm sure it'll be a one-day wonder."

Reb wasn't. Things were, indeed, changing, up on the Hill. Or Marcia was trying to change them. And some of her reasons were very sound indeed. Something was happening in Teren, and Marek couldn't keep sitting on its complacent arse ignoring that. The Council had to engage with the reality of that, and what it might mean for Marek, if the things Reb feared came to pass. That was the fight Marcia was taking on, and it gave Reb a fierce proud feeling when she thought of it.

A sharp rat-tat at the door – finally, a messenger. Reb skimmed the brief message – just a line giving the result, and asking if Reb wanted to meet.

"I'll send straight back." She ducked inside to scrawl a reply, ignoring Alyssa, sitting in the armchair, arms folded and eyebrows raised.

Of course you're welcome to come over, she began, then hesitated. Marcia was pregnant, after all. She was coping fine, and she was only just past halfway, but still. Pregnancy wasn't an illness, but it was a tiring business, and perhaps it wasn't fair for Marcia to be the one marching around the city.

Because the thing was, Reb could go to House Fereno

now. If she wanted. Their – former – liaison was public, now. Discussed by the Council, referred to in the news-sheets. Very, very, public. And Marcia had got away with it, in Council. Reb could just go over there. If she wanted.

She didn't want. She didn't want to walk up to Marekhill and face all Marcia's wealth and power in physical form. She didn't like Marekhill, and she didn't want anything to do with it. Never had. And yet, she and Marcia had had – what they had had together – and they'd agreed to be friends. Marcia had helped Alyssa, without hesitation, when Reb asked her to. She'd refused to disown her relationship with Reb, even though that would have been far easier. She'd stood up for her beliefs about the Council and its relationship to magic, even if Reb herself didn't wholly agree with her.

And before that, she'd lied to Reb. Betrayed her? Maybe. Certainly mistrusted her. Then, after that, she'd apologised, fully, and meant it – and without wanting to buy anything with it. Reb swallowed.

"You got that reply?" the messenger called from the doorstep, shifting impatiently.

I'll come to you. Three bells, unless you tell me otherwise by return, Reb scribbled, sealed it, and handed it to the messenger, together with the fee, before she could think better of it.

By the time she'd finished Alyssa's lesson, taken the ferry over the river, and reached the gates of House Fereno, she was regretting her decision. It was an imposing building of pale-grey stone, wings coming forward at both sides to enclose a front courtyard with a fountain and small flower-beds around it. You could have fitted Reb's house and most of her neighbours down to the Old Market in there. Reb's stomach churned with uncomfortable doubt.

Well. She was here now. She wasn't about to turn back. She twitched her best cloak to settle it and marched up the stone steps to the front door.

"Sorcerer Reb. To see Fereno-Heir," she said firmly to the servant who opened the door.

Their eyes went wide – there was someone who'd read the news-sheets – before they resumed their professional mask, said "Certainly, Ser," and gestured her to a seat in an alcove.

Reb had enough time to gaze around at the marble floors, the beautiful long-case clock, the stairs sweeping up to the next floor… all contrasting so clearly with her own house over the river. She bet House Fereno never flooded in the winter rains; and if it did, it wouldn't be Marcia digging trenches out in the back garden.

And yet… it had worked, for a while, hadn't it? Reb cracked her knuckles and reached to touch the pouches at her belt. House Fereno might represent a lot of power; but so did those.

A door opened and the servant bowed to her. "Fereno-Heir will see you now."

Inside, big, deep windows lined the left wall, looking out over Marek. A couple of armchairs with a small table were grouped to the right, by a ceramic wall-stove, and at the far end were two couches and another armchair, everything upholstered in pale blue. The wooden floor shone with polishing. Marcia was rising, slightly ungainly, from one of the couches.

"Reb! Thank you so much for coming all the way up here."

"Well," Reb said, making her way across the room, "seemed a little unfair for you to be the one doing all the walking, in your current circumstances."

Marcia made a face. "I would say, oh, its not that bad, but honestly, it is starting to be that bad." She sank back onto the couch with a tiny sigh of relief.

Reb took the armchair. "Well, even without that – I gather from the news-sheets that you were up half the night."

"You've started reading the news-sheets?"

Reb, suddenly bashful, shifted in the – very comfortable – armchair. "I wanted to know what had happened yesterday."

"I should have messaged you," Marcia said,

remorsefully, "but then Daril went straight into this whole thing…"

"It sounded… surprising?"

"I was surprised." Marcia admitted. "I am not sure Andreas was, which… well, I haven't spoken to him about it yet. Obviously Daril had it planned." She nibbled thoughtfully at her lip. It was distracting. "I said something to him, last autumn, about being power-brokers. I fear he may have taken that, mm, rather to heart."

"What do you think of the thing itself?"

"Independence? Well, I voted for it. I've no wish to be ruled by Teren." She leant back against the couch. "Not that anyone would have thought about it if Selene hadn't begun pushing for more control. What happens now…well, we'll see. Not much, perhaps. We've been de-facto independent for decades. Longer, even. But then – well. It depends on what Selene – on what Teren – does next."

Reb looked at her, at her focused face as she thought through the issues and tried to plan, and was overwhelmed with a vast surge of affection. "You did well," she said. "You…you know I don't agree with you about magic and the Council. But you did well, trying to get them to understand."

Marcia smiled at her. "Thank you. I really appreciate that." She sighed. "Bloody Daril rather undermined it all, though. No one's thinking about it any more, are they? It's all going to be about independence for months now." She closed her eyes, running her fingertips under them and up to her temples. "One might almost think he'd planned it that way, though that may be unfair." She pulled her hands down and opened her eyes, smiling at Reb. "I will try again, though, even if you and Cato don't want actual representation."

"And Cato won't come anywhere near the Hill."

"Indeed." Her smile deepened, became more affectionate. Reb's heart ached, looking at her. "You will though. Look! Here you are. So perhaps…maybe I'll get some of the Houses to listen to you yet."

"Well," Reb said. "I can't see you giving up. Not your style, is it?"

"I will take that as a compliment," Marcia said, expression wry.

It was true. Marcia never did give up. Except with what had happened between Reb and her. She could have kept asking, kept pushing at Reb to take her back. Reb wasn't foolish enough not to know what Marcia herself had wanted. But she hadn't. She'd apologised, and then she'd left it alone. Because it had been Reb's decision to stop, and Marcia wasn't going to override that.

If anything was going to change, Reb herself would have to change it.

Was that what she wanted? Marcia had lied to her; that hadn't changed. But she'd apologised, and she was...Well. She was still a politician. Reb wasn't foolish enough to expect absolute honesty of her in all her dealings. But she'd refused to lie about their relationship, when it would have made everything easier for her, and that meant more to Reb than maybe it should.

Reb hadn't given her a chance. The moment something went wrong, she'd shut down. Cato had said that, weeks ago, and though she hated to admit it, he had a point.

She might get hurt again. That was always the risk, wasn't it, with other people? Trusting Marcia again meant opening herself up to more hurt. She could just leave. Keep herself closed off and safe.

And yet. Even though the idea terrified her, even though she could feel her breath shortening at the thought of it: she wanted to change. She wanted to try again. She didn't want to give up, not any more. Her hands shook as the certainty settled into her bones. It was always worth the risk, wasn't it, to connect. To try. Even if – even when – people let you down. It was always worth reaching out again.

"Do you," Reb found herself saying abruptly, before she'd worked out her words. "I mean. If. Do you want to try again? You and me?"

Marcia stared at her, wide-eyed, and blinked.

"Or not," Reb added hastily. Maybe she had read this all wrong, after all. "I didn't..."

"Yes," Marcia said, her whole heart in her voice. She leant towards Reb, eyes bright. "If you're sure – I didn't expect – yes, of course. Of *course*. But – " She hesitated. "I let you down, though. I lied to you. Are you..."

"You did. And you've apologised. And – I'm hoping you aren't going to do it again." Hoping. Trusting. Something was shivering under her ribcage: anxiety, or excitement. Maybe both.

"No." Marcia shook her head. "No. I – am trying to be more brave. To – avoid things less. That was the trouble. I didn't know what you'd say, so I avoided it. Turns out that didn't work so well." She grimaced. "On which note – Andreas."

"What about him?" Reb asked cautiously. Was this all about to come down again?

"Well. He's going to be the baby's co-parent, of course. And we've," she hesitated, just for a fraction of a second, then Reb saw her set her shoulders and raise her chin slightly. "We've been involved. You know. Physically."

"I know how babies work," Reb said. She wasn't sure where this was going, but she tried to sit and listen and give Marcia space to say it, and not react until she was done.

"I might not have done it that way!" Marcia said indignantly. "Uh. But I did. And we sort of still are, at least, we haven't *stopped*, at least not in theory, though it's been a while. Oh dear, I'm not saying this very well. It was always friendly and casual, is the thing, it's not like he's going to mind if I do tell him I'm done. I'm not – he's not my boyfriend, or my partner. It's not like I have to cut myself clear of him before I can be with you. Which is the thing, really – I can't cut myself clear of him. He's going to be part of my life, and the baby's, regardless of whether we're, you know. Physically. Or not."

"Of course he is," Reb agreed, relief washing through

her. She'd – expected that already, she supposed. He was the baby's father, after all, and Reb had read the news-sheets; there'd be another baby after this one, too. That was fine.

"You don't mind?"

"I don't think so. I wouldn't expect you to cut off your co-parent and close friend to be with me. Why would I? Of course he's part of your life. And, honestly, I don't think I mind much what you get up to with him. It doesn't affect you and me, does it?"

"I don't think so," Marcia said. "But I won't get up to anything, if you don't want me to."

Reb shrugged. "It's up to you. As long as you've time for me." It was supposed to be – mostly – a joke. It didn't quite come out that way.

"Always," Marcia said, fiercely. Her eyes were shining again. "I just – I wanted to be sure you understood. I didn't want to risk – I said, I'd be honest. I am trying."

"I appreciate you telling me," Reb said. A warm glow was rising up from her toes. "And I don't know what things should look like from here. We've both got commitments, and lives, and all of that." And they were still from opposite sides of the city, and Marcia was still Marekhill, and Reb was still a sorcerer. But maybe…maybe that didn't matter. "We can talk about it. I think we'll probably have to, quite a bit. I just – thank you. For telling me."

Marcia huffed a half-laugh. "I do try to learn from my mistakes."

"I know," Reb said. "That's – one of the things I love about you."

She thought, afterwards, that Marcia might have been the first to move; but Marcia was pregnant, and Reb reacted fast; and in the end they met somewhere in the middle of Marcia's couch, hands clutching at one another as their lips met.

"I'm still not sure how we're going to make this work," Reb said, honestly, a couple of minutes later.

"Me neither," Marcia admitted. "But – I'm willing to

try? If you are? Like you said. We can keep talking about it?"

"I can't think of anything that's more worth the trying." Reb pressed a kiss to the back of Marcia's hand between their interlinked fingers, and basked in her lover's smile.

Marek's new-declared independence might have led to the Teren Lieutenant's departure being brought forward by a couple of weeks, but it had not, apparently, led to the abandoning of all the surrounding formalities. Piath and Andreas had spent a day hurriedly rewriting most of the formal ceremony to bid Selene farewell, which was due tomorrow, and which Marcia was not looking forward to any more than she ever had. Cutting all the formal references to 'Marek, City of Teren' was an improvement, but it didn't make the thing any less tedious.

In the meantime, today was the day for a hurriedly arranged formal visit to each House. In Selene's shoes, Marcia would have cancelled those too; but evidently Selene wasn't Marcia. And to be fair, there was a long-term relationship to be established. Might Selene hope to be in line for the ambassadorship, if she managed this well? She couldn't be looking forward to her return to Ameten, either way.

Selene barely waited to be announced before stalking through the reception-room door. Some kind of functionary seemed to have accompanied her but Selene gestured to them to stay in the hall. Marcia's back tensed; she didn't like Selene's body language at all. Which was ridiculous. She was in her own House, and Selene no longer had any power in Marek. Selene couldn't *do* anything to her.

"Ser Selene," she said politely, unsure if Selene had any other title of her own now that 'Teren Lieutenant' no longer applied.

"Marcia," Selene replied, sitting down in the chair

across from her without waiting to be invited.

They weren't doing 'polite', then.

"I imagine you are delighted by this outcome?" Her voice had knives in it.

"Independence wasn't my idea," Marcia pointed out. Though she rather wished it had been. She certainly wished that Andreas had brought her in on it. Which – she needed to talk to him about, didn't she. Together with a long list of other things, starting with the fact that she and Reb were back together.

"Indeed," Selene said thoughtfully. "No. It's magic you're obsessed with, isn't it. You and your *girlfriend*."

Marcia felt a rush of warmth at the idea that 'girlfriend' was – well, if not quite the word she herself would use of Reb, at least, since yesterday, once more in the right area. It was almost enough for her to stop worrying about the glitter in Selene's eye.

"It is her job, after all."

"Well. I'm sure you'll be glad of that, when I come back."

Marcia frowned earnestly at her. "I'm sure we would always welcome visitors from Teren," she temporized. She had a nasty feeling that she knew what Selene was getting at, but she wasn't about to betray her rising sense of unease. "And an embassy, perhaps," she added. "Perhaps out in the south-west." She regretted that dig as soon as she'd spoken.

"*Embassy*," Selene said with dismissive venom. "Don't be ridiculous. This independence nonsense won't last. I'll be back, and Marek will – rethink its choices."

It should sound like senseless bravado; it didn't. Marcia tried not to show her disquiet, and her annoyance at the way Selene was acting. She was going to rise above this. Assume that Selene was acting out, like a thwarted toddler. *She* was going to be the more grown-up person here.

"I'm sure that once the initial reaction period is over," she said, trying for a polite smile, "we can come to mutually agreeable…"

Selene snorted.

Marcia gave up on being polite and let her rising irritation – and her creeping worry – get the better of her. "Are you talking like this to every Head?" she demanded. "Because you must know you're not doing yourself any good."

"Of course not," Selene scoffed. She sat back in her chair and then, deliberately, slouched slightly sideways, the picture of relaxation. Marcia wanted to stick her with a pin. "But it's not like you can go round telling all the rest of them that I've been threatening you and talking about magic, is it? You may have managed to wriggle out of that, but we both know your reputation is dirt, and we both know you're involved in magic up to your neck. And you bribed my sorcerer away. I don't imagine that would go down well with the Council either."

Marcia gave Selene her best bland face. It was just as well she didn't know about the outright blackmail part of proceedings. Marcia wasn't the first to do something like that, not by a long way, but you couldn't do it and get caught.

"None of them want a fight with Teren. They all want to believe that I'm leaving quietly and it will all be fine. They won't want to hear you causing trouble. Yet again."

She gave Marcia a wide, vicious, smile.

It was true. If Selene was playing gracious with everyone else – well, she hadn't seemed gracious in the moment the night before last, but that could be excused, the same way Marcia had tried to excuse her at first. Selene might have mentioned demons, but the Council would have no desire to engage with that if they could possibly avoid it. Marcia would only sound hysterical if she tried to report this conversation to anyone else.

"So." Selene turned her cup upside down on its saucer. Hot water, smelling of liquorice, spilled out of it, over the inlaid wood of the table. Marcia felt the shock of it through her gut almost as if Selene had upended the cup on her lap. Selene held her gaze. "I will go. And the next time you see me, at the gates of Marek, you will regret all your decisions. Until the demons consume you."

The sheer venom in her tone froze Marcia in her place.

Selene rose and stalked out. She saw the other woman's body language shift as she opened the door, becoming once again the gracious diplomat.

"I believe Fereno-Heir has had an unfortunate spillage," she heard Selene say, and one of the servants hurried in to cluck over the mess and call for cloths.

She wanted, still, to dismiss Selene's threats as the rantings of one who'd lost, and who was petrified of what awaited her back in Ameten.

Wanted to; but couldn't.

Selene had lost, here and now. But if the Archion was still hanging on in Ameten, and if Selene still saw a way to get what she wanted…There was no way Marek could stand against an army, human or demon, if Ameten sent one.

But Selene wasn't Archion, and she wasn't going to be the one that chose how to deal with Marek's independence. She might be in disgrace as soon as she got back. Just because she wanted to return and win Marek back by force, that didn't mean it was going to happen.

Marcia hoped.

More tea was brought, and another plate of little cakes. Marcia took one, put it into her mouth, and chewed without tasting it. She swallowed, sat back, and rested her head against the back of the couch. The little cake sat heavily in her stomach.

There was a lot to worry about. She was halfway through her pregnancy, to start with; she was going to have a baby in three and a half months, which she still didn't feel remotely ready for, even if Cousin Cara was handling all the practicalities. She needed to talk to Andreas about her and Reb, and what that might mean; he was going to be her co-parent, whatever else he was, and there was another child contracted after this one.

She'd managed to save her position as Heir (and *surely* once Madeleine got back she would be Head in reality not only in practice), but Selene was right about her reputation. Marcia was far from certain how that would shake out over the coming weeks and months. Madeleine – her stomach gave a sudden lurch.

Madeleine had spoken of going to Ameten; but surely, now, she'd hear about independence and come straight back? Marcia didn't want her mother and Selene in the same city. But Madeleine would want to be here, involved in all the negotiations around independence. Which there would be a lot of – she'd come home immediately, wouldn't she?

Marcia herself was happy enough about independence, even if she wished she'd known it was coming, but there was a great deal of work to be done, and fast. They needed to build their own relationships around the Oval Sea before Teren had a chance to put their oar in. Marek had the advantage of easy access to the Sea, but they needed to *plan*, and they needed to do it immediately. They couldn't stand against force, but they could try to prevent force being used in the first place. If they had the support of the Crescent and Exuria...surely Teren would think twice, even if Selene did still have the Archion's ear – and perhaps she didn't.

And then, what exactly what Daril was playing at? He wasn't supporting independence purely for its glorious moral value, she was mortally sure of that. He had something else planned; which might or might not be directly threatening to her, but she wouldn't like to count on it either way. Then again...Daril had tied his flag firmly to the ship of independence, hadn't he? If she wanted to keep him from threatening her, or her House; well, if she too was deeply involved in the project of independence, wouldn't he have to leave her alone?

So. All of that there was to deal with, in the coming weeks and months. But for now, Selene was gone – or would be tomorrow – and Teren with her.

The baby moved inside her, and Marcia smiled, putting her hand on her belly, a wave of affection rushing over her. There was plenty enough to worry about – but she was well, and her baby was well, and she had Reb back. Not only that, but Reb was coming over again this evening. To Marcia's own House!

Everything else could wait. Worries about her mother, about Teren, about Selene, about everything – none of it was going away, she knew that well enough. But for now, she and Reb had a night to themselves; and the morning would be time enough for all the rest of it.

ACKNOWLEDGEMENTS

I wrote this before the pandemic, and edited it during. It took a lot longer than I anticipated. But here we are. One more to go!

Many thanks to the 8am Zoom crew for morning edit accountability, and the folks on the awesome writing Slack for all sorts of question-answering and support.

Laura Shapiro, maia sauren, and doop all read an earlier version of this and gave me helpful feedback – thank you! Huge appreciation to Laura for being a fabulous friend and cheerleader whose encouragement pulled me out of more than one slump, not to mention an excellent fic-writing partner. *fistbump*

I am delighted to have another book out with Peter and Alison at Elsewhen, publishers without compare. Hopefully we'll be able to catch up in person again at a con sometime soon! I am grateful also to Tony Allcock for another wonderful cover, and to Sofia for her thoughtful editing.

Finally, much love to doop, Pete, and Leon – I couldn't imagine better people to see out two lockdowns with.

Juliet Kemp, September 2021

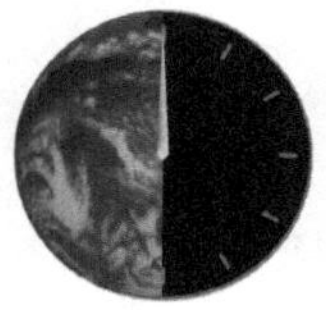

Elsewhen Press

delivering outstanding new talents in speculative fiction

Visit the Elsewhen Press website at elsewhen.press for the latest
information on all of our titles, authors and events; to read our blog;
find out where to buy our books and ebooks; or to place an order.

Sign up for the Elsewhen Press InFlight Newsletter at
elsewhen.press/newsletter

1: THE DEEP AND SHINING DARK
A Locus Recommended Read in 2018

"A rich and memorable tale of political ambition, family and magic, set in an imagined city that feels as vibrant as the characters inhabiting it." **Aliette de Bodard**
Nebula-award winning author of *The Tea Master and the Detective*

You know something's wrong when the cityangel turns up at your door
Magic within the city-state of Marek works without the need for bloodletting, unlike elsewhere in Teren, thanks to an agreement three hundred years ago between an angel and the founding fathers. It also ensures that political stability is protected from magical influence. Now, though, most sophisticates no longer even believe in magic *or* the cityangel.

But magic has suddenly stopped working, discovers Reb, one of the two sorcerers who survived a plague that wiped out virtually all of the rest. Soon she is forced to acknowledge that someone has deposed the cityangel without being able to replace it. Marcia, Heir to House Fereno, and one of the few in high society who is well-aware that magic still exists, stumbles across that same truth. But it is just one part of a much more ambitious plan to seize control of Marek.

Meanwhile, city Council members connive and conspire, unaware that they are being manipulated in a dangerous political game. A game that threatens the peace and security not just of the city, but all the states around the Oval Sea, including the shipboard traders of Salina upon whom Marek relies.

To stop the impending disaster, Reb and Marcia, despite their difference in status, must work together alongside the deposed cityangel and Jonas, a messenger from Salina. But first they must discover who is behind the plot, and each of them must try to decide who they can really trust.
ISBN: 9781911409342 (epub, kindle) / ISBN: 9781911409243 (272pp paperback)
Visit bit.ly/DeepShiningDark

2: SHADOW AND STORM

"never short on adventure and intrigue... the characters are real, full of depth, and richly drawn, and you'll wish you had even more time with them by book's end. A fantastic read." **Rivers Solomon**
Author of *An Unkindness of Ghosts*, Lambda, Tiptree and Locus finalist
Never trust a demon... or a Teren politician
The annual visit by the Teren Throne's representative, the Lord Lieutenant, is merely a symbolic gesture. But this year the Lieutenant has been unexpectedly replaced and Marcia, Heir to House Fereno, suspects a new agenda.

Teren magic is enabled by bloodletting. A Teren magician will invoke a demon and bind them with blood. But demons are devious and if unleashed are sure to create havoc. The Teren way to stop them involves the letting of more of the magician's blood – often terminally. But if a young magician is being sought by an unleashed demon, their only hope may be to escape to Marek where the cityangel can keep the demon at bay. Probably.

Once again Reb, Cato, Jonas and Beckett must deal with a magical problem, while Marcia must tackle a serious political challenge to Marek's future.
ISBN: 9781911409595 (epub, kindle) / ISBN: 9781911409496 (336pp paperback)
Visit bit.ly/ShadowAndStorm

BY DAVID M ALLAN
QUAESTOR

When you're searching, you don't always find what you expect

In Carrhen some people have a magic power — they may be telekinetic, clairvoyant, stealthy, or able to manipulate the elements. Anarya is a Sponger, she can absorb and use anyone else's magic without them even being aware, but she has to keep it a secret as it provokes jealousy and hostility especially among those with no magic powers at all.

When Anarya sees Yisyena, a Sitrelker refugee, being assaulted by three drunken men, she helps her to escape. Anarya is trying to establish herself as an investigator, a quaestor, in the city of Carregis. Yisyena is a clairvoyant, a skill that would be a useful asset for a quaestor, so Anarya offers her a place to stay and suggests they become business partners. Before long they are also lovers.

But business is still hard to find, so when an opportunity arises to work for Count Graumedel who rules over the city, they can't afford to turn it down, even though the outcome may not be to their liking.

Soon they are embroiled in state secrets and the personal vendettas of a murdered champion, a cabal, a puppet king, and a false god looking for one who has defied him.

ISBN: 9781911409571 (epub, kindle) / 9781911409472 (304pp paperback)
Visit bit.ly/Quaestor-Allan

THIEVER

Change is not always as good as a rest

After the events in Jotuk at the end of *Quaestor*, Anarya is no longer a Sponger but is now a Thiever — when she takes someone's magic talent they lose it until she can no longer hold on to it. Worryingly, the power also brings a desperate hunger to take others' talents, just as the false god did. As Anarya struggles to control the compulsion, Yisul is fraught with worry and seeks help for her lover. But Jotuk is in upheaval; the Twenty-Three families are in disarray, divided over how the city should be governed.

In Carregis, the king seeks to establish himself as an effective ruler. First, though, he must work out whom he can trust.

Meanwhile, the priestesses of Quarenna and the priests of Huler are having disturbing dreams…

Thiever is the much anticipated sequel to David M Allan's *Quaestor*.

ISBN: 9781911409977 (epub, kindle) / 9781911409878 (386pp paperback)
Visit bit.ly/Thiever

As Ants to the Gods

Alex Burcher

If they found and destroyed the Scroll they would bring down all civilisation. Would the sacrifice of one man's life save humanity?

Five years after the Great Fire of Lundun, ex-dragoon Laqua is lured into helping the *Keepers of the Light*, a covert band fighting the equally clandestine *Cult of the Death of Hope*. The Cult would bring down the empire of the Moors and, indeed, all civilisation. An empire that has conquered most of Europe, where the language is Arabic and the flag of the falcate moon flies. Where alcohol is banned and hashish legal, prison is unknown and punishment by whip, knife or hook. A world in which the Industrial Revolution is already well advanced and steam engines chug. Where the Norse have settled the New World first. In Lundun, capital of the Tin Isles, the largest mosque looms over St Pauls Cathedral. And Samuel Peppin has given up his diaries to write bawdy poems.

Vital to defeating the Cult is an ancient secret Scroll, the final chapter of the sacred Script, its authenticity assured by the Seal. While the Cult would destroy it, the Keepers intend its dissemination to all. Until they have the means to do so, Laqua is charged with its safekeeping. He falls in with a dour eunuch, a functionary of the Court of the Amir in Qurtuba, and a perfidious, possibly drug-addled, heretic. And what part might a libidinous Norsewoman play? Ahead of him lie spying, fighting, loving, torture and tragedy … and the discovery of a hideous truth.

As Ants to the Gods is an alternate history adventure that challenges some of the orthodoxies and assumptions of Western culture. For adults only, certainly not for the faint-hearted or easily shocked, it is a ribald and irreverent exploration of a world that could have been.

ISBN: 9781911409724 (epub, kindle) / 9781911409625 (520pp paperback)

Visit bit.ly/AsAntsToTheGods

ABOUT JULIET KEMP

Juliet Kemp lives by the river in London, with their partners, child, dog, and too many fountain pens. They have had stories published in several anthologies and online magazines. Their employment history variously includes working as a cycle instructor, sysadmin, life model, researcher, permaculture designer, and journalist. When not writing or parenting, Juliet goes climbing, knits, reads way too much, and drinks a lot of tea.